HAVANA STRIKE

JIM DeFELICE

LEISURE BOOKS   NEW YORK CITY

A LEISURE BOOK®

December 1997

Published by

Dorchester Publishing Co., Inc.
276 Fifth Avenue
New York, NY 10001

ISBN 0-8439-4330-0

The name "Leisure Books" and the stylized "L" with design are
trademarks of Dorchester Publishing Co., Inc.

Printed in the United States of America.

HAVANA STRIKE

AUTHOR'S NOTE

While this is a work of fiction and should be treated as such, the descriptions of the A/V-32A as well as the other technologies, weapons, and craft included in the book are based on a large number of (unclassified) sources. As they are products of the imagination rather than actual sheet metal, in some cases their performance and construction is more idealistic than would be possible given present monetary and time constraints. But that, after all, is fiction's major advantage over reality.

The Pegasus specifically is inspired by work undertaken by, among others, the Lockheed Martin, and Pratt & Whitney companies. The fictional plane is named after the outstanding power plant used by the current generation STOVL aircraft, the Harrier.

Those familiar with both Cherry Point and Jacksonville will realize that I've made some slight alterations to facilitate the action. I figured that since I didn't have to file an environmental impact study, no harm would be done.

With the exception of historical citations, the marine aviators mentioned herein are fictional characters. If anything, their present-day counterparts are several times more heroic.

The CIA document cited at the beginning of the book is an authentic excerpt from the agency's original briefings during the 1962 crisis.

As of this writing, Fidel Castro remains in power in Cuba. While there is widespread dissension to his rule, it appears unlikely that anything but his death will end his oppression. He will never, however, destroy the Cuban spirit, which thrives like a deep-rooted tree despite great trials and deprivations.

I have been privileged to know many Cubans and Cuban-Americans over the years, including several who struggled to carve new lives in the United States after arriving on these shores with nothing but hope in their pockets. I have learned much from them, and owe a special debt to my friends Jerry and Elsa Fernandez—not for information in this book, which they read in an early form, but for their friendship and love. The book's errors are my own, but its truths flow from the hearts of all my friends.

Since I'm thanking a few of the many people who have helped me here, let me add the names of my editor, Don D'Auria, and my agent, Jake Elwell of Weiser & Weiser, both of whom have given me valuable support and guidance. And I must also mention my wife, Debra, without whom I could not have written a word.

To all Cubans: May you live to see the day freedom returns in fact as well as spirit to the island.

SC No. 11173/62
29 November 1962

Central Intelligence Agency

Memorandum: Deployment & withdrawal of Soviet Missiles
and other significant weapons in Cuba
. . .

Conclusion

The Soviet claim to have delivered only 42 missiles to
Cuba, and to have now withdrawn these, is consistent
with our evidence. We cannot exclude the possibility that
more actually arrived, and that some therefore remain, but
we think that any such number would be small. . . .

TOP SECRET

Prologue

Sometime in the near future

Outside, the sun was climbing past the thick, lingering clouds to its zenith, full and strong, the warm rays vanquishing the storm that had raged through the island and the rest of the Caribbean for the past few days. Even for the Tropics, the storm had been unusually brutal. Huge trees that had withstood decades of lesser gales lay scattered like twigs along the shoreline, their uprooted trunks drenched from the deluge. Wide swaths of underbrush were pressed down where the wind had whipped through; even the sugarcane, whose green stalks were sturdy enough to symbolize the undying strength of the Cuban people, had been beaten badly by the hurricane. So it wasn't surprising that the vegetation seemed literally to welcome the sun's re-emergence, plants turning their leaves and heads toward it as it rose. Animals venturing from shelter for the first time in days shook themselves hopefully and stretched their limbs and bodies for maximum

10

exposure, as if the light's energy could be absorbed directly through their skins.

The few people who lived in this forgotten quarter of the island momentarily put off their cares, turning away from the destruction and staring full into the yellow orb that promised yet another chance to rebuild. It was a late dawn, coming nearly at noon, but that made it all the more welcome, and there was not a man in the coastal village at the edge of the charcoal swamps of Playa Girón who did not doff his shirt to exult in the sun's triumph.

But inside this house at the edge of the sea, the blinds and drapes were closed stiffly against the sun, tighter than the windows had been against the storm. The rays were so powerful they burned the white blinds silver, filling the casement with a glow the heavy drapes could not completely contain. A long, narrow band of light seeped through the crack at the middle of each set of five windows lining the room. Five fingers scraped across the darkness toward the large four-poster bed at the far end of the room. Though this was the room's only illumination, it was too much for the bed's occupant, who grumbled every few minutes to one of his many attendants, demanding that something be done about the light striking his eyes.

"Hemos tratado, Comandante," said the doctor standing over him. "We have tried."

"Do not try," responded the dying dictator, President Fidel Alejandro Castro Ruz. "Do it."

The doctor nodded to a nurse, who motioned to an aide by the windows. Once again, the elderly man struggled with the heavy drapes. But the light was simply too strong; the rays plunged past, poking and irritating the stricken man.

"This is what it comes to," said Castro. "This is what I get for outliving them all, all of my enemies, and all of my friends, even Raul. I am left only with shit-eating jackals."

The retinue of party and government officials standing at the far end of the room shuddered.

"Comandante," started the doctor, hoping to cut off the ramble, but he was too late to stop his patient from launching into another fever-driven harangue. Castro had spent much of the past few days this way, the pneumonia ravaging his mind as well as his weakened body. The ravings had dwelled mostly on the first days of the Revolution; earlier this morning he had recalled in great detail the American-supplied B-26s Batista had used to strafe the small rebel band after it came ashore from the Granma at Alegria de Pio in December 1956. With florid shouts he cursed the planes, complaining about the sharp cuts inflicted by the sugarcane that hid him from his pursuers and made escape to the Sierra Maestra Mountains possible. Now he seemed to be recalling a discussion he had had with Che Guevara some years later, a debate between philosophies and realities.

"You do not understand, you do not understand!" he thundered again and again. With each bellow the group at the end of the room took a half-step backward, until the twenty or so men were nearly flat against the wall.

Besides the nurse, there was only one woman here. Thin and short, with dark curly hair and skin tanned to a delicate brown, she stood opposite the retainers, eyeing them with disdain. Though she felt out of place and awkward, a deeper part of her told her she must be here.

"Carla, Carla, come here," demanded *El Comandante en Jefe*. "The rest of you—out. Out! *¡Fuera coño!* Where is Zora? Send her to me at once. The rest of you—out! Carla, *acércate aquí*. Doctor, you too, all of you, out!"

12

The doctor reluctantly led the procession from the room. The men began whispering about how long Castro might last as soon as they were in the hallway; their buzz did not fade until the last one closed the large wooden door.

"My girl," said the old man lying on the bed. His voice had become lucid; the eyes over his long, silver beard clear. "I am glad that you made it."

"The others could not come," she said.

"I know. Everything is chaos. Our friends from the north have seen to that. But you are the only one I wanted."

He tried a weak, ironic smile, as if he were still in control of the situation. Cuba had descended into a state of near-anarchy, rumors of the maximum leader's death flooding through the country in giddy waves. Each ministry had its own favorite son poised to take over; there were countless plans for free and semifree elections, direct and indirect democracies. At least two active coup plots were proceeding from different parts of the military. Castro's own succession wishes were disregarded, washed aside by a flood of speculation and machination. He had known this would happen; his ability to gauge the public sentiment had never left him, even as his position and power eroded with the faltering economy and his fading health. This perceptiveness, which had stood him well through the years of revolution and rule, had turned at the end into a device of self-torture. He knew he had become a relic of the past, in almost every quarter a despised and hated figure.

Carla represented his hope for the future. They had drawn close only in the last few months. He had brought her together with the sons and daughters of his most trusted followers; together they might form the core of a resurrection, a movement that could only begin when his own ended.

"My daughter," he whispered, "come closer to me. Listen to what I say."

With great effort, he held his hand up to her. She took it gently. It was soft and cold. The room, a large refectory turned sick room and furnished with a few spartan chairs, a bureau and the antique bed, seemed to run away from her. A chill whipped through her body; she felt more alone than ever in her life.

"You have your mother's eyes," Castro said to her. Earlier, he had confused her mother with Celia, his lover from the good days; she had not had the heart to correct him. Now, though, she could see that his mind had cleared. She did, indeed, have her mother's eyes.

"She is dead?" he asked.

"Many years now," answered Carla.

"You are so beautiful. It is a shame you have cut your hair. But that is the way with a revolution—I grew mine, you must cut yours. And a dancer's body. You do not have my height, but that is not wanted in a girl." His eyes, which had been dreamy with nostalgia, sharpened suddenly. "Where is Zora?"

"The witch?"

"Do not call her a witch!" Castro thundered. For a brief moment immense energy flickered in his eyes; quickly it receded, leaving him more drained than before.

"She knows," the dictator whispered. "She knows many things."

"They are superstitions."

"More than that. My revenge, and my hope."

"Revenge?"

But the effort had rattled him; his eyes began to lose their focus and his thoughts began to drift. "It is not every man who could father such a daughter," said Castro. His eyes glimmered with pride. "I was

14

already an old man—or so they said." He squeezed her hand with a sudden vitality, then dropped his arm back against the bed. His beard puffed out on top of the covers, moving up and down with his slow, labored breathing. His wheezing sounded like a locomotive grinding its wheels.

"What did you mean by revenge?"

"You must wait. The worms will return, and at first there will be rejoicing. Gradually, the people will realize what they have lost. Then will be your time."

"Father—"

There was a rush of air as the door opened. "Why is it so dark in here?" proclaimed the woman who burst into the room. "The time has come for light."

Carla watched Zora walk across the room, her elbows flaring at her sides as if they were propelling her through water. She wore a long, plain red dress that bulged from her wide hips; her gray hair was tied into a bun at the back of her head. Incredibly, she was a few years older than Castro, but either because of her Santeria magic (as she would have it) or perhaps because the weight of the nation had not worn her down, she looked considerably younger.

"It will hurt my eyes," said the dictator. "Do not open the drapes."

The command did not even slow her down. "You must gaze upon your daughter in the fullness of day," Zora replied.

"It is better this way," rasped Castro.

"It is time for light," said Zora, ripping back the curtain on the first window. Light gushed in, and the room became as bright as the outdoors.

Castro winced in pain. The searching sun found every flaw in his face, every pockmark, the ravaged nose and overworked mouth, the slight depression at each temple, the deep furrows of his forehead. In

15

the harsh light, he looked nothing like the maximum leader, the commander in chief of the armed forces, the leader of the revolution and the Third World, the defiant symbol of Communism, the scourge of imperialism, the last holdout of a defeated idea. He was an old, old man who'd come to the end of his life, painfully aware of his mistakes, struggling to hold on to the belief that his good deeds outweighed the bad. Carla looked down into his face, seeking his eyes, but they were closed tight against the sun.

She stood like that, silent, vainly seeking his gaze, for a long time, as if under a magical spell. Her trance was broken only when Zora squeezed her side.

"It is over," said the old woman. "There is much work to be done. Let us go."

Chapter One

Two years later . . .

Wednesday, July 16
Marine Air Station at Cherry Point. 12:15 A.M. (All times are local.)

Fifteen seconds to pickle.

Problem was, he had a bogey in his mirror, screaming hot and mad for a piece of his backside. The ECM was ringing off the hook and "Gump"—officially, the Co-Command Computer, or C^3, his electronic copilot—was about to have a cow. Marine Lieutenant Edward "Elvis" Garcia leaned his hand on the throttle and said "flare" twice, hoping his pursuer would err and fire heat-seekers instead of closing with his cannon.

He did not. Twelve seconds to target.

"Flares away. Further evasive action highly recommended," squealed Gump in his ear. The words PURSUER CLOSING flashed in bright red on the screen.

The gray outline of Garcia's target climbed slowly but steadily toward the middle of the crosshairs. Had he been delivering a laser-guided weapon, he could have fired long ago, letting the computer fly the bomb toward its target while he juked and jived to safety. But the payload he was aiming at the enemy artillery emplacement was a fat and exceedingly dumb two-thousand-pound iron bomb, strapped to one of the exterior hardpoints on the Pegasus's belly. Nothing to do but hang in there.

And get shot to hell in the process.

Suddenly, he had a brainstorm. He reached forward and hit C³'s kill switch—the only way the machine would let him do something exceedingly brilliant.

Or stupid, depending on your perspective.

"Engine off, engine on," Garcia told the plane.

Without the computer's superego to contradict the commands, the engine coughed dead for a moment, then exploded back on. The A/V-32A stuttered in the air as Garcia struggled to keep it true to target, now just five seconds away.

Smoke and jet fuel burped out of the tailpipe directly into his pursuer's face. It was a brilliant piece of theater, a low-tech screen of mud for his enemy's eyes and sensors. Even so, the dreaded warning UNDER FIRE began flashing on Garcia's screen even before he flipped his computer copilot back on-line. A quarter of a second later, a tracer round flashed past the windscreen. Over the roar of his engines he heard the dull rap-rap-rap of thirty-millimeter slugs crashing into his wing.

The C³ painted his target in gold. Garcia squeezed the trigger to drop the bomb, and in nearly the same moment yanked the stick back as hard as he could. The servos in the base of the stick translated the urgent pull into an abrupt burst upward as Gump responded to the pilot's voice command—"maximum frigging acceleration"—by flooding the Pratt & Whitney F119 power plant with enough high-octane av fuel to keep a dozen 777s aloft for a week. The engine roared its approval.

The Pegasus's abrupt maneuver, aided by its vertical-thrusting turbofan, would have flicked most fighters off its back, but the MiG firing at his tailpipe was being flown by an expert. Hugging Garcia's wake, it followed the marine attack plane as it looped over and rolled flat onto a course the pilot had programmed before takeoff.

"Maximum power, Gump. Get us away on the preset, damn it." Garcia's command was superfluous; the green indicator curve at the right bottom of his screen already showed that the gas pedal was through the floor. Under fire and in its present configuration, the computer would not dare to back off the engine until expressly ordered to do so by the pilot. Nevertheless, the MiG stayed tight on his shoulder, and even as Garcia bent the stick in his right hand to juke his way home, the UNDER FIRE indicator lit again.

The g "button"—a circle above the heading and altimeter crossbars that gauged the gravitational forces acting on the plane and its pilot—began flashing 5, then 7, turning red with the number 9 as Garcia swung the plane as tightly as it could manage to the right. His flight suit did its best to reduce the effects of the high-g maneuvering. Pressure-activated fingers massaged his neck in an effort to keep as much blood as possible in his brain. There was only so much technology could do, however, and as he cut back into what the textbook would describe as a high-speed scissors maneuver, he found his head starting to float. He eased off at the last second, the only way he could maintain consciousness.

The plane on his tail was a MiG-37. Designed

from the ground up as a dogfighter, the MiG was more maneuverable and about five hundred nautical miles an hour faster at top speed than the attack-optimized Pegasus A/V-32A. There was just no way for Garcia's mud mover to outrun it. The one thing he had going for him was his plane's toughness; even though he'd already taken several cannon shots in his wing and fuselage, Gump had yet to report threatening damage.

Garcia ducked toward the ground, hoping his opponent would be loath to follow him into the barrage of triple-A. He also hoped luck and the form-fitted titanium bucket that made up the cockpit would keep his butt from getting toasted.

"Port-wing fuel tank has been punctured," reported Gump. "Taking corrective action."

Garcia glanced toward the operations readouts at the lower right of his heads-up display. The damage message was repeated there.

Not good.

Another message flashed in his display, warning him that the radar guiding the ground antiair guns had locked on the Pegasus despite the best efforts of his electronic countermeasures.

That wasn't actually a big deal. He was now flying so low and slow that all these jokers had to do was point and shoot.

"MiG has broken off," reported Gump. Garcia saw the shadow of the plane turning away in the FLIR display, its engines bright white in the enhanced display. He immediately began climbing hard right, trying to escape the flak.

Too late. Three very big slugs grabbed the plane in midturn, mashing the left main wing and tearing away a good portion of the rear stabilizer.

EJECT flashed in huge red letters across the screen.

"Suckers," cursed Garcia, reaching again for the override switch on the dashboard. He didn't want

Gump to throw him out of the plane before he was ready.

"You know the rules, Elvis," said the flight supervisor over his intercom. "You're dead."

"I could bring it back."

"Bullshit," said Colonel Henry "Bighead" Talic, who was controlling the simulation from a computer station halfway across the hangar. His sinewy fingers pelted the keyboard and Garcia's mock Pegasus took five more shells in the belly.

"Hey, man, that's not fair."

"Too bad, Marine. And what was that bullshit about turning the engine on and off?"

Colonel Talic and the other pilots in the small, elite squadron were waiting at the foot of the steps as Garcia popped the top on the A/V-32A flight simulator. The front end bore about as much resemblance to the actual plane as a bulldozer to a Ferrari, but the interior cockpit was an exact duplicate, right down to the awkward plastic ledge below the right multiuse tube. The tab was the one annoying flaw in the otherwise perfect ergonomics of the cockpit. Garcia hit his knee on it as he pulled himself out of the simulator seat, just as he did every time he got out of the real plane. With his helmet's microphone system still connected, his curses echoed through the hangar.

"Friggin' thing. Frig it to hell."

Talic smiled to himself at the quaint substitution, a habit of Garcia's that had somehow survived more than two years in the Corps. "What was the bit with the engines?" he demanded, screwing his voice back into an annoyed bark.

It didn't have far to go. Though the colonel was barely five-seven, some trick of his anatomy rendered even his normal talking voice as deep as a bear's.

21

"I figured that was the one thing you wouldn't have programmed into the simulation," said Garcia sheepishly.

Talic shook his head. He had been teaching, counseling, and occasionally kicking in the butt eight of the Corps' best and brightest for more than five months, as they and the new V/STOL attack plane grew up together. They were all great fliers, Garcia especially. But they tended to be more aware of the computer systems helping them fly than the planes themselves. A stick-and-rudder man who had flown nearly everything in the Corps inventory, Talic would never trust computing power over sheet metal or carbon-fiber composites. "You try that when you're flying, you'll end up in a dog-food can," he warned.

"You always tell us to improvise."

"Improvise, yes; kill yourself, no. Come on, get your head out of that helmet."

Garcia unscrewed the inputs on his helmet and pushed it gingerly off his head. The helmet duplicated the gear in the high-tech hat he wore in the Pegasus. Like the system first used in Apache helicopters, its sensors responded to cues from Garcia's eyes; he could literally shoot at a target by looking at it. More impressive, a holographic visor array projected a virtual screen of instrument readings; no matter where the pilot was looking in the cockpit, the data would be in front of him at all times. This removed the need for the standard heads-up display on the windshield glass—important, because the lower third of the fishbowl windshield was not pure glass at all, but rather clear LED crystals that functioned as a flatscreen receptor for imaging and radar inputs. A pilot could look at the real world and a computer-enhanced picture of it at the same time.

There were some limits to the power of the sensors—as well as a few lingering bugs in the computer—but overall the effect was light-years beyond the simple avionics Talic had cut his teeth on. The displays were a special boon at night, when many of the Pegasus's missions were expected to be flown.

The helmet used for the simulator, however, wasn't the same one used in the Pegasus. Built before all the systems had been perfected, it was considerably larger and much heavier than the unit it impersonated. It looked like a diver's hard hat from the outside; when you put it on, it felt as if a boa constrictor were making love to your cranium. Garcia had to be helped out of it by two of his wingmates, Buzz Peterson and Linda Weber.

"Finally got you," said Peterson. "It's about time."

"Your hair didn't help you this time." Weber laughed.

Garcia unconsciously ran his fingers through his scalp, inadvertently repeating some of the mannerisms that had made Talic award him his nickname the first day Air-Ground Assault Group Three had assembled. With a blocky face, dark hair, and a boyish smile, he vaguely resembled the fifties rock legend. At just over six feet, he was tall for a fighter pilot, but made up for it with a frame that was wiry even by marine standards. In fact, Talic thought he might weigh as little as he himself did—which wasn't all that much.

But it was Garcia's personality as much as anything that suggested the nickname—brash, a little flashy, full of potential. He had all the makings of a superstar pilot; all he needed was some seasoning.

"Say, Colonel, how about another shot at the Foster?" Garcia asked.

"Not tonight, Elvis. No more encores. Take your bow and hit the showers."

The Foster Torture Test was a simulated attack plan named after a navy captain who had flown hard-boiled sorties decades before in Vietnam. The toughest test Talic and the computer could cobble together, there were a total of twelve separate targets and a veritable armada of defenders to fly against in this high-tech and very serious computer game. In actual fact, it was considerably more rigorous than any likely situation a pilot would find himself in—not least of all because the MiG that had sat on Garcia's tail existed only in the computer and Talic's imagination.

As expected, Garcia's performance was better than anyone else—including Talic—had ever done.

Not that the kid was satisfied.

"Let's go again," Garcia said. "I can do it."

The others laughed.

"We're finished," said the colonel. "It's past midnight. Besides, you got all the goddamn targets."

"Aw, but, Colonel—"

"Enough, Marine. You have to be on the flight line at oh seven hundred hours. You're not just flying for me, you're flying for the President."

"Let me take a shot," said Buzz. "I think I can do better without Forrest Gump screaming in my ear."

"If it weren't for Gump, you would have crashed on the flight deck," said the colonel. "Come on, boys—you, too, Linda. Rack time, all of you. That's an order."

"Sir, yes, sir," said the pilots in mocking unison.

"Fuck yourselves."

"Sir, yes, sir," they snapped back. Recruits fresh off the bus at Quantico couldn't have done it any better.

"Damn fucking brats," snickered Bighead. He smiled as they filtered away. When Garcia filed past, he took him by the shoulder and began walking him toward the door. "Pretty good run, son."

"Thank you, sir," said the pilot in a voice that

sounded even younger than his twenty-four years.

"You should've broken off your attack to duck the MiG at the end," said the colonel. "Then you might have had a chance to live to fight another day."

"Is that the solution to the problem, Colonel?"

Bighead smiled. "There is no solution. You would have been greased either way."

Havana. 5 A.M.

The clock radio erupted with a Poncho Sanchez drum solo. The room shook so violently that Scott McPherson, his consciousness swimming up from the cement tomb of sleep, thought for a moment the downstairs neighbor was testing out a new jack-hammer.

A trumpet and trombone smashed together in a violent duel over the drum. No fan of classical Latin jazz, especially at this hour, Scotty rolled to his right and took a swipe at the radio, more in the way of a symbolic first strike than in hopes of actually turning it off.

He missed. He reached again, his hand fumbling across the table's collection of dolls and doodads until it found the edge of the radio. This was a kitschy device molded to look like a fat chicken with a sailor's cap; the beak tuned the radio, the eyes controlled volume and tone, and the belly flashed the time. The snooze button—the chicken's round blue cap—had been broken weeks ago; to turn off the alarm Scotty had to push a fingernail-shaped switch on the back behind the kerchief. The maneuver required an outrageous amount of coordination.

Which was an explanation, if not quite a justification, for his flinging the entire radio to the floor.

Where it continued to play, louder than before.

Scotty leaned over the edge of the bed, groping for the power cord. By the time he found it, the deejay was proclaiming another "glorious day in the free and easy republic of Cuba, viva La Habana, viva la libertad, viva, viva, viva."

"There ought to be a law against disc jockeys loading up on methamphetamine before noon," Scotty mumbled as the room fell silent. He pulled himself back onto the bed and turned over to fold his body around Esma. His fingers slid down the smooth brushed silk of her nightgown, pausing at the hem. Her thigh was warm, and when he pushed his fingers across it, her skin felt like the surface of the ocean on a hot afternoon. Scotty took a deep breath, his chest expanding against the hard edge of her back. He brought his hand up her leg and belly before continuing to the plump circle of her breast, where her nipple began swelling beneath his palm.

As she pushed her back gently against his chest, Scotty reached down to his thigh, where he unhooked the small holster. Quietly he slipped the leather strap and its palm-size Glock 27 to the floor.

The Glock in his ankle holster, with ten rounds of forty-millimeter ammo snug in its clip, remained clamped to the bottom of his leg. This was Cuba, after all.

Esma's objections to making love to a man with a gun had vanished after someone had tried to take a shot at him two months before. The guns, with their finely filed trigger action and boxy bodies made of plastic, had power far beyond the mere measurements of stopping strength a scientist might assign to their bullets. Strapped to his body, the plastic cannons protected him against the dark fatalism that had wrapped itself around his body. They let him stay here, at Esma's apartment, with the barest of precautions. Even before coming to Cuba, he had begun to live on sheer audacity alone; the pair of small pistols, never far from his reach, even in the bath, were the totems of his courage.

Esma was a totem of something else, something much less expected, something beyond desire that he had not thought possible to feel. He brushed his fingers over her gently, rising to kiss her face with the sweet, light touch of one who has woken from a pleasant dream.

"I hope you did not break my radio," Esma said, drawling the last word in her slow, Spanish-accented English after she returned his kiss. "If you do not like it, you buy me a new one."

Scotty answered by pushing his mouth to her ear.

"You're late already," she told him.

"Late?"

"*Sí.* You were supposed to meet the ambassador at five. You said so when we left the club at three."

"No. I have to meet him at six, Ez." Scotty looped his finger around the string at the top of her gown, pulling it over her shoulder. He began brushing her nipple with his thumb. "Plenty of time."

"*Basta*, lover boy," she said, giggling, then turned onto her stomach. "Your boss is going to fire you if you are late. This is what you told me last night. And then what happens? Antarctica."

"I'd be happy there if you came with me."

"That is one place I will not go." She surprised him by sitting up suddenly and pulling her night-gown back over her breast—though it was obvious she was as aroused as he was. "Take a cold shower. I do not want you fired."

"So maybe I'll take a job with Pepsi."

"Oh, this would be something I'd like to see."

Scotty hesitated a moment, watching the curl of her lips as they failed to completely contain her smile. Then he pulled her on top of him. "Plenty of time," he said.

When Scotty reached the street downstairs, still buttoning his shirt, it was a quarter to six. He

Jim DeFelice

dashed into the road, waving madly; a cabby driving a red Nissan squealed across three lanes to brake six inches from his outstretched arm.

Scotty slid into the back and told the driver in English to stop at the next coffee stand. The driver smiled, then hit the gas so hard the door flew out of Scotty's grip. The cabbie stopped a block away, where a short black man had converted a shopping cart into a mobile delicatessen. A battery of thermoses were filled with allegedly different blends of coffee. Like everyone else in Havana, Scotty knew that aside from the flavored varieties (which went for three times the price of the others, and were incredibly sweet), the differences were largely fictional, aided perhaps by different percentages of water. Besides the coffees, there were a variety of sweets and sandwiches. His favorites were *pastelitos*, or bite-size puff pastries with a guava filling, and he ordered two, one for himself and one for the cabdriver, who etiquette dictated must be treated to the same snack the passenger received. The driver accepted the food and half a cup of "Colombia blend" gratefully, nodding and sipping slowly from the simple porcelain cup the vendor passed into the cab. The china was a holdover from the days of Fidel; all of the "quality" vendors preferred the thick mugs over the disposable replacements common in Miami and elsewhere.

On another day, Scotty might have chatted with the driver, asking where he had lived before Castro died and the country was reliberated. Nearly every taxi driver he had ever met had spent at least some time in America; to a man they were all saving their money either for a Tennessee-built Altima—the taxicab of choice—or, if they already owned one, a fleet of them.

It wasn't idle chatter. Scotty's job as a special aide to the U.S. ambassador was hazily defined, but it

28

primarily revolved around keeping track of the left-wing guerrilla movement. The CIA agent (technically, he was on loan to the State Department and not part of the agency chain of command, a good thing for all concerned) gained a lot of useful information on the terrorists just by talking to *taxistas*, who made it their business to know everything that was going on in the city. The fact that no taxicab had ever been on a block where a bombing occurred seemed to be no accident.

But today, though desperate for caffeine, Scotty was in a hurry. He grunted noncommittally when the driver congratulated the Americans on the abandonment of Guantánamo Bay. It was a common way to start a conversation, even though the last sailor had packed his duffel well over a year before. As the driver started in on the weather, Scotty gulped down the rest of his breakfast and handed the thick white china mug and saucer back to the coffee seller. The taxi driver was obliged to do likewise, though he hadn't had more than a sip or two. The vendor made quite a show of dumping the unfinished coffee in the street; that marked his as a superior operation, for most of the street-side sellers would have poured the liquid back into one of the thermoses.

The clock on the dash read 5:55. "Better go to the hospital," Scotty told the driver.

The man's eyes widened.

"No, no, I'm fine. I have to meet someone there. The new Children's Hospital at the south end of the city. You know where that is?"

"Oh, yes," said the man. He smiled appreciatively, as if Scotty had personally paid the seventy million dollars it took to rehab the ancient facility. "The American hospital."

"Yeah. I'm kinda late."

"No problem."

Jim DeFelice

The man threw the car into gear and began talking nonstop about when the government might set the elections. He seemed to be anticipating a date within a few weeks, though it was difficult to judge how sincere he was. A surprising number of Cubans were actually in favor of an indefinite delay, most likely because they feared there could be even more chaos with a new assembly. And though as a class the taxi drivers were not among the *Habaneros* who thought the old dictator's death was the worst thing that had ever happened to the country, there was still a dangerous number of people who felt that way. Otherwise, the guerrilla movement would have sputtered to death a long time ago.

Scotty rolled down the window and had his ID ready when the guard stopped the taxi a block from the hospital gate.

It was an American guard, wearing the patch of the Eighth Division above his MP armband.

"It's okay," he told the camo-clad soldier. "I'm with the ambassador."

"Sorry, sir," said the guard, whose M-16 was loaded and ready to fire. "No one comes in here."

"Damn it. Check my name against the list. Shit."

Two other soldiers came forward and blocked the cab. A lieutenant scurried down the block in their direction. The cabbie's lips started moving, but no sound came out.

Realizing he was going to have to walk from here, Scotty dumped the fare and a fat tip on the front seat and opened the door. The driver hardly waited for him to step on the pavement before he threw the car in reverse and backed away from the checkpoint.

"Hey," Scotty called to the lieutenant. "You in charge?"

"Yes, sir."

Scotty eyed the soldier suspiciously. The ambassador's guards were marines. Army MP units were plentiful in the city, however, and the officer's drawl had enough Kansas in it for Scotty to relax.

Somewhat.

He flashed the ID at him, making sure that the big .45 in his belt was visible as he opened his coat.

"I'm Scott McPherson. Ambassador's staff."

"Sir, my orders are that no one passes."

"Hey, fuck your orders," said Scotty. "Check your goddamn security list."

One of the soldiers stood to bar his way.

"You're going to get in a hell of a lot of trouble if you shoot someone on the ambassador's staff," Scotty told him, gently pushing his rifle down.

The lieutenant nodded at his man, who took a step back. Even so, the officer followed Scotty up the block and then the hospital driveway, where the ambassador's black limousine was parked in front of a marine humvee.

The lieutenant faded into the background as soon as Malcolm Steele emerged from the car. Ordinarily, his face was a light chestnut color, but anger turned it a deep mahogany, and it was well on its way toward the dark end of the spectrum when he spotted Scott.

"You were supposed to meet me at the embassy an hour ago," barked Steele. "Where the hell have you been?"

"I got tied up with details."

"Screw the details, Scotty. When I tell you to be somewhere at a specific time, I expect to see you there. Smiling. And shaven."

"My razor broke."

"If it wasn't for me, you'd be on a goddamn trash heap pulling your pud," said Steele, abruptly turning toward the hospital door. "Don't forget that."

The caffeine was starting to kick in, and Scotty managed to keep from making a less-than-appropriate response. He was, after all, grateful to Steele, who had indeed saved him from the trash heap—assuming you had a higher-than-average view of Cuba.

"I have an idea about the airplane situation," Scotty said. "If we can't get the MiGs, we get them pilots for those piece-of-shit Harriers you wangled out of the Spanish."

"Another fiasco. Walk with me."

Scotty fell in alongside the ambassador. Steele was right about the Harriers being a fiasco, but to Scotty's mind, the whole airplane situation was absurd. The interim government, claiming it needed more airpower to use against the rebels in rural areas, had put airplanes on the list of conditions for setting elections.

The government claimed it wanted two squadrons of American fighter-bombers. Of course, if those were provided, there was bound to be a huge uproar against "Yankee interference"—which the interim government would use to justify postponing the elections.

Scotty had suggested the Cubans be provided with MiGs, which the air force had operated under Fidel. In fact, a few truckloads of spare parts would probably be enough to get the ragtag force back together.

But there were all sorts of political problems with that, both for the Americans, who were having trouble with a belligerent Russian parliament, and the Cubans, who were not eager to rely on pilots trained by Castro—the only ones who could fly the MiGs.

The Harriers had been Tito Porta's bright idea— a typical Porta idea, since the Cuban-born "consultant" to Steele was always making suggestions that seemed great from a distance and turned to shit when they landed in your hand. Outdated but serviceable, the planes had been donated by Spain a few months before. They could operate from poorly maintained airfields, even parking lots, just the sort of thing you needed in Cuba. Unfortunately, they required special training to fly and were very temperamental. There were only two men on the island at the moment who could pilot them; both were English mercenaries. There were no two-seat training models, and while the Brits claimed this ought not to be a problem, the first Cuban who had tried to fly one had crashed. The planes were so valuable to the government that they forbade anyone who hadn't flown one for over a hundred hours to get within a half-mile radius of the control stick.

"So where do we get the pilots?" Steele asked as they neared the building.

"We borrow a couple of marines from the States. They fly the same plane."

"Borrow?"

"Officially, they come down to train the Cubans. It'd be true, more or less. Eventually, they'd do some training—we could just leave it up to the Cubans to decide how to use them, General."

Steele stopped. He didn't like anyone calling him General in public, though it was an ingrained habit for people like Scotty who had known him before his retirement from the army. The habit had spread through much of the ambassador's staff, and even the deputy chief of mission used it.

"Eventually, the Cubans realize there's no problem with the planes and they'll let their pilots train in them," said Scotty. "Or else they'll all crash."

"Very funny." Steele started walking again.

"The thing is," said Scotty, "from a tactical point of view, this airpower stuff is just bullshit. The guerrillas aren't going to be beaten with this piss here, piss there strategy that the interim government—"

"I need them to set the elections, damn it," said

the ambassador. "We don't have to fight the war for them."

"We're doing a pretty crappy job, one way or another."

"You aren't fooling me with this details bullshit," snapped Steele as they walked toward a knot of officials at the door. "You look hungover as hell, and I doubt you were sounding out anyone in the defense ministry about Harriers in the Trump Havana last night."

"I wasn't drunk," said Scotty. "I was doing my job."

Steele lunged into a round of handshakes with the waiting crowd. "Stay in the background, Scott," he said when he emerged.

"Everybody in Cuba knows I'm a damn spy."

"It's not that. You didn't shave and you're not wearing a tie. You look like a street person," said Steele.

The ambassador's security detail hustled to keep up as Steele made his way into the hospital. Scotty felt sorry for them—Steele had gotten even more demanding and crotchety than he'd been at the Pentagon.

He lingered around the edges as the ambassador greeted the vice president, foreign division, of Real Packages Inc., the first of a group of American businessmen whose arms had been twisted into helping with the hospital renovation. Steele pumped their hands as if gold were going to spit out of their mouths.

From the size and makeup of the crowd, you would have thought someone had discovered penicillin. A throng of local dignitaries, doctors, and townspeople were packed into the hallway and foyer. The ambassador bobbed and weaved, making his way toward the hospital's new emergency room, where the official opening ceremony was to take place. Scotty wondered morosely how many of the people in the audience sympathized with M-26.

The guerrilla movement had taken its name from Fidel's old group, which itself had used it as shorthand for the 26th of July Movement, a reference to the date in 1953 when Fidel and his band of crazies had tried to start his revolution by blowing up an army barracks. That failed attack—it ended up with Castro in jail—was followed by an even greater blunder three years later, when Fidel tried to invade Cuba from a pleasure boat. With typical inefficiency, the asinine and corrupt Batista government had surrounded the rebels in a swamp before finding a way to let their leader escape into the mountains. A series of further gaffes eventually led to Fidel's improbable triumph and reign.

Scotty turned the corridor and saw a throng of people in front of him. He had to push to keep up with the entourage. Though technically the ambassador's personal security was none of his business, he didn't like to get too far away. This wasn't the sort of situation calculated to make anyone comfortable—it was too uncontrolled, and that meant too much of an opportunity for one of the crazies to score points and headlines.

He wondered if he'd been the only person the damn MPs had stopped outside. Half of Havana was here, undoubtedly for the free feedbag Americans felt obliged to offer at these sorts of things. Scotty smelled the heady aroma of strong Cuban coffee and lurched forward, scanning for the inevitable table of rolls and pastries.

Oh my God, he realized, that son of a bitch over there has a gun.

The shadow of the pistol barely registered in his brain as Scotty launched himself toward the ambassador, jumping over the back of one of Steele's security men. He was shouting as he grabbed his

boss by his neck and shoulders, pulling him forward
to the floor. There were screams and then the rapid
report of a nine-millimeter pistol, very large bum-
blebees flitting through the air above him.

Panic.

The security team crouched around them, Uzis
out of their briefcases and Desert Eagle Magnums
glinting purple under the harsh fluorescent light.
But there were too many people here for them to
simply open fire.

Scotty wrestled his Colt from its shoulder holster
and crawled over the ambassador as the gunman
fled through the quickly parting crowd. Two members of the security team were already in pursuit.

"Don't kill him," Scotty yelled as he scrambled to
his feet. "We want him alive."

But they didn't even have a target to shoot at; the
would-be assassin had a good lead, a new clip in his
gun, and serious sneakers. By now the Cuban security people had snapped out of their daze and
were pursuing as well, clutching their M-16s in front
of them as if they were bulletproof shields. They
crouched and fell to the ground in almost comical
slides at the end of the corridor, scrambling once
more to their feet and running down to the left.

Scotty's forty-two-year-old lungs began pinching
his chest as he ran past a nurses' station. He felt
every ounce of fat in his body now, and the wear
and tear that had eroded the bones inside his legs.
His shoulder hurt from where he'd landed when
he'd knocked the ambassador down.

God, you're an old man, he thought as he ran.

His other thought was: Jesus, don't let them kill
the bastard.

Patients and hospital personnel were cowering in
the rooms on either side. Scotty plunged on, hitting
an intersection in the hallway just as gunfire
erupted. He dove forward, sliding into the wall be-

fore realizing the shots were coming from one corridor over. He rolled back to his feet and, nearly out
of breath, trotted toward the commotion. When he
turned the corner, he saw a small knot of men standing over a body in front of the shot-out glass doors
at the front of the hospital.

"Son of a bitch," he said. "Son of a fucking bitch."

He went to the body and knelt down. He felt for
a pulse; it was already gone.

"Fucker's dead. Son of a bitch."

"Hey, screw you, McPherson," said one of the ambassador's bodyguards. "Two of our people got hit."

"None of this would have happened if your intelligence was better," said another of the men.

Scotty, angry but feeling impotent and more than
a little winded, checked the body for ID. It was, of
course, a futile gesture.

"Get somebody to take his fucking fingerprints before the MININT clowns get here," he said, standing.
The abbreviation stood for the Spanish words
meaning interior ministry; though vastly reorganized from Castro's time, the secret police had much
the same sordid reputation among the American
delegation.

"You gonna tell us when to blow our noses, too,
Scott?"

He ignored them, walking back toward the ad-
ministrator's office, where the ambassador's communications man was calling for an incident team
and a helicopter. Steele was on another phone, talking to the embassy, making sure it was clear that he
had not been harmed.

"Dead?" Steele asked, glancing away from the
phone momentarily. Scotty nodded.

Captain Cortland James, Steele's military attaché
and gofer, was standing nervously at the ambassador's side, his Beretta service revolver hanging at the
end of his arm like a dishrag. James, a lock-jawed,

upright officer on loan from the army, bobbed his head up and down like a kid's toy, mumbling something to the effect that everything was under control.

Tito Porta loomed behind the ambassador. Porta, a Cuban of somewhat hazy pedigree, had been on both the CIA's and the State Department's payroll since before Castro's death. In Scotty's opinion, he owed his success entirely to his deep voice, which emerged from the sunken confines of his narrow lips deeper than the croaks of a frog. The overly portentous drone gave the most mundane comment more weight than a bound briefing book.

"Once again, a local intelligence failure," he declared in his Harvard-refined English. His nose twitched up as if the idea of the rebels had physically disgusted him. His glasses were askew and a dusting of white powder had been smeared across the lapel of his powder-blue jacket.

"You finish the donut?" Scotty asked.

Porta ignored him. "The *Fidelistas* must have done this," he told the ambassador when Steele clicked off the phone.

"No way," said Scotty.

Porta looked at him incredulously. "Who else would want the ambassador dead?"

"This isn't their style. Too inept. M-26 wouldn't send a lone gunman to a place like this."

Porta blinked his oversized eyes. "And you are basing this on your depth of knowledge of the Cuban people?"

"You weren't exactly a fortune-teller here either," said Scotty.

"I'll drive the car back to Havana when this quiets down," James told Steele. "You better get out as soon as the helicopter lands."

"No," said Scotty. "Go back by car. In fact, let's get a doctor's car. Better yet, a nurse's."

38

"Why should we do that?" asked James. Borrowed from one of Steele's old commands, he had come highly recommended and was probably a future Medal of Honor winner. Didn't smoke, drink, or curse—his only redeeming quality was a habit of hanging around the casinos, where he had a tendency to lose fair sums. If it weren't for that vice, Scotty would have found him completely nauseating.

"You do the driving, I'll do the thinking, all right Sonny?" Scotty told him.

"That will be a novelty," sniffed Porta.

"That's enough," barked Steele. "What are you thinking here, Scott?"

"This whole thing looks half-baked to me. If the guerrillas were really behind it, I don't see why they didn't just blow up the whole goddamned hospital."

"And why should that lead you to steal a nurse's car?" Porta asked.

"It's not going to hurt anything to play it safe."

Steele thought about it a moment, then went over and found his security team to discuss it with them. Scotty walked into the ward and found a young nurse who was trying to calm some of the others. After he asked how she had gotten to the hospital, they went together to the man who had driven her and two others to work in an ancient Ford Pinto.

The helicopter was just landing as the ambassador unceremoniously ducked into the backseat of the old Ford. James, dressed in borrowed working clothes, sat in the front.

"You better get this straightened out," said Steele, crouching under a blanket. "And if my picture gets in the paper like this, you're going to be selling coffee on the sidewalk."

"You'll always get it half price." Scotty leaned into the driver's window and exchanged a few words in Spanish about how much in debt they were to the old man. The man nodded graciously, shrugging and smiling as if this sort of thing happened every day. There was a look in his eyes, a kind of strength that comes from weathering years of hardship, from outthinking and outsurviving your enemies. Scotty knew Steele was in good hands.

He tapped the roof of the car and it backed away slowly, starting down the employees' driveway back toward the center of Havana.

The helicopter, a bright white Bell Jetranger, kicked up its rotors and began ascending as Scotty walked back toward the hospital. He watched as it climbed and picked up its tail to accelerate. Just then a loud whoosh that sounded like a bottle rocket caught up with it from the west, a dark speck of dirt flying in from nowhere, and the helicopter was consumed by a huge yellow-red fireball.

Marine Air Station at Cherry Point. 6:15 A.M.

The cold water exploded across Garcia's back like a burst from his plane's cannon. Arching his back in reaction, the pilot twisted and stretched the muscles he had just finished working hard in a three-mile run around part of the base perimeter. His right hamstring was a bit sore, but otherwise the early-morning exercise had barely tested him, much less taken the edge off his nervous energy. Garcia, who had not slept since leaving the simulation hangar, was so pumped up on adrenaline he could probably just flap his arms a few times and fly without benefit of the high-tech Pegasus. The last time he'd been this keyed was the morning he first flew a Harrier II.

That thought sobered him a bit. Garcia had been so anxious to strut his stuff he'd practically run into a fully loaded F/A-18 electronic-warfare plane sitting innocently on the runway apron nearby.

Lathered and rinsed, primped, shaven, and practically sterilized, the pilot emerged from the shower a fresh, if somewhat waterlogged, young man. He grabbed his gear—and a pack of Twinkies—and double-timed over to the hangar to get an early jump on the preflight.

With the President due to arrive by Osprey in time for an 11 A.M. flight demonstration, the base was busier than Churchill Downs before the Kentucky Derby. Even the air seemed to have been starched.

Like everyone else at the base, Garcia was excited about the arrival of the President. But that felt a bit theoretical. After all, the commander in chief was only going to be there for a wave and shake, and probably wouldn't even hang around to see the Pegasuses land. Garcia was more concerned about the arrival of his own VIP—his mother, Anna, who would be among the select crowd watching the display. The last time he'd seen her had been after he had graduated from Officer Candidate School, which seemed like twenty years ago now. He hadn't even been a pilot—at least not a Marine Corps pilot. He'd actually soloed in a civilian plane when he was fifteen, courtesy of a friend of his dad's who owned a pilot-training, air-taxi, and whatnot business in upstate New York.

Garcia's father wouldn't be coming today. He'd reacted bitterly when his son told him he'd decided to join the Marines rather than going on to law school after college. During their last argument, the elder Garcia had promised not to speak a word to his son until he left the Corps.

If there was one thing you could say about a Garcia, he was as good as his word, and twice as stubborn.

"You bring those Twinkie crumbs in here, Lieutenant, I'm gonna wax your behind. I just got the goddamn engine juicer back together, and I'll be fucked over with a fishtail if I'm gonna have them strip it out again till this carousel show is packed up and sleeping."

In the unofficial Marine Corps chain of command, Master Gunnery Sergeant Henry Thomas outranked everyone on the base, including the general in charge. Legend had it that Thomas had been present at the start of marine aviation in 1912. If he hadn't actually headed the crew that readied marine Lieutenant Alfred Cunningham's B-1 biplane, he'd undoubtedly taken the engine apart and rebuilt it just before takeoff. The toppest of top sergeants in attitude if not in specific rank, the "gunny" was dressed somewhat incongruously in an immaculately white cleansuit, complete with surgical mask (at his neck, of course) and booties. Thomas stood with his arms folded at the door of the Pegasus hush house—the hangar where the mechanics worked over the planes with more precision than the average surgical team. The sergeant ruled his steel-girdered domain with a personality that was one-tenth proud papa and nine-tenths Attila the Hun. No matter what their rank, newbies to his sphere of influence referred to him as "Master Sergeant." Everyone else called him that, too.

Garcia swallowed the last of the Twinkie and made a big show of dusting his hands. "Hey, Master Sergeant. We all ready?"

Thomas shot him a look. "We've been waiting for you to pull your damn pansy ass the hell out of bed for a half an hour."

"Hey, I'm the first one here. I took a run around the perimeter just because I didn't want to wake you up."

"The day you get up before me," replied Thomas without grinning, "is the day I join the pussy Navy."

"Better not let the colonel hear that," said Linda

Weber, entering the hangar behind him. She swung her arms out as she sauntered in, but her voice was good-natured. "He'll charge you with sexual harassment."

Thomas was a pug of a man, barely five-six but weighing probably two hundred pounds, and none of it beer gut. His face was far too craggy to make a recruiting poster, but it softened noticeably as he turned to confront Weber.

Momentarily.

"Captain, ma'am, if any of these peckerheads ever look at you cross-eyed, you just notify me. I'll rearrange their gonads for them."

"Thank you, but I don't think that will be necessary." Weber turned and caught Garcia with her smile. He felt his legs suddenly lock and ducked his head down, embarrassed at the flush he could tell was filling his face.

"Yo, Wyman, for cryin' out loud, I gotta tell you which end of that damn module is up every time you take it apart?" bawled the sergeant, his bowling-pin legs starting to churn as he threw his body toward the luckless technician. "What, you think you're in the goddamn air force or somethin'?"

Garcia took a leisurely stroll around his Pegasus. The matte-black jet's tail fin bore the low-visibility insignia of VMA-542—the Flying Tigers. The unit had adopted the name of a Harrier II squadron that had stood down a few years before, and had been given temporary permission to dress their black-bodied ships with tactfully brilliant Tiger nose art. The paint would be scraped after today's show, returning it to battlefield trim for the next stage of advanced training—the planes' as much as theirs—out at Yuma, Arizona.

The black, low-visibility paint gave a certain automatic cachet to the jets, but not everyone liked it.

Bighead, for one, preferred the dull if ultrafunctional gray-green "no-seeum" camo of serious grunt whumpers. He was an all-business kind of guy who liked to wax eloquent about ancient A-4s plodding low and slow over the sands of Iwo Jima, shot all to hell by Nazi storm troopers with their Russian SA-6s—or something like that. And there were others who thought the Lockheed-Martin A/V-32A wasn't particularly pretty no matter what color it was painted: A member of the aeronautics press had quipped that the Pegasus looked like a bad accident between an F-22, an X-15, and a kitchen fan.

But to Garcia, the four planes lined up on the smooth cement floor were a serious kind of pretty. The wings were shaped like a succession of softened triangles, as much to lower the plane's radar signal as to aid its maneuverability. A stubby set began below the back half of the cockpit bubble; where they ended a larger, somewhat more conventionally designed set took over. Viewed from the top, the rear end of the jet seemed to have been neatly punched out, the wing material bent upward to make the twin stabilizers. Besides its importance to the plane's flight characteristics, the design enhanced the effectiveness of the low-observable, axisymmetric maneuvering nozzles at the rear. The system reduced the radar and infrared profile of the engine's exhaust—which in other planes was about as subtle as a Christmas tree burning in a living room—to the equivalent of a Bic lighter at a July Fourth barbecue.

But the most striking feature of the Pegasus's design was the Rolls Royce/Allison shaft-driven lift fan wedged parallel to the wings directly behind the cockpit. The fan was housed beneath a flap or window that was closed during normal flight and stealth regimes. Technically, the plane's specs did not call for vertical takeoffs, and while some engine tweaking during the design phase made these possible, they were not part of normal operating procedure. But the fan and a discreet set of maneuvering nozzles helped the A/V-32A get off with a full weapons load from a very short runway. The shortest anyone had tried so far was three hundred feet, but Colonel Talic predicted they'd be using suburban driveways before they finished with their advanced schooling at Yuma next month.

The Pegasus's power plant was a special-model Pratt & Whitney variable-cycle supercruise engine. Once aloft, the plane could dash to almost Mach 1.8 and cruise at something around Mach 1.2, where its fuel efficiency was actually good enough to give it an unrefueled combat radius approaching six hundred miles. Though the radius was short compared to that of conventional fighter-bombers, the Pegasus's ability to operate from forward airfields extended its reach by a large margin.

The plane's physical prowess was matched by its electronics suite, an impressive array of passive and active sensors, including radar detectors, magnified video, infrared and laser imaging, and a sophisticated sound detector system that worked something like a submarine's sonar, tuned to certain preset frequencies uttered by jet and rocket engines. All of these systems were presided over by the C^3 computer, whose liquid-oxygen-cooled parallel processors could have outcomputed a roomful of 1980s-era Crays. The computer's "pilot assistant" mode—"Gump"—was nothing less than an artificial copilot, who communicated in plain English with pilots, kibitzing as well as following orders.

In short, the Pegasus was a spectacular heir to a line of outstanding warplanes produced by the lead contractor, Lockheed-Martin, whose bomber progeny included the F-111 and F-117. With a lineage that included the U-2 and the SAR-71 as well as the F-16 and a substantial portion of the F-22, the fighter-bomber represented an evolutionary leap equivalent to Java man.

Well, his son at least.

Garcia watched the mechanics prep the planes for a few more minutes, then headed toward the ready room—actually a large blackboard and folding chairs at the back end of the hangar. He was about two steps from a seat when Colonel Talic entered the hush house and yelled out to him.

"Yo, Elvis, come talk to me in my office," commanded the colonel, veering to the left with his characteristic march. For just a second he looked like Napoleon, determined to find the shortest route to Moscow.

Everyone within earshot dispensed the mandatory snickers—the office Talic was referring to was the head or men's lavatory, a place he often used for a not-so-gentle deflating of personal ego. Garcia followed along with a mixture of apprehension and confusion—it was far too early in the morning to have screwed anything up.

Talic's remark when he came into the bathroom was even more confusing, and not just because it was uttered in what, for Talic at least, was a soft tone.

"How are you doing this morning, Edward?"

"Uh, fine."

"You get a good night's sleep?"

"To be honest, sir, no. What exactly is this about?"

Talic gave him a smile, then glared at the door as it opened. One of the mechanics did an abrupt about-face as soon as he spotted the colonel.

"We have a slight problem this morning," said Talic, "and I need someone to volunteer to fix it."

"Anything, sir."

"See, that's the kind of can-do marine attitude I appreciate," said Talic.

Garcia felt his heart sink. He had a bad feeling he

had just volunteered to clean out a latrine.

"How do you feel about flying the Gomer?" asked Talic.

Not a latrine, but nearly as bad. Red Gomer Bogey was a Marine Corps Sukhoi Su-27 air-superiority piece of Russian dog shit. It did have an important role in the morning proceedings, however—as fresh meat for the Pegasus wing.

"Major Curtis is puking his guts out over at his quarters. His backup is Bozzone, but he screwed up his shoulder the other day playing football," Talic arched his eyes, "apparently against a few of my pilots, or so I'm told. In any event, he swears he can handle the stick, but the doctor tells me otherwise."

"Aw, Colonel—"

"Now, I want this to be voluntary. Of course, since I do have eight pilots and only four slots, some of our guys will be sitting on the sideline anyway."

But Garcia wasn't supposed to be one of them.

"You don't like the Russkie?" asked Talic. He seemed genuinely surprised. "It's got a lot of balls, Elvis. I'd fly it myself if I weren't leading the flight in the two-seater."

Talic wasn't giving him a snow job; they'd had a long discussion about the jet's handling and other abilities a few weeks before, and it had been the colonel who had suggested Garcia take it up for a spin. He'd flown it several times now in some rudimentary air-combat training exercises. It wasn't a bad airplane, it was just ancient.

Especially compared to the Pegasus. Who wanted to drive a beat-up Hyundai when a Porsche was revving at the corner?

"It's completely your decision," said Talic. "Keeping in mind you're the only other person on the base who has experience in that cockpit. But if I were you, I wouldn't factor that into my decision."

"What would you factor in, sir?"

47

"Nothing except a sheer can-do attitude and the understanding that volunteers are always remembered by their commander when the shit hits the fan."

Or when the time came next week to pare the squadron down from eight to four lead pilots and two alternates. Garcia realized he was a shoo-in for one of the spots; still, it wouldn't do to tempt the Fates.

"I don't have to wear the stupid Russian helmet, do I? It hurts my ears."

"Come on, Elvis, how are you going to get into the spirit of things if you aren't wearing the right hat?"

The Sukhoi looked like the product of a forced mating between an F-14 Tomcat and an F/A-18 Hornet. With boxy engine intakes under its stubby wings, looming twin stabilizers, and a jutting cockpit, she was arguably the best opponent a Western pilot could face when the Cold War wound down.

Now, though, she was a bit long in the tooth. Especially this model, which dated from the early 1980s. Garcia worked his gloved fingers together as he surveyed the panel of dials in front of him. He had flown the Russian hand-me-down only four days before, but reprogramming himself to the cockpit after the Pegasus was not an easy task. As naturally gifted as he might be, Garcia had grown up in the electronic era; analog displays would always seem a bit unnatural to him. The hardest thing to get used to was the attitude gyro on the left half of the dash, for unlike American-style instruments, which showed the world revolving as the plane stayed steady, its shadow aircraft tilted against a constant earth—perhaps more accurate from a philosophical point of view, but disorienting nonetheless.

Technically speaking, the flight controls were

electronically assisted hydraulics rather than the pure fly-by-wire systems Garcia had cut his teeth on, but the difference meant little in practical terms; they were roughly as responsive as those in a Hornet. In fact, though the Sukhoi dwarfed the American attack plane, Garcia had found the performance remarkably similar the first time he took Gomer aloft.

He thought of this as he powered up the Lyul'ka engines. He also thought of a warning from one of his earliest instructors, delivered, ironically, on his first flight in a two-place F/A-18D—don't take shit for granted because you recognize the smell.

Which meant, more or less, that every plane had its own characteristics. The throaty Russian engines reminded him of this, and Garcia proceeded slowly through his checks. Cleared to join the festivities, he ambled over to the end of the runway, aware that he was turning a few heads. Red Gomer Bogey was dressed in colors supposedly based on a Russian naval scheme, but more likely designed to remind anyone who saw it of the marine dress uniform—except for the gaudy Russian star, of course. Her body and wings wore thick bands of different shades of blue; the leading edge of her wings was a crisp red, and her ailerons were tipped with a white sharp enough to make a drill sergeant proud.

Hokey, yes, but then the morning show was the epitome of hokey. The President was going to review a veritable historical parade of marine airpower, topped off by the sleek new Pegasuses, which would chase Garcia from the sky.

Assuming he got the stinking rudders to work right. They seemed stuck. He craned his neck out the cockpit as the tower boomed in his ear, wondering why the hell he was jamming up the freeway.

"Don't you Commies believe in preflight checks before you get to the firing line?" some wiseass cracked over the radio. "Why are you flapping around?"

Garcia kept his mouth shut. He worked through the routine deliberately, triple-checking that everything was kosher. He decided that the peculiar control system had made everything feel slightly sluggish, but the tail fins and flaps were actually OK. Garcia made sure his leading-edge slats were set for takeoff, pushed the gate on the throttle for afterburner, and kicked into the sky.

"Thank you, Grandma Russia," said one of the controllers sarcastically.

"You're welcome, Comradski," replied Garcia.

He came back far sharper on the stick than necessary, showing off the plane's enormous thrust as Gomer shot skyward like a bullet. He took her to about 5,000 feet, then circled to the south in a gentle climb until he reached 10,000. Starting to feel his oats, he did an aileron roll, tucking the Sukhoi to port; he followed with another, then a pair to starboard for balance. The controls were fine, sharply responsive; he plunged into a half-Cuban-8 to prove it. Gravity nudged at him as he pulled out of the maneuver, but he judged it wasn't more than 5 g's, just enough to remind him that Newton and his eccentric laws hadn't gone on vacation.

The proceedings were being choreographed from a venerable C-130 Hercules, which had been borrowed from reserve squadron VMGR-452 out of New York especially for the occasion. Code-named "Senior Warrior," the plane was a combination tanker, electronic intelligence, and command platform—demonstrating the Corps' philosophy about cramming multiple capabilities into a single entity, not to mention the remarkable versatility of the four-engine turboprop first flown in the 1950s.

"Gomer One, this is Senior Warrior. You should

have us in visual bearing three-six-zero at eight thousand feet."

Garcia acknowledged and was vectored over to what amounted to an aerial parking lot just west of the air base. The sky was soon stacked with airplanes waiting for their cue on the dance card.

Red Gomer Bogey's turn came toward the end, but it was a beaut. After the old-timers did standard flybys, the Russian import would slash over the reviewing stand like a Third World egomaniac bent on world destruction. A group of A-6s would scurry in all directions, pretending to be scattered by his attack. A pair of Harrier IIs would scramble off the field, seemingly in chase. Garcia would take a nice, lazy turn out of view and head back—then pretend to chase the Harriers out of the sky. Another turn and he would return victorious—with a quick roll to demonstrate his alleged superiority. As he whisked eastward and climbed triumphantly, the Pegasuses would rise in unison, hover a moment, and then chase Red Gomer Bogey into oblivion.

A circus show, really. But the brass ate it up, and hoped the President would, too.

Garcia, who had a cheat sheet with the maneuver sequence clipped to the right side of the dashboard, thought it would look pretty sharp from the ground; he hoped his mother would be impressed. Unfortunately, there had been no way for him to contact her and she would think he was flying one of the A/V-32A's.

In truth, his mother would know the planes only from the color; he'd told her to watch for the only black planes in the parade. He was just debating whether it would be worth trying to explain what the difference was when Senior Warrior gave him the green light. He rocked forward and the Sukhoi began slurping down jet fuel, settling in for a pass over the runway. The quartet of A-6 Intruders were just entering the demonstration area, and Garcia heard the Harrier II pilots acknowledge that they were ready to play.

Everything was right on schedule.

He spotted the A-6s circling below him as he approached. He took a breath, relaxing, trying to keep his upper body loose, feeling the run he'd taken hours before suddenly in his thighs. His stomach was hollow and empty, and the saliva had vanished from his mouth.

"Here we go," said the lead A-6 pilot, cueing the first dance sequence.

Garcia felt his plane fall away from him as he nosed into a nearly ninety-degree dive, plunging straight for the deck as the other planes rolled into twisting climbs, pretending to run away from him. For a moment, they were strands of rope, entwining themselves in a fluid sculpture, a beautifully fluid entanglement enhanced by the thick red and blue smoke that the Intruders began emitting from special canisters beneath their wings. Garcia flashed toward the earth, passing the other planes and locking his eyes on the altitude bar on the left side of his screen, waiting as the triangular arrow point sank toward his cue to pull out. The g number edged up in the center of the view over the horizon and heading crosshairs, growing by half-points as his acceleration picked up.

At that moment, the young pilot felt very good, very full of himself, enormously proud that he had done so well and come so far in these past few months, proud that he had stood up to his father, paid the price to live out his dream. He'd achieved his most cherished goal, becoming a marine aviator, an accomplishment that an infinitesimally small percentage of men could claim. He wasn't just good enough to be picked to fly the country's newest jet; he had been chosen to show off for the President of the United States. At the last minute, they'd thrown him a curve, put him into an unfamiliar plane; he'd handled the change like a pro—at twenty-four, if he wasn't among the best marine aviators ever, he was well on his way to joining their ranks. His heart beat with an intense, adrenaline-tinged satisfaction.

And then, at the very periphery of his consciousness, at the very height of his hubris, he became aware that something was going dreadfully wrong. The alert buzzer had not sounded, no warning flashed, but he felt something was way out of place. Instinctually, he yanked on the stick, felt the slack helplessness of faint delay, his breath choking in his throat. In the next second his stomach expanded to three times its normal size. The dark brown grain of the earth began giving way to blue, his knee ached, but his butt felt the reassuring pressure of the seat as the Sukhoi grew heavy around him, responding to the commands like a well-trained pony.

In the next second, a dark shadow enveloped the cockpit, gray death stealing in. Warnings were flashing now, buzzers and voices yelling over the radio, but above them all was the loud snap of metal shearing metal, the angry crack of a wing hitting a tail section. One of the A-6s had inexplicably turned in the wrong direction, toward the Sukhoi instead of away. That in itself would not have caused disaster, but the A-6 had entered the demonstration space two hundred feet farther east than it was supposed to be, and the errors were now multiplied catastrophically.

"Full power, full power, full power," Garcia screamed, as if Gump were here to help him fly. At the same instant he literally punched the throttle as the Sukhoi lurched back toward the ground, her momentum thrown off by the Intruder's blow. With his right hand he yanked the control yoke as hard as he could, pulling it toward him as if it were an old-fashioned stick that could be persuaded by brute force.

His airspeed indicator showed over 400 knots; he was going straight in.

Garcia kept pulling. Two or three voices were buzzing in his ears, and the pilot realized that the others would be going on with the show, unaware of his problem.

"Abort, abort," he shouted into his microphone, trying to end the demonstration. "We have a problem."

The brown blob in front of him stopped getting bigger, and blue edged into the top of his windscreen. But with less than one and a half tail fins, the plane's aerodynamic profile was closer to a corkscrew's than a glider's. Garcia fought off a yaw as the rushing slipstream threw wave after wave of g-forces against the stricken plane.

There was barely a half-mile between Garcia and the reviewing stands, dead ahead. A thick mucus in his throat told him he wasn't going to make it.

"Get out of there, Garcia," said Talic, somewhere above him. Garcia heard the words above the roaring din; whether they were real or imagined, he couldn't tell.

Everything ran in slow motion. Garcia saw the crowd out ahead of him. They all thought this was a hell of a show, this hot-dog marine pilot pretending he was going to smack right into them, when all along he was planning to turn off at the last second.

Only there wasn't going to be a turn. A powerful hand had taken hold of the fuselage and was pushing it into the ground, forcing it toward an unrecoverable spin.

I can't hit those people, Garcia thought to himself. I can't. If I punch out now, they're all going to die. The plane will spin itself into them.

Garcia pushed the flaps and stood on what was

left of the rudder. If the plane had been intact and truly followed his directions, it would probably have burrowed itself directly into the ground. Instead it threw its body out awkwardly, skidding but staying out of a spin.

Still sailing toward the review stand.

"Bail out," said Talic. There was no doubt now; his voice was coming over the radio. The colonel must have broken formation to find out what the hell was going on. "That's an order."

Garcia felt the plane slipping into a roll. If he lost it, he'd never get out—and he'd still kill the people on the ground.

He pulled the stick back desperately, wildly, out of control now, trying to bend the plane to his will.

"Elvis! Go!"

Garcia threw his whole body onto the throttle, lunging the engine to the firewall. The plane hesitated for a moment and then shot ahead, clearing the review area and the hangars. Garcia had no notion of where the horizon was, knew the odds of surviving were incredibly against him, but felt an immense sense of euphoria. He had missed the stands.

The President, and his mother, and all the others, were safe.

As gravity threw a black, tightening cowl over his head, he placed his hands firmly on the red handle between his legs and pulled, pulled himself into a bullet as the world broke into a million pieces with the great roar of the final apocalypse.

Chapter Two

The hinges of the heavy door had not been oiled in many years, and pushing it provoked a loud squeal of metal that sounded as if some part of the heavens were being torn in two. Carla de Souza took a breath as she stared into the darkened hallway, reminding her body once more that it would show neither fear nor the anger boiling inside her. To reveal either would be to lose irrevocably, to forfeit everything. She glanced at her bodyguards—only six men would accompany her inside, as agreed—and nodded for them to follow.

Years of dancing had sculpted her leg muscles, and though it had now been nearly three years since she had performed, they had lost none of their tone. But they stiffened reflexively as she approached the door of the old schoolhouse stage, a flutter rising in her stomach. It took her by surprise—nostalgia, the butterflies of a dancer approaching the stage.

Once she had hoped to become a principal of

56

Ballet Havana. Four years before, that dream was all that mattered in her life.

Her tendons ached with the memory, and as she took the knob of the stage door she realized that her opponent was even more wily than she had imagined. For surely Romano had calculated this effect when he asked to meet her here.

Zora had known. She had warned that Romano, as crazy as he was, could not be taken for granted. The witch—Carla had grown to use the term with kindness and awe, rather than derision—always knew.

Without Zora's advice and help over the past two years, Carla would never have survived, let alone gotten this far. But the larger part of her success was innate, passed through the genes. She let her mouth relax, softened the frown as she saw the flickering red light thrown by a dim safety bulb through the stage door. She was ready when the lights flooded on as she walked onto the stage, and so she reacted not by putting her hands to her eyes, but by bowing, the sweeping, gracious gesture of a prima ballerina accepting praise.

Even in the black, bulky sweater and denim pants, her body had an obvious, aggressive beauty; even wearing heavy-soled boots, she moved with the air of someone from beyond this world. Her appearance immediately charmed most of the small cluster of leftists sitting below the stage, especially those who had never met her before.

There was one person, however, she could never win over.

"*Se cree princesa*," spat the tall, bearded figure standing alone in the front row. "She believes in her heart that she is a princess. Or maybe still a ballerina."

Carla signaled to her bodyguards to stay behind, then walked forward to the edge of the stage. "I know who I am. Who is it that you believe you are?" she demanded.

The question was only rhetorical, but there was an obvious answer. For even to Carla, Hector Romano Moncada bore a haunting resemblance to the youthful Fidel Castro, with his field dress, black leather holster, beaked army cap, and unkempt beard. She had heard rumors that the guerrilla leader—her only remaining rival among the rebels—had his underlings refer to him as *El Jefe*, the commander or chief, a nickname taken by her dead father.

Romano was discreet enough now to say nothing, though she wondered how his ego bore the discipline.

"You have overstepped yourself," she told him. "Attempting to assassinate the American ambassador was foolish. Why have you tried to take action in Havana, when the council has not approved? Your area is in the mountains. Go back there."

"You are the council," replied Romano. "And you are not my leader."

"Groups join me of their own will. The Jackal is with me."

"He has three men."

Carla did not answer immediately. The fact that Romano had been able to launch the attack demonstrated that he had far greater resources, and perhaps influence, than she had thought only a week ago. As a woman, even as Castro's daughter, she could never trust that her position as leader in the movement was secure.

"The government has used the attack to press for American arms and air support once again," she said, characteristically relying on the force of logic. Reason had been almost as important as violence in her rise.

"What does that matter to me?"

"It will matter a great deal when the bombs fall on your head. You are the most vulnerable to airplanes. They would not bomb my people in the cities."

"The instant the United States Air Force attacks me, I have won. The country will rally to my side."

Carla had informants and even agents in the provisional government and the U.S. mission to Cuba, and so she knew that the North Americans would never commit their own air force to the fight. Nor did she share Romano's optimistic assessment of the propaganda value of an explicit U.S. role in the conflict. In fact, she suspected the initial attitude of much of the country would be favorable toward the Americans.

She had learned much in her two years of struggle.

"You have grown soft since the first time we met," taunted Romano. He stroked his beard with his fingers—a mannerism stolen directly from her father. "You forget the most important lesson—without risks there will be no rewards."

"¡Basta! Do not tell me about risks. I have taken more in the past two years than you have taken in your lifetime."

"You are a dancer, not a leader. Still beautiful, but only a dancer."

Carla struggled to control her anger. At times like this, Zora had said, look for the motive. Why does your opponent seek to provoke you? What is the logic?

But there was no logic in Romano, nothing but blind madness. If the movement were ever left to him, it would disintegrate into a mindless bloodbath. Its true goal—the preservation of her father's reforms, her father's justice—would be lost.

"I lead M-26," she said, her voice cold and measured. "I will allow you to operate in the mountains,

59

where you always have. If you wish to join me, then we can discuss other arrangements. Otherwise, stay out of Havana—stay out of the west entirely."

"I will fight where I please. Your own troops wish me here. Ask them."

Carla laughed. "There are six here. Ask them yourself."

"Your attempts to win a truce," said the bearded rebel, "are foolish. Politics and democracy are not the answer."

"I will be the one to decide my strategy. You can follow me or go back home, as you please."

"Come, now, I am here to make peace between us." Romano opened his arms wide. "Perhaps I will join you after all. Let me embrace you as a sister."

Finally we have gotten to the reason for the meeting, she realized. He is crazy, yes, but he always has a plan.

Everything now became clear—the attack on the ambassador had been meant as a signal to her, a demonstration that he was far more powerful than she had thought. And now he would make some magnanimous gesture. He was angling for a position on the council after all.

Perfect. That was precisely where she wanted him—in plain view where he could be easily countered. Her lieutenants would be able to begin working on his cadres, something that had been impossible up until now.

He had underestimated her, thinking he could manipulate her so easily. Very well—she would play the role he wished.

"I do not care to embrace you," she said.

"Come, now—as a sister. Shake my hand at least."

Carla watched as he walked up the stairs at the side of the stage. She knew that he would pull her toward him. She felt her bodyguards tensing in the shadows and wagged her fingers at them—a subtle, prearranged signal that everything was under control.

Even so, her fingers reached to her sweater as he approached. A small but very sharp knife welded to a set of brass knuckles rested there; she curled her hand into them, just in case.

Romano took her hand, then, as she knew he would, pulled her toward him. The smell of the jungle rushed at her; with it came a long-repressed memory, her father hugging her as a toddler.

He could be my father's reincarnation, she thought to herself, pushing away. My God, have I been around Zora so long that I have absorbed her superstitions?

"See? I'm not that bad," said Romano, smiling. "To prove it, I will offer you a gift. Not tribute—but a gift."

"What will you get out of it?" She tried to make her voice hard, but in truth, even as prepared and practiced as she was, it faltered.

"Only your goodwill."

"And what will this gift be?"

"A deal with my Russian contacts."

"What Russian contacts?"

"The mafiya has been supplying me for many months."

"With antique weapons?"

Romano shrugged. "If I had more money, I could get better weapons. I will admit this one thing—your resources are better than mine. The Russians seem to think that you will pay a good price for weapons such as the missile that was used against the American ambassador's helicopter."

Carla would indeed. She would pay even more for airplane parts, as she had a pet plan to use some sympathizers in the old air force to bomb the provisional government buildings. Her one failure had been to develop trustworthy relationships with any

Jim DeFelice

Russian—a legacy, perhaps, of the split between her father and the ex-Communists at the end of his life.

"How much do they want for such things?" she asked.

"You will have to deal with them."

"They don't trust you?"

"Trust isn't an issue. They charged me five thousand dollars for the missile I used. I do not know if they will give you a similar deal or not."

Carla nearly gasped. It was an offer she couldn't afford to ignore. She wondered, though—it seemed a price even Romano ought to be able to afford.

"The Russians have many things for sale," said Romano. "I do not particularly like those people, but they may be useful in the short term."

Their faces were only a few inches apart. She could feel the heat of his body—the burning fire of hate that he must be concealing—in the dank air. He was jealous of her, he would always be jealous of her, for she was the legitimate heir, not he. He was only a man with a beard.

A crazy man with a beard.

"What do you get out of this?" she asked him.

"I offer you friendship," said Romano. "We will always have differences, but our forces should work together."

"Join the council, then."

"Perhaps in the future." He broke her gaze. "Victor Padilla will contact you and set up a meeting. He has the details."

"Who is Padilla?"

"He has some affiliation with Eagle's Blood," said Romano, waving his hand dismissively at the guerrilla's ostentatious nom de guerre. "Otherwise, I do not know him. The Russians have many people willing to help them, from the old days."

Carla took a step backward into the darkness as she considered this. Eagle's Blood—his real name

62

was the considerably more pedestrian Juan Pérez—ranked among her most loyal followers in Havana. But he had not told her that he or any of his people dealt with the Russians, an oversight he would have to explain.

"We will see how this develops," she said, curbing her anger at Pérez for the time being. *"Viva la Revolución."*

"Viva la Revolución," Romano echoed.

When she pushed the door open to emerge from the building, Carla startled a group of seabirds that had been roosting in the nearby yard. They took to flight en masse, and for a moment it seemed as if a thousand doves were fleeing the earth.

It was a good thing she had not taken Zora with her to the meeting, she realized. The old woman, horribly superstitious, would have shuddered at the portent.

Grover Cleveland High School, New Jersey. 9 A.M.

The dank odor of mildew and sweat, peculiar to high-school locker rooms, tickled Steele's nose. It was about as pleasant as the scent of skunk on a bird dog, and Steele—who long ago had hunted wild turkeys in woods a few miles from here—tried to screw up his stomach against the stench. It didn't help that James, his aide, sat on the locker-room bench a few feet away shoving Dunkin' Donut munchkins down his throat. The young captain was oblivious to everything, and probably considered it an honor to meet the President of the United States in the basement of a high-school gym.

Steele did not. Nonetheless, he was grateful for the audience with his old friend, and mindful that the location—far from view of the media entourage that traveled with the President—had been chosen for reasons beyond convenience.

D'Amici was, as usual, running late. He had spent the night near Trenton, having addressed a party fund-raiser there earlier in the evening. Now he was scheduled to thrill a group of ninth- and tenth-graders in the auditorium upstairs before setting off for the Midwest.

Far away from Cuba. Steele glanced over at James, who nearly choked on his donut as someone opened up the door. A tall Secret Service agent wearing an immaculate dark blue suit with a minuscule red pin in his lapel strode into the locker room, followed by a shorter man in corduroys and an open print shirt. He smiled behind his wire-rimmed glasses and held his hand up to Steele.

"Hey, General," he said as he approached the ambassador.

"Dr. Blitz. You haven't succumbed to the Washington dress code yet."

Blitz clapped the general on the back. Officially, Michael Blitz was a White House deputy chief of staff; unofficially, he was the President's chief foreign policy troubleshooter. A college professor with a doctorate in post-Marxian Marxism, he had written a few impressive articles for *Foreign Affairs* but brought almost no other credentials to the job when hired at the beginning of the administration—except for the fact that, like Steele, he had known Jack D'Amici since grammar school. Blitz's name was a source of endless amusement to Beltway insiders since he was a teetotaler, but otherwise he had proven an excellent choice, precisely because he had remained as unconventional as ever.

"When's Jack getting here?" Steele asked.

"He ought to be down in a minute," said Blitz, glancing around. "This is James, right?"

"Pleased to meet you, sir."

Blitz shook his hand, then pulled Steele aside. "You're sure about this pilot thing?"

"As sure as I can be. Assuming you're not up for detailing a wing of F-16s."

Blitz made a face. "The pilots are a problem, Malcolm. Big problem."

"As big as getting MiGs?"

"No, but big enough. Whose idea was this? McPherson's?"

Steele almost blanched. "It doesn't matter. It's my idea now," he said quickly.

"McPherson's a good agent if you keep him reined in," conceded Blitz. "But he still pisses some people off."

"This is my idea."

Blitz leaned against one of the lockers. Thirty years before, he'd played free safety for a high-school squad that used facilities just like this. Take away the beard, maybe a few pounds—and put back a lot of hair—and he'd still look nothing like a football player. "You know, Malcolm, if the Cubans would just schedule elections, the guerrillas will shrivel up. This attack the other day aside, they're on a downward slide."

"Why do you think I want the pilots?"

Blitz shoved his hands into his pockets and began rocking sideways on the balls of his feet. "How do you answer a congressman who says U.S. personnel shouldn't be directly involved?"

"They're going over as instructors. The planes are already there. They're apparently a bitch to fly—which it might have been nice to know before the deal was put through."

"There may be some flak out of the Joint Chiefs," said Blitz, in a way that made it seem as if he were hovering on the edge of supporting the project. If he went for it, the President would. If he didn't, it would take all of Steele's persuasive powers—and

Jim DeFelice

probably some begging—to get D'Amici to sign off.

Not that it was worth begging. But if they were going to move the interim government off the dime, he needed to do more than open new hospital wings.

"The chiefs are a pain in my butt," continued Blitz. A smile slowly stole over his face. "Maybe we can lose the paperwork and bypass them. Make it an NSC project. Another personnel loan. By the time they get wind of it, our guys'll be home. Right? What's this going to last? Two months? Three?"

Steele wasn't so far removed from the army that he didn't immediately realize cutting the JCS out of the loop was a bad idea. But before he could say so, the door opened and the President of the United States entered with his entourage.

Jack D'Amici ignored the stagnant smell as he strode with his long legs toward his two old friends. Maybe the air smelled cleaner when you were President, Steele thought.

"Malcolm, how the hell are you? I hear you have people shooting at you from all directions."

"Fine. The gunman and the missile both missed."

"Don't cut it so close next time. Olissa will kill me if anything happens to you."

"Yes, sir, Mr. President."

D'Amici smiled at Steele. Without exception, all of his friends called him Mr. President to his face, even in private. He was somewhat amused by it—and probably would have drop-kicked them if they hadn't.

"Good job keeping it out of the press," added D'Amici.

One of the few advantages of censorship, Steele thought—but didn't say. That was one of the differences between being a general and an ambassador.

"You and Blitz work that problem out?" D'Amici asked.

66

"Not entirely," said Blitz. "We were just getting to the election date."

"Getting a date is not going to be easy," said Steele quickly. "They have all sorts of conditions."

D'Amici put up his hand. "Malcolm, we all have our problems."

Blitz, standing behind the President, shook his head violently. Steele ignored him.

"The situation is very complicated," said Steele. "And the pilots, that's only part of—"

"It's pretty damn big from my point of view," snapped D'Amici. "Why the hell do they keep stalling the elections?"

"They like being in power."

The President's laugh shook the metal locker doors. His mood immediately brightened. "So do we all. Get them to set the elections, Malcolm. If you don't, they don't get any aid. Nada. Maybe that's what they want."

"The pilots—"

"No American airplanes. No direct intervention or anything that smells like it. If you can work out an adviser thing with Blitz, fine. Whatever it takes. But, General—Malcolm—" The President put his arm on Steele's shoulder.

Steele hated that.

"We need the elections. And not just for Cuba. The whole foreign-aid bill is riding on it. Everything."

"I'll do my best."

"I'm counting on you. Tell Olissa she still owes me an apple pie."

"She probably has it baking right now," said Steele as his old friend was swallowed up by his security detail.

Infirmary, Cherry Point. 4 P.M.

Garcia sighed and pushed himself off the hospital bed. "Look, Ma, I'm going for a walk. The leg feels fine. The only reason I'm still in here is that I was ordered to stay."

"You have to listen to the doctors. That's what they're paid for. They study all that time."

"I got the world's biggest Ace bandage on my knee," Garcia told her. "What else do you want?"

"You're lucky you're alive. Thank the savior. If every day I did not light a candle for you, *¡qué va!* What a miracle."

Garcia reached out and put his arm on his mother's shoulder, staggering slightly but keeping his balance. To anyone else, he might have admitted it was indeed a miracle that he had escaped alive, let alone so lightly. But he could not say so to his mother.

"You're going to fall," she said, grabbing his side. She was a full foot shorter than he was, but her grasp was firmer than a wrestler's.

"I'm fine, Ma. I don't need any help."

"About time you got out of bed."

Garcia looked up into Colonel Talic's cheek-splitting grin. He turned five shades of red.

"Mrs. Garcia, good to see you again," said Talic. "Hey, don't let me stop you, Lieutenant; keep walking."

"I'm okay," he said, struggling to the chair.

"Colonel, tell him he's supposed to stay in bed. The doctors have given him this order."

"It's hard to keep a good marine down, Ma'am."

"It's an order. I understand the army. He must obey."

"Marines, Mom. Marines."

Bighead grinned at Garcia with a look that suggested he, too, had once had a mother. "How's the leg?"

"It's sore. Too bad I didn't land on my head, huh?"

Talic nodded. His face had begun to grow serious. "Ma'am, would you excuse us for a minute? I have something I have to discuss with your son. It's official business."

Garcia suffered through a kiss on the cheek before his mother dutifully shuffled out to the hallway.

"You don't have to be embarrassed, Lieutenant. She's a very nice lady."

"I'm not embarrassed, sir."

Talic sat on the edge of the bed. For a fleeting moment, something about his expression reminded Garcia of his estranged father.

"Good of your mom to stay," said Talic. "She needs anything, three or four generals will bust ass to help her. Guaranteed."

"Thank you, sir."

"Everybody thinks you did a helluva job with the Sukhoi. A lot of people could have been killed. You're a fantastic pilot, Elvis. I mean that. I couldn't have done a better job. No shit."

Garcia didn't like the direction this was going. He felt a twinge in his knee, grimaced, then quickly flexed the leg to show it was fine. "The doc says I just pulled the ligament. I did worse playing football in high school. I'll be cleared to fly tomorrow."

"Tomorrow? The doctor said that?"

"Well, what he said was, as soon as I can walk, there's no reason I can't fly. And I'm already walking around. Couple of aspirin and I'll be fine."

Talic rubbed his chin with his forefinger. The edges of his temples had turned light red. Garcia had seen the expression creep over his face one other time—a month before when Talic had had to cut the squadron's roster in half.

"I'm not going with you to Arizona, am I," blurted Garcia. It was a statement, not a question.

Talic shook his head grimly. "You're my best pilot. No doubt about it. But the doctors want you to stay the night here. And then there are administrative things to take care of."

Jim DeFelice

"That sucks a bunch of horse bull."

"Marine." Talic must have been made entirely of sinew and bone, because his short, narrow frame was more ferocious than a hissing lion's. His bark literally shook Garcia in his bed. Still, there was a look of regret in his stern expression, and he spoke more softly when he added, "You're due leave."

Though admittedly intimidated by his commander, Garcia wasn't backing down. "That's a hunk of crap. Sir."

"The problem is, and you've known it all along, we have too many pilots for too few airplanes. The production line is stalled."

"But you just said yourself—"

"Personal feelings have nothing to do with this." The tinge of red had spread from Talic's temples to the rest of his face. It made him look older than his forty-two years. The gray in his razor-cut hair was more obvious, and the lines worn by his combat missions in the Gulf War were prominent. "Cuts have to be made. There are plenty of people around who are going to look after you now. They'll do a hell of a lot more for you than I can. That's guaranteed. You have to think long-term."

"But I want to fly now." Garcia started to get up from the chair.

Talic put his hand out and gently pushed him back into the seat. "This is the Marine Corps, son. If the brass decides to put you in a garbage-hauling platoon, you do it and you like it."

Garcia felt impotent. Angry tears were starting to form behind his eyes; he fought them back. "This is an order from above? Am I going to get a desk job? They're not grounding me permanently, are they?"

Talic shook his head. "No. This is my decision. Listen, you earned yourself some leave. Take your time getting better, then take a few weeks off, enjoy yourself. Take your mother sightseeing."

70

"Since when do I have leave?"

"Automatic after a situation like this," said Talic, tapping his hat quickly.

"You don't think I caused the accident?"

"Shit no. I'm telling you, kid, you're on top of the world right now. This is an opportunity. I'm not bullshitting you. Make the most of it," said Talic. "Look, you can fly just about anything. When the next batch of 32s come through, you'll be in good shape to join them. You'll get a promotion, maybe even be put in charge. You'll be in a position to pull strings."

"But that's not for six months at least."

Talic rose. "Look, Garcia. You're going to be a marine for a long time, right? So let's say some general somewhere notices you're available. You take an administrative assignment—"

"Friggin' hell."

"You take an assignment you don't like for a short period of time, say six months, maybe a year. Part of your time will get soaked up talking to investigators and inquiry boards anyway. You blow your nose when you're told to, then you move on. That's the way the game is played."

"I joined the marines to fly, sir. If I can't fly, I quit."

"Grow up, Garcia. Jesus Christ." Talic sighed deeply, as if by emptying his lungs he could discharge the whole thing. "Look, for what it's worth, I think you're a helluva a pilot, and if you need a favor in the future—"

"I need one now."

". . . if you need a favor in the future, I'll help any way I can. The truth is, my pull doesn't amount to much these days."

"Friggin' horseshit. Sir."

Outside of the room, Talic stopped to say something reassuring to Garcia's mother. He had a sense

71

that his very presence scared the woman, and thought of telling her that she could relax; her son probably wouldn't fly too much over the next few months. But as Garcia hadn't taken that as particularly happy news, he decided not to mention it. No sense having the kid explode on his mom.

Garcia's reaction had been about what Talic expected. Not that he blamed him. He'd have had the same reaction himself twenty years ago.

But it was the right thing to do. It made slicing down the size of the squadron much easier, and because of the circumstances, it was bound to help, not hurt, Garcia's career. The kid didn't realize it, but he'd just gotten a serious long-term boost. Four or five generals and maybe an admiral or two would be vying for his services as soon as word got around. If someone had been looking out for Talic like that when he was a kid, he'd be a general by now.

Lieutenant Colonel Henry "Bighead" Talic saw a lot of himself in young Mr. Garcia—too much, in fact. The whole reason he'd gotten the nickname "Bighead" even.

Garcia hadn't grown up yet. He hadn't learned there were limits even to what ability could do for you, or for others. He'd done one shitting hell of a job getting that Sukhoi out of the area; Talic knew that, and he'd made sure everyone else knew that.

But he was worried Garcia would draw the wrong lesson from it. He was worried the young man would have to learn where the fine line of ability ended, where courage deserted you and you had only your blind guts, the way Talic had.

It was an important lesson. But getting it right nearly killed him.

"Colonel? Say, Henry, what are you doing in here?"

Talic swung around and saw Major Christie, a Marine Corps physician.

"Hey, Doc. Just looking after one of my kids."

"Garcia? He did a helluva job out there."

"Is he going to be okay?"

"Oh, sure. He's not my patient, but from what I heard he just pulled the medial ligament, right? Now if—"

"That's okay, Doc," said Talic, starting to back away. "I don't really need the what-ifs."

"Say, Henry, how come you blew off your physical last week?"

Embarrassed, Talic shrugged. "We were flying, and, to be honest, I forgot."

"Forgot? Something wrong?"

"No. Really. Not at all."

There wasn't, at least not that he knew. But Talic was at the point now where he dreaded physicals, and in fact dreaded all encounters with the medical establishment. They were just one more chance at having your ticket pulled. And at his age, that would mean the end of his career and usefulness.

"You set up another appointment?" asked the doctor.

"Have to," said Talic, whacking Christie's back as a good-bye gesture. "Got a few million things to tend to. Take care of my kid."

Ave Club, Havana, Cuba. 11:30 P.M.

The lights of the onrushing traffic came at him like a thousand swordsmen, poking and slashing his overtired eyes. Scotty resisted the temptation to rub them, helping Esma from the cab onto the sidewalk. Her high heels slipped on the smooth marble of the walkway, and she leaned her body into his, the soft crush of her side stoking his desire again. He felt his blood rise, and for a moment he thought of pushing her back into the cab and going home, making love for the rest of the night, kissing every inch of her body for hours, soaking her through the pores of his skin.

Instead, he let her lead the way into the interior of Ave, a small but popular Havana club at the edge of the harbors on the northeastern side of the city. Unlike the Trump, where they had spent the night before, Ave was strictly a Cuban hangout, unknown to most tourists but touted as the place to hear Latin jazz by local aficionados. It had a certain subdued Cuban elegance, even though the furnishings predated Castro. Esma had shown Scotty how to appreciate such things as the intricately worked iron rail at the front of the building, a metaphor for the national character. The thick art noveau chairs inside, painted a glossy black, had held three generations of Cubans; the smooth marble dance floor promised to host many more into the future.

Scotty and Esma swept up the walkway to the thick blue carpet, still with their arms around each other's waist. One of the plainclothes guards nodded discreetly as Scotty strolled by; he was on good terms with the club's security for several reasons, official and otherwise.

Going to places like the Trump, where he could mix with high-rolling Americans and Cubans and listen for the latest intrigues, was part of Scotty's job. Coming here he could be more relaxed; while he still kept an ear out for gossip, most of what he did at Ave was watch Esma.

"*Señor* McPherson, nice to see you this evening," said the maître d', beaming a smile at him as they approached. "A very good night to come—we have Diane Moreno singing tonight. A table near the front?"

Scotty nodded. The fact that the maître d' had been on the CIA payroll for nearly twenty years—and remained so—encouraged the warmness of his welcome, and meant that the table he showed them to was among the club's best.

Fronted by a girlish blonde at a piano, the band on the small, semicircular stage played a bluesy jazz that gave the thick, smoke-laden air of the club a poignant taste. A hundred flickering shadows rose from the table candles, casting ghostlike figures across the embossed plaster ceiling and the frieze of tropical birds that had given the club its name. The place had a haunted feel, as if its door were a portal to a forgotten corner of the late fifties, when gangsters ruled the decadent Havana nightlife and a prescient sense of impending doom and revolution infested even the island's most successful casinos.

Though this was far from the most exclusive hangout on the island, a good portion of the crowd was sipping expensive champagne and a bourbon-spiked rum drink called "Whizz," an invention reputed to be only a few weeks old. Many had managed to find a way to earn a fortune in the twenty-four months since Fidel had died; not a few were former members of the Communist hierarchy, who had paid significant sums to remove those credits from their résumés.

But there were also people like Esma, middle-class inhabitants of Havana finally able to smile. They and their families had suffered much under Castro; in some sense they were learning to live for the first time.

Signaled by the maître d', the waiter brought a straight bourbon and a bottle of champagne to the table, opening the wine with a great flourish. He poured it for Esma as if she were a princess escaping her palace for the night. She beamed up at him, and the man practically fainted in gratitude.

"Another one falls under your spell," Scotty told her, sipping his drink. She laughed and playfully slapped at his hand, her fingernails flicking lightly across the skin.

The lights on the stage dimmed to a narrow point on the pianist. She began working the keys slowly, then leaned forward, her lips practically kissing the mike. The words of an old song made famous by Nat King Cole, "Boulevard of Broken Dreams," sprayed like a lazy machine-gun burst from the speakers. Esma closed her eyes and leaned her head back, swaying to the music.

Scotty, surprised to hear the lyrics in English, took a sip of his bourbon, then reached over to kiss Esma.

"Damn morbid song," he whispered.

"Ssshhh," she said back. "It's not."

He echoed the singer's throaty phrasing. " 'The joy you find you have to borrow?' That's not morbid?"

"Don't be silly—it's about love."

"Oh, excuse me," he said, kissing her again. As he did, he caught a glimpse of Ray Fashona sulking near the side bar. Fashona was the number-two man in the Havana CIA station, and not someone particularly wont to frequent Ave.

Esma took his kiss lightly, sinking deeper and deeper into the spell of the music. Scotty kissed her again, then pushed away from the table, telling her he would be right back.

"I just want a smoke."

It was a lie she heard often. She slipped her hand up his arm, smiling in a way intended to make it impossible for anything to keep him away for too long.

Fashona spotted him as he walked toward the bar, and watched Scotty ask the bartender for a cigar and another bourbon, this one on the rocks. The agent was waiting in the garden terrace that overlooked the club room when Scotty came out, the fat, hand-rolled Cuban in a corner of his mouth.

"Carla de Souza is here," said Fashona, leaning back against the rail. The harbor was visible behind him, and a faint breeze filled the air with the smell of salt and the smoke of a nearby incineration plant.

"What?"

"Yeah, no shit. Got a couple of her guys here, too."

"Where is she?"

"On the far side of the room, near the door. Think the ambassador will believe us now when we say she has MININT in her pocket?"

"God, she's got balls." Scotty looked back toward the bar but of course couldn't see her. "Since when does she go to clubs?"

"Never, that I know of. One of our people spotted her coming in twenty minutes ago."

"Have you told the Cubans?"

"You nuts?"

"I'd be interested in hearing their reaction," said Scotty. He took another peek. "You sure it's her?"

A short, balding man with a thick beard and a perfect Cuban-Spanish accent—though he was originally from Buffalo, New York—Fashona had a way of frowning that would have made the Pope doubt his religion before questioning something he said. "What do you think?"

"Well, let's go buy her a drink, then."

"Standing orders are to leave her be," said Fashona.

"Fuck that. Your boss is away in California for three weeks."

"I was thinking of Steele."

Fashona hung back as Scotty swung back toward the bar.

"I want to talk to her about the helicopter attack. That's American business."

"Wasn't her. She wouldn't have missed."

"Yeah, but I still want to talk to her." Scotty stuffed the unsmoked cigar into one of the ashtrays by the door as he walked back into the building, scanning the bar and then the room, trying to spot the rebel leader. He saw a short, lithe figure in a black skirt get up and begin walking along the far side of the room as the singer's band slipped in behind her solo with a subdued, vaguely Latin beat.

It took him a moment in the dim light to realize it was de Souza. He'd never seen her this close before, but the round nose, the set jaw, the bewitching eyes that made even the fuzzy intelligence mug shots look like snapshots from a model's portfolio—they were all there. There could be no mistake.

The grace and strength of her body set her apart from the pampered women nearby. Scotty began drifting in her direction, then realized that she was walking very fast. He trotted across the long expanse of the bar, trying to duck between the milling crowd.

By the time he reached the lobby, he had lost her. Scotty cursed, then caught a glimpse of a woman that had to be her standing outside the front door. She was talking to someone, gesticulating. He was too far away to see who it was. As he took a step forward, she darted away, not running exactly, but moving with great deliberation. Men were following her. Scotty unconsciously reached inside his jacket, touching his old .45 for good luck as he headed for the door.

By the time he had reached the pavement, he was running. He'd lost her again, but he saw two dark-suited men two blocks ahead, ducking to the right, and he trotted behind them. Before he'd gone three yards, a black Taurus roared around the corner, followed by a red minivan. The minivan threw open its door.

A sharp sensation in his stomach told him to duck. As he dove to the pavement, he saw a man with a Kalashnikov framed in the open car interior, waving the rifle in his direction. Scotty felt his heart sink, the certainty of death stinging his nostrils, pushing back his hair with the tight grip of fear even as he reached for the Colt beneath his jacket. But then he realized the man with the gun was waving with his free hand, and had taken no notice of him. Instead, the two men Scotty had followed leaped into the minivan as its tires squealed, the driver accelerating to catch up to the Taurus ahead.

Scotty reholstered his gun and rose slowly. He shook his head, half cursing, half laughing at himself for being so scared. He turned back toward the Ave entrance, conceding defeat, willing to call it a night.

In the next moment, the block ahead of him exploded. Even as the force of the explosion threw him backward through the air, Scotty cried out for Esma, knowing in every part of him that it was as vain as calling for God to stop the coming of the night.

Chapter Three

It seemed like years before he could get his legs into
motion and run toward the building. By the time
Scotty reached it, smoke and dust were billowing
from the front, and people had begun staggering
from the doors and broken windows. Scotty started
inside, then felt himself being pulled back; he
looked around and realized it was Fashona, who
had both arms around his chest and was trying to
keep him outside.

"Esma's in there," he screamed, jerking from his
friend's grip as he dove toward the cluttered onrush.
The world turned from a fluid kaleidoscope to frac-
tured shades of infinite blackness, a harsh wail
shaking the corners of his skull and vibrating
through every inch of his being. There was not
enough building left for him to know where he was;
he moved through the grayness of hell, devils leering
through flames and piles of rubble. He found himself on his knees, gasping for air; he rose and con-

tinued to search the ruins, stepping now over dead bodies and parts of bodies. He walked endlessly, unable to stop calling her name; he walked and he searched and he yelled and he walked and he found himself on the floor, this time on his hands and knees. He thought he saw her smiling at him, and indescribable joy leaped in his chest. Scotty reached to kiss her and found himself coughing up blood, back out on the sidewalk, rescued by one of the army of firemen responding to the scene.

Fashona grabbed him before he could go in again, pressing his arms around his back and slapping him several times before Scotty heard the words.

"She's here, Scott. They've brought her out already. She's here."

Finally, he understood. Scotty pulled his jacket around his torso, though it was still quite warm out, and began walking calmly. Despite the continuing rush of emergency workers and vehicles, Scotty descended into a quiet plane, a massive space devoid of other people. The night sky spread out overhead, stars sprinkled in the high ceiling of a magnificent cathedral. The altar lay somewhere in the distance, austere and majestic.

Bodies and half bodies were arranged in neat rows at the street intersection where Scotty had lost de Souza. There were not enough blankets to cover both the dead and the living, and so the dead were left defenseless against the night, wounds gaping. He moved between them, knowing by some instinct where Esma was. He did not look at her body as he sank to his knees; he did not look at her face as he reached his hand to her singed dress. Eyes closed, he felt the hem, grasping it lightly in the way he had done so many times when they were alone together, on nights when she had fallen asleep in a chair or perhaps on the bed, exhausted from her day. The fabric was smooth in his fingers, so silky that it con-

vinced him for a moment this was another of those
times; she was here, sleeping only, lulled by the
blues singer into a restful catnap. A miracle had occurred; some nondescript pillar had blocked the
force of the explosion and rendered her unconscious but unharmed.

It was a reassuring fiction, and as he moved his
fingers ever so gently across her dress, Scotty struggled to maintain it, despite the tears in the clothes
and now the oozing wetness of death that brushed
against the edge of his fingernails.

He could not keep his eyes closed forever, as hard
as he tried. His lids lifted themselves against his will,
and in the blurry second before tears obscured his
vision, he stared into the tortured, broken eyes of
Death.

Cherry Point Infirmary. 6 A.M.

His mind muddied by painkillers, Garcia woke
thinking he was at home in his boyhood bed. The
nurse who had prodded his arm smiled gently, and
for a long moment the pilot wondered what strange
shape his dream was taking.

"You're wanted downstairs, Lieutenant," said the
woman, her stiff white uniform teasing the soft
curves of her body as she bent over him. She
brushed her hand gently over his forehead and he
realized he was awake—in more ways than one.

"I have a wheelchair here," said the young
woman, standing back. "You'll want your robe."

Embarrassed as well as disoriented, Garcia fumbled to cover himself, then stiffly got out of bed, his
injured leg just one of the many complaining parts
of his body. Though he wouldn't admit it to the doctors, the ejection had wrenched his shoulder, and
there was a knot the size of Minnesota in his neck.

The nurse put her arm out to help him as he stiff-legged to the wheelchair.

"Have to make a morning call?" she asked.

Garcia gave her a puzzled look. In her early twenties, blond, with a delicate, powdery pink face offset by sinewy forearms and biceps, she might have passed for one of those angels his mother was always invoking—or at least the star of a television aerobics show.

"Do you have to go to the bathroom?" she said, explaining her question.

"Yeah, I guess. What is all this?"

"You have a visitor downstairs."

"What time is it?"

"It's just six."

Garcia's brain was still not completely functioning by the time he was wheeled off the elevator into one of the subbasements. The nurse handed him off to a marine sergeant in dress uniform. His freshly laundered jacket and trousers filled the corridor with the inky smell of starch, and Garcia wondered again if this was all just a particularly convincing dream.

"Sleep well, Lieutenant?" asked the sergeant as he wheeled slowly down the dimly lit corridor.

"I guess. What's going on?"

"Just following orders, sir. I haven't a clue."

The corridor was lined by insulation-covered pipes and empty gurneys. At the far end of the hall, two marine guards made a show of pulling back their rifles, officially welcoming his approach. Loitering nearby was a man in a rumpled black suit who looked like Arnold Schwarzenegger's half brother. After frowning in Garcia's direction, he spoke into his cuff and nodded at the sergeant, who spun Garcia's wheelchair around and backed carefully through the double doors into a room crowded with immense washing machines.

"Lieutenant Garcia, sorry I had to wake you up."

The sergeant swung Garcia's wheelchair around, and Garcia saw that the gruff voice that had greeted him came from a tall African-American in his fifties or sixties, with close-cropped gray hair and fierce, penetrating eyes. The clipped tones of his voice seemed military, but he was wearing gray slacks and a sports shirt. Behind him was another black man, considerably younger. Dressed in an ill-fitting gray suit, the younger man hovered instead of stood, his limbs seeming to vibrate with nervous energy.

"Sergeant, you're dismissed," said the older man. "Tell you what, boys, you can wait outside, too. Captain."

The younger man, obviously the captain, moved toward the door. Garcia was surprised when two plainclothes bodyguards—surely that was these gorillas' function—emerged from the shadows. He wondered what in hell he had fallen into.

"Relax, Lieutenant," said the older man. "I'd offer you some coffee or something, but I'm afraid this is all rather hastily arranged. I'm on a tight schedule."

Garcia nodded. He had no idea what he was supposed to do. He clearly hadn't been brought to the hospital laundry room to be offered a plum job assignment. The only thing he could think of was that the man before him was somehow part of the investigation into the plane crash, and that he was going to be pressured into giving incorrect testimony. The idea revolted his sense of duty and honor, but even as he resolved himself to tell the truth no matter what, he felt the sinking feeling of a trapped man.

"My name is Malcolm Steele." Steele held out his hand to Garcia. His handshake was warm, firm but not overbearing. "I'm the American ambassador to

Cuba." Steele stood back, smiling. "I was in the service myself. Army."

"Cuba?"

"Friend of mine asked me to take the job, or I'd be on a golf course right now." The ambassador smiled, as if he'd made a joke. "I understand you had a mishap the other day, and handled it extremely well. How badly were you hurt?"

"Not at all, sir. I can get up."

"Let me see."

Garcia pushed himself out of the wheelchair slowly. "I'm a little shaky, but that's because they gave me some drugs to sleep last night. I didn't want to take them, sir, but the doctor—"

"Just walk a little for me, would you?"

Not knowing what else to do, Garcia took a few dancing steps. He tried willing away the pain, hoping the wincing didn't show.

"I'm supposed to tape it up before I walk on it," he said as he moved. "But the doc says that it's just a bad pull, not even a tear."

"I've seen the charts." Steele frowned. "You can sit down."

Garcia remained standing. "It doesn't hurt at all, sir. Not really at all."

The room exploded with a laugh that made the sheets flap. "Not at all, huh?"

Garcia felt his face redden. "No, sir, it doesn't."

"Okay, Lieutenant, I'll accept that at face value for the moment. But sit down."

Steele folded his hands in front of him and he began to pace in the manner of a college professor about to make a difficult point. Garcia slipped into the wheelchair.

"What we are about to talk about is both completely off the record and very, very confidential. Not even your unit commander knows the specifics of what we're discussing. And he is not to. No one is. Do you follow?" Garcia nodded warily.

"I understand your parents came from Cuba," said Steele. "Have you ever gone there?"

"No, sir."

"Have you ever thought of going there?"

To be one hundred percent honest, he hadn't. In fact, it seemed like about the last place on earth he wanted to go. Especially now. Sitting in the middle of the warm, humid room, his nostrils smarting with the smell of bleach, Garcia suddenly envisioned himself chained to a Caribbean desk, in charge of locating stray paper clips at the embassy.

"Sir, with all due respect, I think that the United States Marine Corps has invested quite a bit of money in me as a pilot, and I've just reached the point where I'm starting to put that into effect. I'd rather fly a Beechcraft than be stuck behind a desk."

"I'm not asking you to sit behind a desk." Steele scowled, and seemed on the verge of dismissing him. Instead, he shook his head and said something to himself before continuing. "I don't know what the hell they teach you nowadays, but the first thing the army told me when I stripped off my civvies back in the prehistoric days was to keep my head down until I know where the gunfire is coming from."

"But—"

"Shut your trap and listen to me. I have a proposition for you that is strictly voluntary. You listen to it, and then make up your mind. But it stays completely within the four walls of this room. Understood?"

Garcia, smarting from Steele's harsh tone, nodded.

"I'm going to assume for argument's sake that the ligament in that leg is more or less okay, or will be within a few days, which is what the doctor told me. Though, frankly, the man seemed to have a stethoscope up his ass. Assuming it is okay, I'm here on behalf of the Cuban government, looking for volunteer pilot instructors.

"These are old planes," Steele continued. "Not what you're used to. Early-model Harriers. I don't know all the details, but I've been told you're checked out on them. I've also been told you can fly anything that has wings on it. That true, son?"

The word "fly" was all Garcia needed. "I'd like—"

The ambassador was too set on his course to stop talking. "This isn't a marine operation. You'll be on unofficial loan to the Cuban government as an adviser. As quietly as possible. There's no need to lie about it; you just keep your mouth shut. Anyone asks you a question, you refer it to your commander or to me. The maintenance crews are civilians. You'll be training Cuban pilots. There's a guerrilla war going on down there. The press hasn't played it up too much, thank God, but they use real bullets, I can guarantee you that."

"I'll do it, sir. Absolutely. I volunteer."

Steele practically crossed his eyes frowning. "You sound almost eager, Lieutenant."

"I am, sir."

"You in some kind of mess up here?"

"No, sir. But my squadron didn't have enough planes for pilots, and my colonel, my commander, sir, said I'd probably get desk duty. He strongly hinted that, sir."

"Figures." Steele shook his head. "Every stinking service has its head up its ass. Well, in any event, my aide will give you some details; the rest you'll hear in Havana. We want you there by five o'clock."

Not only did Steele's tone allow no further questions; the ambassador promptly strode for the door as soon as he finished speaking. Garcia sat alone in the room, wondering what the hell he'd gotten himself into.

Jim DeFelice

Havana. 11 A.M.

Somewhere in the blur Scotty had found a bar and started to drink vodka. The liquor filled his head with something that felt like Styrofoam. He could hear through it. He could see through it. He could even think through it. But he couldn't feel. Cars and trucks rumbled alongside him on the busy city street, people bumped against him, but he felt nothing.

It began to rain. The wind shook the palm trees like so many dirty mops. He looked across to the left and saw the ocean, waves swelling like angry horses bucking beneath their riders. He remembered walking down here to the Malecón, but had forgotten whether he came with a purpose or not. If he had had a reason, it was gone.

The rain fell in huge Caribbean gushes, soaking his clothes, drenching his hair and cheeks. Scotty walked on, not slowed by the weight of his sodden pants and sport coat. He walked, and as he walked he grew more and more numb, and finally he realized where he was going.

Nodding at the doorman in the vestibule, he ignored the man's puzzled expression and questions, going instead straight to the elevator. His key turned the lock to her apartment silently, and as he pushed it open, for a short second, for a hair's width of a moment, he fantasized that nothing had happened, that he would find Esma here, sleeping late, playing hooky from work.

Scotty stood silently in the doorway, surprised that even with the rain a tremendous amount of light streamed through the windows of the living room. He could hear his heart pounding somewhere beneath his heavy breath, but he felt as foreign to his body as a man in a grave. Slowly, he walked into the apartment, saw everything neatly arranged. He passed through the bedroom, moving stiffly, unaware of the puddles dragging behind him. He sat on the edge of the bed, trying hard not to breathe, for with every breath he smelled Esma's perfume.

He closed his eyes, but no matter how often he opened them, the room was the same. The blouse and pants she had worn to work the day before were still folded neatly on the small armchair. Her spare pocketbook lay open on the dresser; her black shoes—"Ten dollars American; I got them from a vendor"—waited next to the door.

The phone rang. It startled him. He stared at the handset until it stopped.

When the room was silent, Scotty went to the bathroom and turned on the shower. There were things he had to do. Notify her family. There must be an address book or something in the desk somewhere. Someone would have to arrange the funeral.

He stripped off his clothes, put the .45 on the toilet seat, then carefully unholstered the plastic Glocks. The pistols did not have real safeties, merely a lever in the trigger that helped prevent accidental firing.

It would be so easy to use one. So useless.

The phone rang again. He placed one of the tiny guns on the floor and hung the other beneath a shower cap at the far end of the tub, out of the spray.

He couldn't help but remember the first time Esma had seen him do this.

The water came out so cold, he barked. That was the sound he made; not a scream, not a complaint—a bark. Then the hot water scalded him. Scotty stayed beneath the spray, accepting it all.

When finally he got out of the shower, the phone was ringing again. He went to the bedroom and picked it up; without saying hello, he held the receiver to his ear.

"Scotty?"

It was the ambassador's secretary, Marge.

"Scotty, is that you?"

"Yeah."

"I've been trying to get you everywhere. Are you all right?"

"Yes."

"I'm sorry about Esma. I heard what happened." She paused to let him speak; he said nothing. "The ambassador needs to speak to you. He's still in the States. Can you hold on the line while I ring him?"

"Okay."

"Do you have a scrambler?"

"You're being polite, right?"

"Scotty?"

"Wait a minute." He let the phone drop on the desk and went to the closet, where he kept his bag. Keeping a scrambler here was against regulations, even though it wouldn't work without his security card. He retrieved the card from his wallet, then clipped the device into the line.

While he waited for the ambassador to come on, he picked Esma's blouse and pants off the desk chair. He leaned over to the floor and gently placed them down, then slid into the chair, his towel unwrapping beneath him. He was naked except for his guns, bare armor against threats that now had no meaning.

It was nearly fifteen minutes before Steele came on the line, but Scotty sat motionless the whole time, staring at the framed Monet poster across from the bed.

"Scotty, where the hell have you been?" barked Steele. "I have two pilots on the way to Havana. I want you to hook them up with our friend Mr. Hill and smooth things over with the Cubans."

"Why me?"

"Because it was your goddamn idea and I trust you not to screw it up. You have a problem?"

Scotty looked around the room. It was cold here, becoming foreign already. "No."

"I wangled some ordnance that ought to make the Cubans happy. Wait until they bring up the U.S. planes before you mention it."

Scotty listened without comment as the ambassador detailed the munitions and some other items.

"Scotty, are you there?"

"Yes, sir."

"You're calling me 'sir'? What the hell's wrong with you?"

"I'll get on it."

Scotty hung up the phone. He remained in the chair for a long time, gazing at the dappled, glittering colors of the Monet landscape. Summer had been caught at the moment when ripeness began to hint at decay.

When his eyes had finally lost all focus, Scotty snapped to with a start, shuddered, rose, and slowly gathered his things, preparing to leave Esma's apartment forever.

Cherry Point. 1 P.M.

Garcia couldn't get his mother on the telephone before she left her hotel, so he ended up having to wait for her in the hospital lobby. He had already gone over to his quarters and taken care of his gear and the miscellaneous odds and ends that typically accompanied a new assignment. In this he had been assisted, briefly, by the ambassador's aide, who had turned out to be an army captain. Garcia thought it best not to ask why he was in civilian dress.

A three-by-five-inch piece of yellow paper was folded in the top breast pocket of his shirt; it represented the only written version of his orders in existence. It read:

THIS CONFIRMS VERBAL CONV. W/ NSC STAFF.
ALL PRIORITY. REF. OPERATION DUCK WALK.

Captain James had handed it to him before vanishing. Garcia hadn't even needed to show it when he checked on his plane or went to make sure his trunk—already in Yuma, as it turned out—could be retrieved and put into storage. His entire conversation with the logistics officer had lasted five seconds.

"Everything is under way, Lieutenant. You'd best meet your plane on time," snapped the major. Garcia had never met the woman in his life, but he promptly nodded and did an about-face—which was not necessarily easy on crutches. Making his way over to the mess to get something to eat, he decided he would ditch the damn things before he left for Cuba.

His plane wasn't due until three, which meant he had to spend time with his mom. Garcia wasn't sure what, if anything, he could tell her about where he was going. Talking in riddles would worry her, and with the plane crash she had undoubtedly already worn out her rosary beads.

The fact that it was Cuba made it even more impossible to say anything. The country had never been an easy topic between them, a looming shadow filled with inconsistencies, dangers, and mystery.

When he saw her walking through the front entrance of the hospital, he realized how much she looked like the pictures of her aunts and mother she had shown him when he was a child, the faded photos of old women in the old country. Her tight, tinted curls formed a hood over her head, like that a monk might wear on the way to prayers; the deep lines on her face showed she had probably not slept since coming down.

A set of black rosary beads were threaded through the fingers of her left hand. She did not see him at first, and walked quickly past the front desk toward the elevator.

"Mom," he said, rising on his crutches from the chair where he'd been sitting. "Hey, Mom—over here."

She turned, disoriented for a moment, an old woman caught in unfamiliar surroundings. Then she was his mother again, a torrent of words exploding from her mouth in a jumble of Spanish, English, and something in between.

"What are you doing out of bed?"

"I'm fine. I'm released. I already have orders," he told her as she folded her arms around him in the middle of the lobby. Garcia fought off the feeling of intense embarrassment. She might not get a chance to see him for many months, he thought to himself, and he owed her this small indulgence.

Belatedly, she stuffed the rosary beads into a pocket of her light jacket, as if she did not want him to know she had been praying for him. "Released? With orders? ¡Ay, Dios mío! Who says? Let me talk to the doctors."

"No, look, Mom, I'm fine," he said, stepping back and dancing a little as he held the crutches to the side. Garcia was careful to keep most of his weight on his left leg and conceal the pain with a smile. His knee was so heavily taped it wouldn't have folded if he'd jumped out a three-story window and landed on it. "I'm leaving this afternoon."

"You should be in bed," his mother insisted.

"I tried to call you at the hotel. What were you doing, praying for me at church?"

"And what if I was? A prayer couldn't hurt. When was the last time you said the rosary?"

Garcia smiled at her, glancing around. No one seemed to notice—or at least they did a good job pretending not to. "Want to go for a walk?"

"A walk? How are you going to walk?" She waved

her hand at him. "You should be in bed."

"Come on, let's get some air." Garcia, working the crutches, led her out the door to a VIP golf cart with his personal travel bag. He'd borrowed the vehicle from the MPs—base security was more than eager to help the man who'd prevented their jobs from becoming a monumental nightmare.

"Hop in," he said, pushing himself behind the wheel.

"What's this?"

"I'm going to give you a tour. You want to see the hangar where my plane was?"

"Sure," she said.

Garcia laughed. The note in her voice reminded him of the way she had agreed to see the first car he had ever owned, as if she were summoning enough resolve to successfully pass yet another difficult rite demanded of mothers. He waited for her to seat herself, then wheeled the cart over toward the hush house at the far end of the base, watching from the corner of his eye as his mother gripped the side of the seat tighter than a vise grip on a bolt head.

The main hangar—empty now that the Pegasus squadron had moved on to Arizona—had been left open. Garcia pulled inside, stopping the cart roughly where his plane had sat.

"It's a very nice building," said his mother. "Very big."

"I was hoping for a souvenir," Garcia said, getting out slowly. But he couldn't find one, not even a spare bolt or clipped piece of wire. The place had been swept clean.

"Why do you want a souvenir?" his mother asked. "When you leave a place, you don't need to be reminded of it. Even if it is your home."

Garcia said nothing as he crutched his way across the smooth concrete of the hangar, back out to the apron. The best he could do was a small pebble lying in the crack. Cratered with holes, it seemed almost like a piece of smelted iron ore, though it was gray and as light as a piece of paper. He leaned down and picked it up, holding it in his palm.

"We filled our pockets with sand from the beach at La Concha near Havana," said his mother. Her soft voice startled him, and he looked down into eyes that were younger than any he had ever seen. "Your father said we would make our own Cuba wherever we went. We would never go back."

The eyes started to cloud with water.

"You can go back now if you want," he said softly. "There are flights every day. You could see it again."

She shook her head. "No. Never. Your father is too proud."

"Castro is dead."

His mother spit. "Never say the devil's name out loud."

"He's dead, Ma. Gone."

"His evil lives on. I hate the man. He will reach out from the grave to strike us all."

Garcia had heard this sentiment many times in the past, and knew well his father's insistence that America was his home and he would never return to Cuba. Usually he laughed at his mother's superstitions, but today he couldn't. He let the stone fall from his hand.

"You never told me about the sand," he said.

"Oh, yes." His mother was smiling, even as a single tear slipped down her cheek. "I have it at home in a jar. Near Mother Mary on the bureau. I will show you when you come home next."

It was a tremendous, almost unprecedented revelation. Garcia placed his hand on her shoulder. An only son, he loved his parents, even his father, deeply, but his relationship with them had always been one of silences and even walls. The older Garcias had seen much suffering in their lives, and the stoicism with which they bore it had been passed to him before birth.

His parents had been nearly twice his current age when they landed in America. The first two years were very difficult; though they had relatives, they were both far too proud to accept charity, and they immediately began looking for work. His father had been trained as a biologist before being stripped of his right to teach by the regime. In America, however, he did not speak English well enough to get a position at a drug company or as a teacher; he took a job sweeping the floor of a drugstore.

It was his wife's surprise announcement that she was expecting long after the time most women stopped having children that made him give up his attempts to return to research. Instead, he eventually worked his way into a position as a druggist's assistant, and graduated, at the age of fifty-four, from pharmacology school. It was a struggle that never ceased to impress his son, more so because, even at the most bitter point of their estrangement, the elder Garcia had never once said he had sacrificed his own future to make sure the boy had food to eat and a roof over his head.

"Here," said his mother, pressing something into his hand. He looked down and saw two neatly folded hundred-dollar bills.

"Mom—what's this?"

"Money for you. Spend it on something nice."

"I don't need money. The marines take care of everything."

"Everything? How can this be? On a night off, dinner? Bus rides? A movie? Maybe with a girl, huh?"

He knew better than to try to give her the money back. Even if it had been her last dollar—and with his father now a franchisee of the company where he had begun, it was far from that—she would have slit her throat before willingly taking it back.

"Thanks."

"You should come home soon."

"When this mission is over."

"And where are you going? You didn't even tell your mother."

"Down south. I'm going to be training pilots."

"Florida?"

"It's an easy gig," he said, evading her question. It wasn't exactly a lie, though it was very close.

Would he lie to her if she asked a direct question about Cuba?

No, he couldn't. But he could laugh, say Cuba was the last place he wanted to go, which was more or less the truth.

She didn't ask. Instead, she surprised him by mentioning his dad.

"Your father is very stubborn," she said. "But he loves you."

"I know he does, Mom."

"He was very worried about the plane crash."

"So why didn't he call?" said Garcia sharply.

"He said he would be here tomorrow."

"What? He's coming here?"

"That's what he says. And when he says something, it will happen."

"Jeez, Mom, I can't wait. I have orders. I have to leave this afternoon. There's no getting around it."

She nodded sadly. "He said he would come."

Garcia looked up as he heard the distinctive four-engined whine of a C-130 landing on the main runway a few hundred yards away. He glanced at his watch—it was nearly three.

"I have to get over to the airfield," he told her, heading to the cart. "I think that's my plane."

Matanzas Province, East of Havana. 3 P.M.

The minivan bounced back and forth across the disheveled road, tossing its occupants up and down

97

like a pair of dice in a game of craps at one of the capital's casinos. Carla had a difficult time keeping the car steady; fury trembled in every inch of her body.

The announcer on the radio began repeating the story of last night's explosion. Just as he reached the news of her death, Zora reached across from the passenger seat and turned the radio off.

"*¿Por qué?*" Carla asked. "Why turn it off when it's just getting to the good part?"

"You don't want them to think you are dead."

"Oh, yes I do. I want Romano to think I am very dead."

"He will realize you are alive soon."

"By then it will be too late for him."

Carla reached for the radio. Zora took hold of her hand gently and said, "The wise man does not listen to the sermon preached at his funeral."

"That's because he's already dead," said Carla. Nonetheless, she let the radio be.

For all her caution, Carla had escaped the Ave explosion only because of a hunch. When Padilla suggested the site, she agreed, considering it safer to meet in a public place than in a secluded spot she did not control.

Her concern had been with the government, not Padilla. While the management paid M-26 a considerable sum to avoid "problems" and the club was considered something of a demilitarized zone, there was always a small percentage of doubt and danger. But her spies inside MININT had not discovered any plan to capture her; besides, jail and a trial would give her a platform they clearly wanted to avoid.

Carla had arranged to be given a table near the stage, because it gave her the best view of the side and back doors. More than a dozen of her rebel guerrillas were posted around the room. Two escape plans had been worked out, and if government troops appeared on the block she had enough fire-power outside to turn back a tank. She came to the club nearly an hour before the scheduled meeting in case an ambush was planned en route.

But as she sat at her table, listening to her men via a shortwave-radio setup, she considered the situation more and more carefully. When Victor Padilla failed to show up five minutes before their appointed time, she decided to leave, something inside her sensing a trap.

"Zora, you are very quiet this afternoon. Are you trying to decide where your magic failed?"

"My magic has not failed," Zora said. "You have seen its power many times. Why do you still doubt it?"

"You know a great deal about the world, about politics and people," Carla told her. She spoke from the heart; Zora had become almost a mother to her. "Yet you ascribe everything to your saints and their cards."

"The cards are symbols," said Zora. Usually when she defended her religion, she spoke forcefully; today she seemed considerably subdued and resigned. "I have explained this to you many times."

Carla didn't bother answering. The attack must have shaken the old woman deeply, she realized, for otherwise Zora would be spouting some nonsense about how life-force spirits are reincarnated and indestructible. Santeria was an amalgam of superstitions that combined parts of Catholicism with a voodoo-like African religion. Most of the "magic" associated with it was benign, and in her more generous moments even Carla would admit that if you threw out the arcane rituals and other garbage, there was a great deal of wisdom and commonsense advice attached to the stories and lore.

But she wasn't in a particularly generous or even talkative mood. Carla drove on, focusing her mind on the steps she had mapped out. She must act swiftly and decisively; the psychotic earthworm who opposed her must be ruthlessly crushed.

A dusty turnoff loomed on the left; she yanked the minivan off the highway just ahead of a pickup truck. The truck's driver leaned on his horn and squealed his tires as he swerved to miss her. Carla drove up the dirt road, gaining confidence as she saw the two gray Toyotas parked before the squat red farmhouse at the peak of the small hill. She slowed as she neared the foot of the driveway, rolling down her window. The metal stock of her Heckler & Koch machine pistol felt warm against her thigh after she swung it up from the door pouch, just below the window. The men guarding the house were trusted comrades, but this was no place to be taking chances; Carla kept her finger against the MP-5N's trigger until she spotted Peter at the doorway, waving his hand to signal all was clear.

"I will wait here," Zora said when she parked the minivan. Carla nodded; the old woman would not be particularly useful inside.

As Carla closed the van door, she wondered if Zora was not perhaps feeling somewhat smug, thinking Carla had brought these problems on herself by going against her advice. Zora had argued against the overtures of peace to the government.

The path to the doorway was overgrown with weeds. Three or four clumps at the side were thick with dried blood; Carla barely noticed them as she brushed past, striding quickly into the house. One of her men—a boy really, barely old enough to shave—nodded at her in the foyer.

"*Comandante,*" he acknowledged, clutching his M-16 awkwardly as he cast his eyes to the ground. He was the son of a man who had died several weeks before; Carla patted his shoulder silently, then turned to José, who appeared from inside. Though well into his fifties, José had a long blond ponytail and was the very picture of a devoted freedom fighter, with a grizzled, scar-ridden face and a well-developed torso beneath a half-opened campaign shirt. He grinned, exposing a perfect set of gold-capped teeth, then swept his body down in a salute.

"*Comandante*."

"Very good, Captain. Take me to your prisoner," she told him.

"We are glad you weren't hurt," said José as he led her to the basement.

"Has he talked?"

"He refuses."

As she descended the stairs, Carla reached into the pocket of her fatigue jacket and took out a long switchblade. She held it unopened in her right hand, the machine pistol in her left, as she approached the prisoner. Bound and gagged, he sat strapped to a metal kitchen chair against the back of an animal stall.

The farmhouse was built into the hillside; behind her, a door led out into an overgrown field where a family cow had once grazed. The open door and the bare, overhead bulbs furnished the room with a brown, foreboding light. The floor was packed dirt; it smelled of mud and centuries-old rot.

Carla motioned to the guard to undo the man's blindfold and gag. The prisoner blinked his eyes several times, but otherwise offered no recognition.

She placed the barrel of her MP-5N against his cheek. "Do you know who I am?" she demanded.

"You are de Souza."

"You will call me *Comandante*, in respect."

"I have respect for only *El Jefe*."

Even as the last words came from his mouth, José slapped his face. The blow knocked his head sideways against the gun, drawing blood from his

101

mouth, but the prisoner's expression remained stoic.

"My father is dead," said Carla softly. "*El Jefe* is no more."

"You are certainly not him," replied the man.

Carla raised her hand, or her soldier would have delivered another blow.

"You were under Pérez," she said.

"He was a traitor to the Movement, as are you."

"He is a dead traitor now," said Carla. She had killed Pérez within an hour of the bombing, despite his protest that he knew nothing. "For whom did you blow up the casino?"

He did not answer. Carla flicked her wrist, and the switchblade opened. She held the edge of the blade against the man's cheek.

"How did Romano contact you?"

No answer.

"How many others in Havana are loyal to him?"

No answer.

"Where has he gotten his weapons from? The Russians tell the press they are not dealing with him, but the weapons we have seen are Russian."

No answer.

"The rumors, then, are they true? Does he have caches of arms in the mountains?"

When he made no sign that he would speak, Carla began to draw the blade across his cheek. It took a moment for blood to appear. She waited for it to pool, waited until she knew he would feel the heavy wetness. Then she put the knife on the other side of his face.

"Come. I have much information from my ministry spies and the Americans. I have spies at the embassy itself. You are not saving Romano. But if you save me time, I will make it worth your while by sparing your life."

His lip twitched, but he did not speak.

This time she pulled the knife faster, applying more pressure so that it cut deeper.

"Victor, why do you want to die? You should co-operate with me. I am the leader of the Revolution, am I not? I am *El Jefe*'s daughter. How could you have allegiance to Romano?"

He shook his head. She could see the pain of the cut welling in his eyes. She could see, too, that he would remain defiant until she killed him. Still, she considered that it was only fair—only just—to offer him mercy.

"There was an explosive among your things when my men apprehended you. I am told it was very old. Does Romano have other stores?"

She laid the tip of the blade against the edge of his cheekbone, directly beneath his eye. Despite her effort at control, she could feel the fury rising in her body. Carla gripped the knife more tightly, forcing her emotion into her thumb and fingers, where it might be contained.

"Did you think of the innocent people in the building before you exploded it? In the apartments above, there were families with children. Was it fair that they died? Was it just?"

She was surprised when he opened his mouth to speak. "There is much suffering in the name of justice."

"You placed the bomb to remove the support of the building, and to send fire above. You knew that many people would die, not just myself."

She could feel his resolve ebbing, starting to run from his chest to his feet. Carla increased the pressure of the blade on his cheekbone. He gulped involuntarily. She smiled, withdrew the knife, then put it against his Adam's apple.

"Tell me, my friend, did Romano contact you directly, or are there others involved? That's all I ask. You will be free to go."

"My life would be worth nothing, even if you kept your word."

Carla began to laugh. "And what do you think your life is worth now? Anything? I can kill you, I can have my men kill you—or perhaps I will have you bundled and dragged back to Havana. Do you think the Americans would save you? Would they give you one of their trials? Their justice?" She saw the look in his eye hardening; whatever slight possibility there had been that he might give up was gone. "No, that is too good for the killer of innocents. Cuban justice is all you would deserve."

Carla pushed the knife tip into the valley of his neck, hard enough to feel the quick pulse of his blood, but not enough to draw blood.

"Tell me what I want to know."

"I will tell you nothing."

In that instant, the knife slashed straight across his throat, deep and hard. She took a step back, still holding the knife out, and savored the surprise in his eyes, the blank shock of death. He had expected her to hurt him, but not to kill him.

Not at that moment. No one ever expected death when it came, no matter how resigned to it.

It took a second for the blood to spurt. Carla turned to the side and wiped her blade against the prisoner's pants leg. Calmly, she returned the knife to her pocket.

Victor Padilla began to gasp, choking for life. She watched the blood pour out, then grabbed his hair and held the face up so he would look into her face as his life ebbed away.

"Romano owes you a debt of gratitude," she told him as she placed the barrel of her gun into his eye socket. "Unfortunately for him, he will not live to appreciate it. But let there be no mistake about who killed you. My mark is well known."

The quick burst of three nine-millimeter rounds

rattled the low rafters, and by the time Carla emerged from the house she was covered with a thin layer of ancient dust.

Southeast of Havana. 4:35 P.M.

Two hits of speed and sheer momentum propelled Scotty as he drove toward the small airstrip about forty miles outside of the capital. Most of the booze had worn off hours before, and his head was churning with a rush of fevered energy and the broken slivers of different plans. It was a good thing the Ford he'd borrowed from the embassy car pool was an automatic; his arms and legs were out of whack and he had trouble stopping the car in time at the airport entrance. Fumbling with his wallet as he tried to pull out his credentials, Scotty felt a surge of nausea hit him. He bit the inside of his cheek, waved at the guard, made his way past the shiny chain-link fence toward the dilapidated warehouse buildings near the dirt strip. The airplane he was to meet was a C-130 Hercules; he knew from Africa that the cargo plane could land and take off on a cow path. That had made a lot of things simpler— by avoiding a "real" airport, he didn't have to wrestle with three layers of bureaucracy to get the plane down and unloaded.

Two large tractor-trailers with Pepsi logos were parked on the grass apron near the end of the runway. They did actually belong to a soda distributor, even if they were currently manned by members of the defense forces.

As he rounded the far end of the perimeter roadway, Scotty saw a gray, four-engined airplane lumber over the western hills, heading for the strip. The C-130 looked like a broad-shouldered linebacker, its motors filling the sky with the drone of a thousand bees as it skimmed in. The pilot didn't even bother

Jim DeFelice

doing a circuit to survey the field—he just plopped down and taxied toward the trailers, as nonchalant as a teenager stopping by a 7-Eleven.

Built nearly fifty years before, this particular plane had served in a variety of roles, including a short stint testing the feasibility of the model for aircraft-carrier duty. That Cold War experiment—not particularly successful—was etched somewhere in the memory of the landing hydraulics, which screeched unmercifully as the plane ground to a halt not ten feet from the trailers. Scotty stopped the car and put his hands to his ears involuntarily, hoping not to shield out the noise but to keep his skull from splitting in half.

The Cubans jumped to work unloading the plane as its huge rear ramp hit the dirt. Scotty hustled up to the cargomaster, who was trying in pigeon Spanish to make sure he had the right group of clandestine teamsters at his door. Even covert activities have paperwork, and by the time Scotty had signed the man's forms, the Cubans, lacking a forklift, had broken apart the skids and were three-quarters of the way done packing their trucks.

Scotty tried to ignore the rough handling the crates of ammunition were receiving. Trotting down the cargo ramp, he looked for the pilots he had come to retrieve. A tallish, thin man in a green jumpsuit was standing with a bag not far from the popped bay door of the Hercules. Scotty couldn't believe this was one of the pilots—the kid looked barely old enough to shave. With a shock of short, oily black hair swept up at the front and gawky gestures, he reminded Scotty of a junior counselor at a kids' summer camp.

"Which one are you?" Scotty demanded.

"Sir? I am Lieutenant Edward Garcia, United States Marine Corps, reporting for duty."

"Can the Marine Corps bullshit. You're a civilian

106

as far as anyone here is concerned. And bag the lieutenant crap, too. Where's this Dalton character?"

Bewildered, Garcia said he wasn't sure who or what Scotty was talking about. His curses growing in variety, Scotty went and checked inside the plane, then talked with the crew. Nobody knew anything about Dalton, a marine reservist who was supposed to arrive with Garcia.

Pissed that he had yet another loose end to tie up, Scotty waved for Garcia to follow and walked to the Ford. It was only when he opened the car door that he realized the kid had a serious limp.

Scotty had done a lot of ops work in his career, and had had occasion to drink with more than his share of pilots, military, civilian, and everything in between. To a man, their swagger and smile preceded them; they shared a certain hitch in their giddyap that told the world the turds they plopped were made of gold.

But never had he met one with a limp. And a grimace where his shit-eating grin ought to be.

The kid was not only green, he was a gimp.

Scotty stared over the top of the car at him, wondering if he had been sucked into someone else's bad dream.

"Hey, no offense, Junior, but what gives with the leg?"

"I screwed it up bailing out the other day. It's getting better—this morning I was on crutches. Figured I could leave them home."

"Bailing out? Oh, fuck." Scotty shook his head. "You got any civilian clothes in that bag you're dragging?"

"Yes, sir."

"Well, get changed. You can't go into the hotel wearing a flight suit."

"Here?"

"You want me to close my eyes?"

Garcia didn't answer, and mercifully took little time losing the flight suit and putting on a T-shirt and jeans. He looked very American, but at least he didn't look as if he'd just come from Iwo Jima. Something else Scotty appreciated—he kept his mouth shut, at least until they got onto the highway.

"My friends call me Elvis," said the pilot.

"What do you do, sing a little song for them?"

"Frig yourself," Garcia snapped back.

"Frig myself? Frig?" Scotty's laugh was so cathartic it was almost uncontrollable. "Jesus, kid, you're something. You sure you're old enough to fly?"

"I can fly anything you throw at me."

"Yeah, well, that's a fucking relief. I'll sleep well tonight."

Scotty took a deep breath, feeling the amphetamine unsettling his stomach. He knew he was going to crash soon—he hadn't slept now in almost thirty-six hours—but he had enough energy for one more chore.

"This probably ain't none of my business," he said. "But how the hell are you going to fly with that leg?"

"It's not that bad. I just have to adjust the tape and grab some aspirin. Besides, all I got to do is train people."

Scotty snorted. "Is that what they told you?"

"More or less."

"Kid, I'm gonna give you some good advice. Don't believe anything anybody tells you here. This is Cuba. It's got a hell of a lot of potential, but there are all sorts of people standing in the way of it. Including us."

Garcia didn't answer. Scotty wondered how long it would be before Steele was asking for a volunteer to accompany a coffin back to the States.

"What were those AGM-65s for?" Garcia asked.

"AG-whats?"

"The Maverick missiles loaded in the back of the C-130. You're not a pilot, are you?"

"Are you kidding? I hate flying." Scotty shook his head. "I'm just an errand boy here. What's wrong with the missiles?"

"Those models are intended for tanks. From what I've heard, M-26 doesn't have any."

"You know a lot about the guerrillas, huh?"

"I know that they don't have tanks. Or is that something else I shouldn't believe?"

Scotty smiled to himself, thinking how Steele would take the news about having wrangled worthless missiles. The fact that the pilot knew at least a bit about M-26 elevated his opinion of him.

Slightly.

"They don't have tanks," said Scotty. "At least not yet."

"What, are they are on order?"

"The cover story is that you're an American businessman here to consult with a new Cuban air taxi, Libre Habana. You'll be working with a British colonel, or ex-colonel, whose name is Hill. He's a prig and a prick. None of the Cubans like him, which probably means he knows what he's doing."

"What kind of shape are these planes in?"

"I haven't a clue, except that they fly. Personally, I think the whole project is a waste of time."

Garcia frowned but didn't say anything. Eventually he turned to the side window, staring out as they drove.

"Say, listen, I have to make a little detour," Scotty told him after about ten minutes of silence. "You don't mind, right?"

"Not if you don't mind telling me your name."

"Scott McPherson. I'm a special aide to the ambassador."

Garcia held out his hand, but Scotty just nodded, keeping both hands on the wheel as he swung off the highway onto a narrow, freshly paved road in a new subdivision just south of Havana. American-style raised ranches, most still being built, fanned out like a Levittown in the making. These gave way to a mélange of pseudo-Tudors and vinyl-clad Victorians, also in various stages of construction. Then came the new houses of the truly rich, or at least the much better connected. These faced the road behind stucco walls topped with glass shards and punctuated by heavy iron gates and uniformed guards, whose scowls warned of easy trigger fingers on their M-16s. The development was known, derisively, as Little America; created within the last eighteen months, the entire population consisted of returnees who held important corporate and, in a few cases, government posts.

The house Scotty was headed for predated the others by about twenty years, though it was no less pretentious. Once used as the headquarters for the state energy ministry, its roof gouged a symmetrical four-cornered hole in the hillside. The two armed men standing at the gate looked in at him curiously, then nodded when they recognized him, scurrying to open the gate.

"Where are we?" Garcia asked.

"Near Havana," said Scotty. "Got to see a friend of mine."

He drove through the gate, past stands of exotic, imported lilies, and up a long, pea-gravel driveway.

"There's a gun in the glove compartment," Scotty told Garcia. "Take it out, please."

The pilot, not entirely sure what was going on, jumped involuntarily as the ancient Colt automatic fell out of the glove compartment into his lap.

"Careful, I've never been too sure about the safety. They claim they last forever," added Scotty, reaching to take the gun, "but I don't know how long forever is supposed to be. I have a bad record with safeties."

"What the hell are we doing?"

"You are sitting in the car." Scotty saw a figure emerge from the house. He slammed on the brakes and threw the transmission into park. He was out of the car, leaping onto the verandah, before Saul Virgilio knew what was happening.

"Who the fuck blew up Ave?" he said, pointing the gun into Virgilio's throat. "Who was it?"

"Jesus Christ! What the hell are you doing, Scott?"

"Who blew up Ave?"

"What's with the goddamn gun?"

"Answer my question."

"We're cooperating fully—"

"No you're not. I talked to Franklin at the FBI two hours ago and he tells me he can't even get an appointment to take a piss."

"You fuckhead—you can't do this to me."

"Did you guys try to blow up de Souza?"

"Shit."

"Virgilio, you know what a forty-five slug will do to that little brain of yours? It's gonna look like applesauce. You know applesauce, right? You were born in the States."

Scotty had his left arm cocked across Virgilio's chest. His knee was tight against his groin, ready to strike, but the pistol was really all he needed. Virgilio's hands were quivering back and forth like the pens on a seismometer during an earthquake. He'd never been very good under pressure.

"You're out of your fucking mind, Scott. When the ambassador finds out—"

"You answer the question now, or I blow your brains all over the pretty flowers."

There was a commotion inside.

"My wife is coming out."

"I don't mind an audience."

Jim DeFelice

"It's okay, honey," Virgilio said loudly. "I'll be inside in a minute. Make dinner."

"Who's out there with you?"

"Just someone from the office."

"Saul?"

"Don't come out!" he yelled desperately. "I'll be right in." When his wife didn't answer, he looked back at Scotty. "You don't scare me."

"Then why are your pants wet?"

"You're fucking crazy enough to shoot me, aren't you? We're all on the same side here."

"No. You're on your own side. I know about the payments from the Gambino brothers. Now, tell me—who blew up Ave?"

"We don't know."

"Why was de Souza there?"

"No one's sure."

"That's not the right answer."

"It's the truth."

"Was it someone in MININT?"

"That's insane."

"Who would want to kill her, if not you guys?" Scotty eased back slightly, though he was still holding the pistol to Virgilio's throat. Virgilio was a lot of things, but he wasn't a very good liar, and Scotty judged that he wasn't lying now. "Who?"

Virgilio shook his head, exasperated. "I don't know."

"Why is the news reporting she was killed?"

"How do I know? That's not my department."

"Is it just their ineptness, or are you trying to flush her out?"

"Believe me, she's not taken in by easy tricks. You've seen that yourself."

"Then where did she go?" Scotty asked.

"If I knew where she was, I would arrest her for the bombing." Virgilio's breathing was starting to slow slightly, though it still couldn't be called normal.

"I thought you didn't want a martyr."

"We think she did it. We could blame the bombing on her."

"Why would she go there if she was going to blow it up?"

"Maybe to make it seem that she was innocent. It had to be her; it wasn't the government. Why is this important to you, Scott?"

"Where are you looking for her?"

"I think she went east."

"De Souza? East? Why?"

"You know, we really don't have the network of spies you think we do."

"Don't fuck with me, Saul." Scotty wagged the pistol under Virgilio's chin. "You owe me for a lot of things. Guatemala, for example."

"I know it, I know it. I'm not lying to you. I pay my debts."

"Yeah, right." Even so, Scotty released him.

"I would have told you this if you came to the office," Virgilio said, trying to straighten out his clothes.

It was such an obvious lie, Scotty didn't even bother refuting it. "It's more fun this way," he said, pulling open the car door. Two men with machine guns belatedly appeared from around the corner of the house. "Man, you ought to pay those guys a little more," he told Virgilio as he slid behind the wheel.

He was just about to shift it into reverse when he realized that Garcia was standing half in, half out on the passenger's side.

"Come on, Junior, time to go."

"Shit" was all Garcia could say. He repeated it when they reached the highway. "Shit."

"Well, your vocabulary's starting to improve.

What's wrong? You look like you gotta take a dump."

"Was he a guerrilla?"

"Nah. They'd never take anyone as corrupt as him. He used to be CIA. Now he's part of the antiterrorist section for the Ministry of Interior in Havana. We're old buddies."

Havana. 5:45 P.M.

Confused, his leg throbbing, Garcia got out of the car and struggled to haul his bag from the trunk and into the Paramount Hotel. He was surprised when a porter appeared and took it from him. Even more surprising was the fact that the staff knew his cover story better than he did. When Garcia introduced himself, the clerk at the desk brushed aside his Spanish and answered in perfect English.

"Yes, we have been expecting you. Your suite is on the third floor, with a view of the ocean, *Señor*. Do you need anything for your leg?"

"Aspirin would be cool."

"Of course. The bellhop will show you upstairs, and room service will bring some aspirin. Is this your first trip?"

"Yes."

The clerk winked at him. "Your parents are Cuban, *sí*?"

"How did you know?"

"I understand these things," said the man in Spanish. "Enjoy your business here."

Garcia took this as an indication that either there had been a security breach or his Spanish wasn't completely inept. Hoping it was the latter, he hobbled along to the elevator.

The clerk hadn't been exaggerating when he called the room a suite. The bathroom alone was bigger than his quarters at Cherry Point; the jets on the Jacuzzi looked nearly as large as the vectoring thrusters on the Pegasus. There were two bedrooms, as well as a large room in the middle that could have served as an off-hours club on a good-size base. The television was a monster fifty-four-inch model with over a hundred channels available, all but three piped in from the States. The refrigerator was stocked with a variety of booze, beer, and American soft drinks. The room-service menu sat on the desk, with a handwritten note saying everything was complimentary.

When Garcia pulled out his wallet to tip the attendant for his bags, the man waved off the money. "All paid, all paid," he said. As he was backing out the door, a room-service waiter appeared, carrying a bottle of aspirin on a tray as if it were haute cuisine. He, too, refused a tip.

Garcia sat in a warm tub, letting his knee revive. The aspirin soon took hold, and whether it was stubbornness or the recuperative powers of youth, he decided that he felt nearly as good as new. After fifteen minutes he toweled off and retaped his knee, deciding to put it to a real test by going out for dinner.

Though he was hungry, it was not food he was truly after, but Cuba. What he had seen from the car had, frankly, been rather disappointing; so far the mysterious island of his parents' youth had all the charm of an American suburb. He felt an uncontrollable urge to explore, to walk the streets where his parents walked—even if he had to do it by hobbling along.

McPherson had told him to stay put until Colonel Hill contacted him. But he didn't figure that meant he couldn't go out to grab a bite to eat.

Besides, who was going to stop him?

He found a long line of taxis waiting near the front door downstairs.

"You can have the car for an hour for twenty dollars," explained the doorman as he waved the line forward. "And do not tip more than five dollars."

The driver's name was Junior Brown. A short black man, he spoke English without a Spanish accent, and surprised Garcia after he slid in by announcing that he was from Duluth.

"Minnesota?"

"The same," said Junior. "I came down here last year kinda to bum around, and then I saw I could make a fortune doing this. Where are we going?"

"I'd kind of like to just drive around for a while. I've never been here."

"Hey, no problem. Sit back and let Junior Brown give you the grand tour, including popular points of interest and disinterest, complete with running commentary and no singing."

Garcia leaned out the window, absorbing the city and the humid air around him. As they drove, his disappointment grew.

Even allowing for their exaggerations, the city he was passing through was grossly different from what his parents had described in the passing bits of stories that were told not as remembrances but as examples of how he ought to live his life. It was grayer, dirtier, considerably less alive than even their brief descriptions. The crowded shops, the street vendors, even the long lines and the bus stops seemed to have all been painted dark brown. The buildings were pockmarked with bullets and worn by the wind. The gossipy chatter and music of the streets had been replaced by car horns and cranky exhaust systems. To Garcia, Havana bore the worst aspects of an American city, beaten down by decades of neglect and paralyzed by the past. Even the areas of town Junior proclaimed as "reborn" seemed nothing more than drab blotches of tan and black, speckled with a few bright pennants and wall signs. Painted-over slogans from the Castro era ("Commander in Chief! Give the Orders!", "Nobody Surrenders Here!") haunted the sides of buildings like the old dictator's ghost. Metal grates marked off the remains of a burned or bombed-out storefront.

Even the evening crowd along Malecón Boulevard on the waterfront, to Garcia's increasingly jaded eyes, seemed bored and boring. No wonder his father and mother didn't want to come back.

Junior drove slowly along the six-lane avenue parallel to the sea. It was lined with vendors at metal snack tables, offering such things as T-shirts and used books, trinkets and shoes. A middle-aged man called as he passed that he would give him twenty dollars for his "tennies." Garcia, unsure precisely what the man wanted, shook his head.

"He wanted to buy your Nikes," Junior told him.

"How the hell did he know I had athletic shoes on?"

"All Americans wear sneakers the first day," replied Junior.

"What if I didn't?"

"Then he would have sold you a pair for thirty bucks." Junior laughed. "You'd better be careful down here. Most of these guys are pretty damn honest, but if you're used to American prices you're just a fatted calf. And every so often, you run into someone who worked for the regime."

"The regime?"

"Uncle Fidel. Those guys are all scumbags. So what are you doing down here, kid? Come to make your fortune?"

"I'm here on business," said Garcia, sliding back.

"Lot of money to be made. Place is booming. Kind of like the Wild West, though, especially when the guerrillas act up. Nobody likes them, but you can't beat the entertainment value."

Junior backtracked, heading south and then back in the general direction of Centro Habana, the part of the city that included the capital and several large parks and monuments. The capitol dome—a copy of the Washington capitol—seemed gray and dirty in the failing light, and Garcia's disappointment continued, becoming now almost a stubborn depression.

Junior turned down a side street, then hit the gas to veer out of the path of an ancient, Czech-built bus that had wandered into his lane. It looked like a plodding dragon, bright red with a checkerboard tail. Fresh paint made the scars of two decades' worth of city driving appear as if they were part of the design. The placard on the back proclaimed Pepsi the number-one drink of the post-Castro generation.

Garcia's mood finally began to brighten as the cabdriver entered the precincts of La Habana Vieja, or the old city. They drove slowly past Parque Central, with its laurels, poincianas, almonds, and innumerable palms; it would have been difficult not to be impressed by the natural beauty here. And as Junior plunged deeper into the narrow streets that made up the city's most historic section, Garcia began admiring the old cars, relics thirty and forty and in one or two cases fifty years old. Many were in near showroom condition, shined and polished, untouched by the squalor and dullness reflected on their gleaming surfaces.

"This is San Cristóbal, the Cathedral," Junior announced, gesturing out the window. "Christopher Columbus was buried here. At least they thought it was Christopher Columbus. Turned out to be the wrong guy."

Junior then launched into a pirate story, inspired by the Castillo de la Fuerza, a block eastward. He told the story as if he had been on the beach in the 1530s when a group of buccaneers sailed in and sacked the place, leading the inhabitants to build the fort.

A growl from Garcia's stomach ended the tale mid-swashbuckle.

"You hungry?"

"Kinda."

"The best restaurants are all down here," Junior advised. "Two blocks over is an excellent Chinese."

"I don't want Chinese food."

"Casa Borghese's down this block. Man, their linguine with pesto is blowaway."

"I want Cuban food."

Junior frowned into the mirror. "Mostly tourist traps. Overpriced and crowded."

"Well, take me somewhere that's not. I want a real restaurant, with authentic food."

"Like mom used to make, right?"

"Something like that."

The driver shrugged his shoulders and concentrated on his driving for a while, pushing the car away from the harbor, deeper into residential Havana. The buildings reeked of a boring sameness, but Garcia noticed that the paint—though dull brown—was fresh. Finally, after a number of turns Garcia could never have retraced, Junior stopped in front of a small, dilapidated walk-up. "You sure about this?"

Garcia looked at the building's peeling brown paint doubtfully. "Is it hard to get a cab around here?" he asked.

"It's impossible," said Junior. "I'll come back in two hours and pick you up."

"Really?"

"Hey, man, the one thing you can count on in Havana is a cabbie's word. Go ahead."

Garcia gave him the twenty and an extra ten, then got out. A riot of conflicting odors met him on the sidewalk.

"It's downstairs," said Junior, pointing. "Remember, two hours."

A hand-lettered sign on the iron railing near the stairway read *"restaurante."* Garcia hesitated before pushing open the large oaken door, which was secured by a black metal push-lever. Once inside, however, he was welcomed by three people: a waiter, a young hostess, and a man who said he was the owner and loved everything American. Twitching his white whiskers into a smile, he led Garcia toward the back of the long but narrow room, seating him next to one of the restaurant's two other occupied tables.

The waitress swirled her short green dress as she walked toward him. She nodded quickly when the owner snapped his fingers and told her to bring a carafe of wine. Garcia could barely understand his rapid-fire Spanish as the man described the dishes; finally he stopped him and said in Spanish that the *zarzuela,* a shellfish stew, would be just fine.

"Green sauce or red?"

"Green."

The owner approved the choice with a vigorous nod, as if his young customer had shown the wisdom of Solomon in selecting. He disappeared into the kitchen, and Garcia soon found himself staring at the waitress's breasts while she poured wine into his glass. They were about the size of oranges, thick and round beneath the dress top. Even if he hadn't spent the last several weeks like a monk at Lent, he would have developed a serious case of lust.

"You are from up north?" the girl asked in Spanish, setting the small pitcher down. Her straight hair was pulled to one side. Though she wore no makeup, her creamy skin had a warm glow in the restaurant's soft light. He figured that she was nineteen or twenty.

"*Sí,*" answered Garcia. He added, in Spanish, "I'm here on business."

"Not many Americans come to our restaurant," the waitress answered. She held her small tray in front of her stomach, as if she were ashamed of it and wanted to shield it from his view. But her stomach was flat, not even nudging the tapered waist of the short dress. "The food is very authentic Spanish. As you would get in Spain."

Her enthusiasm had an odd effect—it made him tongue-tied. The only word Garcia could manage was "great"—in English, which the waitress only vaguely understood.

With two native speakers to test and tutor him, Garcia was reasonably skilled at Spanish, but he'd momentarily lost the ability to put a sentence together. He might not even have been able to do so in English. Words floated into his head, all variations of "beautiful eyes," and none really appropriate as innocuous conversation starters: *ojos bonitos, ojos hermosos.*

And so he sat silently, staring. The waitress lingered, smiling back until a call from the kitchen ended the standoff. Garcia felt like kicking himself in the butt.

"The *zarzuela* was a good choice. The one thing that you can count on in Havana is fish."

Garcia looked over to see the woman at the next table smiling at him. About his age, perhaps a year or two older, she spoke English with a light, clipped Spanish accent. Her dark brown hair, not quite shoulder length, was bobbed back and tied with a clasp, leaving a broad, smiling face, thick lips and a large nose. When she smiled, she closed her eyes to a squint and held her hand up, as if beckoning him.

"This restaurant has always been a good one. My father says it was open even before the Revolution. I heard you say you were American," she continued,

Jim DeFelice

extending her hand to shake. "Would you mind if I practiced my English with you?"

"No, not at all," said Garcia. She smiled at him and glanced down briefly out of shyness before again looking into his face.

"My name is Maria Letra. And you?"

"Edward Garcia. I'm here on business."

"And what do you do?"

"I'm a consultant. I was just . . . kind of visiting right now," he added quickly, afraid he was going to say too much.

"Who—whom—are you visiting?"

"Just the city."

"The entire city?"

Garcia nodded. He felt trapped by his cover story, helpless to fend off her questions if she pursued it. But she began talking about how beautiful summer could be, with its flowers and growing cane. And this year it did not seem to be raining very much.

Her bright yellow dress matched the color of the place mats, though it did considerably more for her than the table. Her skin, darkened by the sun, glowed warmly, and if she was not quite beautiful— certainly no match for the waitress—there was an openness in her face and manner that made her easy to talk to.

Or listen, as Garcia was finding that he had little to say except "yes" and "no." He looked up and saw the waitress approaching, a large platter in her arms. As she bent over the table to put it down he stared at her breasts, and it was only by some fluke that he managed to come up with words as she straightened.

"*¿Qué son estos?*" he asked her, pointing to the small plates that were crowded into the large platter. "What are those?"

"*Tapas*," said the waitress. "Try them; they're very good."

122

"They are like appetizers," said Maria Letra. "That one by your elbow is snail. Don't you recognize it?"

"Snails?"

"They're delicious. Try the sauce. Here—" She got up and took the small seafood fork, poking it into the snail and retrieving the morsel. She swished it in the sauce, then handed over the fork and motioned with her hands for him to try it.

The waitress suddenly receded from his view. All he could see was Maria, who he realized was considerably more beautiful than he had thought. Her flowery smell reminded him of the scent an old girlfriend had worn, though there was slightly more musk to it, something more earthy.

"Do you like it? The snail?"

It could have tasted like dog meat and Garcia would have answered yes. In fact it was very good, the sauce peppery from the garlic and spices.

"This would be great chili," he said without thinking.

She smiled and looked at him as if he were joking. "It is a great delicacy here. *Señor* Fernandez is trying to impress you."

"He succeeded," said Garcia. "Here, come eat with me," he added. "You can share my dinner."

"No, I couldn't."

"Come on," he said, standing. "You wanted to practice your English."

"All right, then."

Sometime after the owner had come and pinned a bib on him for the *zarzuela*—Maria laughed when Garcia's first reaction was to jump back from the table—he found himself talking about his disappointment at the dreariness that seemed to have consumed much of the island. When Maria volunteered to show him "the real Cuba," he accepted without hesitation, though he had no idea when he might be able to take up her invitation. And as he

lingered after finishing dinner, he nearly forgot
what the horn outside meant, and had to struggle
to make it to the door in time to keep Junior from
going on without him.

Garcia was still orbiting under the influence of
Maria's cheekbones when the taxi pulled up in front
of the Paramount. "Look for me in front of the Hotel
Nacional," Junior advised. "Anytime you need me,
that's where you find me."

"Thanks," said Garcia, leaning over the seat to
give him another tip.

The driver grabbed his hand so hard, Garcia was
jolted forward. The smiling, jovial face had suddenly hardened into something quite dangerous and
foreboding.

"Listen, kid, one thing—you got to be careful in
Cuba. Havana especially."

Garcia pulled his arm back, but Junior's grip was
not that easily broken.

"No one's going to believe you're a tourist, and the
business stuff won't get you very far. So watch yourself."

"What do you mean?"

Junior only smiled. "You know what I mean. Just
be careful, okay? You seem like a nice guy."

Garcia slid over to the door and let himself out.

"Mr. McPherson sends his regards," said Junior
through the window. "And suggests you take his advice to heart from now on."

Garcia, partly mad, partly embarrassed, walked
through the plush hotel's automatic door. The wine
he'd drunk at dinner made his knee feel considerably better, and as he leaned against the wall in the
elevator, he decided that another session in the
warm Jacuzzi might just cure it for good.

The door to his suite swung open easily. Garcia
reached for the light, then felt a sharp pain in his

leg as he was yanked forward. Hands pressed him toward the ground; he jerked his elbows out and twisted, unsure of who or what was attacking him. He tried to roll to his stomach, but his attackers had too much of an advantage; an elbow crushed into his neck and the fight began to drain from him. He roared as he made a last-ditch effort to escape. His flailing left fist caught something soft, and to his great surprise he found himself back on his feet, dragging someone as he stumbled toward the door. Garcia began yelling; a hand groped for his mouth. He bit the fingers hard. Their owner screamed. Blows landed on his shoulders, but he struggled onward, grinding his teeth against the fingers. The hallway was just in front of him; he reached out his hand for the doorjamb, hoping to pull himself outward. As he did, something hit his good knee very hard and he felt himself tumble forward. As his hand groped for the molding on the entry, he was pulled back inside and rolled onto his back. The door slammed, the lights came on; two men pressed their bodies against his.

"*Basta. Basta.* Don't kill the bloody idiot."

A tall, thin man in plain green fatigues stood over him. A pencil-thin mustache lined his lip, but his scowling face was dominated by a jagged scar that ran from his right ear down to his neck. Fiftyish, his shaved head accented the angles of his skull; together with his austere body, it made him seem as if he were made of wood. He jabbed the air with a cigar that was as fat as he was thin.

"Let him up," said the man in a pronounced British accent.

Released, Garcia jumped up, ready to fight again. But his bad knee had begun to throb, and when one of the men grabbed his shoulder, he stopped. Dressed in the same simple but freshly starched khakis as their leader, the four men who had attacked him seemed to all be Cubans.

"You're stupid, but at least you've got fight in you."

"Did McPherson send you, too?"

"Hardly. My name is Colonel Hill. Which one are you? Garcia or Dalton?"

"Garcia."

"Well, Garcia, if you fly as well as you fight, you'll do nicely." The officer sat down on the couch. "So where the bloody hell have you been?"

"Getting dinner."

Hill's expression implied that he was only vaguely aware of the concept. "This is a difficult country. You can take nothing for granted. It appears one way on the surface. Beneath it can be very different. The guerrillas are detested by nearly everyone, yet they have ample weapons and can strike anywhere they please. And within the temporary government . . ." The colonel shook his head. "The person bringing you dinner may bring you poison as well."

"I had to eat somewhere."

Hill waved his hand at the men who had accompanied him. "Dismissed." Without a word, they filed out of the suite.

"Why'd you have them jump me?" Garcia demanded when they left. "They could have gotten hurt."

"You need to learn several lessons, my young friend. You may get killed if you're not more careful. You may be killed anyway." Hill got up and walked to the refrigerator. He helped himself to a small bottle of Scotch. "They ought not to chill these bloody things. Absurd notion, chilled Scotch. Do you want some, Lieutenant?"

"No." Garcia sat in the thick leather armchair. He was sore and bruised, but too proud to admit it by taking inventory in front of Hill. "Are they the people I'm going to train?"

Hill laughed. "Train? Is that what they told you?"

"I'm supposed to help teach pilots on the Harrier."

"Tell me, Lieutenant, how long did it take for you to learn to fly the A/V-8A?"

"I haven't flown the early models," snapped Garcia, angered by the patronizing tone. "I flew the A/V-8B. And the Pegasus."

"Not my point." Hill slugged the Scotch directly from the bottle. "Though your ambassador would have done better to recruit someone familiar with the plane."

"I can fly it."

"No doubt. Once you get used to an engine that is considerably underpowered, and a wing that has the lifting characteristics of a tea biscuit, I am sure you will do just jolly. On to my question—how long did it take until you were proficient?"

"A flight or two."

"Oh yes. A prodigy, are we?" The small bottle empty, Hill reached into the refrigerator and took two more. "Here," he said, tossing Garcia a short, thick brown bottle of beer. "Hatuey is supposed to be Cuba's best beer. *La Gran Cerveza de Cuba.* I think it's pisswater, myself, but you Americans seem to like it."

Undecided what to do, Garcia twisted off the top but didn't drink. Hill drained another Scotch.

"I speak Spanish," said Garcia.

Hill wasn't impressed. "You're not going to be training anyone, Lieutenant. Not for a good long while. The Cubans have forbidden it, because the planes are too precious and they don't trust most of their pilots. Besides, there's no time, and there are no bloody trainers. We have eight—no, excuse me, seven—Mark 55s that the Spanish navy graciously gave the Cuban air force because even the scrap dealers turned up their noses. Four of them are actually capable of flight."

"Four?"

"You don't really need to know all the bloody details, do you? It might become necessary to kill you."

"The ambassador told me—"

"Oh yes, I'm sure the good ambassador told you many things. Did he mention he was nearly assassinated the other day?"

"No."

"They did a bloody good job keeping that out of the news, I must say. We'll begin training tomorrow morning. You'll be at the flight line at six. At five, someone will knock on your door—two knocks, a pause, then two more. Anything else, shoot first. You have a side arm?"

"In my bag."

"Carry one with you at all times. Here." Hill slipped a small automatic from his pocket. "You'll find this convenient." He tossed it at Garcia. "I have a small holster for it; you can wear it at your belt, beneath a shirt. I suggest you spend some time target shooting. Your afternoons and evenings will be free, at least until the Cubans manage to find us more fuel."

"I can shoot pretty damn well," said Garcia.

"Oh yes, you marines all think you're riflemen, don't you? Well, don't kill anyone who's not a rebel. And if you do happen to shoot someone, make damn sure to tell the police he told you he was a rebel before he died. Deathbed confessions are very big here."

The gun fit snugly in Garcia's palm. The black, brushed steel felt cold in his hand, the thin trigger icy. The gun was completely devoid of markings.

"Who makes this?"

Hill almost smiled. "It's Czech. A Vzor. Brand new. Five shots in the clip. Very soft recoil, and reasonably accurate. The only difficulty is the lack of a safety. A shame. I assume you'll be careful."

Garcia immediately took a more respectful attitude toward the gun, placing it down on the coffee table before him.

"We fly from a scrub field at a place called Jardín Pequeño—the little garden, which I can assure you it is anything but. There's a strip barely suited to our needs; apparently the Cubans believed what the Spanish told them about the airplanes. The missions are straightforward bombing runs. Most of our action is in Camagüey and on the southern coast, where the guerrillas are strong enough to operate in the open. The pigs haven't gotten antiair missiles yet, according to the drunken sot of a Cuban colonel who's supposed to be our coordinator. Really, why can't you bloody Americans find competent people for your puppets?"

"You're saying you're not competent?"

Hill laughed. "Touché, Lieutenant, though I daresay I'll be considerably better paid than you for my troubles. A word of advice—I don't mind a sharp tongue, but if you use it in front of the ground crew I'll cut your balls off. Now, where is this Dalton character?"

"I don't know anything about him."

"He's some sort of marine as well, though he at least is supposed to be old enough to shave." As Garcia felt his face turning red, Hill added, "Oh, don't be so bloody sensitive. Come on, I'll buy you a drink on the ambassador."

Sierra Maestra Mountains, Southeast Cuba. 11:15 P.M.

The eyes followed him. They were deep and dark, eyes of great love, of fathomless power. The eyes saw into the crevices of his soul, saw across the petty disturbances of the day, the slights, the insults, into the great depth of his timeless being. The eyes followed him and inspired him, were there even when he could not see them. *El Jefe* had given him these eyes; *El Jefe* had made the eyes his legacy and his destiny.

The radio had declared Carla de Souza dead. Hector Romano Moncado did not feel elation at her death, though she represented the last barrier to his success. He felt sadness—she was, after all, El Jefe's daughter, and it was unfortunate that he had found it necessary to kill her. He was El Jefe's true heir, but she was a link to him, flawed certainly, but a link nonetheless. Romano had seen something in her eyes, a shadow there, a hint of what he saw now, staring into the mirror on his wall, the mirror that told him *El Jefe* flowed through the timeless ether and was in his soul.

Romano had been able to gather many tokens in the two years since the Revolution had begun in earnest. He had several pieces of the yacht *Granma;* he had the commander in chief's desk chair. He had the caches of old weapons and this complex.

Beyond it all, he had the hatred. He savored it. On the wall was a picture of Kennedy, the original, the first devil. Romano turned from the mirror and laughed at it. He did so as often as he could. Kennedy was the model—*El Jefe* had had his revenge against him; he had ordered him dead, and it had been made so.

Now more was required, more blood for the sins of every American who had followed, for every worm who had returned to destroy *El Jefe*'s revolutionary paradise.

Romano had done much during his recent trip west. Luring Carla into his trap and setting the stage among his followers to succeed her were his major accomplishments, but he had done many other things. Not his least significant acquisition was the object in a plain manila envelope on the desk. He went to it now, unsheathing a pair of photographs of D'Amici—the present president of the Yankee bastard imperialists. They had been supplied by a spy in the devil's own embassy.

Carla's spy, now his.

He laughed, remembering the man's rage when he discovered the pictures were all that he wanted. "You demanded a face-to-face meeting for these?"

But few understood the importance of tokens. They dismissed the beliefs they did not understand as superstition, as "Santeria, the Cuban voodoo."

El Jefe did not dismiss it. *El Jefe* knew.

Romano took one of the photos and folded it carefully. It would remain with him, to remind him of his duty. It would keep him from weakening, as Carla had. She had started with all the advantages, the lineage, the best men, the best advisers, and even so, she had lost the fire. Everyone knew it.

He took the second photo of D'Amici and placed it on the desk with a piece of incense and a holy card, as he had been instructed. He lit the corner on fire, staring as the flame consumed his enemy.

Soon flames would consume more than just a photo.

Chapter Four

As Hill had told him in more colorful terms, the early Harriers did not have nearly the same thrust as the models Garcia had flown, nor did their wings provide as much lift. Still getting used to the difference after two days of nearly nonstop flying, the young pilot spent several minutes programming and rechecking the flight data in the inertial navigation system, which gave him a precise set of specs to follow on the takeoff run. Checks completed, heads-up display in short-takeoff mode, Garcia waited at the end of the runway for clearance while the Rolls Royce F402 engine hummed behind him, its turbines spooling like a team of baseball players doing warm-up calisthenics.

Garcia's work area was cramped and crowded. Owing its origins to the 1960s, the cockpit had all the ergonomics of a telephone booth. The narrow front windshield was dominated by the HUD, or heads-up display, which despite its obsolescence did

132

a reasonable job of supplying pertinent flight information. Below it, the center console arranged itself around a circular moving map display. The dial for the inertial navigation and attack system was just above this, slightly obscured by the HUD gear. The altimeter sat on the top left side of the panel, with the artificial horizon just below it.

If Garcia extended his left arm about halfway, his fingers brushed into the radio controls; he could practically work the throttle with his elbow. The right-side console panel hosted a gaggle of controls, including a switch that every so often seemed to adjust the air conditioner, though generally in the opposite direction than what was needed.

But Garcia liked the stick or control column, which was a lot simpler than the one in the A/V-8B or Harrier II; maybe because of this it gave him a better feel for the plane.

The plane's onboard computer was primitive compared to the Pegasus, but it did the job well enough, crunching input data that included the runway temperature as well as takeoff weight and altimeter setting. It told the pilot to set his nozzles at fifty-five degrees once his speed reached eighty-five knots on the four-hundred-foot takeoff roll. That meant that the four vectoring nozzles beneath the belly of the craft would spin a little more than halfway through their rotating arc for takeoff. Though called nozzles, they looked more like giant exhaust outlets beneath the wings, which was essentially what they were. During takeoff, exhaust gas from the engine would be routed through them, helping provide the extra lift that enabled the bomb-laden plane to get airborne at such a short distance.

As the Cuban sergeant commanding the flight line swung down his hand, Garcia cranked the nozzles into position and slammed the throttle full-bore. The aircraft stuttered forward, smoke pouring in a huge fog around it, gurgling like an old hen, not quite sounding as if it really felt like working today. But once the plane got moving it decided to make the best of it, sniffing between the potholes to pick up speed.

Garcia reached his left hand to the vectoring control, getting ready to pull it back to its stop as the airspeed shot toward eighty-five knots. The lever was finicky; it stuck for a moment as he pulled. He yanked back, then immediately feared he had pulled it past its catch. The mechanism, which looked like a flimsy thumbnail screw, proved considerably stronger than Garcia thought, and the plane slid merrily upward, oblivious to its pilot's momentary rush of anxiety.

Garcia told himself to relax. He turned his attention to his stick hand, remembering an early instructor's admonition to hold the control "like a baby's hand." The metaphor wasn't particularly precise—Garcia couldn't imagine what a toddler would be doing in the cockpit—but it reminded him to guide the plane, not muscle it into the sky. Clearing the end of the field, he gently jabbed the switch to take in the landing gear, then nozzled out, pushing the nozzle-control lever steadily back into position for level flight.

With the nozzles now pointing to the rear, the Rolls Royce's energy was devoted entirely to forward flight, and the Harrier steadied into an easy climb. The ship had become just an ordinary, almost easy-to-handle airplane. Garcia took two very long breaths, banishing the premission fuzzies.

"Nicely done, Matador Three," said Colonel Hill. His aircraft was already orbiting overhead. "Handled like a veteran. Come up a bit and give Ferguson and Mr. Dalton some room to maneuver. Let's see if they do as well as you."

Garcia glanced briefly at the altimeter "clock" on

the panel in front of his stick, superstitiously making sure the altitude there agreed with the reading on the "ladder" in the heads-up display. Leaning forward on his sturdy, if worn, Martin-Baker ejector seat, Garcia took a shot at adjusting the air conditioner.

"See those mountains over your right wing?" Hill asked over the radio. "That's where we're headed."

"Acknowledged, Matador One," said Garcia. Hill was a good pilot, but his style as a commander left considerable room for improvement. He was somewhat indifferent about radio protocols, and briefings amounted to the kind of instructions kids used for touch football games—jog down to the Chevy, hang a left, wait for the ball.

Ferguson dialed in, announcing with apparent relief that he was airborne. The fourth and final pilot, Jason Dalton, came out last, cursing the old Harrier profusely. Dalton, an ex–marine aviator now in his late thirties, had seen action in the Gulf piloting an A/V-8B. He hadn't made it to Cuba until Sunday morning, and had spent nearly all of his time running down the early-model Harrier, which he had flown early in his career. He called it a death trap, and had the statistics to prove it.

He did everything but cite them now as he badmouthed the plane into the air.

"I have a station wagon that has better thrust than this sucker," he complained.

"Matador Four, if you would like to get out and walk," Hill told him over the radio, "be my guest. Otherwise, drop your American attitude and get to work."

Their inaugural target was a building about four hundred and fifty kilometers away, near the coast east of Santa Cruz del Sur. Hill had not bothered to tell them why they were attacking it; Garcia suspected he didn't know.

Each Harrier carried a five-hundred-pound bomb beneath each wing and a pair of four-tubed Zuni rocket launchers. Their game plan, such as it was, called for a plain-vanilla run at the building, two planes at a time from opposite directions diving at about forty-five degrees from fifteen angels, or 15,000 feet.

The rockets were to be held in reserve, though Hill hadn't said for what. Garcia had never actually fired the unguided five-inchers, which though potent had been considered outmoded by the time he joined the Corps.

The pilot's perch was considerably lower in the AV-8A than it was in later planes; the view was severely limited, and rather than looking out on top of the world you felt as if you were sitting in a tunnel. But Garcia found the challenge of the old plane invigorating, and he was especially glad to be flying without Gump on his back. He checked his fuel on the right panel and jostled himself in the seat, maintaining his position in the wedge formation Hill favored—essentially a variation on the time-honored flying wing. The wingman trailed the lead plane at about a forty-five-degree angle 9,000 feet to the rear. It was not a premier air-combat position, but then they weren't expecting any rebel interceptors. With his commander's plane as a reference and without the need to watch for enemy interceptions, Garcia's job was easier than if he'd been steering a commuter plane.

The group reached 18,000 feet, a precaution against the remote possibility of sophisticated antiair guns. Garcia, after double- and triple-checking his instrumentation to make sure he knew where everything was, tilted his wings to do some sightseeing. The island glittered green and gold in the early sun, a fertile jewel in the shimmering, unbroken Caribbean.

The scene was so peaceful, he was almost taken by surprise when Hill called for combat separation. Garcia righted himself and notched the throttle, closing the distance between himself and his leader as they prepared for the final approach.

Unlike the Pegasus, whose computer could actually drop the bombs for him, Garcia was essentially on his own once the bombing run began. He would fly the plane downward until the building appeared in the middle of the HUD's targeting pipper and then pickle off his bombs. While it wasn't anything more than generations of other pilots had done, the fact that he had only a hazy description of the building to go by added an interesting degree of difficulty to the task.

Garcia edged his fingers on the control stick, starting to get nervous again. Even with gloves, his fingers felt cold and slightly stiff.

"Begin," was all Hill said as he slid his plane away to start the attack. Garcia rolled his Harrier on its side, starting into a dive that would take him down into the target at the northwest. Hill would come in from the northeast about two seconds ahead of him; the effect would seem something like a crisscross from the ground. The other two planes would then repeat a similar maneuver a few seconds later.

Garcia's airspeed cranked up quickly, approaching and then running through five hundred knots. His attack angle was forty-five degrees; sharp, but not so sharp that he would have to wrestle the plane to hold its attention. At 10,000 feet, he saw the building, fat, tin, dumb, with no idea it was about to go boom. He narrowed his eyes and saw only the windshield in front of him, the gray and green shades blurring with the vibration of the plane, the ghostly white lines of the aircraft's targeting computer slowly pushing the cue toward its target. These were long seconds, for as it approached 8,000 feet the plane became infinitely vulnerable; any decent antiair gun could slice him in two.

Garcia came on patiently, holding the aircraft steady, telling himself this was no different from the practice runs he'd done in the A/V-32A simulator, no different even without Gump, without any sort of electronic countermeasures, sitting in a thirty-year-old collection of sheet metal that was starting to complain about the rapidly rising airspeed. He edged his thumb toward the black button on the stick as the air-to-ground reticle—the circle floating in the middle of his heads-up display—marched slowly toward the short, straight line where he had placed the building. When they touched, it would be time to drop the bombs. Gently, Garcia coaxed the circle into that line, touched it, jiggled it smack into the middle, then swallowed it whole.

In the same instant he pressed the button to release his two bombs, Garcia realized that his altitude, rather than being at the specified 8,000 feet, had fallen below 6,000. He yanked back on the stick and juiced the throttle, sending the Harrier screaming skyward.

Something happened then, something he couldn't quite comprehend. As his eyes danced around the complicated cockpit, he felt the jet rock beneath him. For a half-second he nearly lost everything. He had no point of reference, no place to return to; a dizzy emptiness hit him square in the chest and his head swam. Panic—dark, black panic—grabbed the back of his neck with stone fingers and clamped down, choking everything. His body floated, his spinal cord trembling with a succession of paralyzing spasms. He could move no portion of his body. He could not even think about where he was or who he was, let alone what to do.

The blue sky brought him back. The lovely, endless sky vaulting overhead caught him. She pulled him toward her like a mother wrapping her arms around a child who has just taken his first short steps. The sky swept him up just as he was about to despair, grabbed him before he could fall into the abyss.

The unexpected high-g effect of the bombing maneuver began to dissipate as Garcia gained altitude. Some unconscious part of him had hit the flares, sending them out in case a guerrilla had fired a Stinger or something similar at his tail.

He began breathing regularly again. He saw his instruments, saw the ladder marking 10,000 feet and climbing steadily now. In the distance he heard, or thought he heard, explosions, almost as if they were afterthoughts. He spotted Hill's plane and gave the commander his "tallyho" call, signifying that he had dropped the bombs and was away clean.

Tallyho. He'd said that, hadn't he? With a British accent? Like Robin Hood?

"Very good, Lieutenant," Hill told him. "Sit tight now."

"Acknowledged," Garcia said, turning the plane into an orbit that had not been briefed but was the logical thing to do. His throat felt absurdly dry; the words coughed out awkwardly. He marched his eyes around the instrumentation as deliberately as he could, studying each device, assuring himself that he was fully in control.

He took stock of himself, ashamed and frankly surprised that he'd been caught unprepared. Despite the precautions built into his flight suit, the sharp jerk of gravity as he had pulled up the plane had affected the flow of blood to his brain; even though he'd felt that pull a hundred times before, it had somehow managed to catch him off guard.

It wasn't his unfamiliarity with the plane; he'd pulled this same maneuver three times yesterday without vertigo or anything approaching it. And in fact the normal force at pullout—it might have been a bit higher since he had muffed the approach just a bit—was four g's, child's play to an attack-jet pilot.

What was different was the fact that for the first time in his life he'd tried to kill someone.

When he realized that, he realized something else—having made it through once, he would make it every time from now on.

The other pilots checked in; all the bombs had been dropped, and no one had been fired on. Hill told Garcia to follow him down for a visual recon run.

"Stay with me, now. We'll go as hot as we can. This is where it can be dicey."

They dipped their wings and dove in. Even before they came back toward the target, Garcia could see the heavy smoke; as they zipped past he thought he caught sight of flames as well. Hill declared their mission accomplished, and with their rockets still unfired, they saddled up to return home.

They were about halfway back when the radio jumped to life. Between the hurried Spanish, recognition codes, and static, Garcia lost most of the conversation between Hill and the ground controller, but the upshot was clear—they were being asked to support a ground action. A group of rebels had surprised a government supply convoy in the hills seventy kilometers to the north.

Garcia glanced at the fuel indicators. The Harriers had a loaded combat radius of just under five hundred kilometers. There was enough juice left in their jars to angle there and back home, but not enough for a messy food fight.

"Let's make this quick," Hill told his pilots. "Ferguson, you find this on your map board?"

"Got it, Commander."

"Follow me precisely," Hill told the flight. "No hotdogging. I don't want anyone ending up part of next year's sugar crop."

The Harriers banked northward. Garcia had only the haziest notion of where he was and where he was going; the plane's moving map was of little help. But his adrenaline was surging. Literally flying on the edge of his seat, he hunched himself around the control stick, willing the old jump jet forward.

Ferguson and Dalton had slightly more fuel, and Hill sent them ahead to make the first run, a column of smoke pointing the way like a homing beacon. The government truck convoy was sitting dead on the highway, taking fire from three sides. Their relief column, which included several American Bradley fighting vehicles given to the Cubans only two weeks before, was making its way up the roadway several miles to the west. If the Harriers could interrupt the rebels' attack merely by diverting their attention, the reinforcements would have a chance to save the convoy.

Under the best circumstances, a rocket run was a low and slow affair, with the pilots waiting for the last possible minute to launch the big Zunis before breaking off. Banking with Hill while they waited for the others to make their run, Garcia saw that the conditions were far from optimum. There didn't seem, at least from this altitude, to be any concentrated positions to fire at, and the rising hillside behind the rebels meant the pilots would have to stand on their pedals, goose their maneuvering jets, and maybe throw out an anchor to get up after the run.

But Garcia's heart was pumping so fast he would have flown the Harrier down a manhole to get at the enemy. As he tacked back to get into position, he saw the muzzle flash of a heavy gun about two-thirds of the way up the hillside, directly across from the lead vehicle in the wrecked supply convoy. He made a mental note, taking it as his target.

Jim DeFelice

"Make your run as quickly as possible," Hill ordered as he pitched forward. "Don't take any chances. Pop the rockets and get away."

Garcia shot into his attack and felt the acid begin to burn through his stomach. His knee had stopped aching long before; his hands weren't cold anymore. He pushed the Harrier's nose toward the highway, swinging his rear end around and aiming for the furrowing thick pillar of black smoke rising from the lead truck, a finger beckoning him to a party. Garcia felt his confidence growing as he came on, his airspeed nicking down to three hundred knots. He tucked his left wing and leaned on the seat, as if this would make the plane follow. He spotted his target dead ahead.

Then he saw the red and yellow sparkles, the pops in the air. He was being fired at. Real stuff coming in, black and gray tufts of burnt air appearing all around him. He bored through, on the edge of his seat, holding, holding, holding as the leading edge of the plane passed through the curtain of smoke from the wrecked truck. The gun he'd spotted was nearly at eye level, so close he could spit on it. Garcia jammed out the rockets, then pulled himself and the plane hard to the right, scrambling to get away.

He fumbled in the crowded cockpit, fighting the g's, reaching to fire off more diversionary flares. But he'd used them all on the bombing run.

There was no time to curse, and in any event the flares were unnecessary, as these rebels did not have ground-to-air missiles. The engine strained, and his knee began to feel limp with the pressure of working the pedals.

But his head stayed clear, and he was calm, completely in control. His airspeed jumped, and the plane seemed to levitate, his plane now, completely his.

Garcia looked back as he circled and saw men

142

running near the gun emplacement he'd just attacked. The ground nearby was burning.

Then he saw the muzzle flash again.

"Son of a bitch," he said, dipping his wing and screaming back toward the hillside in a straight drop. He flicked on his cannon and began firing the rounds way too soon. But even as he realized his mistake, he saw that it could help him; the gun drew an exploding line in the terrain more definitively than Gump could have done. He flew the line down the ridge, right into the emplacement, holding the control column with both hands as the attack jet began to complain loudly about the swirling wind currents near the ground and hillside. Garcia ignored it, ignored the bullets bursting around him, ignored everything—including Hill screaming in his ear. He danced his cannon right into the howitzer on the hill, saw the ground erupt with it, saw hell open up and take the damned bastards to their reward.

Or maybe not. He was past too quickly to see exactly what happened.

"Garcia, get your damn ass out of there," Hill yelled at him. "This is a direct bloody order. We've barely got enough fuel to get home. Get!"

Garcia didn't have to check the fuel indicator to know his commander was right. Continuing to climb, he swung his eyes toward his compass. He couldn't see the other Harriers, and had momentarily lost his direction. His heart was running in his ears, and he could feel his lungs gasping for breath.

Even so, he felt uncontrollable elation, a wild, orgasmic, and even disorienting high. His hands were tingling with it. If he'd flown into a brick wall at this moment, he would have died in ecstasy.

"I'm about ten o'clock," said Hill, sensing his wingmate's confusion. "Follow me. Tightly."

"Gotcha," said Garcia, seeing the plane at last.

Jim DeFelice

When he finally fell asleep early Sunday morning, Scotty crashed a mile wide and a continent deep. Except for brief trips to the bathroom, he stayed in bed for nearly forty-eight hours, drifting through various layers of unconsciousness. Distorted shadows hovered over his head, but for the most part his rest was mercifully free of distinct dreams. He rolled over and over, wrapping himself tighter and tighter in his sheets. Then, somewhere in the ocean of restless fatigue, his brain sensed danger and woke him with an electric bolt of fear.

His hand was already reaching for the Glock on his thigh when he recognized the face looming over his body as Ray Fashona's.

"How the hell did you get in here?"

"I told you your security was lax," deadpanned Fashona. The CIA assistant station chief waggled Scotty's key in front of his short beard, smiled, then turned and gestured to a man behind him. "This is Esma's brother. He wanted to talk to you about the funeral. I couldn't get you on the phone. I'll be downstairs if you need anything."

"You don't have to wait around."

"Oh yeah, I do. Ambassador wants to see you. He's spitting bullets."

"Fuck."

Fashona faded into the distance as Scotty blinked repeatedly to focus his eyes. A short, squat man with light skin stood in the corner of the room, head stooped, shoulders drooping. His nose was flattened at the corners like Esma's, but otherwise there seemed little resemblance. Clutching his legs together, Scotty sat upright on the bed. His hand was still near the Glock, though he trusted Fashona to have checked the man out extensively before bringing him up here.

144

"*¿Habla español?*" The words dribbled from the brother's mouth.

"*Sí,*" said Scotty. When it was obvious that the man would not begin speaking on his own, Scotty told him, in Spanish, what the doctors had said to him—Esma had died instantly. It was a lie he was eager to repeat.

The truth was harder. He wanted to say how much he had loved her, how beautiful she was, how even at this instant the room was full of her. The words wouldn't come. He watched the man nod, listened to the details of the funeral: a small church in a town ten miles away, 1 P.M. tomorrow. The family hoped he could make it.

"*Gracias,*" he told the brother.

The man seemed ready to say something. He took a step toward Scotty, reaching out his arm, but suddenly changed direction, veering from the room as tears welled in his eyes. It was only after he left that Scotty realized his own cheeks were wet.

East of Havana. 10:15 A.M.

Garcia was flushed with excitement when he landed at the far edge of the strip, even though there was barely enough fuel in his tanks to fill a coffee cup. The pilot popped the canopy, removed his helmet, and lifted himself out. Pausing half in and half out of the plane, he slapped his hands together and savored the light breeze that rippled across his flight suit. Forgetting his knee completely, he eased over the side and jumped down to the ground.

Whether it was the leftover adrenaline from the mission or the regenerative power of the Caribbean, his leg didn't hurt a bit. He flexed the muscles in his back, starting to stride toward the office inside that served as their operations room.

Hill intercepted him.

145

"What the bloody hell was that all about?" demanded the commander. "The cannon run, you fool—what the hell did you go back for?"

"There was a gun placement on the hillside. My rockets didn't take it out."

"The next time you fly, Lieutenant, you do exactly what I say."

"But—"

"There *are* no buts," said Hill. "The next time you do something so stupid, I'll shoot you down myself."

Hill stomped away without saying anything more. Garcia, not sure whether he should feel angry or chastened, followed inside to a debrief that barely deserved the name. Still obviously peed, Hill asked the other pilots if they had anything to report. His tone told them quite clearly that they didn't.

"Tomorrow at six-thirty A.M. Don't let there be any surprises until then."

"What'd you do to piss him off?" Dalton asked as he, Garcia, and Ferguson were being driven back to Havana.

"I took a swipe at a howitzer with my cannon."

"That's it?"

Garcia, sharing the backseat with Ferguson, shrugged.

"He told you just to make one pass, didn't he?" said Ferguson.

"Well, he said one pass with the rockets."

"One thing about the colonel—he's not much on military formalities, but if he says something, he wants you to do it precisely."

"I wanted to take out the gun."

"Anytime you take the plane close to the ground," said Ferguson, whose words were washed by a thin, Northern Irish brogue, "you're making it very easy for the rebels to hit you. We can afford only high-payoff attacks. We're all the Cubans have."

"There wasn't any antiair. The rifles they were firing weren't going to take me out."

"A commie with an SA-7 or 14 could break you in two at that altitude."

"I thought the rebels don't have any missiles," said Dalton pointedly.

"They haven't fired one at us yet," said Ferguson. "But I wouldn't stop letting off my flares. They're the only thing we have plenty of." He laughed bitterly, adding, "Garcia probably used the month's cannon allotment going after the hill."

"I was going after a rebel gun."

"The most important thing is keeping yourself alive," Ferguson said. "You'll understand what I mean after a few more missions. Right now it's still a jolly high. Reality sets in. The commander is a good man in a jam, I'll tell you that. I've seen it. Or else I would never be here."

As Garcia digested that, Dalton asked if the others had had engine problems.

"What do you mean, problems?" said Garcia.

"Mine coughed a couple of times while we were coming back. I thought for a second I was going to lose it. I told the crew chief about it when I landed, and he just shrugged."

"It's probably not his fault," said Ferguson. "That sounds like the fuel."

"The fuel?"

"You wouldn't expect it to be the purest, would you? We lost an engine because of it the first week. At least according to the mechanics."

"Are we going to get that fixed?"

"The tanks have been cleaned several times, and the men practically strip the planes after every flight. It's much better than it was," said Ferguson. "Just one more attraction to lovely Cuba."

Not even the unwelcome news about polluted fuel could dampen Garcia's mood. Despite the earwashing administered by Hill, he was feeling high about the mission and wanted to share a bit of it—the high, that is.

And he had a good idea how to do that.

"Here we go, lads," said Ferguson when they pulled up to the hotel. "Should we meet up for a drink?"

"Sounds good to me," said Dalton.

"I don't think I can make it," said Garcia.

"Don't tell us you have a date," said Ferguson.

"I might."

"This isn't one of the Malecón moths, is it?"

"A whore, you mean?"

"That would be the word," said the Irishman.

"No. No way."

"I'll lend you some rubbers," said Dalton.

"Thanks, but I won't need them."

"Going bareback, huh?"

"Come, now, Jason," Ferguson said to Dalton. "The lieutenant's a wholesome lad. He won't be doing any porking until the second date."

"You have to watch these quiet types," Dalton answered. "They're the ones who get into trouble."

"If you want any pointers, we'll be glad to help out."

"Thanks, but I think I can handle it myself."

"Oh, we're sure of that," said Dalton, who laughed even harder when it was obvious that Garcia didn't immediately catch the joke.

U.S. Embassy, Havana. 10:20 A.M.

Though irreverent and slightly eccentric, Scott McPherson was one of the best CIA field agents Malcolm Steele had ever known, one of the few who combined top-notch ability with an almost unstoppable will to accomplish a mission and a finely tuned sense of morality and ethics.

At least he had when he worked with him before Cuba. Steele had known when he asked him to come aboard as a freelancer on loan from the Agency that McPherson was going to be a bit of a project; he'd had a bad experience in Angola and had taken it exceptionally hard. Still, the agent was far from the biggest reclamation project he'd ever signed up.

But at first it seemed like a serious mistake. It hadn't been a nightmare, exactly; more like a constant trial, especially the first six months. He seemed to have settled down over the past year or so, but this . . .

"Threatening a Cuban government official? With a gun? Are you trying to get yourself killed, Scotty? Or just cause an international incident?"

"I'm trying to solve a crime."

"Who the hell told you to?"

"Excuse me, General, I thought that was my job."

"What, to police the entire island of Cuba? This is an internal Cuban affair, Scotty. Not American business."

"M-26 was involved, and as I understand my nebulous job description—"

"Nebulous job description? Don't give me that shit, McPherson. You want to go back to the CIA, just say the word, you're there."

McPherson rolled his arms together and tucked them against his chest. His big .45 bulged beneath his unbuttoned jacket. Steele knew the gesture well, knew the apology that was coming and could have recited it himself.

"Maybe I went overboard," the agent started.

"Maybe?"

"The thing is, Carla de Souza was in the club right before the explosion. She either did it, or she was the target."

"Why would she go there if she wanted to blow it up?"

"Exactly. And who would want to kill the head of M-26?"

Steele didn't give in. "That doesn't justify holding a gun to the head of a government official."

"Actually, it was the throat. And you know, technically, Virgilio isn't really Cuban."

"Don't give me bullshit, Scott. He works for the Cubans, and he is an official in their government." Steele scowled, then shook his head. "Did they do it or not?"

"I don't know. They're acting as if they have no clue. Maybe the report on the explosives will tell me something. I have a couple of other ideas to check."

"Scotty. I know what this is about. I'm sorry for you." Steele hesitated. He knew McPherson had lost his lover in the explosion and that his over-the-top episode was motivated by anger and probably revenge. But the former general wasn't the kind of man who could plod into the messy mud of personal relationships; he could barely talk to his son about the younger man's marriage, even though they were fairly close.

And McPherson didn't volunteer to make it easier. "This isn't personal," he said flatly.

"Either way, there's a line, Scott. Don't cross it. Even I don't have infinite patience."

"All right, General. Listen, I'm sorry. I went too far."

"Apology accepted," said Steele, talking to McPherson's back. He shook his head, then reached to his intercom. "James, get in here. Now."

Matanzas Province. 11:35 A.M.

Che Guevara, his face heavily veiled by obscene graffiti, leered from the billboard as Scotty turned off the highway. The Guevara billboard was reputed to be the only one left in Matanzas Province; a MIN-

INT official who had been with Scotty the first time he passed it claimed that the government left the graffiti-encrusted visage as a reminder to people of how bad things truly had been, a not-so-subtle rejoinder to criticism of the "temporary" regime. More likely, the local government was waiting until the market for kickbacks improved before executing a work order.

Scotty reached into his pocket for the directions to the district police station. When he unfolded the sheet in his lap, he discovered a small amphetamine pill; he started to lift it back into his pocket, then changed his mind and held it in his hand instead.

He'd already taken one of the pills this morning, justifying it as the only way he was going to make it through the day.

Scotty had had a problem with the pills in Angola after the fiasco. By the end he'd been badly addicted, taking four or five of the damn things every three hours.

But another pill wasn't going to hook him. He didn't have any others on him—the rest were back in his office at the embassy. His head suddenly felt cloudy, tired. He needed to think. He needed something that would help him figure out who killed Esma, something that would tell him whom he was going to kill.

Whatever it took to get there, he would make it. After that—it didn't matter anymore.

He swallowed the drug.

The Ave bomb had been placed in a truck parked in the basement garage. The device was powerful in its own right, but it had apparently been placed to ignite some propane canisters stored in an area directly above; the combination ignited a brief but intense fireball. While the nightclub had obviously been the target, nearly half of the hundred people killed had lived in the apartment building that rose over the club.

The truck was owned by a plumbing company, which in turn was associated with Juan Pérez, an M-26 council member who used "Eagle's Blood" as his nom de guerre. According to the MININT E-mail system, Pérez had been picked up early that morning by the police in Matanzas Province. Alerted by his friends in the CIA basement, Scotty grabbed an embassy car and set out to talk to *Señor* Pérez before MININT rendered him useless.

The way Scotty had M-26 diagrammed, Pérez was one of Carla de Souza's underlings. Assuming for the moment that MININT hadn't tried to take de Souza out—and despite what he had told the ambassador only an hour or so before, Scotty was still considering that at least a slight possibility, despite the number of innocent victims—Pérez's fingerprints on the attack made things interesting.

Was he acting on her orders, or trying to assassinate her and take over? It played either way, but Scotty saw de Souza as too powerful, and too Machiavellian, for any of her underlings. Bombing the Ave might fit into her recent zigs aiming at forcing a political solution to the conflict, with elections and the establishment of a legal political party fronting for M-26. The explosion—which had been covered not only in the local media but in the States—made the guerrillas seem considerably more powerful than anyone believed.

Under that scenario, Carla had planted the bomb to make herself look more powerful. Her presence at Ave would link her to it, as if she were thumbing her nose at the authorities.

The district police station was not only located exactly where his directions said they would be—a minor miracle—but the detective in charge of the shift was affable enough to put down his rum and

Coke when Scotty walked in, and even offer him a drink after he flashed his embassy ID.

"Later," Scotty said, explaining, in Spanish, that he had come because he was looking for a *Fidelista* known as Eagle's Blood. Unsure of how mentioning the central bureaucracy would play—some district police agencies resented it, others were tightly connected through family lines and friendships—he said neutrally that the interior ministry had suggested the district police would be helpful.

"That is a lie, I am sure," responded the detective, in English. "And because of that, I will do everything I can to assist. Would you like me to take you to him?"

"Yeah, shit yeah."

"All right." The detective turned on his heels, heading toward the back of the cluttered room. Scotty, surprised that the man was so cooperative, followed through the dusty room. The tight desks with their wire baskets wheezed under the load of unread bulletins and reports, a curious contrast to the neat bulletin boards lining the back, where suspects' photos and rap sheets were pinned in meticulous order. There didn't appear to be anyone else on duty, not remarkable in itself, but it made Scotty wonder how a notorious rebel could have managed to get himself apprehended in such a sleepy burg.

The detective pushed open the back door with a smile, ushering Scotty into the hallway. For just a second a touch of vertigo shook the agent's head, and a tinge of acid in his stomach warned him this was going so smoothly it must be a trap. The drugs had already made his heart accelerate, and now it pumped like the hammer on an old-fashioned alarm clock. He jammed his right hand into his shoulder holster for the .45, and had the gun unsheathed but still under his jacket as the detective pushed open a door at the end of the hallway. Scotty thumbed off

Jim DeFelice

the safety, sweat starting to pour out of his body. He slammed the door wide open with his left hand, keeping the big Colt tight to his side so it couldn't be pulled or knocked from him.

"*Señor,* I do not think you will need to use that on him," said the detective, turning toward Scotty, his hands open apologetically.

The man who had called himself Eagle's Blood lay stretched on a wooden table in the middle of the room, a large, gaping hole where his right eye had once been.

Sierra Maestra Mountains. Noon.

Luck was with them, luck born of patient preparation. Carla had not neglected to cultivate contacts among all of the island's disparate rebel groups, and while Romano's had proven by far the most difficult to infiltrate—his followers tended to be as fanatical and loony as he was—there was still a man whom she could count on for information, if little else. From this man several months ago she had learned of a certain barber Romano visited in the small village several miles from his mountain stronghold. Like everything else Romano did, the habit stemmed from superstition—the man was alleged to be the grandson of a barber who cut Fidel Castro's hair during the fifties revolution.

Carla doubted the authenticity of the story, but not its power on Romano. And as this was the morning of his monthly pilgrimage to the shop, she established her ambush accordingly.

It was a delicate thing to arrange. She could not send more than one or two of her men into the village itself; strangers were easily spotted. And as small as the place was, there were two ways out of town back toward the mountains.

"Zora, you are slipping," she told her adviser when

the old woman recommended they join the squads on the northern route. "Our friend would take the most direct road. It is what my father would do."

Zora nodded in the manner she always did when she thought Carla was wrong but not worth correcting. Nonetheless, within a half hour of Carla's receiving word that Romano had left the barber, the lead vehicle of his bodyguard entourage sped up the highway. They let it pass, a calculated risk—there was always the possibility that Romano was in it.

Ten minutes later, the main body of his caravan— a motley collection of trucks and two old Mercedes sedans—began rounding the climbing curve where three hundred of Carla's men lay in wait. The opening shot was the most devastating—a rocket blew up the lead truck, incinerating in one massive shriek all twelve of the soldiers piled into the back.

Romano's weapons were very old, but his fighters were as committed as any to the Movement. They thought at first that they were fighting government troops, and they responded with great vehemence, their ancient Kalashnikovs and Tokarev pistols spitting furiously.

Carla, her flak jacket open and her machine pistol clutched in her hands, waited for her mortars to finish firing their ten rounds apiece before leaping from her position to lead a second wave of her men into the assault. She had perfected this technique in numerous ambushes of government troops and police stations. Her fierce, heedless dash rallied not only the men who followed behind her as planned, but anyone in the first group who had started to flag.

There was more to her charge this afternoon than mere adrenaline, more than just purpose. She felt a certain lust, an emotion of extreme hate. She fought against it—she knew that to win in the long run she must be beyond hate—but she felt her lungs and legs give in to it as she plunged toward the firefight.

The stock of the Heckler & Koch MP-5N nudged against her rib cage as she pulled the trigger. The gun's nine-millimeter bullets embroidered a death line across the top of the first sedan. Still running forward, she released the submachine gun's spent clip, jamming another into the magazine in one smooth motion. They were winning, they had won—she stopped and yelled at Romano's men to surrender, to give up, they were all comrades.

But the firing continued. She ran back up the road, where one of her men had fallen. She leaned down and, instead of comforting him, took a grenade from his jacket. She cocked the pin and threw it at a clump of trees beyond the vehicles, where Romano's men had tried to set up a defensive position.

Even as she did, she wrestled with herself. I am out of control, she thought. My men are out of control. We must have discipline. We have beaten them; they are surrounded. I must offer them a chance to join me for the greater good.

The grenade exploded, but it did not end the shooting.

"Stop!" she shouted to her troops. "Hold your fire."

As the gunfire began to die down, Carla signaled to one of her lieutenants to check the vehicles for signs of Romano.

"I am Carla de Souza, your leader. I have no quarrel with you men, only with Hector Romano Moncada, who has become a traitor to our Movement by putting his ambition above the people's justice. Those of you who join me will be treated like the comrades you are."

She took a step toward the side of the road, the Hecklar & Koch pointed downward in her right hand. It was a dangerous moment, her flak vest open and of questionable value. Any of Romano's men, Romano himself, could kill her.

But she had to deal with them this way. She set an example, the leader. She projected the aura, the essence of control and invincibility. Of all of Zora's lessons, this had been the most critical. It was the thing she shared completely with her father.

She took two steps forward, could see several of Romano's guerrillas watching her. Her lieutenant shouted from the back of the second sedan. Before responding, she tried to look at each man she saw across in the woods individually, fixing them with her eyes and her will. Then, calmly but hopefully, she turned her head just enough to see her lieutenant.

He held out his hands. Assuming he had been a passenger, Romano had escaped from the car alive.

Slowly, she turned her head back to the guerrillas in the woods. "Come out, Romano," she said mildly, as if speaking to a frightened child. "Where are you?"

She was just starting to curse herself for losing him when a bearded figure rose from a clump of bushes.

"So, ballerina, you are not dead," he called.

"Your assassins missed. Have your men drop their weapons and they will not be harmed."

"Will you kill me then?"

There was something so strangely innocent about the question, the words and their tone, that instinctively she answered, "No."

He threw down his gun and climbed up to the roadway. His men stayed behind him, but they, too, were dropping their weapons.

"You are weak," he said when he reached her. "You have lost the Revolution."

Carla looked at him. She felt for a moment that she was confronting a ghost of her father.

"You're wrong," she said. The words were a bare whisper. She felt suddenly emptied of everything, the adrenaline, the energy, and ferocity that had driven her. Even the renegade emotion of revenge was gone.

Romano grinned and started to his left, back in the direction his caravan had come from.

"Where are you going, Romano?" she said, lifting her gun.

He stopped and turned toward her. "You will not shoot me, ballerina. This thing I know."

Had he turned swiftly, had he laughed, had he done anything characteristic of his overwhelming and insane ego, she would have had no difficulty emptying the submachine gun into his body. She would not have cared whether she struck him in the back or the front or the side. The fact that she had told him she would not did not sway her. She would have shot him for vengeance, for anger, for retribution; she would have killed him because he was a threat to her, to any possibility of the Movement's achieving an end beyond merely destroying the country she loved.

But he only stared at her. He did not urge his men to fight on or even join him; it was evident he was utterly alone. His large, deep eyes reflected her sorrow, not his overweening pride. Slowly, ever so slowly, he turned and resumed walking away, back toward the town, a solitary figure, a ghost that had come this way triumphantly decades before and was now banished to the past.

"Let him go," Carla said to her men. "See to our brothers and comrades."

She watched him vanish into the distance, then raised her arm as Zora approached, brooking no comment.

* * *

By the time Carla had her column reorganized and on the road to Romano's headquarters, her units had already secured it. The commander of the small force that had stormed the former school building was a man named Peter Fuentes, an American émigré whom she had made a lieutenant only two months before. His high-pitched voice over the scrambled radio reminded her of a jack-in-the-box.

Everything seemed surreal, much like the day her father had died. Carla's mind drifted back there briefly, returning to the doubts she had had. She had not even been political until he called her to him a few months before his death. He had imbued her with the spirit of his revolution and justice, made her see how she must fight to keep it alive. He had acknowledged the excesses, told her to go beyond them; he had faith in her.

The skeleton of M-26 was formed by her father and some associates before his death. She inherited it, but not easily; there was much resistance to a woman, even though she was *El Jefe*'s daughter. Slowly she found her way, and then fought to get beyond the outlined path her father had left her, to the true essence of his bequest.

She had realized the limits of the guerrilla campaign even as it succeeded. With Romano's defeat, she was in absolute control; it would be clear that objections to her authority would not be tolerated and would be, frankly, pointless. The attack on her at the Ave would have a twofold effect—any guerrilla who knew who had launched it would see how futile it was to oppose her, how charmed her life was. And the rest would think, as the government now seemed to, that she could and would bomb and destroy anything she wished.

But that was not the way to win in the end; destruction would not preserve the Revolution and the dream of everlasting justice. She could never per-

159

suade the people of Cuba to join her against the American oppressors, largely because they did not view them as oppressors. They viewed them mostly as benign, in some cases as friends and supporters, in others as bumbling but not dangerous interlopers. And while the interim government was corrupt and lazy, the vast majority of people would not take up arms against it, especially if elections appeared likely.

If those elections were held without her, she would lose. She had to act quickly, bluffing the government and the Americans into accepting a provision in the constitution that legitimized her Social Democratic Justice Party. The minute hand of the clock had now swung around to a time when it was finally possible.

She sat silently in the back of her minivan, watching the jungle blur into a stream of green, brown, and black. Zora breathed heavily beside her, the old woman's breath a kind of chant designed, no doubt, to keep evil spirits away.

"Be careful," Carla told the driver when his abrupt steering jostled her from her reverie. "I do not intend to inspect his medical facilities from the patient's point of view."

The young man—he was actually her own age, though by now she thought of herself as approaching sixty rather than her late twenties—apologized profusely. She leaned forward and put her hand on his shoulder, telling him not to worry. Sitting back, she suddenly felt uncomfortable. When inspecting her submachine gun failed to vanquish the feeling, she turned to Zora.

"Tell me what you are thinking," she said to the old woman.

"I am not thinking."

"Then what are you doing?"

"I am looking at the jungle."

"Nonsense. Your eyes were staring straight ahead."

"I can see the jungle through the windshield."

"You think I should have killed Romano."

"I cannot say."

"That is what you think, though. You feel it will be interpreted as a weakness."

"Do not assign me your own thoughts."

The van stopped suddenly and one of Carla's camouflage-clad troopers came running up from ahead. She jumped out of the van, gun ready.

"Commander, we are in complete control," said the soldier.

"Very good," she said, snapping off a salute. "Where is Fuentes?"

"Completing the search of the facility. The road ahead was mined. Your driver must backtrack and come around from the other direction, but if you wish you can walk with me this way."

Leaving Zora and the car, they proceeded down a steep, narrow pass to a brick school building, incongruously large given its location in the desolate mountains. Built in the seventies, the school had been among the buildings the defense ministry had prepared for "special contingencies"; it had in fact never housed schoolchildren. Carla felt a vague satisfaction as she walked through it, remembering her father's achievements in education. She told herself she must fight this nostalgia; the most difficult battle was still ahead.

Fuentes met her at the head of the stairs to the first basement. "There is quite a bunker here," he said. "Wait until you see the extent of it."

"Good work, Commander. 1 need to establish a communications center quickly."

"Gotcha," he answered. He was forever mixing English slang into his Spanish, managing to sound a bit goofy at both. "Romano's office was down here," Fuentes added, pointing the way. "Wait until you see it. What a crazoid."

Carla followed silently down the steel steps to basement level two, then walked swiftly along the smooth concrete to a small, cell-like room guarded now by two of Fuentes's men.

Fuentes swung open the door from the hall.

"Wild, huh?"

Carla took a step into the room, its air permeated by incense. Huge posters of her father covered the wall. A ten-by-twelve photo of John F. Kennedy hung by itself on the wall to her left; the photo had been slashed and covered with dried blood. The center of the room was dominated by a marble table that was more altar than desk; the charred scraps of another photo sat in the middle of it. Next to the photo was a dead falcon, its neck wrung. Part of the belly had been plucked, and the raw flesh bitten.

Carla by now was well-versed in the trappings of Santeria rituals, and hardly surprised that Romano would have practiced them. But one of the holy cards used as tokens in the practice caught her eye on the small dresser in the corner.

It was a Virgin Mary of Padua, neither a common prayer card nor a familiar token in the arcane rites that combined a mystic Catholicism with older, more primitive beliefs, matching the Catholic saints to Yoruba deities.

It was, however, a card that Zora used in her practices.

Shielding Fuentes's view with her body, Carla swept her fingers across the table, scooping the card up.

"Commander, Commander," called one of the men from down the hallway. "Quickly! quickly! We have made a great discovery!"

She shoved the card into her pocket and went to

join the others, pretending for the present that she had not noticed this devastating sign.

Havana. 5 P.M.

Garcia hadn't been this nervous since he asked Lisa Leterri to go to the senior prom. He shaved twice; through some miracle he managed to avoid cutting himself. Thankfully, he had a bare minimum of civilian clothes with him, or he would have changed more than the three times he did, growing more and more despondent each time he examined himself in the suite's full-length mirror. He fixed his short hair, muffed it to appear more casual, fixed it again. He wore his watch out with his eyes, and put a serious dent in the carpet as well, trying to work off his nervous energy. But he managed to wait until exactly 5 P.M. before going down to the lobby, where they had agreed to meet.

When he didn't see Maria in the lobby, he went outside to wait. He was no sooner out the door than a shiny black Jeep pulled up in front of the hotel, its horn blaring.

"Hey there," said Garcia, climbing in. "Perfect timing."

Her blue cotton skirt was rolled up over her knees, and Garcia had a difficult time trying not to stare as she pulled into traffic.

"Nice car," he told her. "Where are we going?"

"I am going to show you the real Cuba, as I promised," she said.

"We're leaving the city?"

"What time do you have to be back?"

"No time, exactly, but I have to be up early in the morning. And, uh—"

"Oh, don't worry. I'll return you in one piece."

Maria had a grandmother who lived about thirty miles south of Havana, in a house that had been in the family for at least a century. Before Castro, the home had been part of a large farm, but Maria skipped lightly over that, telling him instead how quiet it still was. "They roll cigars in a small factory nearby," she said as they drove. "My grandfather, when he was alive, went there every day and bought two cigars. Sometimes I would go with him, walking along the road. I still remember the way he held my hand, and the smells. He was so proud, picking me up to sit on the bench while he chatted with the women who rolled the leaves."

Garcia listened intently to her stories, feeling as if he had entered a dream. The fat Caribbean sun nudged his shoulder, telling him how lucky he was to be here. His nervousness evaporated beneath its weight.

The large brass bracelets on her arm clanked when Maria turned the car off the highway, passing a small strip mall of two or three stores. If it weren't for the bicycles parked neatly by the door and the signs in Spanish, it would have looked precisely like any roadside plaza in an American town.

"See these houses?" Maria pointed across his body, perfume rising from the thin cotton of her shirt. "Three years ago, there was nothing here. A long time ago it was a farm for cattle—there were not many like that in Cuba. But then, Fi-del." The name of the dictator unfolded in two long syllables from her mouth like a curse. She jerked her hand back abruptly to the wheel. "They made everything sugar. Of course, this is not good land for sugar, but who could tell them that? My grandfather complained bitterly—but only to himself."

She smiled at the memory of the old man.

"It's good land for houses," she added. "At least people have a place to live now."

The homes were smallish prefab structures that were manufactured in an American plant and shipped over by boat, part of an assistance plan aimed at relieving the island's chronic housing shortage. To Garcia's eyes, they seemed small and cramped, but for Cubans consigned for years to tiny apartments or crowding in with relatives, they were palaces.

Despite or perhaps because of the nearby construction, the road became bumpier and bumpier as they drove. Maria continued onto a dirt lane that took a winding path up the side of a hill. Though the road was narrow, she drove as fast here as she had on the highway, revving the Jeep through its gears as competently as a fighter jock might put an airplane through its paces. At the top of the hill stood a large, two-story farmhouse painted yellow with green trim. Very old, it was made of wood, and had an enormous porch with thick pillars and broad, gray floorboards.

"This is my grandmother's house," said Maria. "Come on."

Garcia followed her out of the Jeep, through a carefully cultivated garden of perfumed roses and jasmine that draped over the fence posts and onto the house. Small yellow birds about the size of finches—Maria called them *tomguínes*—whistled as they watched him walk up the steps to the house. Maria practically ran as she pulled open the wooden screen door and entered the large front hall, skipping lightly over the floor as she went inside.

"*Nana, Nana. ¿Donde está mi bella Nana?*" Maria sang. "Where is my beautiful grandmother, the light of my life?"

"*Aquí! Aquí!*" came a voice from the back of the house. "And my grandmother still has sugar on her tongue."

They met near the back of the entry hall, Maria folding her arms around a short, smiling woman in a black dress.

"What is this with your hair?" Maria said, pointing at the long gray locks that hung to her waist.

"I washed it. You're just in time to braid it for me."

"First you must meet my friend," Maria said, curling her arm around the old woman's and leading her toward Garcia. *"Eduardo Garcia."*

"¡Qué gusto!" said the woman, taking his hand. She offered her cheek; Garcia, not knowing what else to do, kissed it.

"You are so bad," Maria scolded her. "He hasn't even kissed me yet."

"A shame," said her grandmother.

The two women spoke together excitedly, their words a rapid-fire song. A canary inside began tweeting, and Garcia felt as if he had been transported into a magical kingdom filled with flowers and happiness—to say nothing of beautiful women.

"My grandmother insists that we have something to eat," Maria said. "She was making chicken and beans for supper—you will stay, no? And then we will go into town for a stroll."

They ate at a peeling white table in the middle of the ancient porch. Garcia felt like a patron in an exclusive restaurant, fussed over by the two women. Maria pointed with her hand as she told stories of her grandparents. Her mother had died when she was young, and she'd spent much of her youth here. She spoke in Spanish, because the old woman did not speak English; Garcia had trouble with a few words but would not admit it for all the money in the world.

Maria brought him a cold beer to drink as she braided her grandmother's hair. The old woman beamed at him, but was somewhat reserved now; she did not ask about his parents, nor what had brought him to Cuba.

The village Maria took him to was nothing special; a small town like thousands of others, she said.

The buildings were mostly made of cement and covered with stucco, one and two stories tall; a few of the more important structures had been built with bricks, and one or two very ancient ones were made of wood. All were bright and freshly painted. A battery of clay pots sat in front of nearly every one, with garlands of flowers and plants adding a festive air to the street.

Everyone they happened to pass seemed to know Maria and stopped to greet them. As soon as they realized that Garcia was American, they switched from their rapid-fire, "r"-rolling Spanish to English despite his protests. They were without exception complimentary of the United States, and in general told stories about relatives or friends they hoped would one day return. The chamber of commerce could not have arranged a better plan to woo a visitor.

After an hour or so of walking, Maria led him to a small café opposite a newly built church, where they sat under an awning and shared an American wine cooler.

"My family, before Castro, was an important family here," said Maria. She frowned as if she had eaten something disagreeable. "Not exploiters, though. My grandfather worked alongside the others in the fields and was known throughout the town as a just man; he had a great reputation. This is one reason the house remained his. He was also a rebel sympathizer, though I think he played both ends, no? Against themselves?"

"Was it bad under Castro?"

"¡*Dios!*" She waved her hand briskly, as if she had just stuck it in a pot of boiling water. "At the end, no one could eat. There was nothing. There were no jobs, no hope. But it is over."

"Some people want to return to communism."

"Never. Cubans are not so stupid that they would

have something like that again. At first, maybe, Castro did one or two good things. Batista was a joker. That is how Fidel came in and fooled so many. But to return to that—never."

"What about the rebels now?"

"What do you know about the rebels?" she asked sharply.

"Nothing."

"You should not concern yourself with Cuban politics. Let us talk about something else."

Garcia wondered what her reaction might be if he told her how he had spent the morning. "What else do you want to talk about?"

"How long will you be in Cuba?"

He shrugged. "Maybe a long time."

"And what will you do here?"

"I'll find something to keep me busy."

"I know what you're thinking."

There was something soft in her eyes as she spoke. Garcia leaned across and kissed her. Her lips gave way gently, the sweet coolness of her drink melting into the warm smoothness of her mouth and tongue. She reached her arms around him and they embraced.

Suddenly she pulled back. "Eddie—a gun?"

Garcia, unsure for a moment what she was talking about, looked at his waistband before realizing he had the Vzor and its pouchlike holster there. He had gotten so used to carrying the palm-size weapon over the past few days that he had nearly forgotten it.

"It's just a pistol," he said apologetically.

"Why do you carry it? Are you thinking I am going to rob you?"

"No. Not at all. It's just—I've heard Cuba is a dangerous place."

"Ridiculous. Would you carry a gun back home?"

"I've seen, I've been told, anyway, that Americans are in danger."

"That is nonsense. The *Fidelistas*—is that whom you are afraid of?"

All he could do was shrug.

"The rebels are nothing. They have weapons, and here and there are people who support them, but mostly out of fear. Real Cubans detest and despise them. We hate the bastard Fidel and what he stood for."

Her anger welling up, she rose from the table. He put his hand out and caught her arm.

"Hey, I didn't mean to offend you."

They looked into each other's face, each unsure of what lay behind the surface. Finally she slipped back into the chair, still staring at him.

There was nothing else to do but kiss her. Warm and deep, it stole all other memories from him; it was as if she were the first woman he had ever been with.

Soon she was talking again, and as they laughed together Garcia ordered a second round of the wine coolers. When the sun nudged against the horizon, they left some money for the bill and got up. She surprised him with a long kiss that tasted of the wine, the sweetness rushing to his brain.

"You're younger than me, you know," she whispered when their lips parted.

"How do you know?"

"I'm very observant."

"How old are you?"

"You should never ask a woman that question," she said, swirling up from her chair. "Come on, now—it is time for you to be back in Havana."

"Maybe I can be a little late."

"Do not believe everything you have heard about Cuban girls," she warned him, taking the car keys from her pocketbook.

* * *

Jim DeFelice

La Carretera Central (The Highway to Havana). 11 P.M.

Scotty shared a few drinks with the detective,
largely, he told himself, because it was necessary to
get the man to talk to him. But the officer added
little of any importance, even after taking Scotty to
see another body with de Souza's characteristic
death insignia found in an abandoned farmhouse
farther east. The corpse's well-tailored, if now thor-
oughly disheveled, suit made it seem obvious he had
come from Havana; beyond that, he had not been
identified. Scotty had no doubt that he, too, would
be found to have M-26 ties and somehow be connected to the bombing.

MININT had laid claim to the bodies and an official from Havana told the district officer its men
would arrive "within the week" to take charge of the
investigation. That passed as high priority for the
ministry. It was fine with the detective, who in any
case would have expended far more effort over his
rum and Cokes than the crimes. As far as he was
concerned, more rebels should kill each other and
save the government the expense.

Having drunk enough to dull the first pangs of
amphetamine withdrawal, Scotty headed back to
Havana. Waves of emotion, followed by drug-
induced shakes, racked his body; he wanted revenge, he wanted another hit of speed, he wanted to
somehow fight his way to the other side of the despair over Esma's death. For a while, he thought he
would drive straight to the ocean and plunge in.

Scotty tried to divert himself by listening to the
Ford's radio. Music gushed from the speakers, an
old mambo exploding in a nostalgic mood so heavy-
handed even a gringo could close his eyes and pretend it was the late forties again, Cuba in its prime.
Waxing nostalgic was about the last thing he wanted

to do, and Scotty flung his fingers out at the buttons, searching for another station. A talk program filtered in. One of the government's mild critics was saying that Cuba had suffered so much but was coming back; it would come back, if these damn rebel bastards would just stop their attacks and the interim government would get out of the way. It was all the Americans' fault for not putting it straight.

Scotty gave up and turned the radio off. He rolled down the car window. There was a slight chill in the breeze, enough to scratch his eyes, prop them open at least. He pushed the car back toward the city as fast as it would go, struggling to keep his head clear of even the most innocuous thought. Without realizing it, he decided that he was not going to go home tonight, that he would go straight to his office in the basement of the embassy, load up on speed, and work until he dropped.

He was going to catch de Souza somehow. He had formed a theory to explain the execution of the two men: She had killed her accomplices to disguise the fact that she had planted the bomb. She was setting herself up as a good guy, someone who fought for justice. There would soon be a communiqué announcing that she had discovered who set the Ave bomb, and had delivered their death sentences.

But what if she had killed not patsies, but the men truly responsible? What if she had been the target?

Then he wouldn't even have revenge to cling to.

He didn't want to think of that. Scotty drove on into the city, wheeled past the security posts, parked the car, jogged to his office downstairs. The oppressiveness of the bare gray concrete walls and the dull-red industrial carpet helped him focus now, surrounding him like a cocoon. He was a solitary miner, descending into the earth to pound his section of stone.

He slid into his chair, pulled open the bottom

drawer, and took out a prescription bottle filled with amphetamine pills. His hand shook as he opened the cap; the tablets spilled all over the blue paper of a report that topped the mess of intercepts and other documents on his desk.

The paper was an FBI forensics report detailing how the Ave had been blown up. Scotty began to sort the pills on top of it, counting them so he could ration himself. Some letters on the report below caught his eye. He stopped, pushed the pills aside, and began reading, feeling finally the depth of the hole he had fallen into.

He realized more than Esma's death had taken him there.

The plumbing truck had been packed with Russian-made high explosive. The explosive was very old, pre–C-4, and had not been used before by M-26 in Havana. Indeed, the setup for the attack—the target, the method, the device itself had no precedence in the long campaign against the government in Havana and the bordering regions, as the report's author painstakingly pointed out.

This argued against MININT, of course, which would have wanted to make the attack look like a guerrilla bombing in case something went wrong. But it also discounted de Souza.

It could be explained, Scotty had felt, by the fact that she wanted to make it seem as if she wasn't the perpetrator. But as he reread the technical findings of the report, his doubt grew.

The detonators had been fashioned from ancient Soviet grenades, antipersonnel devices that dated from the fifties. Though highly unusual, there was little doubt, because the forensics lab had identified the wax that was mixed with the grenade's high-explosive charge.

The technique and the ingredients themselves

172

seemed extremely peculiar, but Scotty had seen it done before.

It was a coincidence, he told himself as he sat upright in the chair, stiff but shocked now into full wakefulness. Just some fit of chance.

If so, it was the kind of coincidence God makes, his long finger poking you from behind to tell you there is no escaping the sins of your past.

Scotty pulled the phone toward him and called the FBI's joint task force center, located several miles outside of Havana, where the report's author worked.

"He won't be on duty for hours," the desk agent told him.

"Give me his home phone number."

"He ain't going to like you waking him up. He's not a morning person."

"Fuck him and give me the phone number."

The explosives expert answered the phone on the seventh or or eighth ring.

"Are you sure it was CK-2?"

"What?"

"The wax in the detonator that blew up Ave. Was it CK-2?"

"Who the hell is this?"

"This is Scott McPherson at the embassy. Have you ever heard of the Fidelistas using old Russian grenades to make bombs?"

"That's not my job."

"You're sure it was CK-2?"

"Hey, listen, if you want to do the analysis yourself—"

Scotty hung up the phone. He looked down at the pills, still untouched, then back up at the blank white walls, shaded a dim yellow by the single incandescent lamp on his desk. Newspapers, pamphlets, fliers sat in disordered piles around the room, the only furnishings besides the desk and chair. Scotty rarely used the office, except to think, or hide.

He couldn't do either now. He picked up the phone again and dialed information in the States.

The number was familiar. It echoed in his head as the telephone company's computer repeated it. Under different circumstances he had punched the number many times before, only to hang up before it rang.

This time he stayed on the line.

A man answered. He hadn't expected that.

"I need to talk to Isha," Scotty said, fearing he had gotten the wrong number. The man asked for his name.

"Scott McPherson."

There was a grunt of recognition, though Scotty had no idea whom he was speaking to. Then came a pause, followed by a rustling of bedcovers or blankets. Then Isha's voice.

"Scotty?"

"Isha. Are you okay?"

"Am I okay? Scotty, why are you calling so late?"

"I need to ask you about something—I need information about the grenade that used CK-2 wax."

"I'm not part of the program anymore, Scott."

He didn't speak. He knew she would, eventually.

When she did, her voice was more awake, but infinitely more wounded, sadder, without defense.

"The wax was mixed with high explosive to make the grenade. It's distinctive because all of the wax came from a specific place in a two-year period when the grenade was made. I assume that you're calling because the grenade was used in a bomb."

"As the detonator."

"How old was the main explosive?"

"Old. Hard to tell. It was definitely Russian, though."

"I would guess both were stockpiled in the late

fifties or early sixties. The precise method was included in a Russian manual at the time. Why do you
need me to tell you this, Scotty? You know it all
yourself."

"Can you get the grenades on the black market?"

"Why would you?"

"Could you?"

"Highly unlikely. If you had them lying around,
maybe. That's the only reason you'd use them. If you
were going to buy something, you'd—"

"Were any shipped to Cuba in the sixties?"

"Cuba? Is that where you are now?"

He said nothing, though out of duty, not choice.

She sighed. "Of course. It may have found its way
into the army, or the training camps the Russians
helped fund. For exporting the Revolution. Long
gone by now."

He could almost see her shrugging, biting at her
lip the way she always used to when she realized the
statement she'd uttered wasn't entirely definitive.

"Who would be a likely suspect?"

"Someone old, been around. An instructor or a
student from one of those camps. Be in his fifties or
sixties by now, at least. Older, maybe. Or someone
with access to the stores. Or who wanted it to look
like that. There's much better stuff around these
days, Scott. Fiddling with that particular grenade
wasn't difficult, but it can still be dangerous."

"I'm sorry about Darren." The words finally burst
from his mouth, steam finding a weak spot in a
worn pipe. "I'm truly sorry. I never told you."

"You don't—"

"I sent him there. I shouldn't have. It was my mistake, a mistake I shouldn't have made."

"It's gone now, Scott." Her voice broke. She put
the phone against something, maybe a pillow. He
waited for her to speak again. When she did, it was
not as forced as he thought it might sound. "The job

175

here is a breeze. I teach suburban kids how to be angry about their past."

He tried to copy her enthusiasm, though he knew it would sound false. "You're good at it, I bet."

"A lot of the white kids hate me their first day of class. I win them over, though. They end up blacker than me. It's fun. The dean despises me, but he can't touch me. It's delicious." She laughed, then added, "Thank you, Scotty."

"I didn't have that much to do with you getting the job."

"No, I meant for calling. You know something? I think I'm pregnant. I have an appointment with my gynecologist tomorrow. You're the first person I've told, besides my husband, Dante. Did you know I got married?"

"He's a lucky guy."

Scotty wished her well, and she wished him well, and then he said he had to go and hung up. Standing over the desk, he carefully put all of the pills back into the bottle. Then he walked to the men's room in the dimly lit corridor of the embassy basement. For a second he hesitated, took a leak first, then steeled himself and flushed the whole thing, bottle and all.

Scotty washed his face in the sink and left it wet. Somehow he managed to avoid his reflection and went back out into the hall, turning up the corridor to the passage that led to the CIA station at the far end of the basement complex. It was an immense underground office, guarded not by marines but the agency's own men. They nodded at him and punched the access code to let him through the glass-and-steel mesh door that led to one of the largest agency installations outside of the U.S.

He passed into one of the monitoring rooms, where the station received satellite imagery from

NSA headquarters in the States. While a number of Cubans believed that the Americans had live surveillance of nearly every square foot of the island, the reality was far different. Three months before, one of the new stereoscopic KH-15 birds that worked a vast swatch of the earth's midsection had become disabled; its replacement had a limited view of the island. Even before that, for security as well as practical reasons, there were no real-time feeds, and the optical and laser imagery available was comparatively limited. Between the jungle, vagaries of cloud cover and weather, and, more important, the type of war the guerrillas were fighting, the imagery wasn't nearly the omnipotent weapon rumor made it out to be.

Scotty walked through to the communications area, stopping briefly to check for recent cable activity before going over to the records room and the two Sun workstations that were connected by double-key-encrypted, high-speed links to the CIA's extensive archives. The duty officer was a lanky red-haired woman with the improbable name of Sylvia. She was thirtyish, not particularly good-looking or outgoing, with eyes that were tiny dots within the reddened circles Scotty associated with a lifetime of peering at minuscule lines of print in dimly lit basements. He launched into his request as he entered the room, not waiting for her to look up from her desk.

"What I want to do is correlate everyone in MININT with ties to the early days of the Revolution, especially anyone who would know anything at all about explosives."

"You shouldn't be able to find any correlation," she told him, still staring at the stack of printouts on her desk. A wisp of her long hair drifted across her face, linking the freckles like a jagged scar. "That's been searched like a million times. It's been

Jim DeFelice

cross-checked against the military, against—"

"Yeah, but I want to check it again," said Scotty. He pulled over one of the wheeled chairs and sat, stretching his legs. "What I think is, somebody in MININT was indirectly connected to one of Fidel's guerrilla camps."

"Why MININT?"

Sylvia seemed almost shocked when, instead of telling her with curse-laden sarcasm to mind her business and get to work, Scotty slowly explained that he was now convinced that Carla de Souza had been the target of the Ave bombing, not its perpetrator. And while she had killed two of her own people in the past few days, the people who most wanted her dead were in the government, not the Movement. It seemed likely to him that someone in MININT had a link to a Castro-era weapons cache, and the place to start looking was in the records.

"It may not be MININT at all," Scotty admitted. "But I have to start somewhere. If there's a right-wing hit squad operating, it may not have any connection at all to the government."

"I thought there was no right-wing movement on the island," said Sylvia.

Scotty shrugged. She was actually echoing his own assessment, prepared in an official report not three months before.

"We can do an historical check if you want," she said when she finished. Pushing her chair back to the Sun workstation, her fingers began keying commands. "But you know it's going to be useless."

"What won't be?"

"I'm supposed to finish cross-checking the embassy phone logs tonight to make sure no one's making personal calls," she said. "The deputy chief of mission is on a rampage—"

"You really don't think that's more important than this, do you?"

She sighed, then began working her way through the Cuban archives, performing various searches. There were absolutely no hits with MININT; she began expanding out into lists of government officials, present and former military members. It was slow, dull work, even if the computer did most of the slugging. She hunkered over the keyboard, punching the letters and numbers, her head bobbing back only occasionally. Scotty watched the deep bags of her cheeks as her expression went from a frown to a deeper frown. She buried herself here, in this bunker, for hours and hours and hours; it was an act of denial or despair he'd never understood until now.

Something in the way her eye caught him when she glanced upward unlatched his tongue. He told her the story unbidden, without preface or explanation.

"I knew it was a setup," he said. "I knew they had something going on. We had been tracking these guys for months, out of Russia and through Africa. What we were really after was a warhead from an SS-11. I don't know if you're up on your Cold War ICBMs." He didn't bother explaining how easy the warheads were to steal and rerig. "Anyway, my task force tracked it down there with a bunch of other goodies. Luanda, Angola. Hell of a place. I'd been authorized to go get it pretty much however I could. My team was pretty small, so I hooked up with some in-country people, as well as the agency area desk. My munitions expert was a woman named Isha Brown, and it happened that she was engaged to one of the guys on the African side, a man named Darren Ali."

At the name, Sylvia jumped a little, finally recognizing the story. Her reaction slowed him, but only for a moment.

"I needed a fresh face, so I got Darren in as a buyer. He was good, man, he had real ops talent

179

nobody had ever tapped. So la-la-la, and we're maybe two days away from wrapping it up, when they call and ask for a meeting. It was bad, I knew it was bad, and I had to make the call. If I pooped the tent, all our work would go down the chute and we'd probably never get the warhead. But if I sent him in, they'd be watching him with a microscope.

"I figured—hey, he has a knack, you know? He had a silver tongue. So I took the chance. I sent him in without any backup or surveillance. It could have been safer that way for him; less could go wrong.

"The first I heard of the bombing was a radio report. We ended up losing the warhead and everything else. By the time we caught up with the son of a bitch who had rigged the bomb, he'd taken cyanide. That was a little bit of satisfaction, at least, seeing how he'd died."

Scotty remembered very exactly, but did not describe, the blood curling from the bloated lip of the sixty-five-year-old former Russian army major who'd rigged the explosive and masterminded the warhead sale. The device had never been recovered.

"There was a bunch of other stuff. Anyway, that's why I got sidetracked off the ladder to the stars. The big reason, anyway." The dryness in his throat was like a snake, slithering back and forth. "I guess there's some version of that floating around in the Company, huh? You've probably heard it all."

"I don't know that anyone blames you."

"Oh, yeah they do. I do. Anyway, Ave was blown up with a bomb that was kicked off by the same kind of grenade. I lost—" He stumbled, not sure how to describe what Esma was to him. Finally, her bare name slipped out of his mouth, floating across the mechanically cleaned air of the small basement room. "Esma—she got blown up with the same stuff. Poetic justice."

Sylvia, her body stiff, stared at him the way a cat

might watch a bird it couldn't reach. "It wasn't justice," she said finally, before returning to the computer.

After a while, Sylvia became truly creative in her search parameters, checking lists with all sorts of variables, but got the same result—nothing. Culling through some of the printouts she dumped, he thought he spotted one or two government officials with links to the early days of Castro's export-the-Revolution days, but nothing that would give him a real lead to follow on the bombing. After two pots of coffee, the search degenerated into reading old situation reports from the sixties and early seventies, along with occasional distillations from Fidel's own files. While it was interesting in a way, Scotty realized he was mostly wasting time. But since he didn't want to go to sleep and didn't have a clue what to do next, he read onward.

At some point he found a report stolen from the Cubans in the early seventies that outlined the likelihood of Russian KGB agents trying to infiltrate the Cuban government apparatus. The attempt seemed to have been dealt with quickly, and Scotty would have nudged the report away had he not seen a very familiar name among the possible suspects—Manuel Letra. It was the same name as the current head of the broadcast ministry.

Surely a coincidence, he thought at first. The minister had been among the many thousands of exiles who had escaped Cuba and made a new life for themselves in Miami. He had been an outspoken critic of the regime as well as a successful businessman, qualifications that had earned him his job. He was an important man in the new Cuba, a man with both a fortune and a future.

And, as Sylvia's manipulations of the relevant records eventually showed, he was the same man who had once been suspected of being a KGB agent.

Chapter Five

Wednesday, July 23
Havana. 6 A.M.

Technically, the information about the minister should have been turned over immediately to the Cubans. Even if it didn't prove Letra was connected with the rebels, it demanded an explanation. All high-ranking members of the interim government were supposed to have taken an oath swearing they had had no connection with the Castro government. At the very least, Scotty should have informed Steele that he had potentially damaging information about one of the government's higher officials. But it struck Scotty that if Letra had somehow been connected with the Russians in the old days, he might know something about the ancient cache of weapons that had been used to make the Ave bomb. It was a long shot—more like a hundred-yard Hail Mary pass—but it was a lead nonetheless.

Besides, telling the Cubans would mean he'd have a really long report to write.

So after going home, taking a shower, and loading

up on coffee—caffeine was now the one drug he would allow himself—Scotty went to the broadcast ministry offices to talk to Letra. Surprised to find the office already open for business, he walked into the lobby of the three-story building without passing a guard. The floors in the stucco-covered building were plushly carpeted. The retro-Deco furniture in the lobby glittered with a prideful glow ordinarily associated only with private businesses and homes. A mainland company—rumor had it that it was somehow connected to a relative of the head of the U.S. Senate's foreign relations committee—controlled all of the government cleaning contracts, with generally dismal results.

Scotty's embassy ID was sufficient to have him pointed to Letra's suite, which occupied the entire third floor. Letra's secretary had not yet come in, and Scotty walked through the outer office to a large, light-filled room dominated by leather furniture and an elaborate ebony desk. Letra, whom Scotty recognized from the newspapers, was working on something at his desk.

"*Señor* Letra," he said, stepping into the room.

Letra looked up with a scowl. "You're early," he snapped in Spanish. "Sit down. What did they tell you?"

Even if Scotty had been inclined to tell Letra he wasn't whom he was expecting, he didn't have the chance. The minister launched into a tirade about how he loved his daughter, though it was impossible to govern her. "She is headstrong. She thinks because I am so old that I cannot see with these eyes. My health is excellent—I have the body of a man of forty. This Garcia, he is not who he says he is, that much I know."

In Cuba, Garcia was a name like Smith in the United States; there were at least twenty living on every block in Havana. Still, Scotty felt a strange suspicion come over him, and waited with a certain fatality to find out whom Letra meant. And so he learned that the minister had caught wind of a fledgling romance between his only daughter Maria and a young North American whose last name was Garcia. The man had told her he was a businessman, but he did not appear on any of the government lists of permitted foreign agents, where in theory he ought to have shown up if he were truly a man of substance.

Letra had asked MININT for an investigator, and while he was surprised to see a man who was so obviously an American, perhaps it did make sense that someone from *el norte* would be sent to find out information about a fellow countryman.

"*Señor* Letra," said Scotty finally, putting up his hand.

"You are going to tell me that your family has been in Cuba for centuries, no doubt," said Letra dismissively. He reached to the desk and took a pad. "This is my daughter's work address. The young man, I believe, is staying at the Paramount Hotel. His first name is Edward. You can expect my daughter to object if you speak to her; never mind that."

Scotty leaned forward and took the piece of paper from the minister. Obviously he'd underestimated the kid.

"Why are you not doing your job?" demanded Letra. "Get going."

"You didn't allow me to introduce myself," Scotty told him. "My name is Scott McPherson. I work for the American ambassador."

"You're not from the Ministry of the Interior?"

"No," said Scotty.

"There are Yankees all over the place there."

"I'm not one of them."

"You sound almost Cuban." The minister shifted in his desk chair. Frowning, he reached into a small humidor and took out a cigar. He did not offer one to Scotty. "You must understand, I hold nothing against the young man who is seeing my daughter," said Letra.

"Of course not."

"This doesn't have to get to the ambassador."

"Who said it would?"

"What is it that you want?"

"I need a history lesson."

"History?"

"In Russian hand grenades. Ones that can be used to explode larger bombs. I understand the process is dangerous, but very simple to execute if the grenade mechanism is properly handled. Assuming you have the right grenade. That's critical. There are only one or two you can do it with, apparently."

"I have no idea what you're talking about."

"Your KGB instructors never told you?"

Fear spun through Letra's eyes so fleetingly that Scotty might have missed it had he not been watching carefully. "I have no idea what you're talking about."

"Up to you. I guess I should have gone through channels with this anyway."

"Corruption is a very American disease."

"I'm not interested in extortion," said Scotty, starting to rise. "Just information."

The minister pushed a finger through his thick gray hair. "My opposition to Fidel is well-known," said Letra.

"Your background in the KGB isn't known, though, is it?" said Scotty. "I figure that in order for Fidel to think you were a double agent, you must have been a member of his security forces to begin with."

"No, you have that wrong."

Scotty shrugged. It was a calculated gesture, a cliché almost, as was his step toward the door. But they brought the desired result.

"Sit down," said the minister. "Tell me what you want."

Scotty slid back into the chair. He waited, watching as the minister marked the contours of his face with his thumb, the way a priest might granting a sinner the last absolution.

"I was sent to Russia as a young man," said Letra finally. "We were sent—I would not expect you to understand what we had to put up with. The poverty of the country? That was nothing. The young people who complained toward the end of Fidel—" He glanced at his desk as he spit the name of the dictator from his mouth, expecting perhaps to see it land there and grovel. "They complained of stupid things. He was an evil man—do not believe these few who say now the good things he did. A leech and a bloodsucker. He lived on the soul of Cuba. And I do not think he converted at the end—that is a story for old women."

As he spoke, the minister's face tinged redder, small blood vessels appearing in his cheeks. His Spanish became quicker and harsher, the words flying from his mouth like darts.

"Young people my age were brainwashed. We were turned against our families. It took me until my trip to Russia to understand. Once I could slip away from our chaperones, I saw firsthand where the Revolution would lead."

Scotty listened quietly. He had a sense that most or even all of what the minister said was true, but it was always what a man left out that was important.

"When I was twenty-three, I found the courage to denounce the regime," concluded Letra. "My eyes were opened. You know my history from there. No doubt you have a file on me."

"Why did they think you were a double agent?"

"I denounced Fidel. In Cuba, that was more than enough."

"But the KGB?"

"I assume it was because I was sent to Russia as a young man. They needed some pretense to disgrace me. I became a nonperson."

Scotty realized the irony—the government had undoubtedly expunged his records as punishment, which had opened the way for him to return and hold a position after Fidel's death.

"You were a member of the party," Scotty said, guessing, though it was hardly a stretch. "And of course you worked in one of the ministries."

Letra deflected rather than denied the assertion. "They put me on an enemies list and let me work the harvest," he said. "Then I found a way to leave."

Scotty nodded. "I assume you hate the guerrillas."

"Of course."

"You would love to assassinate their leader."

"Don't be absurd. Which is it? Are you charging me with being a Communist, or a right-wing reactionary?"

"Neither."

"Then what do you want?"

"How possible do you think it is that there are old caches of Russian weapons on the island?"

Letra seemed genuinely surprised by the question. "There are all sorts, as you must know. Why is this of interest to you?"

"I'm looking for caches from the early sixties that haven't shown up anywhere. Russian-made dynamite, grenades."

"That old? I don't know. I suppose, perhaps in the mountains. The guerrillas in Sierra Maestra have made use of some old weapons there. Fidel was always paranoid that the North Americans would invade." He smiled wanly. "That wasn't just paranoia, was it? Especially after Playa Girón, the Bay of Pigs.

There were civil-defense brigades, naturally. There must be stores of weapons hidden everywhere. The government captured many after Fidel's death, but he was like an old woman, hiding things everywhere. What is it that you are doing? Fishing?"

"I'm investigating the Ave explosion. I thought perhaps you would know something about it."

His face said he did not. Scotty, though not convinced, had gone as far as he could this morning. He rose to go. He was almost to the door when Letra spoke again.

"I fight every day for democracy. You don't know how hard I fight. My whole life has been devoted to it. If my enemies find out about this charge," he added, the harsh control so evident in his voice lifting ever so slightly, "they will use this information against me."

"Everybody has enemies," Scotty said. "The question is, how many friends do you have?"

"And you are one?"

"You better hope so."

Havana, En Route to Jardín Pequeño. 6 A.M.

"Oh man, I'll tell you, I could get used to this." Garcia slid into the backseat of the minivan, holding the coffee he had taken from the hotel restaurant. He cradled the fine porcelain in his hands, sipping the thick Cuban coffee while he watched the porter stow two briefcases in the luggage compartment behind him. The briefcases were empty, but they were essential to the elaborate pretend-opera the pilots were playing. Any passerby would think Garcia, Dalton, and Ferguson were part of the army of visiting businessmen looking to make a mint in Free Havana.

"Ain't bad at all," said Dalton, climbing in next to Garcia. "You know what I had for dinner last night?

188

Lobster. I love lobster. I didn't even know you could get fucking lobster in Cuba."

"I hope the pair of you don't think this is going to last," said Ferguson, taking his place in the front. His face was ragged, a hodgepodge of bleached and reddened blotches. He suddenly began to cough, and leaned out of the car to get rid of the gobs of heavy mucus his lungs fetched up. When he regained control of himself, he sat upright and pulled the door closed with as much dignity as he could muster.

"Missed you at breakfast," Dalton told him. Though not a world-class ball-buster, he did like to twist the knife. On the short side at five-six, he had a baby face and overactive eyebrows that added to his impish appearance.

"Screw yourself, Yank," replied Ferguson. He lifted the lid off his large Styrofoam cup, jostling the tea bag inside. He settled the cup between his knees, then fortified the liquid with the contents of two small, airline-size bottles of Scotch. Garcia and Dalton had witnessed this ritual before, and said nothing.

"Where the hell is the damn driver?" Ferguson grumbled, recapping the tea. "No wonder the Cubans are losing this half-assed war."

"I understand they're winning," said Garcia.

Ferguson snorted in contempt. "You can't win a war you're hiring foreigners to fight."

The conversation was cut short by the arrival of the driver. Though casually dressed in jeans and a T-shirt, the middle-aged man was actually a major in the Cuban defense forces. Taciturn and exceedingly businesslike, he spoke into the microphone of his portable radio at regular intervals, one or two words at a time.

It took about forty minutes to get from Havana to Jardín Pequeño and its semipaved airstrip. During

Castro's early years, the base had housed units of the Cuban army; it had been used sparingly since the end of the regime. Besides the Harriers and their support personnel, there was a battalion-size contingent of the Cuban army there. The airplanes were using a hard-dirt runway that probably had not been utilized since the early days of flight, and even then had probably been considered less than ideal. But that was what the A/V-8A had been created for; if you avoided the potholes and didn't mind the dust, the short, narrow strips were more than enough for the planes.

Garcia watched through the window as the city gave way to a beautiful, verdant countryside. All he could think of was Maria. They'd set up a tentative date for tonight. He wanted to take her to one of the nightclubs he'd heard about, though he would be content to stare at her for a couple of dozen hours. The infatuation was not just sexual. She seemed almost magical when she spoke, her eyes glittering, her words dancing, whether in English or Spanish, in a song that seemed at once wise and playful.

"Hey, watch what you're doing with that coffee, lover boy," said Dalton, steadying Garcia's arm. "You're dripping that sludge all over the floor. It'll rot right through."

"Sorry."

"How was your date last night?"

"It was okay."

"Only okay?"

"Yeah, you know. Okay."

"Okay okay? Or just . . . okay?"

"What are you two clowns babbling about back there?" asked Ferguson.

"Garcia hasn't debriefed us about his date."

"He's wise to keep it to himself," said Ferguson. His sour mood started to lighten, now that he'd drunk about half of his Scotch-laced tea.

"It wasn't a date. It was more like a tour."

Dalton laughed. "Oh, that's what they're calling it these days."

The teasing ended abruptly as the minivan turned off the highway onto the access road to the base. A caravan of Cuban army trucks—all of Russian vintage—were lined up along the side of the road, facing the base. The driver slowed but did not stop at the checkpoint, two soldiers waving him onward.

"What the hell's all this about?" Dalton asked, pulling himself forward on the seat.

The driver didn't answer. They drove into the compound, heading toward the area where the Harriers were parked.

Not being an air force base, the installation did not have regular hangars, and the Harriers and several Cuban helicopters had been housed outside, with no effort to camouflage or hide them. The army had posts surrounding the base for security, but they were very vulnerable to the sort of random mortar attacks the rebels apparently liked to use, attacks that had pockmarked the base and its runway.

Something had done considerably more damage the night before, as the three pilots realized when the van rounded one block of buildings and saw the burnt-out wreckage of a Bell Huey helicopter. Behind it, the base defense-force headquarters was in ruins.

"It's about bloody damn time you got your butts out here," said Hill as the three pilots slid out of the car. "What the hell have you been doing?"

Garcia stared at the wrecked building, feeling something like shock. Dalton walked toward the twisted remains of the helicopter. The fire had shrunken it to a third or quarter of its normal size; charred and twisted, the skeleton reeked of carbonized metal and melted plastic.

Belatedly, Garcia thought of the Harriers. He turned and saw that they were all still standing at the far end of the field, parked along the runway where the crews had been working on them yesterday.

"Bastards came in at two A.M.," said Hill. "Fortunately, there weren't many of them, or these apes would still be fighting them off."

Garcia started walking toward the fighter-bombers. Debris from the fighting was strewn indiscriminately along the field—spent shells, shrapnel, even a pair of rifles.

There was something else in the grass twenty yards from the Harriers.

"Shit," yelled Garcia, running toward the body. With his service side arm inside his bag, his only weapon was the tiny Czech pistol in his belt. He removed it as he ran, though he realized it was of dubious value except at very close range.

He didn't need it. From ten yards away he could tell the man was dead. Khaki pants and dark green shirt were stained black with a thick cake of blood. His face had wrenched itself into an expression of unnatural horror. Garcia stopped, staring at the man's bare feet, which looked almost pink in the tall grass.

"He's dead," he said to Dalton, who was the first to reach him. Dalton immediately turned away. "I guess we better get someone to take him away," Garcia told Hill.

"What are you talking about?"

"This man," said Garcia. "The Cubans must have missed him."

"Bloody hell, don't you know anything? You think he came in here without boots on?"

"They leave the guerrilla's bodies to rot," explained Ferguson. "As long as it's convenient."

"That's not right."

"This is bloody war, you idiot," said Hill. "Grow up. Come on, all of you—we have to get into the new base as soon as possible. The Cubans want a mission this afternoon, the bastards."

Sierra Maestra Mountains. 9 A.M.

Now that he had fallen, now that Carla had struck, Hector Romano Moncada felt entirely at peace with himself. For this, too, had been part of the plan, unforeseen though it was. He had been too prideful, taken his victory over her too much for granted. And now he had been beaten.

But not vanquished. Not, in fact, defeated. *El Jefe* had been routed severely in his early days, only to come back. Romano was merely following in his path.

Perched on the ledge of a mountain cave overlooking the Caribbean, Romano took a long, deep breath of the salty air. He had made his body perfect, sacrificing all physical pleasure so that he could become the vessel of history, the vessel of his great hero's soul. He had thought that *El Jefe* had already come to him—surely the many sacrifices had made him think so—but now he realized that it had not happened until yesterday on the road, when he rose and confronted de Souza. Her eyes had flashed with defiance—with the light of her father—and then drained into mere buttons of coal. The spirit had passed in that moment, not before.

Now he understood everything. Already, his people were moving to restore him to his rightful place. By tomorrow night, all would be ready.

And then he would carry out *El Jefe*'s last wish. He would exact revenge against the gringos. And *El Jefe* would live forever.

Jim DeFelice

The Outskirts of Havana. 10 A.M.

For just a flicker of a second, Scotty thought of blowing off the funeral. He had any number of excuses; he didn't even have a black suit. But duty pulled him toward it, duty and sadness that only grew deeper as he tried to avoid it. And so after wasting more than an hour trying to surreptitiously scare up some reference to the explosives used in the bombing in the CIA files, he took a brief walk down by the ocean, steeled himself, and drove toward the small church just outside the city limits.

The car Scotty had borrowed from the embassy pool was a Chevy, the only one in the inventory and perhaps the only one in Cuba. He swore as he drove that it would be the last time he ever used it—not only was the bulky car an obvious target, but it sucked gas like a wino locked in a liquor store. The steering wheel had all the precision of a bumper car's. The air conditioner was stuck on high; he had to regulate the temperature by opening and closing the window.

Not surprisingly, his sport coat was soaked with sweat by the time he found the church. Esma would have laughed, then found some secret place for him to take a bath. She had a knack for finding luxuries in the most unlikely places.

Was that true? It seemed as if it were, but his mind had started to play tricks, magnifying her memory, making her more beautiful, more perfect. Not even Esma could have found a bath here, in this dry and dusty poor town, outside the city's shadow.

He parked the car in a lot across the street from the church, an old structure built of brown-and-red-flecked bricks. Not fancy but far from neglected, it was one of the churches Fidel had allowed to be resurrected toward the end of his regime, after the Pope had visited Cuba. The building bore the scars

194

of the Revolution as many of the older Cubans did—with pride tinged by sorrow.

The lot was empty, and though paved, strewn with sand. For a moment, he feared he had misunderstood the directions, though it was obvious a funeral was taking place here—the hearse and an ancient black Lincoln were parked in front.

But of course he had the right place. Scotty walked up the two short steps to the abbreviated narthex at the entrance just as an organ began wheezing inside. He stood in the center of the open doors at the back as the congregation rose, all eyes riveted not on the altar but on the polished rosewood box the embassy had paid for in the center aisle. A Cuban flag was draped across the end of the casket where Esma's feet would be; the casket was closed.

The organ filled the church with a paralyzing dirge. The music mocked his resolve as he stood frozen on the rim of the incense-filled nave. A hole opened in his chest, and his life ran into it, sucked down like the water from a bath. Everything he had lost in the last two years, everything of any value to him—love, job, future—whirled down that drain; he stood an empty man, bereft of energy and hope.

He had loved Esma, and now she was gone. He had, not long before that, loved the CIA, his work and his country, in a different way, and those were largely denied to him as well. Because of his mistakes in Angola—and his failure to take hold of himself immediately afterward—his ability and judgment would always be questioned. Once he was a darling fast-tracker with ties to the administration and Congress; now even the few men still willing to employ him had question marks in their eyes.

He had no home, no family to speak of, and even the small pleasures he might seize now would be forever tinged with sorrow. He wanted revenge, but he could not even, at this moment, feel anger. All he could feel was a useless but overwhelming self-pity.

Shaking, in desperate need of something, drugs, alcohol—though he ordinarily didn't smoke, a cigarette—Scotty started to back away from the mass.

The priest stopped him. He had entered from a side door in the sacristy at the front, and walked before the altar in his mourning vestments. Nodding at the gathered family, he walked to the coffin, intending to bless it; his eye caught the figure at the back of the church. The priest lifted his hand, gesturing for him to approach.

Scotty found it impossible to disobey. Pulled forward, he walked stiffly but surely as the priest completed his blessing and took his place on the altar. Pausing by the coffin, Scotty fingered the cloth of the flag lightly. He felt an arm on his shoulder; Esma's brother ushered him to a seat in the first pew, next to her mother.

Not a Catholic, and not overly religious in any event, he followed along, standing, sitting, or kneeling with the others. The emotion that gradually took hold of him and replaced the empty weariness of his soul was not heavy sorrow. There was sadness, a great deal of it, but what wrapped itself around him was more stoic, less indulgent. If it did not completely vanquish the self-pity, it nonetheless moved it away, made it less relevant. As the ceremony continued, Esma's mother put her hand in his, cooling his warm fingers.

At one point everyone was looking at him, and Scotty realized that he was expected to do a reading. He got up awkwardly, escorted to the podium by one of the ushers. The priest handed him a small pamphlet and nodded.

Scotty was surprised to find the words in English.

He began haltingly, with a voice that seemed to come from someone other than himself:

> "Rest in the Lord, and wait patiently for him: fret not thyself because of him who prospereth in his way, because of the man who bringeth wicked device to pass.
>
> Cease from anger, and forsake wrath: fret not thyself in any wise to do evil.
>
> For evildoers shall be cut off: but those that wait upon the Lord, they shall inherit the earth."

Havana. 11:10 A.M.

Steele felt his eyes starting to glaze over as the Cuban official continued. Carlos Lupa was a member of the temporary government who functioned as the treasury secretary. His official title ran to a full paragraph, but the ambassador was convinced that Lupa's real job was to bore the hell out of him at least twice a week, haranguing him about how much more aid the island's economy needed to turn the corner to prosperity.

He was in fantastic form this morning, filling the large, high-ceilinged conference room with airy predictions of how the Cuban budget deficit would be wiped out by the end of the decade. The informal session had been going on for nearly forty minutes, and while Steele greatly admired the sleek marble floors and the superbly crafted archways of the ministry building, he could think of half a dozen things he had to get done before noon, when he was scheduled to take a conference call with Blitz and the head of the NSC.

"I don't disagree with anything you say, Mr. Minister," Steele said for the thirteenth time, trying to interject. The attempt failed as miserably as all of the others; Lupa continued speaking in grand sentences of the "superior attitude of the Cuban working man and woman, which makes prosperity a sure thing."

Steele rolled his eyes. It didn't help that Tito Porta was sitting next to him on the leather couch, bobbing his head up and down like a golden retriever. The ambassador valued Porta's advice mostly as a counterweight to Scott McPherson's, and in the absence of Scotty found him a grating annoyance.

"Enough, please," snarled Steele finally. Even in an informal, off-the-record meeting like this, his tone was an enormous breach of diplomatic etiquette, but in truth, the Cubans were used to it by now. "What you are saying is absolutely true, and it strikes me as all the more reason for the temporary government to set a date for the elections."

"But, Ambassador, the attack at the hospital proves how virulent the guerrillas are. As a former military man, I am sure you understand. That is why we are so thankful that you are our ambassador, with your special understanding for such matters."

"I appreciate your confidence," said Steele.

"We are very embarrassed by the attack, but we must face facts. It pains me to say this, but things are more dangerous now than ever."

Steele, in fact, thought just the opposite. According to a secret U.S. opinion poll taken last week, public opinion was running over eighty percent against the guerrillas. The only thing as unpopular as M-26—at least in the Havana area—was the interim government.

"I'm not saying that the rebels have been crushed," said Steele as patiently as he could. "What I am saying is that if you hold elections, it will be a huge blow against them."

Lupa squinted behind his oversize wire-frame glasses. In just the last six months, he had gained an enormous amount of weight, so that he reminded Steele of a Butterball turkey, fattened for Thanksgiving. "I do not see your point, Mr. Ambassador. The rebels will disrupt the elections, and they will once more claim a victory."

"They won't disrupt elections they are part of," said Porta suddenly.

Steele turned to him with an exasperated expression, dumbfounded by the inappropriate remark.

Lupa could have chosen to ignore the comment, especially as it had not come from the ambassador. Instead, he put down his coffee cup stiffly, taking advantage of it to end the discussion.

"That was out of line," said Steele quickly. "Mr. Porta does not speak for the United States."

"Our meeting is at an end," said Lupa.

Steele jumped to his feet so quickly that everyone in the room gasped, including the two plainclothes Cuban secret service bodyguards near the far wall. It took every ounce of the general's considerable self-control for him not to explode.

"Minister, I must remind you that you said the elections would be discussed after the defense forces had air support. You now have that support. The government must live up to its end of the bargain."

Lupa looked down at Steele's hand, which was pointing a not-unthreatening finger. Steele lowered it.

"Mr. Ambassador. I understand that you were appointed because you are a personal friend of the President, and that this closeness was to show how important Cuba is to the United States. I know that you are not a professional diplomat, and so I will overlook this breach of decorum. But let me assure you, no Cuban government, interim or otherwise, will allow itself to be dictated to by the United States."

Steele sucked in a lung's worth of the hot air. "I apologize if my comments sounded like an order," he said. "I am merely trying to review our commitments. I believed, as you said when we started, that this entire conversation was off the record. And I remind you that Mr. Porta does not speak for me or for the government."

Lupa smiled. There was nothing Steele could do now but bow out of the scene as gracefully as possible. The United States was spending several million dollars a week, effectively propping up the interim government, and had about as much leverage with them as a homeowner with an overbooked plumber.

"As for the airplanes, they are not what we requested," said Lupa.

"They are the best we can do for now," said Steele.

Lupa held out his hands in an empty gesture, then turned and left the room. His men followed, leaving the ambassador and his aide alone.

Steele turned to Porta. The Cuban was trembling. "Too soon?"

"No, you did it perfectly." Steele sighed. McPherson, with his sneering attitude, would have carried it off better, but the immediate result would have been the same. Steele hoped that by raising the possibility of rebel involvement in the elections, the government would move to hold them quickly, sensing that the United States might begin to demand that as well. It would take several days to see if the veiled threat had any effect.

"Perhaps if you bring American planes—"

"Oh, don't be ridiculous, Tito. You know what effect that will have. If you were a guerrilla, wouldn't you pray every night for proof that the Americans were persecuting you?"

Porta shuffled along to the car, too cowed to say anything else.

Havana Strike

Whether it was the mass or the fact that he was just tired, Scotty felt incredibly calm after the service. Declining an invitation to return with the family to a small reception, he got into his car and started back toward Havana.

He still intended to find out who killed Esma, though in an inexplicable way revenge itself was no longer important. The bombing had somehow become a theoretical problem to be solved, a scientific equation detached from him.

No matter what theory you favored—a MININT hit, a guerrilla rebellion, de Souza trying to demonstrate her power—all of the theories intersected at the head of M-26. The easiest way to find out who set the bomb was to ask her.

She would be difficult, but not impossible, to find. Fidel's bastard daughter would be on her guard more than ever now. But she was brave enough to take foolish risks. Anyone who was brave was vulnerable.

If he found that she was the bomber, would he kill her?

Almost certainly, despite the consequences.

If she were killed, she would become a martyr and inject the rebel movement with new energy. That was one reason the Cuban government had never moved against her personally.

Certainly, if an American killed her, she would become a powerful symbol.

He would find her, and she would tell him, straight out, whether she had planted the bomb or not. From what he knew about her, she would not shy from that.

It was preposterous, but no more preposterous than other things he had done in his career. The commendations in his folder were earned from action, not words. He could do it, if he put his mind to it.

There were other things to do. The pilot, Garcia. He had to be warned off Letra's daughter before the ambassador found out.

And there was, of course, the rest of his job. There were intelligence estimates to write, advice to give. Scotty snickered out loud in the empty car, then turned on the highway toward the airport where the Harriers were based. Garcia first.

He would find the bomber. There was time.

When Scotty first saw the caravan of military vehicles on the highway, he was still two miles from Jardín Pequeño, and he didn't connect the two. But it was obvious as soon as he turned off the highway that something was going on at the base. He passed through the sentry point and got halfway to the building used as a kind of field office by the Harrier commander before he saw the ruined building and realized what had happened.

He immediately thought of Garcia's girlfriend and her father. He resisted jumping to the conclusion that one or the other was involved in the bombing only because he had dismissed the possibility that Letra was a secret guerrilla or sympathizer. But it was too neat a coincidence not to bother the hell out of him.

The small squadron had already left for a new base; after a perfunctory conversation with the Cuban military commander detailed to clean up the mess, Scotty drove back to Havana, looking for the address of the building where Ms. Letra was employed.

It wasn't hard to find. Channel 17, one of a dozen television stations started since the end of the regime, had taken over nearly half a block off Avenue Menocal in Central Havana. A curious mixture of old and new, the television offices had been constructed of steel and glass inside the exterior shell of three separate but adjacent buildings. The design had a slightly disorienting effect, as if you had knocked on the door of a medieval castle and found yourself in NASA's Houston Control instead.

Security at all broadcasting facilities was tight, and it didn't help that Scotty's .45 set off the metal detector as soon as he walked in the door. While there was no question about his identity, Scotty had to submit to the indignity of a frisk, which turned up the small Glock at his ankle. The other, near his groin, would have set off the detector on its own—the slide, barrel, and much of the firing mechanism were, after all, steel, and then there were the bullets—but the security thugs put a little too much confidence in their searching abilities and didn't pass him through a second time.

Even so, Scotty felt somewhat more paranoid than normal riding in the open elevator up into the metal-spoked guts of the building. Two behemoths flanked him, mandatory escorts for any visitor, even a government minister.

Especially a government minister.

Knowing that her father held an important position in the interim government, Scotty expected Ms. Letra to be an anchorwoman or at least a correspondent. He was surprised to find his guides leading him to the bookkeeping department. Partitions of smoked glass, augmented by massive Steelcase filing cabinets, cordoned the area off, making small offices out of the large open floor. There were no doors per se; his burly companions stopped a few feet from a partition and pointed Scotty toward the area where Ms. Letra worked.

Maria Letra was sitting at a glass-and-steel desk, slumped slightly back in the plush, black leather chair. Though she was facing the entrance to her cubicle, her eyes were staring above, covered by her hands, which slowly moved back to stroke her hair. Mascara had run from the corners of her eyes; she had only recently stopped crying.

Scotty stood for a moment before speaking, studying her, planning his attack. There was no easy way to know who was a member of M-26 and who wasn't.

She looked down and jumped back in her chair, startled to see him.

"I knocked, but I guess you didn't hear," he lied, speaking in English.

"What do you want?"

Scotty took a step forward, unsure why Garcia would be attracted to her. Though she must not be thirty yet, in the hard, unflattering wash of the overhead fluorescents, she looked old and beaten. Her body was not unattractive—her long legs were obvious beneath the glass of her meticulously ordered desktop—but it seemed to Scotty that the good-looking Garcia could probably have a bevy of prettier women tugging at his heels simply by clicking his fingers.

"My name is Scott McPherson. I'm from the embassy."

As he was speaking in English, it was obvious which embassy he meant. But she looked at him blankly.

"I understand you've been spending some time with an American named Edward Garcia."

She pulled herself up in the chair, self-consciously pulling down her skirt. "What business is that of yours?"

"His air base was attacked this morning, for one thing."

"His base? He told me he is a businessman, a consultant. Was he hurt?"

"No. Apparently not."

"Oh." She sighed to herself, seemed relieved—but only for a brief moment. "You don't think I did it, do you?"

"Who have you told you're seeing him?"

"What is this, an inquisition?"

When Scotty didn't answer, she scowled. "Is that all? I have business to attend to."

"What did you do yesterday?"

"Yesterday? I worked. Then I took Edward to see my grandmother. He was back by nine. Ask him."

"Your grandmother?"

"Yes. Is that against the law now? Does the embassy want to interview my grandmother as well?"

Maria Letra practically spat the word "embassy."

"What do you know about M-26?"

"What do you mean?"

"I think that's obvious."

"Only what I read."

"Have they approached your father?"

Her lip quivered, and she shook her head. "My father? Why?"

"Did you talk to him about Garcia?"

"Why?"

"He wanted me to investigate him."

She shook her head ever so slightly, speechless for a minute. "When? When did you talk to him?"

"Around seven this morning. When did you tell him about Garcia?"

"He's dead," she said, starting to sob. "He—he killed himself. They just told me. I thought you knew."

San Pietro. 2 P.M.

The squadron's new base had been a military school, and came with a short but nonetheless real airstrip, whose two thousand feet could handle C-130 cargo planes in a pinch. That meant takeoffs and landings would be considerably easier. It also meant supplies could be airlifted in, avoiding not just highways vulnerable to guerrilla attack but, more important, the bureaucratic and political infighting that governed weapons allocation in the country. A short time after Garcia and the others set their Harriers onto what now felt like a luxuriously spacious concrete runway, a C-130 screeched down and unloaded several packets of American iron bombs and the as-yet-unusable Maverick missiles that had come to Cuba with Garcia. More important, a second plane delivered enough cannon rounds to allow the Harrier pilots to use their weapons whenever they pleased—assuming they had no plans to do so beyond the next two weeks.

Two platoons of soldiers had been flown in to act as sentries; though he saw them mostly from a distance, Garcia was considerably more impressed with these troops than the guards at Jardín Pequeño. The men were part of an elite Cuban force that compared loosely but not unfavorably to the American 82nd Airborne; they established a perimeter and moved two oldish but nonetheless potent light tanks into commanding positions roughly at either end of the field. These hand-me-down M48s with their 105mm, laser-guided guns could send a squad of bad guys to hell in a hiccup.

If the airstrip and its facilities seemed massive after Jardín Pequeño, the pilots' quarters were anything but. Ferguson, Dalton, and Garcia were bequeathed a two-story brown box of a building about twenty yards from one of the two hangars—not particularly a quiet place to spend off-duty time. But given the size of their rooms—cloistered nuns lived in more spacious cells—that probably wasn't going to be much of a problem.

Even worse, Hill had told them they were to be confined to the base for "the immediate and intermediate present." Whatever the fuck that meant, as Dalton grumbled to Garcia while they walked the perimeter of their new base, trying to find something worth paying attention to.

"We get to shovel around with our fingers in our noses and our heads up our asses all day," Dalton complained. "Either that or drink rubbing alcohol with Fergie. Shit, we probably won't even have enough av fuel to do more than one mission a day. Think we can adapt those engines to drink diesel?" he added as a fuel truck belonging to the Cuban unit passed by. "Oh yeah, I forgot—they already are."

Garcia shrugged.

"Christ, what the hell are we going to do here?" Dalton continued. "Just imagine how exciting this will all be three days from now, when we know these rocks by heart." He picked up a stone and hurled it beyond the fence—an area that, no one had told them, had been mined.

Both men dove for cover as the rock hit a particularly fussy triggering device. When they realized what had happened, they began laughing uncontrollably.

Dalton talked about his seven-year-old daughter and his recently divorced wife as they headed back toward the Harrier hangar. He was starting to sound homesick; Cuba seemed to have changed his opinion about his marriage and his life in the States.

Cuba had had an effect on Garcia as well, though in a very different way. For most of his time in the marines, he hadn't given his parents much thought at all, except in abstract ways—or, at times, defiantly. He had felt his achievements as a pilot were a direct answer to his father. Growing up, he had had to listen to interminable speeches about the hardships they'd undergone, etc., etc., and out the ears. The stories had been imparted as little morality lessons: "How can you bring home a B in English? I studied nights to perfect my English . . ." The implication was always that his road was an easy one, and he should walk down it quicker and happier. He resented it greatly, and he resented his father's unyielding calculus of what was right and wrong, how much he should achieve, and how great a man he should be.

But now that he was here, and especially since his visit to the countryside, Garcia was starting to think about the stories in another light. While there was still anger toward his father and his seemingly dictatorial ways, Garcia had begun to understand him as he never had before. His dad had waged an enormous struggle to survive; his whole life, his whole future, was at stake in everything he did, every choice he made. If he was rigid now, it was because he had had to become that way to survive.

Maria had somehow helped him understand that. Not because they had spoken directly about it; except for saying that they had once lived in Cuba, he hadn't mentioned his parents at all. But in the way she talked about the regime and the hardships it imposed, in the way she had shown him the land and talked with her grandmother, he saw what his parents had given up to survive. As good as America had been to them, there was no erasing the pain they had suffered or replacing what they had lost.

He'd talk to them about it, eventually. Right now what he wanted to do was talk to Maria. He had to at least tell her their date was postponed. So when he and Dalton reached the hangar, he left the pilot to trade barbs with Ferguson and the ground crew while he went to the squadron building and looked for a phone.

Unfortunately, the only one in the building seemed to be in Hill's office.

On his desk, in use.

"Hey, Skipper, we working today?" Garcia asked when Hill came up for a breather.

"What do you think, Lieutenant?"

"I haven't a clue."

Hill scowled, consulting a ragged legal pad for yet another phone number.

"Say, Colonel, you mind if I use the phone at some point?"

The commander shot him a glance that would have killed Dracula. "Our location is a national secret, Lieutenant. As little as that may mean to the Cubans themselves, it carries weight with me."

"I wasn't going to tell anyone where we were."

Hill continued to glare, but nonetheless handed him the set. He remained sitting at his desk, and didn't take any of Garcia's subliminal hints about visiting the head for a few minutes.

It didn't matter. Maria wasn't around and Garcia ended up leaving a message with her secretary, who promised to reach her at home "no matter what."

"Thanks, Colonel," said Garcia when he hung up.

"Always happy to play Cupid," said Hill sourly. "Don't break too many hearts, eh, Elvis?"

Garcia felt his face turn red. He wondered how Hill had heard about the nickname, which he hadn't shared because of McPherson's strong reaction. "It's mine that's in trouble, sir."

"No doubt."

Hill was in a slightly less sarcastic mood an hour later, when the pilots assembled for a briefing not only on their late-afternoon mission but on their overall situation. Something must have happened to put him into a particularly loquacious mood, Garcia thought, because the session bordered on being informative.

The tough thing was figuring out whether that was a good or bad sign.

As of tomorrow, the war plan would call for two sorties a day, morning and evening. This was well within the planes' capacity, Hill felt obliged to add. In theory, the Harriers could be fed and burped with the engines running on the runway; the British had done so during the Falklands War.

No one, Hill especially, believed that theory, especially since their ground crew was undermanned. Even in their heyday, the planes were noted for having particularly fussy engines. But the commander pressed on without a trace of his customary irony. "I am not going to ask you or the airplanes to do anything you're not capable of," he said. "Our fuel stores have been increased, and more bombs are on their way. We may even boost the mission rate once we're assured of additional jet fuel."

"Are you betting the Scotch or the fuel gets here first?" joked Ferguson.

"The fuel."

"Is the fuel going to be clean, or the same polluted crap we're using now?" said Dalton.

"We won't fly if it's not up to snuff. Our Sergeant Brice will see to that."

"I don't know about that," said Dalton. "I had a hiccup or two yesterday that Fergie says was probably bad gas. I talked to Brice about it, yesterday and again this morning. He didn't seem all that concerned."

"Come on, now, Jason," said Ferguson. "He did say he would strip the system. They rechecked it again after they got here."

"We've fixed the fuel problems," snapped Hill. "Any pilot who has a problem with his aircraft should point it out immediately."

"At twenty thousand feet?" Garcia joked, trying to break the tension.

"How come we're boosting the mission pace if the war's going to be over in a week?" said Dalton, who wasn't in much of a mood for laughing.

"It may very well end soon. But until it does, we will do what our employers want."

"Your employers," said Dalton. "Garcia and I are over here on the American plan."

"Is there something wrong, Dalton? You seem to be colicky today. Were you burped after your bottle?"

"What are we bombing this afternoon?" asked Garcia, still trying to keep things light. "Another farm stand?"

"I don't like the idea of being stuck out in the middle of nowhere," said Dalton. "How the hell long are we going to be confined to the base?"

"It's for your own good," said Hill.

"My father used to say that when he sent me to my room without supper."

"If you keep complaining, I'll give that a round," said Hill, brooking no more interruptions as he proceeded to the mission briefing, delivered in his usual terse format. A former church in the foothills of the Sierra Maestra mountains was being used as an ammo dump; they were going to take its roof off. The mountains rose from the southern coast of eastern Cuba, not far from the abandoned U.S. naval base at Guantánamo. The region was the wildest in Cuba, with portions a tropical rain forest—and another patch nearly a desert. The rebels had been strong there since Castro's death; indeed, Castro himself had launched his own successful revolution from a camp in the region known as Pico Turquino—blue peak or blue mountain—in the 1950s.

Hill drew a flight plan that he said would have them swing in from the ocean, dogleg around, and come down at sixty degrees to deliver their packages. The angle was a bit sharp, but as long as they watched their toes—the colonel's phrase—it ought not to present a problem.

A pair of external wing tanks would be strapped to each wing to extend their range.

The rebels in Sierra Maestra were allegedly even less organized than the particular group they had struck yesterday; not only did they lack antiair missiles, they probably had nothing heavier than old Kalashnikovs.

"Still deadly, make no mistake," added Hill, whose real fear was actually the venerable and deadly ZSU-23-4, a Russian 23mm antiair gun that could be aimed either by radar or by eye. The guns had a nasty habit of turning up where they weren't expected. "We will make our drop at five thousand feet for maximum effect. Let's make a show of it," he said, jumping off the edge of the desk and heading toward the planes.

"You ever sit through lamer briefings?" Dalton said to Garcia as they headed for their planes. "Every answer to every question is the same. What's our course? Close your eyes and follow me. What happens if we have engine problems? Blow your nose and contact me. Yeah, right."

"You're exaggerating," Garcia said.

"Not much. That stinking dogleg takes us around the mountain for nothing. Sixty degrees? Shit, we're going to have to stand on the controls to get up. Those old planes will come apart. And why the hell are we dropping at five thousand feet?"

"Maybe he doesn't want you to miss."

"Shit. We'll be scraping snow off the peak when we pull up."

"I don't think there's any snow on them."

"You get my point. Hell, Garcia, maybe he wants to give you another chance to use your cannon."

"What are you worried about? This is going to be a picnic."

"Oh yeah, right. You think we'd be bombing someplace if these guys weren't a threat?"

Havana Strike

Not knowing what else to do, Garcia shrugged in exasperation. "You should have brought it up."

"He was already on my case. He doesn't like me. He treats Ferguson a lot better, and he's a . . ."

Garcia rolled his eyes, encouraging his friend to leave the blank unfilled.

The four Harriers stood in a row at the edge of the airstrip. A thousand-pounder nestled between the cannon pods under each belly; the cigar-shaped drop tanks were flanked by rocket launchers under each arm. They looked as awesome as the day three decades before when they were delivered to the Spanish Arma Aérea de la Armada. Ned Brice, the cockney crew chief Hill had recruited to keep the old-timers airworthy, stood to the side, beaming proudly.

Brice was something of an old-timer himself. He claimed to be fifty-three, but looked closer to eighty. Whatever his age, his lungs were in good condition—as Garcia found out when he bent down to shake the port outrigger wheel on his plane during his walk-around.

"What the hell you trying to do, son, break m'plane?" Brice shouted in his ear. "Leave that job to da damn rebels."

"They won't have the chance, Chief," Garcia told Brice. The old mechanic seemed to know a lot about the Harriers, but he had a ton of problems—besides the finicky planes, he had trouble communicating with the Cubans assigned to help him. He also seemed to share Ferguson's habit of nipping drinks on the side. And as Dalton's complaints had hinted, the old-timer wasn't particularly responsive to the pilots.

His walk-around and preflight complete, Garcia tucked himself into the cockpit, ran through his checklist one more time, then started trundling to the takeoff line. The Harrier seemed at dash-one

213

this afternoon: everything ripe and up to spec. Garcia's preflight butterflies were minimal, though he felt the mandatory flutter when the flight-line controller gave him the "kick your ass up and the hell out of here" sign.

Juicing the engine, he started Matador Two rolling ahead on the concrete. Either the Harrier was gratified to be working with real concrete or she was particularly anxious to blow up bad guys, because the plane thundered upward a good thirty feet before the computer's specified clear point, moving more like a rushing bull than a slick, controlled showman. Garcia steadied her, banking around the strip to join up with Hill, who as usual had led the group into the air.

Once they were all airborne, the commander directed them to the southeast, over the open water. Still gaining altitude, they flew due south several minutes before gradually turning eastward. The mountains were near the coast of the island, and in a relative sense were not that far from Guantánamo Bay.

The big red Caribbean sun flooded into their cockpits as they flew, washing everything with its penetrating light. The rays were so strong that Garcia could imagine himself basking in them as he flew an old-fashioned open cockpit biplane—at considerably lower altitude, of course. It was a fantasy he hoped someday to indulge; he'd never flown a biplane.

There was little chatter this afternoon, the pilots sitting alone with their various thoughts and preoccupations. Garcia thought of Maria; the memory of her laugh and the way she smiled kept floating up with every glance at the compass or fuel gauge.

When Hill executed a sharp turn to the north, the other planes hustled to fall into formation. Garcia checked his instruments carefully as they crossed back over land. Thanks to the external tanks, he had plenty of fuel; the engine was cooking up a storm, and the radar was as clear as the endless blue sky around him.

An odd thought occurred to Garcia as Hill made another sharp turn, this time to the east, starting the dogleg that would take them to the beginning of the bomb run: Was it a sin to bomb a church, even one being used by terrorists?

Garcia wondered how many Hail Marys his mother would ascribe for penance on that one.

As Hill nudged the flight downward, Garcia realized that their final approach would be made out of the clear sky between the mountain pass directly opposite the sun. He guessed that the commander had decided to order the dogleg and steep angle because the route made it difficult for a ground gunner to aim. The gray-white silhouette of the planes would be hard to make out against the whitish sky; after they pickled and shot upward, the fat red blob of Father Sol would blind any ground gunner trying to aim at them. Since they were worried not about radar but visually aimed guns, these old-fashioned tricks were an excellent idea, shaving the percentages ever so slightly in their favor.

It was pretty damn smart, actually, to have figured it out so precisely. So why the hell didn't he just explain that to Dalton?

Because Dalton hadn't asked, Garcia told himself. Hill wasn't an idiot, and he wasn't a prick; he just wasn't used to discussing every little facet of his thinking. Not exactly the classic commander, but not a fool either.

As the planes moved into a combat spread, Garcia could feel sweat starting to trickle along the skin at the back of his ear. As Hill's tail swooped downward from his windshield, the stomach flu of nervous tension hit his gut like a Mack truck. He tipped his

215

Harrier forward, double-checking that he had already thumbed the HUD into ground-attack mode. The hot sun washed inside the cockpit, slipping off as the plane angled into the attack. Garcia curled his fingers on the yoke, took two breaths, nudged the throttle ever so gently, more as a psychological device than to adjust his dive. His heart was starting to race, and he felt a jittery excitement rising in his chest. As the ground began to blur, Garcia heard his breath building into gulps in his mask. He counted out loud, a trick he'd heard somewhere that supposedly prevented hyperventilation.

The cue on the HUD slid toward his target, the pipper ratcheting in as he pushed the Harrier home. Everything was a hum, a strain, a loud whoosh of air brushing past the fuselage. The turbulence of the wind in the mountains formed an irregular slipstream against the stubby wings and irregularly shaped belly of the old jet; the universe around him began to shake like an out-of-control washing machine.

Then he hit a clear space. The sky opened up, and for just a fraction of a fraction of a second, there was nothing in the world except Garcia and the gray steeple of a small, hillside church.

Now, a voice told him.

It was his own voice, speaking out loud. The bombs were dropping, he was coming up, pulling up, yanking on his yoke, pounding it with all his might, laying on the power, shooting off his flares, jolting away into the sun.

Garcia broke to the right as planned. As far as he could tell, no one had fired at them. Beginning to bank to the southeast, he heard a series of secondary explosions through the rushing static in his ears.

Sure as hell weren't prayer books. Garcia took his time, sailing gently into a wide orbit at just over fifteen thousand feet, not a care in the world. He was just about to call in when the radio crackled.

"Lead, I have trouble here."

The words took Garcia completely by surprise. They belonged to Ferguson.

"Engine's cutting out on me. Shitting hell. I can't get altitude."

Garcia quickly pulled his plane tighter in the circle, looking back for where Ferguson should have been. He found the Harrier quite a bit lower, the pilot struggling to coax power from the failing engine. Dark smoke was pouring out of the tailpipe.

"Have you been hit, Matador Four?"

"Negative. Just having all sorts of problems with this bleeping engine. I don't know if it's the fuel or what."

"Where are you?"

"I got him," said Garcia, who had already dipped his wing toward the ailing plane. "You have black smoke coming out your rear end."

The smoke meant it was unlikely to be a momentary annoyance. Garcia took a quick peek at the gauges monitoring his own engine's performance; she was running fine.

"Can you make it back to base?" Hill asked.

"I'm not sure what the hell happened," Ferguson said. "But the engine temperature is climbing and I feel like I'm in an oven. It's coughing like hell."

"You're going to have to bail out," Hill told him. "Now."

Ferguson had already reached that conclusion. He steadied the plane and did his best to head it back toward the west. Garcia, drawing almost parallel to the stricken plane, glanced at the yellow handle between his legs that activated his own ejection seat. It was only for a moment, but when he looked back, Ferguson was already hurtling through the open air.

*   *   *

At least everything worked the way it was supposed to. Garcia kept a healthy distance from the billowing parachute as it dropped toward the jungle, but was still close enough to see the pilot pulling at his lines, making an effort to steer his descent. He imagined he could hear the string of curses.

During a U.S. operation over hostile territory, elaborate rescue procedures were de rigueur. Not only would rescue helicopters be on alert, but special-forces teams would generally be available to suppress any local ire.

Needless to say, the arrangements were more primitive here. The Cuban air force did, in theory, have a helicopter assigned to them—but the helicopter was covering the entire province, and could be alerted only through several levels of intermediaries. If there were special forces, Hill had never mentioned them.

Garcia followed the chute down, watching Ferguson land in a cultivated field that had been cleared from the edge of a forest valley. Garcia turned his attention to the surrounding countryside, trying to see if anyone had noticed the parachute. That would be problematic—there was no way to tell from here, or even on the ground, whether someone approaching Ferguson was friendly or not.

"Keep the area clear," Hill directed, winging his way back toward the church they had hit to see if anything was coming from that direction. "Have you picked him up on victor yet?"

Victor was the VHF radio band. As soon as the chute opened, Garcia had dialed over to the distress frequency. But the line remained empty.

He dropped his Harrier into low gear, a knot or two above stall speed, tiptoeing back toward the area where the chute had landed.

"This is Ferguson," the voice crackled. "I'm in one piece."

"The helicopter is on the way," Garcia responded, determined to sound as optimistic as possible. "I don't see any locals."

"I guess that's good."

"There's a line of trees to your east," he told him, leaning the Harrier over to get a better look. "You see them?"

"There's trees all over the place."

Garcia, hoping not to give too many details in case the guerrillas were monitoring the transmission, tried to think of a way to tell Ferguson where to go without making it obvious where he was. Cut away, the pilot's chute drifted back toward what seemed from the air a thick jungle, the starting slope of one of the mountains.

"There's a clump of trees in a field in the direction of your home island," said Garcia, realizing that he sounded more silly than cryptic. "Sit there. I'll keep you company."

"Raw-ger," said Ferguson.

Garcia laughed at the funny inflection, hoping the downed pilot had meant it as a joke. He drew another slow circuit in the air, flying a lazy eight. His job was simple—stay in contact with Ferguson and do his best to keep him safe. On the other hand, he didn't want to draw too much attention to him. He climbed back upward, trying to strike a balance between two irreconcilable demands.

Hill and Dalton, meanwhile, broke off. They were going home to refuel and rearm, in case the helicopter took even longer than they expected.

"Assume anything coming close to him is hostile" were Hill's parting words. "Shoot first; we'll apologize later."

Garcia pushed back in his seat and took a God's-eye view of the situation. Ferguson's Harrier had pancaked into a hill about three miles away, and was still on fire. If the local guerrillas hadn't seen

Jim DeFelice

the chute—a bit optimistic, but he had to put his hope somewhere—they would probably head for the plane and conduct their search from there. So Garcia ambled over and checked the nearest road for activity.

From 8,000 feet, the motley greens and browns arrayed below seemed like pieces of paper spilled out from a portfolio of construction paper. The thin line of the road snaked out from the hills like a child's untied shoelace.

Three hillsides away, the church/ammunition depot was still burning.

"Still there, my white knight?"

"Oh yeah, fallen hero," said Garcia, snapping back as peppy as he could. "Any action?"

"Negative. Knee hurts a bit from the fall. How much longer?"

"Hard to give you an ETA," Garcia admitted. "I'm yours for eternity."

"Appreciate that."

Garcia started to say something encouraging about how quickly his knee would heal, but then decided against it. Radio transmissions ought to be kept to a minimum. He did another medium-altitude orbit, then took his plane down to survey the countryside near the church again.

It was almost too quiet. One of the reasons the rebels were able to operate out here was the sparse population and rugged terrain, made nearly impenetrable by the interwoven jungle, hills, and mountains. But it was not quite empty. There was a cluster of houses just two miles from where Ferguson had gone down; someone was sure to have seen or at least heard something. Garcia wondered if the natives were being careful, or just too busy to notice that a war was taking place in their backyards.

Ferguson's voice, cracking with fear, startled Garcia. "What's going on?"

220

"Something wrong?" He dipped his wing back in the direction of the downed pilot.

"I'm hearing strange noises, like a thousand trucks."

Garcia and his Harrier flashed down in a dive so steep he had to practically stand on the controls to level off. If he'd been able to crank open the cockpit bubble and reach out, he could have grabbed a tree branch from the mountainside as he flashed by.

The Harrier's cannon was charged and ready to fire. Garcia rocked upward and then banked around toward the road. But there was nothing there.

"Fallen hero, fallen hero, do you read me?"

"What's coming for me?" Ferguson demanded.

"Where are you hearing these noises?"

"All over the place. I'm not sure. The south. That mountain I missed coming down."

The panic in his voice was obvious. Worried that his comrade was starting to wig out, Garcia thought back to his brief survival-school stint, trying to formulate a response. But there was little he could say that wouldn't give Ferguson the idea that he thought he was nuts.

"Garcia?"

"Fallen hero, your perimeter is clear," he said. "Hang loose, man. It's under control."

Garcia poked the Harrier's nose back earthward and took a low pass intended to reassure the downed pilot. He didn't have an unlimited supply of fuel, and these accelerated hops were a good way to drain the tanks. He thought of suggesting that Ferguson shift his position—moving around would at least get his mind off bogeymen—but he didn't want to risk locating him for anyone monitoring the band.

But what the hell was the pilot hearing? The jungle to his south seemed thicker than a Berber carpet and three times as inert.

"You're safe," he told Ferguson as he climbed up over the hillside and climbed back to altitude.

"Okay," was his weak reply.

Nearly ten minutes later, Garcia heard the wing's call sign crackling through on the rescue band. He exchanged verification with a heavily accented voice who informed him he was flying for the Cuban air national guard in Rescue Twelve. Slightly suspicious, Garcia put the gas pedal to the firewall and hopped out to look for him. Sure enough, he spotted an ancient Russian-made Mil Mi-14 lumbering from the west about ten miles away. Fat and squat, the helicopter looked like a bus with a rotor on top.

Garcia circled back and took a dash for Ferguson. His fuel was approaching bingo; he had at most five minutes to linger before he'd have to return to base.

"You awake down there?"

"Affirmative," said Ferguson.

"Helicopter's on the way."

"Is that what all the commotion is about?"

"Uh, yeah," said Garcia.

"It's coming from the southeast?"

The helicopter was still a good distance away— and west, not southeast, heading across the open field. Garcia couldn't figure out what the hell Ferguson was hearing.

Maybe the noise was echoing against the mountains. Poor guy must be going out of his mind, Garcia thought. More than likely, he needed a serious drink.

But just as he was starting to tsk-tsk over the need for more temperance videos in the RAF, Garcia caught a glint through the jungle canopy. With a start he realized there was a road down there, hidden by the thick growth.

About the last thing he did consciously was curse himself for his stupidity. Everything else was automatic—he dove, readied the cannon, told Ferguson to run from the trees to the clearing, directed the helicopter in, all in the same moment.

The steady thump-thump-thump of the cannon pod strapped to the plane's belly filled his ears. The green below him disappeared, replaced by a typhoon of smoke and dust.

There were at least three vehicles there, two pickups and something like a jeep, and these weren't good guys—the air around him ignited with small-arms fire, gnats trying to catch up to him.

He couldn't hear the commotion over his cursing. He made himself hoarse with it, screaming out his frustration and stupidity as he wheeled back for another pass, not giving a shit what happened to him, determined only to obliterate the bastards below.

He'd screwed up. He should have looked at the damn jungle harder, relied on his eyes instead of assuming everything was cool. He was too used to computers and fancy gizmos that did your looking for you.

The helicopter and Ferguson were talking. Garcia knew that the pilot would have to run from the trees to the field to get picked up. The guerrillas were now only a few hundred yards away. He made another pass, then pulled up sharply, planning to roll back and clear out the field for the helicopter.

He never made it. Just as the Harrier's nose jerked upward he felt a heavy thump behind him. In the same instant, his stick got unbelievably heavy. Instinctively pouring on throttle, Garcia heard the low echo of an explosion to his left, the kind of sound thunder makes when it's less than a mile away.

This wasn't thunder. It was a Russian SA-7 shoulder-launched surface-to-air missile, and the sound had accompanied the removal of a good portion of the rear of Garcia's plane.

Chapter Six

The canopy ripped off above his head and a tornado of wind rushed around him, biting and pushing like sharks in a feeding frenzy. Garcia, confused and disoriented, looked up and saw the sky turning from blue to dark gray, suddenly filled with storm clouds. He wondered why he hadn't been ejected from the plane yet, and struggled against the wind to find the yellow handle that controlled the explosive charges that would send him surging upward. If the ejector didn't work there was no way he could escape the force of the wind rushing across the plane, pushing the Harrier toward the earth with the grim momentum of an unstoppable meteorite.

Only when he looked down to guide his trembling fingers did he realize he had already been blown clear. His gloved hands were a shaky blur, and at first he thought they were covered with blood. As he fought the wind to bring them up and see how badly he was hurt, the parachute harness finally jerked his body backward. The strong pull was the first familiar thing, a shock that put him back in control.

He had gone out somewhere around five thousand feet, his plane heading almost due north. He wasn't sure how far he might be from the field where Ferguson had landed; it must be several miles, though he hadn't had an opportunity to get the tape measure out.

The helicopter would still be in the area, and assuming it picked up Ferguson without too much trouble, would soon turn to looking for him. Hill and Dalton ought to have fueled up by now; they'd probably be on their way back.

It was difficult to bend his neck, but he could tell by flexing his various body parts that he had come away from the plane in one piece. Not even his knee, bound in athletic tape, seemed to hurt.

Garcia twisted around in the harness, trying to orient himself. The sun was to his left, just ducking behind the mountains. The helicopter ought to come from the southeast, behind him. Hill and Dalton would be coming from the west, most likely, directly ahead.

Gee, guys, where the hell have you been? By the way, Commander, that intelligence on the rebels not having antiair missiles? I'm thinking it's not entirely accurate.

The ground rose toward him at a steady, even alarming pace, vast tufts of green beckoning him with all the welcome of the jaws of hell. Garcia finally spotted an opening in the tree cover—what seemed to be a medium-size farm hacked into the base of a mountain.

That was the good news. The bad news was that it was off to his left, and the wind, pushing in his face, was sliding him farther and farther away, back toward the looming mountain and its tree-covered crags.

There wasn't much hope of steering the large rescue chute, and Garcia wasn't exactly practiced at using it. He gave it a stab, however, leaning his body and trying to swing his legs in the direction he wanted to land. This had about as much impact as whistling while walking down a dark alley in the middle of the night, but at least it took his mind off the fact that he was almost certainly coming in for a rough landing.

And just when he had all but healed from his last crash.

Thirty feet from the ground, the wind gusted and threw Garcia back from the worst of the mountain and the low-lying jungle. He saw a wooden fence and stream in the distance. He tucked his arms and legs together and closed his eyes, thinking that some miracle had occurred and he was going to be deposited unharmed at the edge of the field.

Just then something smacked across the front of his helmet's crash shield. Something else hit him in the back and the side; he felt himself twisting through the rough arms of the trees, then jerked back at the chest, hauled momentarily into light unconsciousness.

By the time he stopped falling, Garcia found himself dangling in the middle of a group of trees perhaps twelve feet off the ground. In truth, he had been extremely lucky, for aside from a few scrapes and bruises, he had managed to escape injury. But dangling helplessly in the harness instilled neither confidence nor a sense of good fortune.

After issuing the mandatory string of curses, he set about the business of getting himself down. The last thing he wanted to do was jump; the ligament in his knee, even though taped, was sure to rip this time instead of stretch. He pulled up on the harness, testing to see how strongly it had caught; he was rewarded with a swing that sent him smack into the tree trunk.

His curses were more heartfelt than before, even including a "fuck" instead of his customary "frig," but he managed to keep his voice at something quieter than a shout. The indiscriminate stream of indignation became something of a song that he hummed to himself as he twisted in the harness and hugged the tree. It was just thin enough for him to shimmy down, at least in theory. He managed to get his legs around the trunk. Getting out of the harness while clinging to the tree took the moves and concentration of a circus contortionist.

Several times Garcia had to stop, not merely to rest but to laugh; even considering the fact that he might be shot at any moment, his tangled predicament was as funny as a Three Stooges routine. Twice he thought he was free, only to discover yet another part of the harness holding him in place; by the time he reached the ground, he had been part of the tree so long he thought he'd grown roots.

In fact, if his watch was to be believed, less than twenty minutes had passed since the guerrillas' missile took hold of his tail. Freeing himself of his helmet and gloves, Garcia fired up his radio and broadcast a quick message to tell his rescuers that he was indeed alive.

The radio answered with the silence of a banished ghost. Garcia checked his watch, deciding to wait exactly three minutes before broadcasting again. The helicopter surely must be nearby, though the fact that he didn't hear it—or the Harriers that ought to be providing cover—wasn't a big morale booster.

The second transmission also went unanswered, as did the third. Garcia bent to the ground, intending to scoop out a hole for his helmet so he could hide it. But after one tentative shovel, he realized there was no way he was going to get the parachute out of the tree; that was more of a billboard than the helmet would ever be. Carefully, he placed it shield down so there would be no reflection off the visor, as unlikely as that would be through the trees. Then he made another broadcast.

Nothing.

He couldn't spend the rest of his life waiting for the sound of rotors in the distance. Sooner or later, the people with the missiles were going to come looking for him. Garcia guessed that his plane had crashed on the other side of the mountain; it would be quite a while before anyone on the ground reached it, much less found him. But it was hard to quantify how safe that might make him.

The farm he had seen while descending was probably a mile away, at most. If they had a phone there, he could call for help.

Of course, if they were rebel sympathizers, they might use the phone, too. Assuming they thought he was worth keeping alive.

Not every Cuban was a rebel, Garcia reminded himself. In fact, most weren't. The people he had met in the small town yesterday had been extremely friendly, and Maria had told him that only a very, very small portion of the population opposed the present government. Most people liked Americans.

On the other hand, Hill had told them that as a general rule, the farther from Havana, the less support the interim government had. If you go down, he warned, always assume the locals are hostile until proven otherwise.

As he debated with himself, he realized the shadows were falling across the forest edge at the base of the mountain. There was no sense staying here; even if the helicopter came to look for him, it couldn't land. Twirling a rescue line through the trees would be ludicrous. The field he'd seen was the best place for a pickup; he'd best survey it.

Garcia looked up at the curled mass of fabric in the branches overhead. Thanking it for saving his butt, he began walking in the direction of the farm.

A few hundred yards down the hill, he found a stream. Garcia knelt, cupping his hands for a drink of water. As he crouched forward, he heard something rustling behind him. Garcia dove to the ground, fumbling for the service Beretta in his holster.

A guerrilla could have fired a full chip, reloaded, and emptied a second before he would have been able to get off a single shot.

But it wasn't a guerrilla. As he rose to his feet, Garcia realized it was nothing more than the wind.

No way he could sit out here all night. His mind was already making enemies out of the shadows.

Garcia tried another fruitless transmission, then crossed the stream toward a ramshackle fence that marked the edge of the field. He kept his gun in his hand as he walked through the thinning trees. No more dumb-shit moves, he told himself.

Getting his tail waxed by the guerrilla missile probably qualified as the dumbest dumb-shit move of all time. He could practically see Bighead shaking his head. Oh sure, they told you there's no air-to-air defenses. You believed that? Let me sell you a bridge, kid.

Mr. Hot Shit Pilot, Mr. Top of My Flight School Class, Mr. I Saved the President Himself—wanked by a goddamn shoulder-fired bottle rocket. Talic had been right to drop him from the Pegasus team.

Out of nowhere a scene from his teenage years hit him. Garcia was sixteen or seventeen, just learning to drive, and he'd creased a panel on the family car by getting too close to a guardrail. Confronting his father, he felt an angry, guilty tear just starting to form behind his eye.

And his father said, in a very firm but not threatening voice, "There's no sense feeling sorry for yourself. Tell me how you're going to fix it. That's what you should do."

At the time, the attitude surprised him—his father was a ranter, not the calm, pensive type. But the moment had had tremendous impact, and it encouraged Garcia now, made him stop beating his head with his mistakes and resolve to push on. He wasn't going to worry about which way his luck was running; he was going to do something about it. He wasn't defenseless—he had both his service pistol and the small gun that Hill had given him. He had his survival knife, the radio, and—maybe as important as all the rest—a small stash of pin money.

And good looks. Maybe he could charm some pretty *señorita* into helping him.

He laughed, and laughing gave him even more confidence. And with confidence came a plan.

The best thing to do was to go directly to the house that went with this farm. He would ask to use the telephone. If they let him, that was great. He'd be their best friend for life.

If they hesitated, he'd pull the gun.

Of course, it would help if he knew who the hell to call. But that would take care of itself.

Hey, worst-case scenario, he thought as he began trudging toward the wooden fence, he could call Cherry Point. Wouldn't that be a pisser?

The field had been plowed within the past few weeks, and smelled of fertilizer. Garcia walked along the edge, following both the fence and the overhead wire. Twice he stopped and tried broadcasting his distress signal, without result.

Walking, he kept his footfall as light as possible—not so he wouldn't be heard, but rather so he could hear. His ears strained for the sound of a helicopter, and he hoped at any moment for the familiar whoosh of Harriers streaking overhead.

He listened for other noises as well, like those that would be made by the pickup trucks he'd seen searching for Ferguson.

The fence came up to a dirt road whose clay surface was a bright red. Garcia walked in the grass alongside it, trying his best to keep from making any tracks. A squat shadow stood against the hillside a few hundred yards away. It was dark, with no lights inside, and when he was close enough to be sure it was the house, he had a fleeting hope that it might be temporarily unoccupied—but with a working telephone. As he got closer, though, he spotted a flickering shadow inside.

"We push on, right, Dad?" he said, as if his father were trudging along with him, encouraging him, lending him courage. He hid the radio in a small clump of grass near the road, figuring he could retrieve it if necessary. Tucking his service pistol into the top of his boot, he pulled the baggy pants leg down to conceal it, more or less. Then he took the Vzor and double-checked to make sure it was loaded. The gun fit snugly in his hand, which he put in a pocket in the side of the jumpsuit. Walking toward the cabin door, he stuck his other hand in his pocket as well, figuring it might look more natural: He was just a regular Joe who'd fallen out of the sky in the Cuban mountains; must happen all the time around here, no?

A middle-aged woman in a plain cotton dress opened the door. She was holding a hurricane lantern in her hand.

"*Buenas tardes,*" he said. "*¿Puedo usar el teléfono?*"

"*¿Qué?*"

"*El teléfono.* May I use your telephone?"

"We do not have a telephone," said the woman in

231

English, holding the lantern up to look at him. "Humberto!" she called. "*¡Ven acá!*"

"You speak English?"

"Who are you?" asked the large man who appeared behind her. His English was heavily accented, but clear enough. "What do you want?"

"Excuse me, I'm sorry for bothering you," said Garcia, firmly gripping the pistol but keeping it in his pocket. "I wonder if I could use your telephone."

"Why?"

Garcia held off pulling the pistol out. Once it was out there was no turning back; he'd probably end up having to use it. He decided to flash it only if his plea for help was absolutely refused.

"I have had difficulty with my airplane," he said, speaking far more slowly than necessary. "I have to phone my superiors."

"Is it you who caused our power to go off?" asked the woman.

"I don't know. Maybe the guerrillas did. We didn't bomb a power station or anything."

"And who did you bomb?" demanded the man.

"Please, let me use your phone."

"And will you shoot us with your gun if we refuse?" asked the woman indignantly. "I see it in your pocket."

He pulled it out, feeling slightly silly, even embarrassed. "I don't want to hurt you, honest."

"We have no phone," said the man. "This is Cuba, not Miami."

Garcia was unsure whether to believe them or not. Before he could say anything else, the pair began speaking together in Spanish so rapid and accented that he could understand only the gist.

What he could figure out, at least, sounded positive—he was an American, and the least they could do was give him something to eat.

It was the stuff he couldn't figure out that troubled him.

"I would be very grateful for your help," said Garcia. "I'm sorry about this gun."

"Then put it away," said the woman. "Or we will not help you."

"How do I know there isn't someone waiting inside to hit me over the head when I come in?"

The man laughed. He pushed the door open, then took the lantern from his wife's hand and shone it around the sparsely furnished room.

"There's no one here," he told him. "We are not sympathizers. Follow me and I will show you the rest of the house, if you wish. You might as well come in, since you've caused us so much problems already, wrecking our electricity."

"How come you speak English?" said Garcia, still holding his ground.

"Do you think Cubans are like Americans, who can afford not to educate themselves?" answered the woman. "How come you speak Spanish?"

"I didn't mean to insult you. I meant, did you live in America?"

"Do we look as if we did?" asked the woman in Spanish. "Do you think our other home is a mansion on the beach? Are you putting away the gun or not?"

Garcia slipped it into his pocket. He, too, spoke in Spanish. "I'm sorry if it made you nervous."

"And if a Cuban knocked on your door in America in the middle of the night, how would you react?" asked the man. "Would you be nervous?"

"I would welcome him inside," said Garcia. "My parents are from Cuba."

His answer seemed to confirm something the man had thought, and he nodded tentatively. It was only then that Garcia decided he was safe.

When he had taken his second step into the room, a powerful arm gripped him around the back. The shock made him reach again for the gun. But it was only the woman, pulling him along to the kitchen. Garcia was given a seat at the head of an ancient farm table, whose painted enamel top was worn clear to the metal.

"I guess I'm lucky you don't have an electric stove," he told them as the woman busied herself with the plates and pots.

"An electric stove," said the man, as if the item were a pot of gold. "Where do you live in Miami?"

"Not everybody in America lives in Miami," Garcia told him. "My family lives in New York. My parents moved there after they escaped."

"How did they leave the island?"

"In a boat."

"Well, I wouldn't have thought they flapped their arms," chided the man.

Between gulps of beans and rice, Garcia told them the story of his parents' escape and arrival in America. Both the man and woman listened intently, nodding and asking questions. Garcia had to admit that he did not know the specific answers to most of the questions about his parents' time in Cuba; it was not something they had spoken of.

He devoured two bowls of food before either of them began to eat. Struck by how friendly they were toward him, he asked what they did. The wife had been a schoolteacher; the husband was still a farmer.

Their son had tried to escape to America many years before. He had not been heard from; they believed that he had drowned.

"I'm sorry," said Garcia.

"Don't be glum," said the man. "There is always hope."

They weren't lying about there being no phone in the house. After some discussion, the man offered to take him to a friend's house in a town several miles away. There was a phone in a store nearby, and the friend knew the owner quite well. They believed he would be sympathetic toward an American.

"You're being so kind to me, and I don't even know your names."

"Humberto Remírez," said the man, laughing as he pointed to himself. "And my wife, Dalia."

"I'll make sure you get a reward," Garcia told them. "I'll ask that you get one, at least."

"We don't want a reward," said Mrs. Remírez.

"Getting our electricity back would be nice," replied Mr. Remírez. "That would be more than enough."

Mr. Remírez was pulling on his boots when there was a knock on the door. Before he knew what was happening, Mrs. Remírez was pushing Garcia into a closet.

"Be quiet," she said.

Inside the closet, he listened as the couple went together and opened the front door. He felt a burst of relief when he heard Mrs. Remírez greet one of the callers as the chief of police; obviously Colonel Hill had alerted the authorities to look for him.

But as he reached for the knob, he realized something was wrong. They were arguing. Mr. Remírez's voice quickly rose above the others. He had seen no one, he expected no one. Even if he had, he would not turn them over to a Communist bastard.

There was more commotion. The police chief said he had a dozen men with him and a dozen more on the way. They would burn down the house.

"Go ahead," said Mrs. Remírez in her ever-defiant Spanish. "Take this lantern and start the fire."

"Very well. José—"

"No!" shouted Garcia, opening the closet door. He took a quick step into the kitchen, where he was met by four young men in green rebel uniforms pointing

AK-47s at his chest. "Leave these people alone. I forced them at gunpoint to help me. I told them I would kill them if they didn't hide me."

"You should have escaped through the window," hissed Mrs. Remírez when he was pushed into the front room.

"What are you saying?" demanded the police chief. Apparently he spoke very little English.

"She called me a bastard," said Garcia in Spanish.

Before he could say anything else, one of the guerrillas hit him in the side of the head with the butt end of his rifle. Garcia staggered to his left, then felt another blow take him from the side. He stumbled forward, caught by the police chief. He was thrown to the ground and handcuffed.

The blows made him woozy. He felt himself being searched roughly, then being dragged through the house. Outside, he was lifted into the back of a pickup truck. Curling against the side of the bed, he wedged his foot against the wheel well as the truck started forward. His teeth jangled in his mouth, and he felt blood seeping from his tongue as the vehicle sped up a dirt road. Every so often, one of the two men in the back with him poked his face with his gun, whether to make sure he was still alive or to remind him that he could soon be dead, it was impossible to tell.

Havana. 7 P.M.

Scotty glanced at his watch. The hard plastic seat in the upstairs waiting room of the Havana Police Detective Bureau had worn a wedge across his butt, and was now working on his spine. He'd been sitting here for nearly an hour, waiting to talk to one of the detectives in charge of the Letra case. Several times he'd thought of blowing the whole thing off, but decided that since the detective was probably playing head games with him, leaving would just be giving in.

Besides, he didn't have anything better to do for the moment.

Municipal bus stations had more charm than the twenty-by-ten-foot room with its narrow rows of bright red chairs and well-scuffed tiles. It was the kind of place that made you want to smoke; the ribbed, gray-washed cinder-block walls sucked the life out of the dim overhead incandescents, and the place smelled vaguely of vomit and Lysol. A seventies-era television sat on the top of a particle-wood desk at the front of the room; mercifully, it didn't seem to work.

At least he had the room to himself. Downstairs, besides the usual collection of police officers and petty thieves, the halls and public areas were teeming with members of the media. Neither MININT nor the broadcast ministry would issue a statement, further stoking the frenzy over the government official's death. The street outside was lined with satellite dishes and long television vans.

Most, if not all, belonged to American news organizations. Cuba was a helluva place to be assigned, even on the few days of the month when there was actual news to report.

There were enough bureaucrats and officials involved in the investigation for the rumors to assume truly creative proportions; worming his way through the crowd outside, Scotty had heard one newscaster say breathlessly into a microphone that the minister had been planning to abscond to Spain with a million dollars in a briefcase when a janitor stopped him in his hallway.

He didn't feel obligated to set the man straight. Nor was he necessarily inclined to do the same for the police if they didn't know why Letra had committed suicide.

The door to the detective's office opened, revealing a short man with a round, almost boyish face. He was dressed in a light tan suit; though he must have been wearing it for hours, it looked immaculate.

"*Señor* McPherson, yes?"

"That's right. Gomez?"

"Diego, please."

Scotty followed him into his office. This was marginally better appointed than the waiting room, with a row of bookshelves along one wall but no television. The chair behind his desk was one of the hideously uncomfortable red things that filled the waiting area; there was no visitor's chair.

"Excuse me for keeping you waiting so long, *Señor* McPherson."

"Scotty."

Gomez smiled indulgently. "Are you hungry? Would you like something to eat?"

"No, thank you."

"Pizza? The Brooklyn Shop has very good pies."

"No, that's okay."

"You don't mind if I order one, *Señor* McPherson?"

"Of course not."

Gomez slid into his chair and punched the number on his phone—apparently he knew it by heart. His rapid-fire, slangy Spanish jangled in Scotty's ear only because he had used a seemingly native American English to speak to him.

"Bring in a chair from outside, *Señor* McPherson," the detective offered when he got off the phone.

"That's okay. I've been sitting too long."

Gomez nodded solemnly. Scotty guessed that he might be a holdover from the regime, promoted because of his ability. There was an unmistakable air of professionalism about him, and if he had not been a member of the secret police, nothing would bar him from holding a job in the reconstructed department.

"So, *Señor* McPherson. Why is the American ambassador interested in the death of the minister?"

"The ambassador is interested in all facets of the Cuban government."

"But the criminal investigation?"

"You suspect foul play?"

Again, the paternalistic smile. "We have a good idea of the circumstances of the death. Perhaps you wish to see photos of the crime scene."

"Sure."

Gomez held his stare for a second before reaching for a manila folder on his desk.

"The photos were a little wet when they were given to me," said the detective. "That was some hours ago, but they still stick together."

"I'll be careful," said Scotty, opening the folder.

Letra had blown his brains out with a Beretta nine-millimeter pistol. It was a neat job, as these things went. Expiring, the body had stayed in the desk chair, which confined the blood on the floor to a relatively small pool. Of course, the bookcase and wall behind the chair were a speckled mess, but the antique, finely wrought desk was spotless.

"You have seen things like this before, I imagine."

"A few times," Scotty told him, handing the photos back.

"What precisely is it you do for the ambassador, *Señor*?"

"I'm an adviser. I do a little bit of everything. Kind of like a handyman."

"You are with the CIA?"

"I'm an adviser."

The detective nodded as if the word had great meaning. "And your interest here? Is there something specific?"

Scotty shrugged. "You know the old poem, 'No man is an island.'"

"I do not hear a bell tolling, Mr. McPherson."

Now it was Scotty's turn to nod. "We heard vague rumors. Was there a suicide note?"

"There was."

"What did it say?"

"You can read it for yourself, if you like."

The detective retrieved another folder. In it, Scotty found a piece of paper with blue ink, the words written in a precise hand.

"This is the real note," said Scotty.

"You are surprised?"

"Well, I thought it would be a copy, or in plastic."

"That is the way the FBI advises?" Gomez gave his head ever so slight a shake and tapped his spread fingers almost imperceptibly on the desk. "There were no other prints except those of the minister."

Scotty had already begun reading the text. The note was brief:

Maria—
   It would be difficult for me to explain the vast journey that has brought me to this empty place. I hope that, by this ending, I may prevent you further suffering. Perhaps not, but it seems the only chance. Remember that I love you, and my beloved country, free at last. Give my best to your mother.

Papa

"There are no real mysteries here, are there, *Señor*?" said the detective. "Except for the most basic."

Scotty slid the folder back on the desk. "And what's the answer to that?"

"A lover?"

"I like you, Detective. You have a great sense of humor."

"I understand you were at *Señorita* Letra's place of business when she got the news."

"Shortly afterward," Scotty said.

"How did she look to you?"

"Distressed."

"She and her father were particularly close?"

"I really wouldn't know."

"Not at all? But didn't you see the minister this morning?"

"As a matter of fact, I did."

"Why?"

"It was a personal matter."

"Having to do with your role as a handyman? Were you fixing the doorknob, perhaps?"

"Doorknobs seemed to work fairly well."

"And his daughter was involved?"

"It turned out to be a misunderstanding."

"I see. Was that the ambassador's opinion?"

"As far as I know, the ambassador doesn't have an opinion. Probably won't have one, one way or another. Except that the death of a prominent man is always a tragedy, no matter what the circumstances."

Gomez finally permitted himself a frown.

"You know, *Señor* Gomez—Diego—standing outside, you hear a lot of different things. One of the rumors was that your minister had stolen money from the government."

Gomez waved his hand dismissively, leaning back in the plastic chair.

"Another was that the minister was connected with M-26."

"I had not heard that, but I doubt it's true."

"Because he was involved with a right-wing movement?"

"Which movement would that be?"

"That's what I was wondering."

"There are none that I know of, *Señor,* and I would know of them."

"Are you sure?"

"Is that what you are thinking, Mr. McPherson? That Cubans cannot be trusted? Do you think that when we say we love our country, it is a lie? Do you believe that we are either country bumpkins, boobs with shit on our boots, or else evil blackguards, up to no good, our sympathies turned this way and that for the sake of a ten-dollar bill?"

There was a knock on the door; the detective's pizza had arrived.

"I have no doubt that your ambassador would invoke diplomatic immunity if I attempted to hold you for questioning."

Scotty shrugged. "We can find out if you want."

"That won't be necessary. If I thought you knew anything of value, I would have had you arrested long ago." He got up from the chair. As Scotty pulled open the door, the detective stopped him. "The next time you come into a police station, please leave your guns at the desk. All three of them."

"I'll try to remember."

"Are you sure you don't want any pizza?"

"Nah. Makes my stomach growl in the middle of the night."

From the police station he went back to the embassy to write up a brief report. Steele would be impressed, which would make it easier when he spent the following day—and maybe beyond—in the eastern provinces, looking for de Souza.

He mentioned the suicide note in his brief report, but not what it referred to. Some word of it might leak from one of the staff—Scotty was thinking specifically of the snake Tito Porta—and what would the sense of that be?

He also left himself out. And the pilot. Kid owed him a big-time favor.

"Yo, Scott?"

Scotty snapped around, startled. "Jeez, James, you scared the piss out of me. Don't you knock?"

"I did."

"Yeah, all right. What do you want?"

"Boss wants you right away."

"I was on my way up to see him anyway." Scotty gathered the white legal pad he'd jotted his notes for the briefing on. "I got the whole dope on Letra."

"Letra?"

"The broadcast minister killed himself. Don't you watch the news?"

"No, sir."

"Not going to get your medal of honor that way. This isn't about Letra?" he added as they started down the hallway.

"No. It's a pilot named Garcia."

"Aw, fuck," he said.

"You know about it?"

"More or less."

"He was supposed to be a better pilot."

Scotty grabbed his shoulder. "What do you mean, 'he was supposed to be a better pilot'?"

"He got shot down a few hours ago. I thought you said you knew all about it."

Sierra Maestra. 11 P.M.

Considering that a few hours before he was trying to blow them up, the rebels didn't treat Garcia all that badly. Aside from the blows at the farmhouse, and some rough treatment as he was pulled out of the back of the pickup, the guards handled him almost gingerly.

After the initial surprise, Garcia realized this was probably because he was valuable property—a hostage who could be used to demonstrate the sheer righteousness of the guerrillas' cause and methods. Slumped in a small wooden chair in the corner of the dank room where he had been placed, Garcia considered how best to destroy that image. He expected that they would set up a video camera, and a soft-spoken rebel would ask questions off camera. He would refuse to answer, of course; they would more or less be counting on that.

At some point, they would hit him, being careful to avoid his face. They would use just enough force to get him to cooperate.

His job was to make them lose their control. If he could show the world a black eye, then he would have stolen their victory.

Every second of his Marine Corps training was filtering through his head. Not just the lectures on dealing with captors, either. His first days of slogging through the mud and rain, running in full gear so long and hard that his lungs nearly exploded— the memory of those physical limits came to him now and encouraged him.

Make it through this, his drill instructors had promised, and you can make it through anything.

Garcia knew he could withstand the beatings, at least to the point that they began to inflict visible damage. He wasn't sure he could make it through the isolation, though. He sat in the dark, unlit room for hours, handcuffed to the chair rails. The dim hall light gave him just enough illumination to see the cement floor; he studied it carefully, memorizing the imperfections.

He tried hard to keep his thoughts concentrated on the physical things in front of him. Anything else would weaken him. Even the memories of basic training might kick up enough nostalgia to soften him. The enemy would exploit any vulnerability.

Most of all, he did not want to fall asleep. If he fell

asleep, they might take him by surprise. Staying awake became his first battle; in the dark of the room, fatigue grew heavy on him. He twisted his neck around, trying to keep it from kinking. And he did what he could to ignore the growing pressure in his bladder.

He had to be tough. He was a marine. He was Lieutenant Edward Garcia, son of Roberto and Estela.

To get more from him, they would have to grind him down. Each blow they landed would be a victory.

But inevitably the doubts crept in, circling like wolves around a dying fire. He began to long for his captors to appear, even if all they wanted to do was torture him. At least that was something he could react to, instead of the loose vagueness of unquantified fear.

By the time the door finally opened, Garcia had lost all sense of time, and was drifting toward sleep. The light stabbed his eyes and brought him back; he looked up with an expression that was half scowl, half squint.

"So they are sending boys against us now? American boys."

The light was so strong he couldn't see anything more than shadows before him. But what caught him off guard was the fact that the clipped Spanish words came from a woman.

"Untie him and get him something to eat. Then bring him to me. Take care that he is unharmed," said the woman, who vanished even before the men with her jumped to obey her orders.

"You are a damn lucky pig, gringo," said the man who yanked at his wrists to unlock the handcuffs. "Any of a dozen men would chop your head off. It would be a pleasure."

"I would strangle you with my hands," said another. They were speaking Spanish, and did not seem to realize Garcia could understand them. The pilot immediately decided to keep that a secret—a first victory in what would be a long war, one he would by all odds lose.

The men grumbled among themselves whether they ought to just kill him anyway. There seemed to be some resentment against the woman who had commanded he be fed, though there was no question that she was in charge.

Garcia felt better now, if only because he was at least moving. His boots had been taken from him, and the combed concrete floor of the underground bunker stung his feet. He knew he was at least two stories below ground. It hadn't been possible to get a good view of the building from the outside. There wasn't all that much to see now, either—the facility was obviously large, with several intersecting hallways, dozens of rooms and stairways that seemed to lead down as well as up. But his captors did not like his eyes wandering, and finally one took his head and forcefully pointed it toward the ground.

The four men who were escorting him were younger than he was, in their early to mid teens. Marching to the end of the corridor, they took him down a flight of stairs, then across a short distance of a long hallway to a medium-size room with two large tables, obviously a cafeteria. Like the other places he had seen, it had a concrete floor and whitewashed walls. There was no decoration, or even color.

"I wonder if I could use a bathroom," he said in very deliberate English when one of the guerrillas pointed at a chair.

"Bath?" repeated the man.

"I have to take a leak. Pee?"

The man asked him in Spanish whether he had to take a piss, but Garcia feigned not to understand.

Eventually they got the idea, and he was led to a small room back off the hallway.

It looked to him as if it had been a janitor's closet. There was a sink but no urinal. A putrid odor permeated the walls, and the guard pointed at a pail in the corner.

By now, Garcia would have pissed on the bare floor. As he let loose into the bucket, he realized that he had learned an important lesson. He must eat and drink sparingly, lest his captors use bathroom privileges as a weapon.

He was still fairly full from his meal at the farmhouse, but even if he had been starved it would have been easy to resist the shriveled pieces of chicken that were waiting on the table when he returned. There were no knives and forks; Garcia picked up a hunk of meat and chewed it slowly. Noticing that one of the guards was eyeing the food jealously, he pushed the plate in his direction; the man flushed and turned around abruptly.

Dried out and stringy, it tasted more like a rumor of chicken than the real thing. Belatedly, Garcia wondered if the food had been drugged.

Garcia finished the piece of chicken. There were still three more pieces, but he pushed the plate away, then looked up at his captors, shrugging to indicate that he was done. Frowning, they took him back to the stairs, then down another level.

He filed away the few details of the place that made an impression—the smooth grayness of the walls, the creak of the peeling black metal fire doors at the bottom of the stairs, the wide concrete floors. The light was supplied by overhead bulbs protected by metal screens; every so often, the lights flickered briefly, though not enough to activate the yellow bulbs boxed with emergency batteries next to them.

They descended another set of stairs, wider than the first, and now the drab gray gave way to bright blue paint. The lighting on this lower level was fluorescent, and if not quite bright, certainly more ample than above. The dank smell was less pronounced, and there were posters on the wall, sixties-era artifacts that proclaimed, in Cuban Spanish, the need for struggle and sacrifice that would lead, inevitably, to victory.

Nor was the hallway mostly empty like the others—people were scurrying back and forth through open doorways, carrying yellow pads and folders beneath their arms, moving with the determined gait of dedicated office workers; Garcia might have been passing through the lower-level offices of a Fortune 500 company. The bare concrete beneath his feet had been replaced by indoor-outdoor carpeting, and when he was ushered through a doorway at the end of the hall it changed again, this time to an elegant, if worn, Persian rug. A young man dressed in fatigues and a flak vest met them inside; he told them to wait, banged on a black metal door, and then disappeared inside. He reemerged quickly, waving them in.

Sitting at the desk in the far end of the room was the woman who had come to his cell earlier. An old black woman filled an armchair nearby, her flowing print dress a sharp contrast to the black dungarees and T-shirt worn by the younger woman.

The light here, far better than in his cell, made it clear how beautiful the woman at the desk was. With her short curled hair and her sharp though tired eyes, she possessed something innately attractive.

The woman waved her hand and dismissed his guards.

"Sit," she told him in English.

"Where?"

"There is a chair behind you."

Garcia reached back and pulled the metal chair

toward the desk. He considered lunging at her but decided either she or the other woman must have a weapon trained on him.

"What is your name?" Her voice was calm and even, as if he were here for a job interview.

"Edward Garcia."

"You are an American?"

"Yes."

"A member of the military."

"I'm a volunteer."

Her lips parted for a sardonic laugh. Lightning danced in the black holes of her eyes.

"Oh, yes, I am sure. A man comes to you and orders you to volunteer. Our government employs a similar system. Do you think, Edward Garcia, that we are completely ignorant here?" She pushed her chair and rose from the desk. "Do you know who I am?"

Garcia shook his head.

"My name is Carla de Souza. I am the daughter of *El Comandante* Fidel Castro, the father of our country. I am the head of the Revolution. *¿Comprendes?*"

Garcia tried not to alter his expression.

"Oh yes, I know you speak Spanish. Do you think we would not gather information on you? Do you think that the day you stepped foot in Cuba, we did not begin a dossier? We have computers, too. I have hands and ears all over this island, to gather information when I request it. You have no secrets from me."

"If you know so much already," said Garcia, "you can let me go."

"Oh, we will have uses for you. Perhaps we should use you as a training exercise. How would it feel to be hunted through the countryside? Would you like to feel that? I have felt it, Eddie. It isn't pleasant."

"You can torture me, but I won't give you anything useful."

She folded her arms in front of her chest. Garcia thought she was contemplating something; if so, she gave none of it away, her eyes studying his face, measuring his body. Her own was lithe; even its simple movements as she paced before him betrayed grace and a special strength. But when she spoke to him again her voice betrayed nothing but venom.

"You are lucky, pilot, that I have use of you, or you would already be dying a slow death. Do not do anything to make me change my plans for you. Paco!"

The door to the office opened and her flak-jacketed assistant appeared.

"Take him back to his cell. Make sure he is comfortable. For now."

Carla remained at the desk, silent, brooding, long after the pilot had left. It was set now; the future would move ahead. She glanced upward and saw the old witch studying her from across the room.

"You stare at me with those leopard eyes, Zora. I will not change my plans. It is the only way."

Zora made a light sound with her lips. It could not quite be called a sigh, but Carla recognized it as a sound of exasperation.

"To negotiate with the earthworms is to admit that they have won," said the old woman. Her enormous body lay slumped and motionless in the chair, but her eyes darted with emotion. "It is the same as surrender. The struggle is an eternal one; it cannot be given away with a handshake."

"It will not be."

"They will not hold elections."

"They will."

"And how could you trust the results?"

This was all familiar territory—Carla had come to

her conclusions nearly six months before, and discussed the implications in great detail with Zora. Still, and despite her increasing irritation, she felt a need to try once more to win the old woman to her side.

"If what you say is true," said Carla, "then the momentum of history is on our side. Our most important goal will be to survive. With the party legitimized by a constitution, we will take the fight to a higher plane."

"The saints will not allow you to surrender."

"Which saints are those, Zora? Your prayer-card gods?" Carla bit back her rage; she had almost mentioned the card she had found in Romano's lair. She was not ready to, not quite yet. For all her anger, it was a sadness she did not yet want to drink.

"Do not denigrate what you do not understand. The forces at work here are eternal."

"No, old woman, no superstitions tonight. I have too much to do."

Zora rose slowly from the chair. Despite her age, despite the trembling that took hold of her hands as she raised them, she was still an imposing presence. While Carla did not fear anyone, she came closest to fearing Zora.

"It is too late," said Zora when she reached her feet.

"What is too late?" Carla demanded. "The hour? The Revolution?"

Silently, the old woman began walking to the door. Her thick legs moved very slowly even at the best times; now she moved as stiffly as a glacier pushing itself uphill.

"I am going ahead with my plans," Carla said. She could feel her resolution beginning to slip as she spoke; her lip literally quivered. This caused her to explode in anger, as much at herself as at her friend. "Get out! Get out of my sight! Take yourself and your superstitions, and confine them to your room. Do you hear me? Out! Out!"

Zora, giving no sign that she had heard, left the room.

When she was gone, Carla went to the desk and pounded her fist on it so hard she dented the thin metal. She stood looking at the indentation, wondering what she had become.

"Zora," she said softly, as if the old woman were still with her. "Come, I apologize. Let us be friends. I have learned so much from you. Despite everything—despite your betrayal, I do love you."

She spun around in the empty room, her motion a mocking satire of the pirouettes she had spent her youth perfecting. The air ran out of her; she sank into the upholstered chair.

Her course was set. No one, not even her beloved Zora, could alter that. She would save her father's revolution; she had sworn to do so, she had fought to do so, she would do so.

But there was a vast distance left to go. And there was much evil left in the way. The contents of the bunker were proof of that.

Chapter Seven

Thursday, July 24
Havana. 4 A.M.

There were dreams. They were not unpleasant. Tangled glimpses floated up from the distorted shards of memory—Esma and Scotty walking through Old Havana, Esma laughing on the beach, Scotty buying her an ice-cream cone. The sum total of his life drifted in from the vast ocean, leaving pieces of seaweed limp on the rounded rocks.

"Yo, Scott. Hey, man, ambassador needs you. Yo."

Scotty shook himself awake with a jerk, his first instinct to grab for the Glock at his thigh.

"What are you going to do, shoot me?" Cortland James asked. The ambassador's aide stood over the couch, one hand on his hip, the other cradled around a large cup of coffee.

While James obviously hadn't taken the nap Steele had suggested, he looked none the worse for it. Still dressed immaculately in his brown suit, his face was unwrinkled and his eyes wide open as always. The only visible concession to fatigue was the absence of a tie around his neck. His collar remained buttoned, straining the flesh beneath it.

Scotty pulled himself up on the couch and looked at his watch. He'd been asleep for a little over two hours. "Jesus, James, what are you doing, popping speed so you can bet on the European horses again?"

The young aide's brown face turned a shade of purple. "What do you mean?"

"I always wondered how you could pull those all-nighters at the Trump's roulette wheel and look like a business executive the next day, that's all." Scotty reached down to fish for his shoes. Something in his back creaked. When he stood, James was still staring at him. "Relax. I won't tell anybody you're a druggie. You'll still be a general before you're thirty."

James—who Scotty knew never even took aspirin—marched angrily out of the ambassador's waiting room toward the conference room. Scotty rubbed his eyes and went in the opposite direction to the secretaries' suite, knowing that Marge or someone else had put up a fresh pot of coffee. By the time he got to the conference room, the rest of the ambassador's situation staff had gathered.

"I hope you're all rested," said Steele. The ambassador also seemed not to have taken a nap in the two-plus hours since the last session broke up, but unlike his young aide, he bore the evidence emphatically. His voice was hoarse and his eyes red; his Georgetown University T-shirt—his son's alma mater—had a coffee stain near the collar.

"We have the latest laser-radar, as well as the afternoon's photo shoot. The U-2 overflight has been scheduled for daybreak. We're going to decide on priorities for it, though frankly I'm inclined to tell them to shoot the whole eastern end of the island."

Scotty, whose seat was next to Steele and opposite

James, pulled the laser images from their thick folder and slid the large stereoscopic viewer over the panels to examine them. The viewer enabled the images to be rendered in 3-D without the aid of a computer; the mountain literally loomed before his eyes as he pressed his face into the glass.

As impressive as the images were, their usefulness was severely limited. One of the KH-15 satellites that produced them—the new satellites worked in pairs, vectoring laser rays from different angles— was a spare, operating from an extreme southern orbit. But even the original had never been intended to cover Cuba, and its path could be modified only slightly because of other priorities. The computers did their best to compensate, but the result was an image skewed toward a northern perspective; most of the valleys and even some of the mountainsides to the south and southwest were in shadow.

The images showed the destroyed ammo dump, which was still smoldering several hours after being hit. The wreckage of both Harriers had also been identified, though the second plane—Garcia's—was partly obscured by one of the shadows. They looked like twisted piles of Tinkertoys.

Guantánamo Naval Base sat empty and unused in the far right-hand corner of the large area image that oriented the series' location. Had it not been deeded back to the Cubans as a goodwill gesture a year and a half before, Scotty realized, the prospects of recovering Lieutenant Garcia would have been considerably better.

Then again, maybe not.

Fashona, who was filling in for the still-out-of-country CIA station chief, sat to Scotty's right. He concentrated on looking at the optical images, which were daylight photographs from an older KH satellite. Intended for strategic surveillance and also not in the best orbit to observe the Sierra Maestra

Mountains, they didn't even show Garcia's parachute.

The interim Cuban government, Porta reported as they examined the pictures, didn't feel strong enough to send anything less than a full division on a search—which would undoubtedly mean such an operation would be fruitless.

"The defense ministry has debriefed the first pilot," said Porta. He took his wire-rimmed glasses in his hand and began rubbing them with his shirtsleeve. "Mechanical failure led to the crash. The cause of the second crash is still unknown, but they have discounted missiles."

"That's absurd," said Scotty.

Porta shook his head. "Do you want me to report what they tell me, or what you believe?"

"You could have told them they were full of shit."

"And that would have gotten me where?"

"Further than we are now. Why the hell won't they just admit someone sold the rebels missiles?"

"There's no evidence."

"My ass."

"All right, we're all tired," said Steele. "Scotty, can you make out anything from the KH-15 photos?"

"Nothing new. The U-2 should run tracks around his Harrier, east to west. That should give us more than enough coverage. We'll find the parachute, at least. Or broken branches. A UAV at low altitude might be useful, too."

"I've already asked," said Steele. "There's a marine Pioneer aboard the Shreveport coming through the Canal. It's on the way."

"Oh, that'll help," said Scotty sarcastically. Pioneers were small, unmanned aircraft, or UAVs, that could be used to provide battlefield reconnaissance of highly dangerous areas. The Shreveport was a landing assault ship that might be immensely useful, not only because of the UAV but because it would come packed with marines. Unfortunately, it moved only a little faster than a glacier in winter; by the time it got close enough to launch the Pioneer it would be Labor Day.

"A prompt offer to negotiate would make the most sense," suggested Porta.

"Why the fuck would we do that?" Scotty asked.

"It will show M-26 good faith."

"What for?"

The curly ends of Porta's hair seemed to twist with the heat coming off his head. "Because we want our man back alive."

"The last thing we want to do is go whimpering to them. They'll assume we're in a weak position. We want them to think we're on their ass about this, and it's in their interest to give him up," said Scotty. "There's something going on inside M-26," he added, looking at the ambassador.

"In what way?" Steele asked.

"My thinking is that someone was trying to assassinate Carla de Souza when they blew up the Ave the other night. If that's so, there's a power struggle going on, and it will influence whatever deal they want to make. Assuming the kid's still alive." Scotty took a gulp of his coffee. He could tell Marge hadn't made this batch herself—too weak. "If he's in the hands of a splinter group, they'll be anxious to do a deal. They'll want to show they're influential."

"Splinter group," said Porta. "There is no such thing. De Souza controls the council, and the council controls the entire movement."

"MININT seems to think she blew up the club herself, Scott," said Fashona. "It fits with the attack on the ambassador."

"I don't buy that. She has no motive and didn't claim credit for it afterward. For either one."

"She rarely does."

"She doesn't make a secret of it, though. De Souza

assassinated two men from Havana immediately afterward, and at least one of them was connected to the bomb."

"The Ave bombing is irrelevant to this. Interpreting what M-26 does is like trying to read the stars," said Porta. "De Souza is in full control. We should offer to talk to her, and take it from there."

"Bullshit. What's with you lately, Porta? Your advice is lamer than usual. Maybe you should get the prescription on those glasses checked."

"Scott, that's enough," barked Steele. "We will not initiate contact with the guerrillas, nor will we deal with them on an official level. The second I talk to them, they'll claim the American government recognizes them."

"I'm not arguing for a policy change," said Scotty.

Fashona, stroking his beard, suggested that a special-ops unit be brought into Cuba "as a contingency." Porta had just started to say that the Cuban government would strongly object when one of the CIA technical specialists from the communications section—a telephone operator by any other name—rushed breathlessly into the room.

"Mr. Ambassador, sir, there's a phone call for you," said the man, who seemed to have run up the four stories from his basement lair.

"Who the hell is it?"

"It's a woman, and she says she's Carla de Souza."

Scotty felt his blood pressure jump. "Let me take it, General."

Steele momentarily ignored him. "Are you tracing?"

"We're attempting, sir. But you know the Cubans."

"Is it a crank?"

"We've checked the voice profile against the computer, sir. It seems authentic. At first I thought it was, you know, just a loony, so I flipped it into D channel and then I—"

"Even if she's using a device to confuse the trace," said Scotty, "she won't stay on indefinitely. If I talk to her, you can deny contact."

"Somebody ought to take the call," said Fashona. "Just for kicks."

"Let me do it." Scotty stood, as if it had already been decided that he would talk to her.

"Okay," said Steele. "Let's go into my office, Scott. You're not speaking for the ambassador. Emphasize that. Tape is rolling, right?"

The operator nodded, then ran to make sure he'd remembered to turn it on. Scotty walked inside, his mind narrowing. His hands suddenly felt cold, like ice.

The small light on the telephone flashed bright orange in the darkened room. Scotty pulled out the ambassador's chair and plunked down into it.

"Probably just a prank," he said, looking up at Steele. "I don't trust the Company computers."

The ambassador answered by pointing at the phone. Scotty leaned forward and picked it up.

"Hey there," he said in English. "Who's this?"

"I want the U.S. ambassador," said a woman's voice on the other end of the line. She was curt, spoke English with a Caribbean accent, and sounded wide awake. The connection was a bit tinny, but clear.

"The ambassador is out partying his ass off," said Scotty. "Who am I talking to?"

"You know who I am. Who are you?"

Scotty leaned back in the chair, glancing at Steele. He considered pushing the speaker-phone button but decided against it.

"This is Scott McPherson. I'm a friend."

"A friend of whom? I do not have time for these games. Get me the ambassador."

"I told you, he's out." Scotty shifted in the chair, made his voice sound more serious. "Talk to me."

She surprised him by answering right away. "There is an intersection precisely twelve kilometers from Playa las Coloradas on the highway to El Cobre. Turn left there and drive three kilometers, where you will get further instructions. Start from Playa las Coloradas at noon today, and you will have your pilot unharmed. Earlier or later, and you will have a corpse. One man, no more. Cancel the U-2 flight."

She hung up before Scotty could react.

Steele watched as confusion spread over McPherson's face. Slowly, the CIA agent put his hand over the mouthpiece of the phone.

"You better close the office door," he said.

The ambassador, not sure what he was up to, nonetheless did so, ignoring the questioning stares from the team members still assembled in the conference room. From across the room it appeared that McPherson was still listening to de Souza, but he put down the phone as soon as the door was closed.

"What's going on?"

"We get the pilot back alive if we go out to Playa las Coloradas and fetch him."

"No conditions?"

"Not that she said."

"Where is that? In the mountains?"

"Way down on the coast. Pretty far from where he was shot down."

"You think this is legitimate?"

"Oh yeah, definitely. That's what has me worried. She knew about the U-2 flight."

"The U-2 flight? How the hell could she know about that?"

Scotty nodded. "That's a good question. She

might have guessed. She might have found out from the Cubans."

"Porta wouldn't have told them, Scott."

Steele expected McPherson to disagree. But all he said was "Maybe they have a spy at Homestead."

"There's something here you're not telling me. Out with it."

"Nothing," said the agent. "I'm just surprised that she knew about the U-2, that's all."

Steele rubbed his chin and neck. There were times—about ten a day—when he wished he could just go out and grab some of these motherfuckers and strangle them.

Not a diplomatic solution, but a satisfying one.

Steele waved his aide out of his chair. "I know you don't like Porta. But he's not a fool. He wouldn't have told the Cubans anything I didn't want him to."

McPherson didn't answer.

"I'm going to have to tell Washington about this," Steele said, picking up the phone. "Scotty, round yourself up a helicopter and get out to Playa las Coloradas. Call me before you go—I'll give you a yea or a nay. This is completely unofficial, you understand? You do not represent the embassy or me."

"You want me to go?"

"Well, I can't. Send Fashona in here. I want to know how de Souza found out about the U-2. And James. But no one else gets told. Scott—"

The agent stopped and looked back at him with his haggard face. The traces of youth that had lingered in the corners of his eyes as recently as the other day had been crowded out by fatigue and something more exhausting.

"You're not still taking this all too personally, right? With this Ave connection?"

"I don't think so."

Unconvinced, Steele nodded anyway. He'd never

Jim DeFelice

been very good at playing father confessor, and he knew Scotty had never been much of a son.

M-26 Headquarters, Sierra Maestra. 6 A.M.

"You did not sleep too badly, I assume."

Garcia looked up from the floor in confusion. He had been locked in an empty cell after speaking with de Souza the night before, and fallen asleep on the concrete. A dim, yellowish light filtered in from the hall. A figure—he thought it must be the guerrilla leader herself—stood in the middle of the open doorway.

"You are still with us, are you not, Eddie?"

Garcia struggled to pull himself up. His body was cold and stiff; his head felt as if it had been submerged in a pail of water.

"I thought you would be more impressed if you spent the night as we sometimes do, not on a bed, not with a blanket. But then, you are a marine. This was nothing to you."

Angered at her sarcasm but still groggy, Garcia got to his feet. A pair of hands grabbed him from the back. De Souza—he could see her clearly now—laughed.

"Let him go. He will not harm me. We are going to have an understanding, Lieutenant Eddie and I. Come, Eddie, listen to me. If you are a good boy, you will be released. And then you will do a job for your government. You are quite valuable to them, you know. Unlike the other pilot. Him we found necessary to kill."

Garcia stepped forward in the cell, fury rising in his chest. Before he even realized what was going on, de Souza swung a submachine gun up from her side and put it against his chin. He was completely taken by surprise.

"Do not underestimate me, Lieutenant. At any

262

moment, I can crush you like an insect."

He stood there, the barrel of the gun in his face. He made the mistake of thinking of Ferguson, and felt himself weaken. De Souza shook her head, pity flickering briefly through her face, replaced once again by her haughty smile. "We will have to blindfold you, but it will not hurt." She gave her gun to one of the guards near him, then reached her hand to his arms, pulling forward. Her touch was soft and gentle. One of her men placed a hood over his head as he walked.

"Be gentle with the handcuffs," she ordered. "Leave his legs free. He understands that his life is in our hands. I want you to be comfortable, Eddie. You have much to do today."

Garcia was shaking, though he tried his best not to. He walked from the cell into the hallway, started along by her soft, almost sexual tug on his manacled arms. He wondered whether it made any sense to resist. The gun had been very, very real—he recognized it because it was a weapon also used by the Marine Corps. She had also said he was to be released.

In any event, he was surrounded by guards, handcuffed and blindfolded; there was nothing he could do.

They walked him up two flights of stairs, then placed him in an elevator. Part of this may have been to confuse him—Garcia had the sensation of rising and then falling again before the elevator finally came to a halt. Whether purposeful or not, it disoriented him almost to the point of making him dizzy.

Another short hallway, and then he heard doors creaking, large metal hinges straining. The warm morning air, humid, smelling a bit like rain, swirled across his hooded face.

Garcia was placed in a van between two large, ill-smelling men. As soon as the door was slammed shut, he put his head down toward his knees, nauseous.

He could not surrender so easily. If resistance was useless, still there must be something he could do to fight them. Trying to think of a way to measure the distance from his prison to wherever they were taking him, the pilot began counting as soon as the van moved. At 152, he realized this was useless; they were sure to double back and take turns to throw him off. Still, he counted because he could not think of any other way to resist.

His stomach turned over and over with the jolts of the van. He could close his eyes to the claustrophobic darkness of the hood but not his nose to the odor of sweat and pee. It threatened to overwhelm him.

Slowly and deliberately, he counted to himself. It was all he had. Struggling against other thoughts, struggling to keep his mind free, he counted.

Garcia reached the number 17,003 before the vehicle stopped. He strongly suspected they had doubled back at some point. He had felt the vehicle travel upward and then down again. Clearly they had not gone in a straight line. But he held the number in his mind as if it were the formula for making gold—17,003.

One of the men who had sat next to him pulled him roughly from the van. As Garcia tumbled out, his stomach revolted, forcing a bilious flow from his mouth that soaked not only the hood but his clothes. He squatted with his chained hands against the ground, retching as badly as he ever had in his life.

"Take the mask off him," commanded de Souza. "Clean him up. I need him now."

Two men pulled off his mask and helped him to his feet. Someone shoved a towel in his face; he took it and wiped himself up as best he could. Feeling empty and ashamed, Garcia stepped away from the puddle of vomit slowly. He dropped the towel on the ground and began following along as he was prodded through a narrow, rock-strewn path that had been cut into the stone of the hillside. They walked up about fifty steps, then took a ninety-degree turn and walked up twenty or thirty more. Though still queasy, Garcia felt his strength returning; by the time the guard in front of him held out his hand to stop, he was glad that he'd thrown up, glad to have caused the bastards at least some token discomfort.

De Souza, standing on a narrow plateau above, gestured for him to join her. He walked up slowly, wondering what in hell she had planned. They were about a third of the way up the southwestern side of a mountain, a thick canopy overhead; Garcia realized that the rough path had been constructed to afford maximum protection from prying overhead eyes.

It hadn't been built recently. There was thick moss on the stones and thick weeds between them. De Souza touched his arm lightly, steering him to the right. A series of boulders, as if deposited by a landslide, lay against the hillside. As he began to pick his way over some of the smaller rocks, he realized there was another path through the larger stones. His boots kicking up dust, he walked on toward the face of the mountain, which rose up sharply from this small clove. It wasn't until he was three feet away that he saw a diagonal opening sliced into the hillside, a small crevice invisible until you were right next to it.

He squeezed through, followed by de Souza and her men. The only clue that the narrow cave he entered wasn't real was the smoothness of the rock-strewn floor. The only light was the dim blue haze from the narrow opening behind him, and he put his hands up in front of him as he walked forward slowly, afraid he might walk into the wall. Finally he found another slit to his left and turned into it. His foot tripped an infrared beam at the bottom and the darkness that had been before him brightened into a shimmering blue fluorescent, projected from behind panels in the artificial walls.

"Keep going," de Souza commanded, and Garcia continued forward in the cave. It was fifty yards or more before his legs tripped another electronic eye and the wall to his right creaked open, unlocked. "Wait," she said, and three men sprang forward to push it back, revealing the edges of a large metal-and-concrete bunker.

"Come, Eddie," said de Souza, taking his arm and leading him with a light touch into the complex. "Come with me. You have a long day ahead, and already we are behind schedule."

The red and yellow paint on the railings that lined the nearby walls was old but unworn. A metallic smell hung in the air, and Garcia immediately thought of the hush house at Cherry Point.

There must be a hidden air force here, he thought, immediately calculating how best to play along until they left him alone in a cockpit, ready to fly the plane away or destroy the entire complex.

Then he saw the large block of metal perched on an island rising from the floor. A mechanical arm pointed up at the ceiling. His eyes focused first on the dark teeth in the tongue of the erector, and only after a few seconds did he realize that the black cylinder lying prostrate in the assembly below it was a rocket.

Across from the firing table were three large white tanks, the type that might be used in the States to hold liquid propane.

Or oxidizer and fuel for a missile.

"Take a very good look," de Souza told him. "Make sure that you are able to tell your ambassador everything that you see. You have studied history, haven't you, Eddie? Do you know about October 1962?"

"The Missile Crisis."

"Very good," she said. "You are the son of a worm, but at least you know some history. Do you know your family's history?"

The question surprised him so much that he turned from the missile.

"How much do you know about your father's life here?" de Souza asked. "Do you know anything?"

"My father and mother escaped Castro's repression."

"You forget that we have done research on you, Eddie. I know your grades, I know your family history, I even know your father Roberto's criminal record."

"What?"

"When you see him again, ask him about the man who fixed shoes. See what he tells you."

"What the hell are you talking about?"

"My father released his criminals to be America's problem. Ask your father when you see him again. The man he stole from. History, Eddie, it is very important. You must know it all."

Nearing Playa Las Coloradas. 11:35 A.M.

The helicopter was among the newest in Cuba, a shiny Sikorski that had everything but a working microwave oven—and that was on order.

As far as Scotty was concerned, it could just as well have been a rusted biplane with fabric wings and an open cockpit. He was an equal-opportunity hater of all things with wings, be they airliners, helicopters, or even birds.

He accepted the pilot's offer to sit in the front seat only because no matter where he sat, his stomach would whirl the second the engine did. He tightened his seat belt and did what he always did when he flew—silently cursed the Wright brothers and every arrogant son of a bitch who followed in their footsteps.

It didn't help that the pilot kept pointing out landmarks as they sped toward the mountains. The man spoke very little English, but Scotty couldn't make his Spanish sound lousy enough to get him to shut up. He was very proud of his helicopter, very proud of all sorts of things, including his two-year-old son, whose recent triumph at potty training he detailed in all its glory when the scenery got dull.

In the backpack tucked between his legs was an oversized radio transmitter that tied into the Defense Department's UHF TACSAT satellite communications system. He also had a small geo-locator device that was supposed to transmit his location via a different satellite back to the embassy basement every few minutes, as long as the batteries held out. Otherwise he was entirely on his own.

The fact that de Souza knew about the U-2 flight bothered the shit out of him, but he also realized it could very well have been a guess designed to make her look omnipotent. She was a master at that sort of thing, a woman who could have bluffed a Las Vegas dealer out of four kings while holding a pair.

If she was on the level about releasing the pilot, she was into some new territory. Carla de Souza had never given up anything for free before.

It might fit with her series of communiqués in the weeks before the bombing, which stated that M-26 was seeking "political legitimacy." Giving him away might let her demonstrate peaceful intent, especially if she was worried about a rival snatching him.

But it wasn't a public show; she gained no leverage with anyone, except the American mission.

But wouldn't it make better sense to hold him until the Americans made an attempt at rescue? It offered the sort of propaganda—Cubans against Americans—she would want.

Maybe she figured they wouldn't make that play. Or maybe she was worried about losing him to rivals.

It made sense. De Souza must be at war with her own people. Perhaps they didn't like her talk about becoming legitimate.

So she hadn't been the bomber. Most likely the people she'd killed had been responsible.

Shit.

The helicopter hit a burst of turbulence, and Scotty threw his hands out to steady himself.

"Isn't she a beaut?" the pilot said proudly. "That crosswind must have been fifty knots, but she hardly bucked at all. The finest helicopter in all of Cuba, I guarantee."

Somehow, Scotty made it to the small district airport outside Playa las Coloradas intact. Legs wobbly, he found without great difficulty the car the local police had sent—not only was it the only car parked in the restricted area near the terminal, but it had bubble-gum lights and other equally obvious signs of being a police cruiser.

"I asked for a personal vehicle," Scotty told the officer who had been assigned to deliver the dressed-up Taurus. "Not this."

Crestfallen that Scotty did not recognize the magnificence of the automobile, the man explained that no one in the department owned a personal vehicle. The cruiser was the best they could do on short notice. And the embassy was going to pay for the gas as promised, no?

Worried that he would be delayed, Scotty decided he had no choice but to take the police car. He declined an offer of lunch, and was only too happy when the policeman said there was no need to drive him back to town. Pointed in the right direction, Scotty was soon on the highway, heading toward the intersection where he was supposed to turn.

It was only after he had been on the road for a few minutes that Scotty realized there was a tape in the cassette player.

His first reaction was paranoia—the player could easily be hiding a plastique bomb. He closed his eyes as he drove, momentarily paralyzed by his own astounding stupidity.

Then another thought occurred to him. If de Souza wanted him dead, the cop would have shot him. Or the car would have blown up by now. Using the cassette to trigger it was too chancy; he might not be the music-listening kind.

With a curse, Scotty shoved the tape into the player, and was rewarded with a shrill, ear-popping whistle.

Followed not by an explosion, but Carla de Souza's voice.

"So you see, *Señor* McPherson, if it was my will to have you assassinated, I could have done so at any time. I could have blown up this car, shot down the aircraft that brought you to Playa las Coloradas, or perhaps had your throat slit at the airport. It was my decision, not yours."

Scotty angrily reached for the power button on the tape player. Before he could find it, the tone in de Souza's voice became less mocking, in fact almost sympathetic.

"I am told that you were in the Ave nightclub the night of the explosion, and that the bomb killed someone close to you. I am sorry for that; I am sorry that so many innocent Cubans died there in a senseless attack that achieved nothing. You know by now, or will suspect, that I was the target. I hope you are smart enough to have realized this. I have heard things about you, and I believe you are an intelligent man. I have already dealt with the men responsible. It was part of a misguided plan by Hector Romano Moncada, who tried to raise an insurrection against me. I will not bore you with the details. Undoubtedly you know of Romano. Do not think that his insanity has infected us all.

"When you find our young friend the pilot, he will have a story to tell you. Listen to it carefully. He will also have another tape. You are not being black-mailed, *Señor*. You will notice that the pilot is being released without any conditions. If we all follow our destiny, things will work in the proper way. I trust this.

"The numbers written on the label of this tape are distances and turns. Follow them beginning the three kilometers from the intersection, as I directed you earlier. If you are as smart as my friends at the embassy claim, you should have no trouble deci-phering them and reaching your pilot."

There was a pause, though the recording contin-ued. Scotty imagined the woman sitting at a desk or a table, thinking before going on.

"Are you a student of history, *Señor*? I came to it very late, but the lessons it teaches are inescapable."

"What the hell are you getting at?" Scotty asked the tape player, but it had reached the end of the tape. There was nothing on the other side. "God-damn it," he said, rewinding and then slamming on the brakes because he had gone past the turnoff. "I hate it when these people try and get philosophical."

M-26 Headquarters, Sierra Maestra. 12:40 P.M.

Carla finished giving the small squad its orders and watched them load themselves into the four-wheel-drive. They were brave young men, veterans now of the guerrilla war, but they moved with a clumsiness

271

that was almost comical. She fought back a smile, saluting as they left to take her dispatches to the various units in the western end of the country.

One or two of the dispatches would find their way into government hands. So much the better. They declared a unilateral cease-fire until further notice.

This next phase of the fight would be more a public-relations campaign than anything else. She must—she would—convince her countrymen of her intentions, and then persuade them to see the future. When they trusted her, all would be possible.

Carla allowed herself the luxury of a long breath of the fresh mountain air before retreating back inside, downward to her command center in Romano's cellar. She planned to be out of here before nightfall, but there was still a lot to do. Her job, she mused as she saw the pile of papers and notes on her desk, was largely that of a bureaucratic secretary. The excitement of the past few days was rare, now that the Revolution had reached this stage.

There was no turning back now. Within the hour, the American pilot would be turned over to McPherson.

She could, of course, still use the missile against them. She could take that decision back, if she did so quickly. According to the technicians who manned it, the weapon had been modified so that, once it was properly in place, it could be readied to fire with an hour's notice.

She had debated with herself even after she spoke to McPherson. She could use the weapon as her father had once intended, as Romano had surely planned, for suicidal vengeance. But that would be failure; that would be worse than surrender. It would repudiate everything she had done, and her father as well.

Why did she feel anything toward him at all? He had not even acknowledged her until he was nearly dead. He had never treated her mother with respect. He had made her a prisoner of fate, of history, of the Revolution—of Cuba itself.

But he loomed in her mind, in her soul, larger than life. Carla felt the weight of her commitment to her country as she sat down at the desk.

Her father had made many mistakes in its name. Had she just made her own? Even with her victory over Romano, there was sure to be dissension. True believers did not see the world with clear eyes. They thought first of blood and vengeance, not of life, not of the way history must continue to flow into the future.

It was Zora who had taught her all this. She had only been a dancer, an artist, when Zora first came to her, before her father's death.

But the old woman had betrayed her. Carla reached into her pocket for the mass card, trying to fish up some doubt of Zora's evil. The Santeria superstitions were hopelessly complicated and convoluted, making no sense in any logical way. It was possible, if just barely, that this card meant something different than what she took it to mean. Its presence here could have been mere coincidence.

She knew that could not be. But she wanted it to be, and the only chance for that last small splinter of hope was to confront Zora, as bitter as it was sure to be.

The Foothills of Sierra Maestra. 1 P.M.

Blindfolded, handcuffed, wedged into the van, Garcia sat silently as the guerrillas drove him to the rendezvous. Gone were the brave notions of counting to himself or listening for some detail that might give away the missile's location. All he could think about was his father.

Not think. It was more the opposite of thinking.

Jim DeFelice

A hollow had opened in his brain; a cancer had eliminated his most basic beliefs and undermined his own identity. He remembered he was a marine; if it weren't for that, if it weren't for the few simple ideas about duty and honor pounded into him since he joined the Corps, he might have completely disintegrated in a puddle of water.

Vaguely, he became aware of the men in the van talking. They were debating something, arguing. He heard the words "de Souza," "traitor," and "brother," before a gunshot exploded in the seat in front of him.

Garcia folded his manacled arms in front of his face and dove for the floor as the van swerved. There were two more shots, then gunfire from outside the van, then yelling and screaming as the vehicle screeched to a stop. Garcia tried to push toward the door as bullets shook the van. He heard the swoosh of a rocket grenade, followed by an explosion thirty or forty yards away.

Hunkered on the floor, Garcia had no option but to pray as the firefight crescendoed around him. The rapid bursts and explosions rolled on in waves, one starting before the other died out.

As the gunfire continued, he felt the van rock and realized the door near his head was being opened. Garcia tensed his body, planning to resist—if he had to die, he was at least going to do it bravely. A hand grabbed at the back of his hood and ripped it forward, pulling it off. He pushed his arms down and looked up into the face of the man who was going to kill him.

And saw Scott McPherson.

"Don't just fucking lie there," hissed McPherson. "Come on, before these motherfuckers take us out too."

*   *   *

Scotty pulled the pilot headfirst from the van as another set of grenades shot overhead. Their explosions threw a wall of dirt and rock in the air, but by now Scotty was beyond caring; he hauled Garcia to his feet and began running like hell for the trees. Fortunately, the Cubans were so intent on shooting the hell out of each other that they either didn't see the two men running from the van or couldn't get a good bead on them. A shower of machine-gun bullets ripped through the overhead leaves a few seconds after Scotty reached the jungle, but by then only the luckiest of lucky shots was going to find a target.

Scotty pushed and tugged Garcia with him as he threaded back through the brush toward the bend two miles away where he had left the police car. He hoped like hell they got there before one side or the other won the firefight.

He'd lost his .45 somewhere back near the road when the shooting began. Losing the gun really burned him; he'd had it so long it had become almost a good-luck charm. But there was no way he was going back to look for it. Retrieving one of the Glocks from its ankle holster, he held the small gun in his hand as he ran, careful to keep his fingers out of the trigger guard.

"You owe me big time for this one, kid," he said when he finally thought it was safe enough to pause for a rest. The words came out between gulps for air, and he had to lean against a tree to hold himself up. His lungs were burning, and his thighs weren't feeling particularly thrilled either. "Aren't the fucking marines the ones who are supposed to bail people out?"

"You shouldn't have attacked the van," said Garcia. Unlike Scotty, he had no trouble catching his breath, though his limp was noticeable. "They were going to let me go."

Scotty had to unzip his pants to reach the other Glock at his thigh. He gave it to Garcia. "You told me you know something about guns, right?"

"This looks like a toy."

"Yeah, well, don't lose it. It's all we got at the moment. And I didn't attack the damn van. Apparently our friends had a debate on whether to let you go or not. You're lucky there were a few dozen people tagging along to play bodyguard." Scotty pointed at Garcia's handcuffs. "You got a hacksaw on you?"

"No."

"Just fucking great."

"They released me because they have a missile," said Garcia.

"A what?"

"They have a ballistic missile. It's in a bunker buried in the mountains back there."

"Are you shitting me?"

"Jesus Christ, why the hell would I make up something like that?"

"Hey, don't point that gun at me. The fucking trigger spring's honed to a thread. Did de Souza give you a tape?"

"It's in my top pocket."

Scotty reached inside and retrieved the cassette. There was something else—the handcuff key.

"Jeez, she must have had the hots for you, kid," he said as he released him.

"The hell she did. She put a gun in my face and said she was going to kill me like she did Ferguson."

"Yeah, right. Ferguson's the other pilot who got shot down?"

"His engine crapped out."

"He's back in Havana getting drunk. Come on, let's go join him."

"She lied to me?"

"Jeez, imagine that." Scotty pushed the pilot to get him running again.

A short distance away, Scotty lost his balance at the top of a shallow but nonetheless steep ravine. Garcia slid behind him and helped him up. An occasional burst of gunfire echoed behind them, signaling that their enemies were still busy fighting among themselves.

"Where are we going?" Garcia asked.

"There's a police car on the road that way," Scotty told him. He was winded again and decided he'd better take a rest before continuing. "That's our ticket out of here, assuming we make it. Listen— there's a radio and a locator beacon under the front seat, just in case."

Garcia nodded solemnly.

"Don't worry, kid, I'm not leaving you alone if I can help it. Besides, I'm thinking our friends are busy enough for us to get away. You're damn lucky I decided to meet these bastards in the jungle instead of following instructions," he added, starting to walk. "You'd have been chewed up with the rest of them in that ambush. I expect a card on my birthday for the rest of your life. This makes twice I've bailed you out this week."

"Twice?"

"I'll tell you about it later. How's the leg?"

"It's fine."

"Yeah, right. You coming, or you have other plans?"

Whether to prove that his knee wasn't hurting— or perhaps because Scotty's entire body was—Garcia kept pulling substantially ahead. Scotty had to grab him when they got near the road.

"Hold on. Hold on. Let's make sure we're the only ones who know where I parked."

They weren't. When he crawled forward to investigate, Scotty saw two men huddled near the bumper of the police car, AK-47s in their arms.

"I'll walk back and create a diversion," suggested

Garcia, "then you shoot them when they come to check it out."

"Yeah, good idea. Only one problem," said McPherson, grabbing Garcia as he started to rise. "My .45 is back in the dust somewhere, and this Glock has the accuracy of a spitball over five yards."

"So what are we going to do?"

"We"—McPherson emphasized the word sarcastically—"are going to sit tight while I think of something."

"We can't just wait for them to find us."

"Hey, no shit, Sherlock. Listen, kid, do me a favor and take five, all right? That Marine Corps gung-ho shit only goes so far."

"I'm not trying to be gung ho," said Garcia. "I'm just trying to get us back in one piece. We have to tell them about the missile."

"Wow, I hadn't thought about that."

"Jeez, you don't have to be an asshole. We're on the same goddamn side."

Scotty stared at the two men waiting by the car. They were teenagers, probably without a huge amount of experience. Garcia's plan might work. If Scotty could get close enough with the Glock to catch one off guard, the odds would at least be better than making a mad dash at them.

"Maybe we should just walk through the jungle to town," Garcia suggested in a whisper.

"The nearest town is ten miles away, and there are exactly two people there who aren't part of M-26. Besides, there were at least fifty guys in that group that ambushed your van. I got to believe they're mopping up by now and are on their way to look for us."

Scotty looked at the Glock in his hand. There were ten bullets in the clip, more than enough.

Hell, he wasn't that bad a shot.

"How's your Spanish?" he asked the pilot.

"Better than yours."

"Think you can call out that you're wounded?"

"Socorro, socorro."

"Roll the *r* more. I thought your parents were Cuban."

"They are," said Garcia. He felt a pang because of his father, but pushed it away. "*Socorro, socorro,*" he said again, softly.

"That's good. Don't embellish. Just moan and groan, kind of."

"Where?"

Scotty looked at the road and the guerrillas again. "Here's what I'm thinking. You go down the road about fifty yards, maybe a little more. You do the yelling thing. They go and investigate. I sneak up, jump into the car, run them down."

"What if you miss?"

"I'm not going to miss," he said. "Besides, you'll have the pistol."

"What if only one comes?"

"Then I shoot one and run down the other. He'll be watching for his friend, anyway. All I have to do is get reasonably close to get the odds down."

"I don't know. It sounds like a long shot."

"It's the same plan you suggested two minutes ago."

"That's why I'm worried."

"Jesus, kid, just get down the road and make it look good."

Scotty watched as the pilot pushed back through the weeds and brush. He went at least a hundred yards before edging toward the roadway out of Scotty's sight.

When he began shouting, he sounded a lot like an entire village in pain.

Or perhaps ecstasy.

Jim DeFelice

It took forever to get a reaction, and then it wasn't exactly the one Scotty had hoped for—half a clip of bullets were sent in Garcia's direction while the two guerrillas took cover behind the fender of the police car.

They weren't the bravest rebels in the world, nor were they necessarily the smartest. When they finally figured out that the screams were for help, they jumped off the car and started walking down the road together to investigate. Half crawling, half running, Scotty started moving through the underbrush and then onto the road. He got to within ten yards when one of the men heard him.

His first and second bullets caught the guerrilla on the right side and the man staggered backward, his rifle falling away helplessly. But the rest of Scotty's shots missed as he bolted across the road to the cover of the police car.

The other terrorist, initially confused, recovered enough to dive to the ground, firing his Kalashnikov wildly. Two of the bullets hit the back of the car, one close enough to Scotty's head to make him scurry around to the other side.

There was no way he was going to be able to get into the car without getting wasted by the guerrilla. And he was too outgunned to try to get off a shot. His best bet now—maybe his only bet—was to keep the guerrilla occupied long enough for Garcia to sneak up behind him. He had no alternative—the rebel finally realized that he could fire at Scotty under and through the car, and let off a long burst.

Scotty dove over the embankment on the shoulder of the road, then threw his hands and feet out to stop himself when he heard the AK-47 clicking empty. Adrenaline pumping, he jumped back and reached the roadway just as the guerrilla wrestled another clip in.

The three shots he had left in the Glock sent the man back into the woods in retreat, but he didn't appear to have been hit. And now it was Scotty's turn to reload.

The dead rebel's Kalashnikov, unfired, lay a tantalizing fifteen yards away. There was no hesitation—the anger that had seethed in him since Esma's death took over now, and he bolted for the gun, diving into the dust as the guerrilla in the woods announced with a fresh burst of gunfire that he did actually know how to load a rifle.

Scotty swirled around in the dust and returned fire, lacing the trees with bullets.

When the rebel didn't answer, Scotty ran forward for the kill. There was a moment then when he saw bright red, when everything was a flash of hot fire, and as he reached the side of the road he had only one goal, to kill the son of a bitch who'd tried to kill him.

Then, in the next moment, he saw a dark shadow flashing over his shoulder and felt the hard butt of a rifle end hitting him in the side.

Scotty's Kalashnikov went flying as he fell face-first into the jungle. Another blow hit him, then another. He crawled away, rolled back, put up his hand, and saw the wooden stock being aimed as a battering ram, floating almost poetically in the air, as if it were a benign butterfly passing the time on a hot summer afternoon.

Then there were two shots close together, and the rifle fell to the ground as its owner staggered back, blood gushing from his neck and chest. A second later, the guerrilla fell off to the right, already near death.

"Stinking trigger is pretty easy," said Garcia, looming over him. "I only meant to fire once."

* * *

Jim DeFelice

Zora appeared at the doorway to the command center, an apparition framed by two of Carla's bodyguards.

"You called for me?"

Carla ignored the hint of displeasure in the old woman's voice. "I did indeed." She looked around the small room. "Everyone, please excuse us. No, José," she added to the bodyguard. "You and Ernesto are to stay."

Zora's face flashed with an emotion Carla had never seen before—surprise. It vanished quickly, replaced by understanding, then acceptance. The old witch was stoic to the end.

The other four men who had been reviewing maps with Carla left without saying anything else. She had the sense that they had foreseen what was coming and were only too happy to escape the venom that would have to be released.

Still, I may be wrong, she reminded herself. I must not make a judgment until I am certain. In this case above all others.

"You may sit," she told Zora, motioning toward the chair in the corner.

Zora remained standing.

"It's up to you," Carla said. When the old woman's face showed no emotion, she reached into the pocket of her black jeans and took out the prayer card. "What does this mean?"

"I have told you many times, the cards mean nothing of themselves."

"This one does. I found it in Romano's lair."

The old woman's face remained blank as stone. Carla had her answer now beyond any doubt. A pain began near her right temple, spreading across her head, down her throat, into her chest. She had not felt such a throb since her mother died when she was twelve.

"I have one other question for you," Carla said.

"As you wish."

"The Russian missile—did you know about it?"

"Yes. Your father had it for a very long time."

"Why did you not tell me?"

Again, Zora did not answer. Carla felt anger flashing inside her; she fought to control it. "The missile is a senseless weapon. It cannot get us what we want."

Silence.

"Do you disagree?"

"What you want and what we need, these have become different things," said Zora finally.

"Vengeance and blood? Your family died a long time ago, Zora. And my father is dead—you pulled the sheet over him yourself."

Zora's eyes stared through her. Carla rose and took a few steps to the right, unconsciously stretching her legs as she had as a dancer. She caught herself, smiled at the old habit. Now that it was over—now that the old woman had as much as confessed, she would feel better. The pain was already subsiding. Her duty was clear—Zora would have to be punished for her betrayal. There was great sadness, but at least the doubt, the worry, had passed.

"Do you wonder how our lives might have been different?" asked Carla, indulging herself for one last moment before she gave the order. "No. Your religion makes the past the present, and joins the future into an unbending stream. You have told me that many times. Do I understand it properly?"

"You understand what you can see," said Zora. There was a touch of sadness in her reproach.

"The one person always at my side. And now you have betrayed me. How long were you with Romano?"

"I am loyal to your father and the cause of Cuba. I have not betrayed you, or anyone."

Carla began to lift her hand in dismissal. Then from above she heard the faint report of machine-gun fire. She took a step toward the door, only to find her way blocked by José.

"I am most very sorry, Commander," her bodyguard told her. "But I am afraid you cannot pass."

The Road To Playa Las Coloradas. 2:45 P.M.

By the time they played the tape a third time, Garcia knew the words almost by heart.

". . . The pilot's description should leave no doubt that the missile exists. My people assure me that it is in fine shape, and capable of hitting any target in the United States that I choose.

"But I do not wish to kill innocent people. There are many who say I am justified, that I should seek revenge for the blood of my comrades who have fallen. But the greater good must prevail; we are fighting for the real future of Cuba, the preservation of the people and the Revolution.

"I will turn the missile over to my friend Mr. Mc-Pherson of the U.S. embassy. He is a man who understands us because he has experienced pain. I ask nothing in return. . . ."

Without saying anything, McPherson reached to the cassette player and flipped the tape out before de Souza got to the part where she said a new message with more details would be released shortly.

"You know her?" Garcia asked.

"Oh yeah, we're old pals. Probably sleep together before this is all over," said McPherson.

The tone in his voice made it impossible to ask anything else. Not knowing what to say, Garcia repeated his description of the missile—somewhere between nine and twelve feet around, thirty to fifty feet long, with a sharp nose and small fins at the tail. "It was black, and lying on the back of this long trailer. There were a couple of mechanisms around, but I couldn't tell if it was a launching pad. I saw two tractors, kind of like bulldozers without blades, except they were grayish green and—"

"Tell me something, kid. If we make it to the airport, what kind of plane can you fly?"

"Anything you can steal."

McPherson laughed. Garcia wasn't sure whether it had been a serious question or McPherson was just tired of hearing what the missile looked like. When he spotted a sign for an airport, however, he figured the CIA agent wasn't joking.

Five minutes later, they drove by the turnoff.

"Were you kidding about the plane?" the pilot asked.

"Not at the time. But now I'm thinking we're best off sticking to the ground. I'm afraid your friends know too much about us. They may have set up another ambush there."

"Why would de Souza release me, then kill me a couple of hours later? According to what she says on the tape, she's going to give up the missile."

"She wasn't the one behind the ambush."

"She sure looked like she was in charge to me." Garcia edged into the thickly upholstered seat, wedging his legs against the side of the dash. He'd never ridden in a police car before, and despite everything else there was an overwhelming temptation to turn on the lights and siren. "She was pretty damn good-looking, for a guerrilla."

"You better watch your hormones. They already got you in trouble."

"What do you mean?"

"That Cuban girl you're shacking up with, Maria Letra? She's a minister's daughter. Or was. He died yesterday."

Garcia felt his face turning red. Flustered, he blurted that he wasn't "shacking up" with anybody. But before he could defend Maria, McPherson cut him off.

"Relax, kid. I didn't tell the ambassador."

"Why would he care?"

The agent shook his head. "Are you crazy? He'll take your head off."

"Why?"

"For one thing, somebody bombed your base."

"She had nothing to do with that."

"Uh-huh."

"You're just busting my balls, right?"

"That's what I live for." McPherson turned to look at him. "Keep your mouth shut about it and you won't have a problem. I didn't tell him, and I won't."

"Hey, man, watch the road. Jesus." Garcia involuntarily flinched as the agent returned the car to its lane. "Don't you get us killed."

They drove on for a while in silence.

"You can't take everything at face value in Cuba, kid," McPherson finally said. "I told you that the other day. You never really know who's on your side."

"I know Maria is."

"Uh-huh."

Garcia folded his arms and pushed himself deeper in his seat. McPherson couldn't be right.

But after this morning, he wasn't sure he could take anything for granted. De Souza's revelation— or lie—about his father had unnerved him.

It had to be a lie—she had lied about Ferguson, after all. But the details, the hints about the shoemaker. Lies, too?

She had known his father's name, and where he lived.

Garcia thought of mentioning it to the CIA agent but wasn't sure how to bring it up. Besides, how would McPherson know one way or another? To even mention the possibility was damning his father.

And he didn't want to do that. Not now, not ever.

Probably it was a lie, part of her mind games.

"Don't think too hard, Junior, you'll soil the upholstery."

"Fuck you," snapped Garcia.

McPherson smiled, but it didn't last. His unshaven face seemed to be always on the verge of a tired scowl. "Take a nap, why don't you?" the older man suggested. "I'll wake you in an hour. Then you can drive."

"I'm not tired. Besides, I don't know my way around."

"All you got to do is stay on the highway. It ain't advanced orienteering. Hey, you got a credit card on you?"

"No."

"Shit. And we're almost out of gas."

McPherson was kidding about the credit card, but not about the gas; they coasted into a small barnyard with an Exxon sign as the engine sputtered and threatened to quit. A lone gas pump, at least fifty years old, stood in the shadow of a freshly painted but otherwise dilapidated barn.

The engine finally died about ten feet from the pump.

"They're probably inside, scared shitless because we have a police car," McPherson told Garcia. "At least I hope so. Come on, let's push it closer."

No one came out as they heaved the big, soap-shaped car up by its bumper and eased it forward.

"Should I go inside and see what's up?" Garcia asked.

"No way. I don't like this at all. Remember we're in guerrilla country, and we don't exactly look like neighbors." McPherson reached into his pocket and gave Garcia the Glock that still had bullets. "Get behind the wheel. Somebody comes out and it looks like I'm cooked, take off."

"But—"

"Jesus Christ. Can't you follow a goddamn order? Bring the tape to the embassy. Okay? Goddamn, what a pain in the ass you are."

"Yes, sir." Garcia slid behind the wheel and waited as the agent filled up the tank. He watched him take two bills from his wallet, roll them up, and leave them in the nozzle handle.

"Come on, come on, go," demanded McPherson, pulling open the door. "Get the damn thing started."

The car coughed to life. Garcia stepped on the gas and dirt and gravel went flying everywhere.

"It's hard to tell what the story is sometimes," McPherson explained as they drove away. "Sometimes people are afraid of the police because they had bad experiences under Fidel. Sometimes the police are guerrillas themselves. Out here, everything's all mixed up."

"Most of the people support freedom," said Garcia, repeating what Maria had told him.

"Yeah, but freedom for who?"

The agent angled around in the seat, then took off his shirt to use as a pillow. His torso was marked with several old scars, as well as some fresh scrapes and bruises. "Stay on this road, don't hit anything, and don't use the siren, whatever you do."

" 'Cause it'll scare people?"

"Because it'll wake me up."

Havana. Midnight.

The ambassador's office suite was a study in organized chaos, with secretaries, attachés, assistants, and even a janitor rushing from various knots and computer screens, maniacs on a scavenger hunt in a loony ward. All this activity seemed a bit out of place to Scotty, even though he had expected the ambassador and a watch team to be waiting for his return. The whole world was up here—including a young Cuban woman in an alluringly short red dress, who came running to the elevator as soon as the doors opened.

"Jesus Christ. What the hell are you doing here?" Scotty bawled when he recognized her.

"Maria."

"Edward—"

The pair came together like something out of an old Rock Hudson–Doris Day movie.

Scotty stood back, fuming. "Who the fuck cleared your security?" he demanded. "Who let you up here? Goddamn it."

"Steele said it was okay," said Fashona, appearing in the whirlpool of people rushing from one room to another.

"Have you checked her security?"

"She was cleared to work for a television station and was the daughter of a government official. Jeez, Scotty, don't be so hyper. We have more important things to worry about."

"You don't know the half of it," Scotty told him. He reached out and grabbed Garcia by the arm. "Come on, Junior, the lovey-dovey stuff can wait. You and I have to talk to the ambassador—and girl-friend can't come."

The agent ignored their protests and literally dragged Garcia through the suite, looking for Steele. He found him bent over a map on his desk, listening as Porta murmured in an unintelligible croak.

"Got him," announced Scotty, gesturing toward Garcia.

Steele barely glanced up. "It's about time," he said, returning to the map.

Surprised at Steele's reaction, Scotty put on his

most officious voice. "You're going to want to hear this tape, General. The rebels have a ballistic missile that may have been left over from the sixties. Our friend de Souza says she's going to give it up, but only to me. Personally, I think she's—"

Before he could finish, Steele pointed toward a television/VCR setup on a side credenza. As Scotty turned to look at it, Steele picked up a remote from his desk and pushed Play. A video recording of the island's ten-o'clock news came on, with the anchor talking joyfully about a sugar-crop prediction. Just as he got the words "record harvest" out of his mouth, the screen began to roll. The feed suddenly changed, replaced by a clear but poorly lit scene of a bearded man sitting in front of an old Cuban flag. A viewer could be easily forgiven for thinking the man was Fidel Castro.

"Good evening," he said in Spanish. "My name is Hector Romano Moncada, and I am the leader of M-26. This evening I bring you glorious news of our successful revolution. We have won many battles in the jungles and on our city streets. We have not given up El Jefe's fight. We have inherited his legacy and his greatest weapon. Tonight we issue the American invaders an ultimatum. If they do not leave our island by midnight July twenty-sixth, we will destroy their capital. There will be no other warning. . . ."

Chapter Eight

Friday, July 25
Over the Atlantic Ocean. 3 A.M.

The only plane available for charter back to Washington was an old 707 owned by Warwick Airlines, an off-brand carrier that had been flagged by the FAA for numerous safety violations during the past year. Scotty rationalized those violations as bureaucratic nit-picking all through takeoff, but his logic started thinning the second they ran into turbulence north of Havana. Then a sledgehammer of rain began pounding rivets through the wings so loudly it sounded as if they were sitting under Niagara Falls.

Wrestling his knuckles together, Scotty found he needed an almost absurd amount of willpower to keep himself from grabbing at the liquor cart as the stewardess passed. He checked the pouch of the seat in front of him, looking for something to distract his attention; all it offered was a plastic card telling passengers how to pray in five languages if the plane went down.

He could read his maps and briefing material

again, but he was almost as sick of them as he was of the plane flight. Hours of staring had narrowed the missile site down to two likely spots, but these were based as much on guesses as Garcia's description. They hadn't even been able to decide what kind of missile it was, though de Souza's hints and Garcia's descriptions narrowed it down to a sixties-era medium- or intermediate-range nuke, possibly an SS-4 or SS-5, since the guerrilla leader had gone to great lengths to imply it was left over from the October 1962 Cuban Missile Crisis.

Either missile—and certainly anything later—would put most of the East Coast in danger. The real question was whether it would still fly. But then, you had to guess it would if the guerrillas were killing each other to get control of it.

A team of air force wizards and Phyzine addicts were hard at work back in the States; with luck and enough Jolt Cola, they might have a more definitive site than Scotty had managed by the time the embassy team arrived in D.C. for their 6 A.M. NSC meeting. Hopefully, their opinions would be worth more than Tito Porta's, who when pressed insisted that the most likely place for the missile was San Cristobal—on the opposite side of the island from where Garcia had been.

Porta's inexplicable logic had not kept him from being included in the group accompanying Steele back to D.C. In fact, the Cuban "expert" was now sitting a row behind the ambassador, leafing through a thick stack of guerrilla intercepts. If pressed, Scotty would have admitted that it wasn't a horrible idea, just unlikely to yield anything useful.

Especially on this flight. With every dip and dive, Scotty began mouthing prayers he'd forgotten in grammar school. He needed to do something—anything—to get his mind off the plane.

Steele was catching z's in the back of the plane, as were Fashona and James. The only person up front besides Porta who was still awake was Garcia, sitting across the aisle from Scotty. He stared out the window, enraptured by the artistic way the storm threatened to shear the wings off.

As the plane took a dip that would have given Neil Armstrong vertigo, Scotty decided he was either going to talk to the kid or start drinking again. Miraculously, the plane maintained nearly level flight long enough for him to make it across the aisle unscathed.

"What's causing all this up-and-down stuff?" he asked as he slid into a seat.

Garcia turned a glum face from the window and looked at him a moment before answering. "Storm."

"Yeah, no shit. But how come?" Scotty lashed his seat belt together and notched it as tightly as it would go.

"How come there's a storm?"

"No, I mean, why don't we just, you know, slice right through?"

"Air currents."

Garcia went back to staring out the window.

"So how does it feel to be a hero?" Scotty asked.

The pilot turned back toward him, said nothing, turned back to the window.

"Jeez, kid, now what's wrong?"

"Nothing."

"Hey, listen, you're not pissed about Letra, are you?"

"You're wrong about her."

"How am I wrong? All I said was that you have to be careful, right? I'm not saying she's a guerrilla."

"She's not."

The plane pitched to the left slightly, and Scotty threw his hand out against the seat in front of him. "You've been through worse than this, huh?" he asked as the airliner quickly leveled itself.

"Every day."

"Uh-huh. Well, listen, I like you and all, but we all have blind spots. You're in love with her. You can't think straight."

"What if I am?"

"Shit, I'm not saying she's a bad person, just that you have to be careful. This is Cuba we're talking about, not some town in Iowa."

Scotty started to undo his seat belt to go back across the aisle, but then he reconsidered. Garcia had bailed out of two planes in the space of a week or so and survived. That made him one lucky son of a bitch.

If this sucker was going down, the safest place to be was right on his back.

Sierra Maestra Mountains. 5 A.M.

Knees against her chest, palms flat against the cold floor of the bunker cellar, Carla de Souza stared at the dark space before her. The empty void held no possibility of warmth, no chance of survival.

She was concerned for her country's future, not her own. She would gladly sacrifice herself a thousand times over to preserve one-tenth of Cuba, one one-hundredth of the Revolution. But there was no salve for the madness of the void, no way to cure its dementia. She could only stare at it for hours, feel its emptiness surrounding her.

Carla was aware of her body as she had not been in many years, as perhaps she had never been. She could feel each muscle, each tendon, the soft roll of fat that had grown at the top of her hips, her hollowing cheeks, the cold tip of her nose. She stared, making her mind as empty as the void.

Light suddenly intruded. A precursor, perhaps.

Romano stood in the open doorway, laughing.

The door creaked closed behind him, leaving them alone together in the darkness.

"Good morning, ballerina. Have you slept well? How does it feel to be broken like a toy, treated like the child you are?"

Carla stared at his outline, watching his eyes as they jolted around the cell. Insane eyes, filled with bile and vengeance.

Had her father been this mad?

It could not have been so; surely he had accomplished much as the country's leader. He had been its father; even the Yankees and worms said so, in their denigrating way.

"Now that you know the depth of our power, what do you think? Are you angry at *El Jefe* for not telling you what he possessed?"

She said nothing. How could she speak to the void? How could she speak to the face of evil?

"The Americans will try to delay, but there will not be time for them. When they attack me, I will be justified. My righteousness will be obvious to even the most simpleminded, and all of Cuba will rally to me. The Americans are helpless. They cannot launch their own missile in retaliation. That is the beauty of our vengeance—they can do nothing except writhe in agony."

The words jumped from her mouth before she could stop them. "Hector, you must not launch the weapon. You must surrender it."

"Surrender? I am hours from victory. I would never surrender, even if the entire world were against me."

"There will be no Cuba if the missile is launched. The Americans will take over the entire island."

"Then every Cuban will rise up against them. Don't you understand? That will be victory. That will be the thing that makes our future possible."

"Do you think the gringos will rest until they have

295

killed you? Do you think that they will rest until they have found every member of the movement? Do you think they will permit any piece of the Revolution to remain?"

Somehow she'd gotten to her feet and crossed the blackness of the cell. Romano was only inches from her, so close she could feel his rancid breath on her face.

"Give them the warhead," she told him. "We must win the hearts of our people. That is where the Revolution can survive. Have these years of fighting taught you nothing?"

"Are you surprised, sister, that our father gave the missile to me?"

Carla stepped back. His madness had overwhelmed him; Hector Romano Moncada was not Fidel Castro's son.

"He could not acknowledge me as he acknowledged you." Romano's eyes flickered in the dark void of the cell. "But I came from his seed as surely as you. You felt it, didn't you, when you could not shoot me? We are brother and sister, you and I. But I am the strong one."

Her legs began to give way slowly; she felt herself sinking against the wall, unsure now of everything except the utter darkness of the space before her.

Washington, D.C. Situation Room 3. 6 A.M.

Halfway down the dimly lit corridor, it finally dawned on Garcia that when everyone was talking about going to the "White House," they didn't mean literally the presidential mansion but the office complexes nearby. His disappointment was overshadowed by his awe as he followed along in the ambassador's entourage past a pair of plainclothes guards into a high-tech secure room. At least half the chairs in the large room were already filled, and numerous aides and staff members crowded behind the circle they formed. Garcia nearly fainted when he saw not only the Chairman of the Joint Chiefs of Staff but his own Marine Corps commandant. His hand jerked upward in a nervous, reflexive salute, stopped by Scott McPherson, who had walked in alongside him.

"You don't salute underground, kid," he hissed. "Not here. Just relax. They'll all kiss your ass sooner or later."

Garcia was incapable of responding, and followed meekly to seats near the far end of the room. The hi-tech conference facility, the newest part of the secure subterranean complex euphemistically called "the White House Basement," had more electronic doodads than a consumer electronics show. Each "station" at the large round table that dominated the room had three different computer screens set low into the space in front of the chair, and a complete suite of secure communications.

McPherson showed Garcia how to work the function keys that would bring projections onto his screens. "We'll probably be using this a lot. The Vice President will run the meeting, and he likes maps. He also likes to break things down like a math problem, part A, part B, like that. So if you can work a few letters into your speech, he'll love you."

"You've been here before?"

"Back in the good old days, I was here all the time. Remember, only the VIPs get seats."

"We're sitting."

"No shit. Don't drink the water; it's chlorinated all to hell."

Steele, seated on Garcia's right, shot a warning glare at McPherson before patting the marine pilot's shoulder. "We'll be starting as soon as the Vice President gets here. When it's your turn to speak, just do it plainly, exactly the way you spoke to me in Havana," the ambassador told him. "No one's going to bite you."

They didn't at all, though Garcia noted that the head of the Navy, Admiral O'Rourke, shot him a particularly withering glare when he finished his summary of what he had seen at the missile site. Steele then turned things over to McPherson, whose demeanor suddenly seemed much more like that of a college professor than the cursing swashbuckler who'd rescued him. McPherson's overview of the guerrilla organization, only occasionally colored by four-letter words, was as terse and dry as if he were discussing a corporate takeover at Microsoft.

Then the fun and games started. The Joint Chiefs were not pleased about the Harrier operation, and O'Rourke and an army general criticized Steele and the NSC staff for not informing them of it. The commandant quickly spoke up in defense of Garcia, and there was a few minutes of backtracking as the admiral and general made it clear that they "had only the highest praise" for the Marine Corps lieutenant.

"Better get it in writing, kid," whispered McPherson.

Much of the criticism was directed, more or less obliquely, at one of the President's aides, a man named Dr. Blitz, who sat with his elbows perched on the desk and with a placid frown perched on his lips. Finally he pulled his mike forward and suggested that if the Joint Chiefs were merely interested in character assassination, he would make himself available in an alleyway outside.

The Vice President raised his hand, cutting off an angry response from the admiral.

"The problem, gentlemen, is not whether we should have lent a pilot or two to the Cuban government. It's a good thing we did, or we might not even have known about the missile until it was fired. The problem is, (a) Is the threat real? and (b) How do we deal with it?"

Garcia remembered McPherson's advice about the water as the meeting continued. The first of the arguments—and despite the soothing tones and technical jargon, it really was an argument—concerned the question of whether the missile and the warhead were real or not. A historian hastily summoned from Washington University gave a brief overview of the 1960s Cuban Missile Crisis. The Soviets had sent SS-4s and SS-5s—respectively, medium- and intermediate-range ballistic missiles—to bases in Cuba. Both types used a storable liquid fuel, and were meant to counter American first-strike capabilities, which at the time could have obliterated the U.S.S.R. before it launched a retaliatory strike. The SS-4s could carry a two- to three-megaton yield warhead a little over a thousand nautical miles; the SS-5s threw a three- to five-megaton warhead approximately twenty-two hundred miles. Both types fit Garcia's description, and the oxidizer tanks made it clear that a more modern solid-fueled rocket was not involved. From a visual point of view, the main difference between the two old missiles was about a half a meter's worth of diameter—a difference too close for the untrained Garcia to distinguish.

There had never been definitive evidence that live nuclear warheads had been brought to the island, let alone that they would have left direct Russian control. On the other hand, an individual warhead was small enough that it could conceivably have been left behind. And, as others in the room knew too well, there were a number of Russian warheads currently unaccounted for that could possibly be adapted to the missile if the body but not the warhead had been left.

The best data indicated that forty-two missiles had been brought to Cuba in 1962, not counting surface-to-air weapons and small, "tactical" nukes that the technology of the time could not hope to keep track of. The number, however, was the subject of some debate, and in fact U.S. sources had consistently underestimated the deployment.

The medium- and intermediate-range missiles were under strict Soviet control throughout the summer and fall of 1962, but the command structure and the location raised grave doubts about the other forces, and eventually Soviet Premier Nikita Khrushchev worried that the Cubans themselves were uncontrollable. Khrushchev quickly came to fear that the missiles might bring on the very thing they were supposed to counter, a preemptive attack on the Soviet homeland.

The downing of a U-2—ironically by a Russian crew, though Khrushchev initially believed it had been Castro's doing—brought the matter to a head, and Khrushchev ordered the missiles removed before an American invasion of the island led to a war the U.S.S.R. would lose.

The historian contended that all of the missiles set up by the Russians had been meticulously accounted for. But an air force missile expert immediately disagreed, saying that while the reconnaissance at the time was "state-of-the-art thorough," there were several ways it could have been duped. And, as he and the papers in the inch-thick, bound CIA summary of the crisis noted, estimates of the number of missiles had always varied, and the Agency had not been able to definitively say all missiles were removed when the crisis ended.

A highly technical debate quickly began over which missile it might be. The historian and experts from the air force and the CIA shot questions and opinions back and forth like a rapid-fire tennis match.

"Why is this important?" interjected the Vice President after the discussion had gone on for several minutes.

"If it's an SS-4, then we have to be concerned with its mobility," said the historian. "Whereas the SS-5s were fired from stationary platforms. And, of course, the range is critical. It would make a big difference in siting the Patriot defenses. An SS-4 could go only about a thousand miles; the SS-5 twice as far. In the first case, Washington, D.C., would be just out of range."

Still, the experts could not agree on which it might be. The discussion veered in a different direction as the historian questioned how an SS-5, or SS-4 for that matter, would be fired from a bunker that had no apparent opening.

"There are several solutions," said one of the air force men. "The easiest would be to wire explosives to part of the roof and blow a hole open. That would explain the assembly he saw, as well as the fact that we can't find the silo."

"A mobile missile would make more sense," said Blitz, who seemed to know a considerable amount about the situation though this was the first time he spoke about it. "An SS-4 would be easier to hide and handle, since it was originally designed to be mobile."

"There is another possibility we should consider," said one of the CIA officials in the front row. "The entire thing could be a charade."

A number of others in the room agreed, and neither the historian nor the air force experts could rule that possibility out. The Vice President asked Porta, the only "real" Cuban in the room, for his opinion. Porta—he and James had been relegated to the wall behind the ambassador—fumbled around nervously before managing to say that he did not think the threat was real but could not discount it.

"With all due respect, sir," interjected McPherson, addressing the Vice President. "We can't afford the luxury of hoping it's pretend."

There were some murmurs of assent.

"But even if it's a real missile," said the Vice President, "what are the odds of it still working after all these years?"

A bespectacled NASA expert near the back wall cleared his throat before moving hesitantly to answer. Both SS-4s and SS-5s had been used by the Russians to launch various members of the Cosmos series of satellites, the SS-4s into the seventies and the SS-5s at least into the eighties. Plans for the SS-4 had been given to Iran only a few years before, and were believed to form the basis for its recently revealed medium-range weapons.

"They're small by current standards, but dependable, sturdy little things," said the scientist, as if he were referring to a child's plaything rather than a six-ton collection of tanks and tubing. "With the proper attention, I would think the age of either type irrelevant."

"The rocket itself could have been built during Castro's regime," said Blitz, "based on designs his people might have become familiar with from the Russians. It could even have solid propellant."

"He described oxidizer tanks," noted the air force expert. "Why would they bother faking that?"

"They wouldn't," agreed Blitz.

"Assuming we do have a live missile here," said the Vice President, "how long after they start fueling can they launch?"

"During the 1962 crisis, the CIA estimated that it would take between eight and twenty-four hours to prepare for a launch," said the historian promptly. "Once they were ready, the most they could stand at alert was five hours.

"So if they're going to launch at midnight, July

twenty-sixth," he added, "the earliest they would start fueling would be midnight tonight. And the very earliest you'd want the missile ready to go would be seven P.M. tomorrow."

"They may have modified the process somewhat," cautioned the air force expert. "They've had some time to work on it." He then went on to discuss "fuel modalities"—basically what it would take to keep a forty-year-old rocket's propellant alive. The key ingredient, red fuming nitric acid, wasn't the most stable compound in the world, and the major theorized that it would almost certainly have been updated.

"It's interesting that he gave us such a long warning period," said Blitz. "That would suggest that they're confident the missile can't be found, have radically lengthened the alert period, or shortened the fueling procedure dramatically. Or all three. We could be down to a warning time as short as thirty minutes—barely enough time to get an assault started."

"Romano went public out of necessity," said McPherson. "De Souza forced his hand by releasing Garcia. His own plan was probably different. I don't think we should kid ourselves—Romano wants us to invade. He'll use it as a pretext to rally Cubans to his cause."

"Will that work?" asked the Vice President.

"I don't know," said McPherson. "The rebels are unpopular, but everybody loves a martyr. And viewed from an historical perspective, we don't exactly have the best reputation."

"It's irrelevant," said Steele, his voice so sharp that Garcia jumped. "There's no way we can let that maniac blow up Washington, D.C. Or even threaten to."

The options on dealing with the missile were fairly limited. Antimissile defenses might work, but couldn't be counted on. And while exploding a large nuclear device at the suspected missile site would destroy it, the resulting radiation would devastate the rest of Cuba and much of the Caribbean. As one air force expert put it, with only slight exaggeration, you might just as well target Havana—or Miami.

Which left assault as the only viable plan.

While it was clear what the final recommendation would be, it took nearly an hour more for the Vice President to decide they needed more technical information before they could go to the President with a proper plan. In the meantime, Patriot antimissile defenses would be moved into place. Against a ballistic missile that achieved altitude, the Patriots not only had a low probability of interception, but would also most likely be dealing with an armed warhead; even a direct hit might cause untold destruction. But with better antimissile defenses still years away, the Patriots were better than nothing.

Then again, they said that about prayers, too.

Scotty saw a grim smile of satisfaction come over the head of the navy's face when the Vice President lamented that Guantánamo Bay was no longer available to use to stage the assault. Even with a real crisis facing them, a good part of what was happening this morning was just the usual political bullshit. Scotty couldn't help but feel not only disgust but something like relief that he was no longer part of the asinine power game. He watched as his nominal boss at the CIA, covert operations head Wes Morvin, grimaced when the air force, not the Agency, was told to prepare the report on the missile's probable potency. Morvin even looked a little peed when the Joint Chiefs were told to come up with the plan to take the missile out. The CIA had been dealt a minor role in the crisis, and his disappointment was so obvious that the Vice President asked pointedly if he had a problem.

"No, sir, not at all," Morvin answered. "We will

make our expertise available as we have to this point."

"Great," snapped the Vice President.

That could have been me, Scotty thought to himself. I wonder if I would have been as big an asshole.

Probably.

He glanced over at Garcia, who had lost none of his deer-in-the-headlights look as the meeting dragged on.

"We'll meet at one P.M.," announced the Vice President. "I realize that's not much time, but . . ."

There was no need to finish the sentence.

"Let's go get something to eat," Scotty told Garcia as people began filtering from the room.

"Eat?"

"Yeah, you're hungry, aren't you? Come on, before your boss down there decides to pound a medal into your chest. We're surplus material anyway."

The pilot, looking a bit like a kid lost at a county fair, followed him out into the hallway. Once in the corridor, he hesitated, and Scotty had to wrap his arm around him to get him moving again.

"I think the commandant wanted to talk to me," said the pilot.

"Right. Come on."

"But—"

"Trust me. It's best to keep your head down until Steele works something out with him and the admiral," Scotty said. "O'Rourke is really pissed."

"He didn't seem pissed at me."

"You don't understand Washington."

"But the President—"

Scotty stopped short. The hallway was crowded with aides and NSC staffers. "The President what?"

"The President told Ambassador Steele it was okay."

"Were you there?"

"Well, no."

305

"Then you don't know that, do you?"

"I—but the ambassador wouldn't have—"

"No shit, Sherlock. Now forget you ever figured that out." Scotty pulled Garcia along toward the exit. The kid had the good sense not to say anything else as Scotty led him outside and then toward the city's business section. Scotty, feeling a little sorry for him, explained that the transfer assigning him to Cuba had been run through the NSC staff, kept low-level so that the Joint Chiefs of Staff wouldn't find out about it. Which naturally pissed the hell out of them.

"It's an internal-politics thing, kid. Don't worry about it; as long as you stay away from the admiral, you're fine. The marines will treat you like a hero, and you have some pretty powerful friends."

"Like you?"

"Jeez, don't sound so fucking sarcastic. No, I'm just a turd who keeps floating up in the bowl. Steele likes you, and so will the President. Even that ass-kisser James, and he's bound for glory." Scotty let out a cynical snort. "Come on. You like Chinese?"

"Chinese? For breakfast?"

"Very solid way to start your day. Besides, neither one of us had much dinner."

"Aren't we supposed to . . . report somewhere or something?"

"You've been in the marines too long."

Scotty led him across J Street to a place owned by a former Company informer. Even before he rapped on it the door was opened by a short hostess who had once been employed as a freelance assassin in Hong Kong. Those days were long behind her, though Scotty never liked to encounter her with silverware in her hands.

They exchanged a kiss and a few words, and then Ms. Woo led them to the back.

"You understood what she was saying?" Garcia

asked when she had retreated to the kitchen.

"More or less."

"Wow."

"Don't be too impressed. It wasn't more than hello. What do you want?"

Garcia, confused by the variety and obviously no expert on the cuisine, asked what the cashew chicken tasted like. Scotty called a waiter over and ordered a table's worth of food, which soon began arriving by the armful.

"Try these bamboo shoots," Scotty suggested, waving his chopsticks. "It's like kimchi."

"What's kimchi?"

"Just try it."

Scotty laughed as the pilot spit the burning food from his mouth.

"Too hot for you?"

"Shit." Garcia dropped his fork and grabbed for a glass of water. "Real friggin' funny. Ha-ha-ha."

Scotty worked over a crisp-fried carp with red beans. That was one of the real downsides of Cuba— no great Chinese food.

Esma had laughed when he promised to take her to D.C. just to try some.

One more promise never kept.

But there were other things to worry about. "So what happened to you inside the missile bunker?" Scotty asked as Garcia poked at his food.

"What do you mean, what happened?"

"Listen, kid, you're going to have to level with me. Did something happen that you're not telling us about?"

Garcia put down his fork. "No."

"You were moping about something on the plane. Steele noticed it, too."

"On the plane?"

"Come on. We've been through a lot together,

right? Is there another missile? Did something look phony?"

"No." Garcia's face twisted in annoyed, righteous surprise.

"Look, we're friends, okay? Tell me what was bothering you. Are they threatening your family or something?"

"I was depressed because I got shot down."

"Come on, kid. Tell Uncle Scotty what the real story is. What happened inside Big Rock Candy Mountain?"

"You're an asshole sometimes, you know it?"

"I'm an asshole a lot. But I'm being serious now." Scotty felt his whole body grow cold. He wasn't sure now what Garcia was going to tell him, and he worried that he had misjudged the kid's basic innocence. If the pilot didn't open up soon, he was going to have to take him over to the FBI and polygraph him.

Nothing personal.

"Come on. You saved my life," Scotty tried. "I saved yours. We're friends. Jesus, kid, we got a couple of million people depending on us. Talk to me."

"My—I—they told me my father was a criminal."

"Is that all?" Scotty burst out laughing.

Garcia turned bright red, and for a moment Scotty thought he was going to belt him.

"I'm sorry I'm laughing," he told the pilot. "The ambassador was worried that there was more information about M-26 that you didn't want to tell us."

"Like what?"

"We wouldn't know, right? But you were sitting by yourself, moping. And you seemed troubled at the NSC meeting."

"Like I made the whole thing up?"

"We didn't think that. Listen, kid, trust me. This is a pretty intense time for everybody, right? No one can take chances."

Garcia hesitated before nodding. Scotty could tell he was still considering whether to punch him.

"I didn't mean to laugh at you. What did they say about your dad?"

Stumbling at first, Garcia began by telling him not what de Souza had said, but the stories his mother and father had always told him when he was little. There was very, very little about Cuba, he explained.

The words gushed out, and Scotty saw that despite his effort to appear neutral, Garcia was actually near tears.

"She may have been lying," Scotty suggested.

"I thought about that. But the bit about the shoemaker. It was the kind of detail that seems odd enough to make it true."

"Maybe she was counting on that. A lot of dissidents were jailed. It was pretty much standard procedure, depending on where you were, what else was going on."

"Wouldn't he have told me about it, then? Why did he keep Cuba such a blank?"

A good point, Scotty thought. But hardly evidence.

"Maybe you should ask your dad. I'll find you a place to call him when we go back."

"No way. Not now."

"You shouldn't let it fester. Call him."

"I will." Garcia nodded.

Scotty could see that he wouldn't. "How did de Souza find out? Did she tell you?"

"She said she had spies everywhere."

"Not enough, apparently," said Scotty. "At least not in the right places. Come on. Let's hit the road," he said, standing.

"Can I finish this pork thing first?"

"Nah. We have to get back."

"I thought you said they didn't need us anymore."

Jim DeFelice

"I lied. We're supposed to be in that military planning meeting."

"What?"

"I didn't want your stomach growling in the middle of the meeting," said Scotty, signing the check.

Yuma, Arizona. 9 A.M.

Colonel Henry "Bighead" Talic looked out across the desert as an F/A-18 shot overhead, the throaty roar provoking an involuntary smile on his lips.

"One of yours?" asked Congresswoman Sue Kelly. Talic, while not exactly a giant himself, had to stoop down to hear the petite grandmother's question.

"Oh, no, ma'am," he told her. "Ours are just ahead. That's one of the problems with the A/V-32A, though."

Talic nearly bit his lip trying to get those words back. Sure enough, the congresswoman's face furrowed into a deep frown. She might remind Talic of his great-aunt, but his great-aunt wasn't voting on the appropriations for the Corps next year—including a not-insignificant portion of the A/V-32A's program funding.

"A problem, Colonel?"

"Inside joke, ma'am," he hastened to explain. "Among us old-timers." He cringed, worried that she would think he was referring to her age, not his. "You see, the Pegasus employs what we call a sound-stealth technology. Goes with the low-observable package. She's a good bit quieter than other ships. I wouldn't say she whispers, but she doesn't roar. You'd hardly hear her crossing if she were overhead."

"That's bad?"

"No, ma'am, that's one of the assets of the plane. It lowers the defensive reaction time. That's why that was a joke, you see." The gears in Talic's head

310

were smoking as he worked out the explanation—
not because he was concerned about putting it into
layman's terms, but because he had to do it without
the lubrication of expletives. "Say, for instance, you
and I are bad guys, and we're sitting in our trenches
waiting for the marines to land. We have a shoulder-
launched surface-to-air missile."

"Such as a Stinger FIM-92?"

"Yes, ma'am, exactly." Talic let her have a big
smile. You had to show your appreciation when civilians got the nomenclature right. "Now, that Hornet there, you and I heard her coming a few miles
away."

"We did, Colonel."

"That gave us plenty of warning. We could have
prepared our weapon, set up, maybe even had a
smoke." Talic congratulated himself on having successfully substituted smoking for peeing in his explanation. "By the time we hear the Pegasus,
though, she's nearly overhead. You combine that
with the low radar visibility, and it's a potent
weapon. Adds to survivability and surprise, ma'am,
and they're the name of the game."

"What about your eyes?"

"Excuse me?"

"Won't we see it coming?"

"A lot of our attacks are at night, ma'am. But even
during the day, you adjust your tactics accordingly."

"And a package of thirty-seven planes wouldn't be
noticeable?"

Okay, Talic thought to himself, she remembered
yesterday's briefing about Marine Expeditionary
Units and their support air cover. "Thirty-seven
would be detectable, ma'am, if they all came together. But a lot of those are support aircraft, and
the troop carriers, which are farther back in the, er,
game plan. Surprise would be a factor only in the

initial stages, which is where the Pegasus would strut its stuff."

"I see, Colonel. A sergeant told me yesterday that he could fire a Stinger within two seconds of spotting a plane."

"Oh, he might have been exaggerating a tad, ma'am."

"Still, it does give one pause when a missile that costs less than fifty thousand dollars can destroy a plane that costs half a billion."

"That's why we put such an emphasis on training, ma'am," said Talic, kicking himself for having committed the oldest strategic mistake in the world—underestimating the enemy. These VIP briefings were an important part of his job, and he knew that if did well, he'd be helping not only the Corps but his own career—the day was fast looming when he was either going to get promoted to a Pentagon ass-kisser or asked to take retirement.

He was still undecided as to which fate was worse, though if he screwed this up, he wouldn't have to make the choice.

"Nothing's invincible, is it?" said the congresswoman sweetly.

"Not at all, ma'am. Now, of course, the way the, uh, rear end of the plane is shaped, that cuts down on your IR signature. Plane's almost invisible to a heat-seeker."

"Tell me something, Colonel. There's no metal at all in these planes?"

"Well, there is some metal, ma'am. But a large portion of the fuselage is graphite-epoxy. And of course the wings are mostly another carbon polymer. You see, we're looking to save weight and still have tremendous strength."

"But you use metal in the engine and for the control system, among other things. In the wires and such."

"Oh yes. There are no hydraulics at all; it's entirely electronic."

"Then why did the press boast that there was no metal in the plane?"

Talic had to confess that he hadn't actually seen the story she was referring to. "Just between you and me, ma'am, the press often gets things wrong."

"So I understand. But in this case, I would wager they were working from a press release, which would have been prepared by DOD."

"A little harmless exaggeration, probably," he said, realizing as he did that she was very subtly showing up his own exaggeration about the plane's IR signature.

"I hate it when people aren't precise," said the congresswoman. "Can we see the planes now?"

"Oh yes, absolutely," said Talic, practically running toward the hangar.

White House Basement. 11 A.M.

"It's about time you got back," hissed James as Garcia and Scotty pulled seats toward the large Formica-topped tables in one of the auxiliary conference rooms. "What'd you do, go to the Smithsonian?"

"There's an Impressionist exhibit at the Freer," said McPherson. "Junior likes blurry pictures."

Garcia bristled, but he was still too intimidated by the surroundings to tell McPherson to stop calling him Junior or, worse, kid. He understood that the agent didn't mean it as a slam, exactly—it was one of the nicer things he called anyone. But it still rankled.

McPherson hadn't pressed the phone call home. It was just as well, since Garcia would have refused. He needed time to think about how to talk to his father.

Jim DeFelice

Garcia took a seat next to McPherson and James as an air force intelligence major spread out a highly detailed map showing the possible missile sites. The experts had decided there were a dozen, and they were still little more than guesses. The general whose staff had compiled the list acknowledged there was a possibility—he said as high as twenty percent—that they had missed the location entirely.

Even with the ability to scan more than ten meters below the earth's surface, the laser-radar satellites had yet to find a silo, or even an underground space similar to what Garcia described. The problem remained the position of the northern satellite, which limited the viewing angle.

Airplane reconnaissance, which would have required using RF-18s, was considered too likely to tip the guerrillas off and of questionable value unless the planes got very low—where they were likely to be shot down as Garcia had been. Since surprise was critical to an assault operation and the odds weren't heavily in favor of finding the silo anyway, the flights had been vetoed.

Realizing the guerrillas had probably gotten some information about the limits of satellite surveillance, the group had come to the general conclusion that the missile would be trundled out a side passage, probably with a southern exposure, where it would be fired.

"It would be impractical to construct an undetectable roof to a silo, if you will, that's twenty meters thick," the air force general explained. "That would also explain why they're so confident we won't find them."

"Impossible or impractical?" asked McPherson. There was as much bite in his tone as if he were talking to someone on the street.

"Impractical, not impossible," admitted the blue-coated general, who took the tone in stride, as if he

314

knew McPherson well. "We have had problems with some of the facilities in Russia. But I'd give it ninety-ten in favor of it not having been done. And it would be comparatively easy to move an SS-4. Even an SS-5 could be moved and then fueled."

"Twelve sites is too many," said an army colonel tasked to help coordinate assault logistics. "And we still have to take out the M-26 headquarters at the school."

"We can hit that in a second wave," suggested the air force general. "The fueling time may give us a lot of leeway. If it takes twenty-four hours to fuel and fire, we'll have a day to find it."

"I wouldn't count on that much time at all, sir," said one of the general's aides in a stage whisper.

"Since we have to cut down the sites," McPherson said, "I think we can eliminate anything that isn't near a road that existed in the sixties."

Even so, the best they could do was six locations, including the two McPherson had originally pegged. Garcia followed along as the group adjourned to yet another conference room, where they then met with the ground assault planners.

The planners—they were almost all army—reacted to the number of first-wave sites with incredulity.

"No fucking way we can go in full bore against six sites in the mountains," said a major with the special forces. "Not within that time frame, and not so damn far apart. And look at the weather reports—all kinds of clouds moving in. We won't even have UAVs in the area in time for assault. Jesus H. Christ. You're out of your mind."

"The number of sites has to come down," agreed a Marine Corps colonel.

But no one volunteered to eliminate any other sites. And so when the planning groups presented their plan to the full NSC at the one-o'clock meeting, the Joint Chiefs collectively moaned.

"You're calling for a six-pronged helicopter assault at four o'clock in the morning," said Chairman Wallcox. "On impossible terrain, with growing cloud cover, under the most hostile circumstances possible. We don't have enough men and equipment for three simultaneous attacks, not in the kind of force you're talking about."

Garcia felt like a fifth-grader sitting in a college physics class. True, his preliminary officer training had included infantry work and even some rudimentary exercises, and he prided himself on his ability to grunt it out with the best of them. But the men—and a few women—gathered around the table were specialists in their field, talking in a kind of shorthand. It wasn't the acronyms so much as the knowledge they took for granted, like how impossible a parachute drop would be at point X or how much night-vision equipment would slow down a squad of soldiers. Garcia understood most of the air-support issues, but even his extensive training—and ability—had not yet crafted a mind-set that could view the entire battlefield at once. He was impressed as hell by the quality of the people around him.

And that was what worried him. If all of these brains couldn't figure out how to get the missile quickly, it might not be doable.

The Vice President, sitting at a console almost directly opposite Garcia, listened with palpable impatience as the session continued. McPherson suddenly jumped forward in his seat with a theory—prioritize the sites closest to an old rail line, since that would have been a natural way to move equipment into the mountains.

A new debate started. How close? A mile? A half-mile?

Just as McPherson started to say something, the door opened and the President himself walked in.

Garcia didn't recognize him right away. Everyone around the table was starting to stand, and Garcia instinctively began to rise with them. It was only after the nasal voice he'd heard on television told them all to carry on that he realized who was walking toward him.

"Job well done, son," the President told Garcia as he slapped his arm on his shoulder. "You're getting to be quite a hero. Don't think we're not paying attention."

Garcia sputtered out a garbled collection of "sirs" and "thank you, sirs." Next to him, McPherson barely suppressed a laugh. The President—he seemed taller than on TV—smiled and continued around the table, discreetly greeting others until he arrived at the empty seat between the Vice President and Dr. Blitz. Garcia noticed that Admiral O'Rourke was making every effort to look away as the President approached.

President D'Amici listened carefully as the Vice President recapped the guerrillas' threat. The Secretary of State then made the case for negotiations, but quickly deflated it by saying it would open up all sorts of future blackmail.

"Not an option," said the President gravely. He looked across the room at Ambassador Steele. "Malcolm, tell us about the guerrillas. What's going on?"

Steele gave the President a brief overview of M-26, leaning heavily on Scotty's theory about guerrilla infighting.

"Scott, can you add anything? Is this thing for real?" the President asked.

Garcia felt himself almost trembling, as if the President had called on him.

The CIA agent answered that he couldn't add much beyond the fact that the guerrillas had apparently been fighting over ownership of the weapon, which implied it wasn't imaginary. "Romano Moncada is certifiable," McPherson added. "I'm sure he thinks he's the reincarnation of fuckin' Fidel, and would use it in a blink."

The President didn't react to the profanity, nor to the informality. "You had a little adventure picking up our pilot, I understand."

"Actually, he saved my butt when we were ambushed. He's done a hell of a job."

D'Amici nodded, then listened as Professor Blitz quickly summarized the historical background and the questions about which missile they might be up against. "The bottom line here is, we have no choice but to attack," added the adviser. "We have a window of opportunity because of their fueling situation, but we can't count on it lasting forever, so the sooner we go, the better."

"How safe is this warhead if we attack them?" asked the President.

"In theory, it ought to be inert until well after the launch," replied an air force general. "The Soviet warheads at the time were designed to withstand fairly heavy secondary explosions without going off, and could survive the missile's self-destruct procedure without exploding. But of course, that's only a theory."

"Is that why we aren't thinking about sending some stealth bombers with smart bombs to take it out?"

"That's one consideration," said the National Security Adviser. While obvious defensive positions could be bombed, the penetration weapons that would be needed to knock out a reinforced hangar or silo required a very specific target.

"And not only do we have at least six sites, sir," he added, "but they're on the sides of some relatively large hills and mountains."

Garcia felt the President's eyes sweep over him like a pair of searchlights. "Tell me what you know about the missile silo, son."

Garcia shot to his feet, nearly shaking. He told himself to relax; the man he was talking to was just a regular guy, older and more confident, but flesh and blood, like McPherson or Talic or his father.

Well, not his father.

"Yes, sir. The entrance was dug right into the mountain. The interior seemed to have been reinforced. The walls, at least where I went in, had to be at least fifty feet thick. The roof, though, I'm not sure."

The pilot saw the President's grave expression deepen, the weight of the situation eating into his face. He could tell what he was thinking—there must be a better solution—and the young marine felt himself starting to sink back toward his chair, as if he were personally responsible for letting the President down. He remembered the last seconds in the cockpit of the Sukhoi, when it looked completely hopeless, when he pushed, prodded, and prayed his way to a solution.

"The satellite scanned to a depth of eighteen meters, Mr. President," added one of the intelligence analysts when Garcia finished. "And we have found nothing. But because of the alignment, there were many areas shaded out. There are several ways they can launch the missile, either by moving it or opening a hole in their mountain."

"The fact that there is no obvious silo could also mean that it's fake," said the President.

"That's right," agreed Blitz.

"I don't suppose we can bet the lunch money on that," said D'Amici. He meant it as a joke, and laughed a little, but no one else did.

"The Chiefs think hitting six targets simultaneously is a stretch on such short notice," said the Vice

President. "We have a window of opportunity, so we're trying to give them priorities—maybe three in the first wave, three more in a second wave a few minutes later, and so on. If we start the attack at four, by six A.M. we should have the entire region secure. It's just the first twenty to thirty minutes that will be dicey."

"If we could even prioritize the first three," said an army general, "it would help. But this terrain is going to make it difficult for the Joint-Stars battle-field surveillance components to get any prestrike intelligence."

"Why can't we send in a UAV beforehand?" Blitz asked.

"Nothing's in position with the kind of range and power we'd need," said the general whose team was responsible for the assault planning. "Optical UAVs will be useless at night, and anyway, they'd have to fly so low they'd be heard. Surprise is critical."

An idea burbled out from the depths of Garcia's mind, an insane idea.

"I—" he started, but then he realized how crazy it was, and shut up.

Too late.

"What is it you want to say, Lieutenant?" the President asked.

Garcia looked around the room. The Vice President, Admiral O'Rourke, the Secretary of Defense—everyone was looking at him.

"Nothing, sir. Nothing."

"Go ahead, Junior," hissed McPherson, pushing his elbow into his side. "Talk. They'll listen."

His mouth froze. D'Amici waited another second, then turned to the Vice President to ask another question.

"Sir, excuse me." Garcia balled his fists into his hands, which were straight down at his sides. "But since we need intelligence, your idea about the stealth bombers could help us. Not using the B-2 itself, but the idea."

"Sit down, Lieutenant," barked Admiral O'Rourke.

The animosity in his voice took Garcia by surprise, but stiffened his resolve. "Sir, I could take a Pegasus across the sites for a last-minute scan. It would be just like having a UAV out ahead of the assault troops, only it would be faster, maybe even quieter. If there was any sort of activity, I'd pick it up. Then I could direct the assaults. Or send the bombers in first."

"Shit, kid, why don't you land and blow it up yourself," whispered McPherson.

"I could blow it up myself," said Garcia, who hadn't realized no one else could hear McPherson— or that he had been joking.

The President roared with laughter. For a moment, the grave air that had hung heavy in the room lifted.

"Well, you certainly give your men a can-do attitude, Admiral," D'Amici told Admiral O'Rourke.

"I apologize."

"No, no, don't apologize. I like this young man. He's always thinking. I think going it alone is probably a bit Rambo, don't you, son?"

Garcia, who at this moment wanted to bore himself down into the earth's molten core, nodded.

"But using the plane to scout the sites—that's a good idea, isn't it?"

"Might tip them off, sir," said one of the planners. "Nothing is completely invisible, not even the Pegasus."

"On the other hand, their defenses aren't terribly sophisticated," answered an air force major. "An F-117 could get in."

"The Pegasus is quieter," snapped Admiral O'Rourke, who seemed to have finally decided it would not hurt his future to acknowledge that the marines, and this one in particular, existed. "And we could fit the bomb bay with a sensor package." He turned and consulted with one of his aides, then urged the man to speak to the entire group.

"The, er, designed units haven't reached production, but we could tweak the pod off a standard RA-18. You couldn't send back the telemetry, but you could slave the Pegasus's computer to view a side-looking radar image. It's not foolproof, but it ought to work."

"It would be best to use the two-place model, Admiral," said Garcia, his butterflies and embarrassment banished. "This way, we could have a set of eyes in the backseat. Someone who knows the terrain. They could watch the screens while I flew."

"I volunteer."

The words surprised Garcia so much, he whirled around.

"I know the Sierra Maestra very well," said Tito Porta. "My family is from there."

"That's admirable of you to volunteer," said one of the air force analysts, "but we need a trained operator."

"Excuse me, sir," said Captain James. "But I had a tour as a Joint-Stars officer. Six months."

"Doesn't it fucking figure?" sighed McPherson.

Yuma, Arizona. 1:55 P.M.

As soon as the door to the base commander's office closed behind him, Colonel Talic felt more relieved than he had the afternoon he'd put his A/V-8B down at Al Jubail/King Abdul Aziz Naval Base on the last day of the Gulf War.

He wasn't in any mood to do a handstand, though. If the congresswoman's demeanor made it look as if she had spent the past fifty years baking cookies, her questions showed she might have spent at least half that time moonlighting as a DOD analyst. He'd taken numerous hits. She had even corrected him once on the Pegasus's rate of climb.

And damned if, on reflection, he hadn't realized the Republican from New York cow country was right. While she'd seemed impressed with the planes and the squadron, he knew she wasn't inside telling the base commander what a great squadron leader he was. Forced retirement was probably three days away.

Talic decided he'd take a very long debrief over at one of the base clubs. He had gone about two steps in that direction when he was accosted by Zach Stevens, the wing's S-4 tactical officer.

"Hey, Henry, there you are. I've been looking all over for you."

"Jesus, Zach, you wouldn't believe what I've just gone through," he wailed. "Come on, I'm buying—it may be my last lunch."

"No can do. You can't either, Colonel."

"What's this 'colonel' shit?"

Stevens pulled out a thin Teletype message. "They want the Pegasuses to join up with an MEU in Florida, and they want the two-seater there yesterday."

"The trainer?"

"Yeah. Something big's going on, and nobody's saying what. You ever hear of a marine air station at Jacksonville Naval Base?"

"Give me that paper."

Talic took the yellow slip of paper from his subordinate's hand. The order was terse, classified, and completely illogical.

Which meant it was neither a mistake nor a screwup.

"Round up the pilots," barked Talic, swinging toward his quarters to grab his gear. "Tell Thomas and his boys I need those planes within an hour."

"Already working on it," said Stevens, scrambling to keep up. "But we only have thirty minutes."

"Too bad Elvis missed this. Could have really used him," muttered the colonel as his trot turned into a run. "Goddamn kid's probably catching rays on a beach right about now."

En route to Florida. 3 P.M.

"You're out of your goddamn mind," Scotty told Garcia as they boarded a navy helicopter. "This is the worst damn case of gung-ho disease I've ever seen."

"I'm still pissed at you. You made me look like a jerk in front of the President."

"Like shit. He kissed your ass. You come back from this in one piece, he'll offer you a cabinet post."

"How come you didn't volunteer to come with me?"

"When fucking pigs grow wings, that's when I fly," said Scotty.

"You're going to fly now."

"Yeah, don't remind me." Scotty pushed into the belly of the craft. The ancient H-46 medium transport had held various jobs during its thirty-plus years of service. It had a large rotor at each end, which gave Scotty a certain amount of confidence. His seat, however, was a piece of fabric stretched across a thin tube of metal; he strapped himself into the bright orange shoulder harness as if it were safety netting, and closed his eyes as the helicopter whipped its engines into action.

They were headed for Jacksonville Naval Air Station in Florida. Primarily used for antisubmarine operations, the base was one of several hastily tapped as staging areas for the assault. President D'Amici had reserved final approval for the strike, but the elements had to be ready to roll when he gave the word.

The operation was so complicated that its details were still a jumbled mess, subject to a thousand asterisks and last-minute changes. Fresh satellite intelligence was due to arrive at Jacksonville for Scotty's perusal by 7 P.M., just in time for a high-level conference call among the analysts. Until then, they were sticking with his railroad-track theory in prioritizing the sites.

The helicopter lurched into the sky, leaving Scotty's stomach somewhere back on the tarmac. He cursed himself for eating the crispy carp, even if it had been ordered in the line of duty.

Porta and James sat across from him, studying a detailed topological map that sketched out the possible sites. The two Scotty had initially zeroed in on were near railroad tracks and remained in the top group.

"I think it must be this one," Porta told Garcia as the chopper steadied into cruising altitude. "These rocks are like the ones you described. Don't you think?"

"It's hard to tell."

"I'm positive. You should go there first."

Scotty scowled. Not twelve hours before, Porta was saying the missile was on the opposite end of the island. The man spouted more misinformation than a talk-show host.

But he sure could put his nose up people's asses. He'd probably end up running for goddamn president of Cuba. Or the United States.

And James. *I have Joint-Stars training.* Uh-huh. And Medal of Honor lust. But at least he had the sense to keep his mouth more or less shut when he didn't know something.

The helicopter jerked itself into a banking turn, and Scotty became acutely aware of the canvas holding him in place. He found himself starting to wonder how thin the metal wall behind him was.

That was not a good direction for his thoughts to take.

"So what's the deal on this plane of yours?" he asked Garcia, tightening his grip on the aluminum seat strut.

"You haven't heard of it?"

"Not lately."

"It's a low-observable strike fighter. The Corps version of the Joint Strike Assault plane. A hundred years beyond what I've been flying."

"And you, James, you're going to spin the dials in the backseat?"

James fluttered his nostrils in Scotty's direction. "I'm going to redeem myself."

"Redeem yourself? For what? Because you have a desk job? You fucking guys are too much."

"Actually, the C^3 will do all the work," said Garcia. "All the captain will have to do is watch the displays. They won't even know we're there. By the time they hear us, we'll be gone. A vacuum cleaner makes more noise than a Pegasus in stealth approach."

Scotty rolled his eyes, even though he agreed that the quick, up-close recon made a lot of sense.

"Your parents will be proud of your heroics," said Porta. "It will redeem your family name."

Surprised that Garcia had shared de Souza's accusation with Porta, Scotty shot the Cuban a cross-eyed look, then turned to the pilot, whose face was writhing in embarrassment.

What a mistake telling Porta, Scotty thought. Might just as well put out a press release. Garcia must have figured the Cuban could help him get access to old government records or something.

"I ain't gonna be a hero," Garcia said in a flat tone almost drowned out by the helicopter's engines. "I'm just going to do my job."

Havana Strike

The message was necessarily short.

"Six A.M."

Romano said nothing. He placed the phone in its cradle and handed it to his aide. He thought for a moment of returning to his room, of gathering his thoughts one final time before the fatal hour. But the message meant that the Americans had made their decision and given him eleven hours to prepare. Though that was more than ample time, it should not be wasted.

And so Hector Romano Moncada simply paused as he left the bunker of his command post, breathing in the heavy, expectant air. This was the way history came upon you, moving with expectation and ferocity. His entire life had pushed toward this moment.

The missile would be launched as soon as the American invasion force touched Cuban soil. From that moment on, his own existence ceased to be important. He had prepared for that, even as some small part of him resisted. He could not tell whether it was simply his ego, desiring the adulation that victory would bring, or a true concern for his countrymen, who would require a leader to bring them to the future.

But there was no need to worry on either count. For truly he would be hailed by future generations as the man who kept Cuba free; he would be second only to his father, Fidel. And Zora had promised that of his essence there would be no death; if his momentary existence ceased in the coming battle, his soul would find a new home somewhere else, to lead his people onward.

His eye caught the door as it opened. One of his soldiers struggled from the building with a thirty-

327

year-old machine gun. Tired, the man leaned against the bricks for a rest.

"You there," Romano shouted. "Come, now, you must be strong. There is a great deal to do. We will all rest tomorrow."

"*Sí, Jefe,*" said the man, hoisting the gun over his shoulder, his energy renewed. "Thank you, sir."

Jacksonville Naval Air Station, Florida. 7:15 P.M.

With literally nothing to do until the Pegasuses arrived, Garcia roamed the large naval air station, looking for some place where he could be alone. That was close to impossible—the place was busier than a shopping mall at Christmas. Transports were buzzing in, troops were mustering; D day had been mounted with less hassle.

Garcia's blood roiled with a combination of anticipation and anger. He was pissed at McPherson for telling Porta about his father. He'd trusted the agent to keep a secret—hell, if somebody who worked for the CIA couldn't keep his mouth shut, who could? Worse than that, he'd come to look on the man as something of a friend. Not only had he saved his butt but he'd also kept him from getting into trouble over Maria. McPherson had the totally wrong idea about her, but that was probably to be expected; being a spook made you seriously paranoid.

And obviously not to be trusted.

The worst thing was that he'd probably made some snide-ass comment about it, some stupid-shit joke.

Every so often the anger welled up inside the pilot and he just wanted to punch the stuffing out of something. He couldn't, of course. And so he just walked.

He found himself down by the runway area, admiring a squadron of F/A-18s that had just evicted a P-3 Orion from its maintenance area. The fighter-bombers looked like hungry tigers spoiling for a fight. Their jocks must be inside; Garcia thought maybe he ought to make himself useful by giving them a quick rundown of what they might expect if they were called in for ground support. But when he approached the door to the administrative building directly behind the hangar, he found his way barred by two sailors.

Well, not the sailors themselves. Their rifles were a hell of a lot more impressive.

"Sorry, sir, no one is permitted inside."

"I'm a pilot."

"Begging your pardon, sir," said the sailor, who sure y ranked as the politest swab in the world, "but you're not with the squadron."

"No kidding," said Garcia, starting to push past. The sailor quickly presented his rifle—and not for inspection.

"Hey, it's okay, he's with me," boomed a voice from behind him. Garcia, red-faced, watched McPherson wave his CIA credentials at the sailors like a magic wand.

"Sorry, sir," apologized the guards, stepping out of Garcia's way.

"Hey, wait up, Junior," shouted McPherson, trotting into the building to keep up. "Whoa, slow down. What's up your ass, anyway?"

"You're up my ass." Garcia could feel his anger unraveling. "You should've kept that stuff about my father to yourself."

"I did."

"So what was Porta talking about?" Garcia felt his anger boil in the veins of his neck, then controlled it, though just barely.

"Hey, hey, hold on," said McPherson, grabbing his shoulder as he started away.

As he whirled back around, Garcia thought he might actually punch him.

"Tito Porta? Man, he's got to be the biggest dickhead in Cuba," said McPherson. "Ask anybody—I can't stand the scumbag. I wouldn't tell him the time of day."

"You're a stinking liar."

"Ask your copilot." McPherson stepped back as if to laugh, but didn't. "Listen, I'm not lying to you."

"Don't try acting like you're my buddy," said Garcia, pulling his arm back and continuing down the hallway. "You're not my friend."

"Yeah, well, I'll remember that the next time I save your fucking life, asshole."

Scotty watched the pilot disappear through a set of doors at the far end of the hallway. "By the way, the new satellite images are in. They don't show dick, but they're in."

Walking back out toward the hangar area, he stopped and asked the sailors where he might find something to eat. Pointed in the direction of a cafeteria, he walked behind the hangar area, starting to feel more philosophical about everything. He'd be pissed off, too, if he thought somebody told a stranger about his dad being a crook.

Tito Porta, especially.

But if Scotty hadn't told Porta, and Garcia hadn't, who had?

The information hadn't been included in any of the reports on Garcia's captivity. In fact, there hadn't been a formal report.

Was it in his personnel folder?

Why? And how would it get there?

A bad feeling took hold of him. Scotty began running toward the suite of offices that had been commandeered as an intelligence post.

Porta wasn't there. One of the naval duty officers

said he'd seen him looking for a place to have a cigar.

"Is there a phone around here I can use?" he asked the ensign.

"We haven't set up the encryption facilities yet, sir."

"Just show me to a regular phone. No, wait a second—where's there a pay phone?"

The officer gave him a puzzled look, then directed him to a lounge area two buildings away. Scotty ran the entire way. He didn't want to use the base phone system, worried that Porta or one of his compatriots might have found a way to bug it.

"The line is open," he told Sylvia in the CIA systems section when she picked up, warning her he was speaking on an unscrambled phone. "But I have to know something—did we do a background check on my little buddy Garcia?"

"Hello, Scott," she said sarcastically. "How are you?"

"Come on, the pilot Garcia. Was there a background check on him?"

"I don't know."

"Can you access it?"

"Scotty—"

"You wouldn't believe how important this is."

"Try me."

"An open line, remember."

"I was supposed to go off duty hours ago. We're up to our eardrums, you know it."

"I'll give you anything, Sylvia. Please."

"All right. Hold on."

Scotty waved off a haggard sailor who approached the phone booth. The man's glare made him contemplate just how long it would take to reach the pistol snugged against his ankle.

Too long. Fortunately, the sailor spotted another phone nearby and moved on.

"Wow—you know his father was jailed in Havana?"

"Does it say why?"

"No."

"How come it's in his folder?"

"It's not. Someone ran an inquiry off his parents' names and I picked up the history line when I went to search. Might have been a petty thief, looks like. Why were his parents run against the database?"

"I was hoping you could tell me," said Scotty. "Is it routine?"

"No. He wasn't actually working for the embassy."

"Does it say who asked for the check?"

He could hear Sylvia's fingers clacking against the keys.

"The code is ambassador's staff."

"Staff? Not Porta?"

"Just says staff. Someone did it themselves; we would have used our own numbers. Could be anyone."

Except Porta, who would have had to go to Sylvia's department to ask for anything out of the computer because he wasn't cleared for direct access. And Scotty knew the man had an aversion to computers and wouldn't have been able to word-process a letter, much less work over complicated files.

But then again, he couldn't take anything for granted. "What's the date on the report?"

"Hard to tell. Wait a second. July twenty-second."

"Twenty-second? You sure?"

"I'm guessing. There's no way to tell for sure, except that I know where it is on the master cue."

July 22 was before the kid had been shot down. Scotty's mind raced over the past few days, trying to dredge up some other way of nailing Porta. He remembered the U-2 flight de Souza had known about.

"I know this is a long shot, Sylvia, but can you access the embassy phone logs?"

"Scotty, I have an unbelievable mountain of work here."

"You can do that, can't you? You told me the other day."

"Yes. I can do it."

"Find out if Tito Porta made a call from the embassy yesterday morning around two—somewhere between two and four."

"Why?"

"Just fuckin' do it, Sylvia! God."

She did not like being shouted at. He could tell by how hard she slammed the phone onto the desk.

But she didn't hang up.

"No," she said when she came back on. "There was only one phone call from an embassy phone yesterday between two and four; it was at three-oh-three A.M. Nothing until six o'clock after that, and I checked back as far as one and didn't get anything."

"Who made the call?"

"I don't know. That's the odd thing—it has an access code that's defunct."

"Defunct?"

"Yeah. That's interesting. You can't just fake those. They're based on a coded algorithm."

"Huh?"

"They're generated by code. Hold on a second."

"I'm sorry I yelled at you."

Sylvia typed away without acknowledging his apology. "There are a couple of phony numbers in the system, Scotty. No wonder the department billing is all screwed up."

"Shit."

"They're never made to the same number, but they're all using upstairs phones. The ambassador's office suite."

"You sure?"

"Well, that could be faked, but not easily. Scott, I'm going to have to alert security. That's standard procedure."

"Fine." Scotty was lost momentarily, his mind denying the obvious conclusion. "Just on a wild-goose chase here—call up Captain James's personnel record."

"Hold on."

"You heard me apologize, right?"

"Yes. I just haven't decided whether to accept it or not."

While he waited for her to work the buttons on her computer, Scotty reached down to his ankle and unholstered the Glock. He checked the magazine—loaded and ready to go.

"It's in front of me. What is it you need to know?" Sylvia asked.

"Just tell me when he was assigned to Joint-Stars. That's air force and army Joint Surveillance Target Attack Radar System or some bullshit like that. Battlefield surveillance."

"I'm looking for Joint-Stars. I don't know. Not all of these army gigs are in plain language."

"Look into the comments section. You'd have some air force thing attached maybe, or an intelligence note, or something. Have to be before Cuba, so that's—what, two years now. Actually, you know what, he said the assignment was for six months. You could look for something overseas, Korea or Malaysia. Damn it, I'm not sure."

"Doesn't matter. There's nothing like that here."

"Nothing at all?"

"Not only does a text search fail, but the only assignment Captain James had for more than three months besides an infantry unit right out of officer's training was in the Pentagon. Say, Scott, did you know that he got into a hell of a lot of trouble two years ago over gambling? He was severely repri-

manded, according to this. Jesus, the whole finding's here. You should see how much money he
supposedly was betting. Scott?"

Jacksonville Naval Air Station, Florida. 9:10 P.M.

After he acknowledged the controller's clearance to
land, Talic turned his eyes slightly to the left. The
sensors in his helmet immediately picked up the
movement, and the flat-panel video screen embedded in the lower half of the cockpit glass flashed an
enhanced view of the two Pegasus A/V-32As trailing
his port wing. Gump obliged him with an equally
exact view of the two planes to his right.

"Weber, you should be lining up your approach
by now," he told his pilot. "A couple of people are
going to be watching us land. Let's make it look
pretty."

"Yes, sir. I'm sorry, Colonel."

Talic's smile was interrupted by Gump, beeping
at him because he was almost at the programmed
coordinate to begin his descent.

"Screw you, Gump," he told the computer.
"There's been a change of plans. We're landing in
vertical mode."

"Course change has not been programmed," replied the computer.

"Oops. Looks like I forgot to tell you. What a
shame."

Though he did his best to hide his feelings from
the squadron he was training, Talic hated Gump
and the computer it fronted. If the truth be told—
and certainly it wouldn't be to a congressperson or
just about anyone else—he didn't care for the Pegasus either.

Too much whiz-bang, too much push-button.
Though he'd spent his career on the cutting edge of
Marine Corps aviation, the best plane he'd ever

flown was still an honest old Skooter—an A-4, and not one of the newer models, either.

Pushing the stick in that plane meant something.

He pushed the stick now, and the computer translated his gentle touch into a series of electrons that slapped the flaps and ailerons around. Talic put the two-seat Pegasus into a perfect three-point landing right in front of the designated hangar. The four planes of his squadron came down in near-simulator-perfect fashion behind him.

Popping the canopy, Talic scanned the apron, looking for familiar faces in the crowd of onrushing techies. Most of the support crew had flown out of Yuma ahead of the A/V-32As; with luck, Sergeant Major Pain-in-the-ass Thomas ought to be kicking the shit out of some hapless E-4 by now.

"Jesus, Colonel, what'd you do? Come by way of Alaska? I got a Honda Civic drives faster than you do."

"Elvis?" Talic nearly fainted over the side of the plane when he spotted the lieutenant. "What the hell are you doing here?"

"Waiting for you to hand over my airplane."

Talic, not wanting to wait for the ground crew to roll out a ladder, leaned back in the cockpit and had Gump take enough air out of the landing-gear struts so he could jump down easily.

"You can hurt your knee that way, Colonel," said Garcia, folding his arms around him in a welcoming bear hug.

"Jesus, Garcia, it's good to see you. Shit, you're looking good. Hospital beds must agree with you."

"I haven't been in the hospital, Colonel," said Garcia sheepishly. "I've been in Cuba."

"Cuba?"

"I've been flying Harriers—old Spanish jobs from year one. I got shot down the other day."

"What?"

"A shoulder-fired missile the fucking guerrillas weren't supposed to have," the pilot said. "But that's nothing. You know what's going on?"

"I haven't got a clue," said Talic, surprised not only by Garcia's presence but by the upgraded—or downgraded, depending on your point of view—swearwords.

"Garcia?" asked Linda Weber as the rest of the squadron pilots came up and surrounded the pilot in a team hug.

"You guys are going to want to find some place to eat," Garcia told them. "Then there's a ton to do. I'll fill you in on what's going on, but it's between us, okay? I got a CIA agent on my back, and the ambassador would probably have a fit if he knew I was out here instead of studying maps."

"Ambassador? Elvis, come here with me a minute," said Talic, taking the pilot aside. He waved the other pilots toward the hangar, where a navy lieutenant was just coming to round them up. "What the hell is going on?"

"Bad shit. I'll explain along the way." Garcia eyed his old commander with something more than the goofy grin Talic expected. "Say, Colonel, do me a favor, okay?"

Something odd, hard, in the voice caught Talic by surprise.

"Nobody calls me Elvis anymore."

Talic nodded slowly, surprised that his young prodigy had grown so much in such a short time. There was only one way that could have happened, and as he followed Garcia inside, he sensed for the first time just how serious their mission was going to be.

At roughly the same moment the Pegasus flight touched down, Scotty was taking the stairs up to the intelligence center two at a time. As he reached the landing, he saw Tito Porta just pushing inside the nearest door. He caught the Cuban's arm with a sudden burst of speed and yanked him out into the hallway. Porta got half a shriek out of his mouth before it was abruptly cut short by a nasty jab of the business end of a Glock 26 in his windpipe.

"Tell me, fuckhead, how did you know about Garcia's father?"

"W-what's going on?" Porta stuttered.

"You told him on the helicopter that he would clear the family name. What did you mean?"

"I—"

Scotty ignored the shouts and commotion flaring up behind him.

"Tell me what you meant."

"C-Captain James said—"

Scotty didn't bother to hear the rest. He tossed Porta aside like a child's toy and dashed past the two MPs who had emerged from the intelligence suite.

"Are the phones set up yet?" he yelled to the first intelligence analyst he saw.

"We're just getting them hooked in."

"Give me a working line quick. The whole operation is compromised."

Everyone else in the suite—intelligence officers, analysts, MPs, and hangers-on—moved in slow motion around him as Scotty waited for the communications specialist to dial him into the secure network. "I need Steele," he barked when the line went live. "I need Ambassador Steele right now. Tell him it's Scott McPherson, and tell him it's trouble. Big time."

Scotty pushed the phone away from his ear as the man on the other end of the line started asking questions instead of doing as he was told. Belatedly realizing he was still holding the Glock, he slipped it into his pocket. "Somebody here see Captain James?" he asked his gawking audience.

. "I think he took the maps over to one of the pre-flight areas," said a navy captain. "He was supposed to be fitted for flight gear and prepped on the equipment."

"Fucking shit," muttered Scotty.

"Scotty, what the hell is going on?" barked Steele over the phone.

"James was never assigned to Joint-Stars," Scotty told him.

"What?"

"He's a mole or a spy or something for the guerrillas. Someone has been using bogus codes from the embassy to contact M-26. They've been calling from your suite."

"That could be anyone."

"Someone called at three o'clock in the morning, right before our friend de Souza got ahold of us. That must be how she knew about the U-2. James was awake then. I remember, because he told me he hadn't slept."

Scotty heard Steele call to an aide, telling him to punch into the army's personnel records. He wasn't too happy, and he answered a question to the effect that privacy procedures be damned.

"General?" asked Scotty.

"I have to go through channels, Scott. I'm not exactly in the best spot to do this right now. It's going to take some time. What else do you have?"

A hunch? A gut feeling?

"Nothing solid. James may have been the source for some personal information the guerrillas had on Garcia. It's not clear."

"Are we talking about the same person?"

"It looks like he might have had big gambling debts or something. I don't have all the dope, but there's definitely something there. I know he hung out in the casinos, but like a chump I never figured it out."

339

Scotty decided not to ask Steele if he'd known about James's history—the fact that the ambassador didn't ask any more questions was an answer all by itself.

Stinking Steele. He thought he could reclaim everybody.

Scotty included.

"Why do you think the mission's been compromised?" asked Steele.

"Jesus Christ, General, if a spy was sitting in the middle of the NSC meeting—"

"All right, all right. Where are you?"

"Command center at Jacksonville."

"Is there a General Keller there?"

"General Keller?" shouted Scotty to the room. "General Keller?"

"I'm his aide," said a major, approaching the phone.

"I got his aide," Scotty told Steele, pulling the man forward by the cuff.

"Put him on. Our only option is to push this thing up—way up. Scotty, you better not be wrong about this."

"I'm not, General," said Scotty, handing over the phone.

In the space of only a few hours, the peaceful naval base had erupted into a fierce, if semicontrolled, whirlpool. With just under six hours left for the assault to get under way, the frenzy was reaching high gear.

So was security. While Scotty had passed into the building without any problem, he had to go through not one but two different security posts to get outside its doors. Fortunately, an NSC staffer recognized him at the first post, and his shouted greeting greased the skids past the MPs.

Not so at the perimeter of the Pegasus hangar.

Two unsmiling marine sentries blocked his way.

"I'm with the goddamn CIA," said Scotty, reaching into his pocket. He pulled his Glock out first—and immediately found two M-16s in his face.

"I'm just getting my ID," he said, holding the pistol gingerly by the barrel.

They didn't let him prove it. The pistol was snatched from his hand and Scotty felt himself being pushed to the ground.

"I'm going to let you secure me," he said through his gritted teeth, fighting his reflexes, "because we're in a hurry. And then I'm going to expect a very sincere fucking apology."

"Shut your mouth."

"Would you check my ID?"

One of the marines pulled the laminated tag from his pocket. He looked at it, then took his boot off of Scotty's arm.

"Sorry, sir," said one finally, "but our orders are not to permit anyone on the field or into the hangar."

"I'll recommend you for a medal," said Scotty, snatching the tags back. "Give me my gun."

"Better be careful, sir. Looks almost real."

"Yeah, yeah, very funny, asshole," said Scotty. He took a step toward the hangar—only to once more find his way blocked by the sentry. "Look, I'm sorry if I insulted you. Just get out of my way. I'm in a hurry."

"Didn't you hear us? We have orders not to let anyone pass."

"Screw your orders," said Scotty, whose anger now crescendoed. "Look, you shit-eating jarheads, I have to talk to Lieutenant Garcia before it's too late."

Both marines bristled. "Sir. There are no jarheads in the marines."

"Get your commander on the radio. Tell him

you're pointing your M-16s at Scott McPherson
while a spy climbs aboard your newest fucking airplane, Christ shit-fuck almighty."

The Pegasus engine ripped to life with a satisfying
surge, the huge vertical fan behind the tandem cockpit straining with anticipation. Garcia told Gump to
finish its tests pronto, and the C^3 unit whipped its
chips into a number-crunching orgy. Everything
was dash-one perfect. The control panel blazed with
green lights, and Garcia's fingers itched against the
sticks at the side of his seat, throttle and lift grip on
left, control grip on right. After the crowded confusion of the Harrier cockpit, sitting in the Pegasus
was like sitting in a living room, or at least a very
well-ordered den.

Garcia hadn't had a chance to grab one of the
squadron's laptop computers to record the essential
flight-plan data prior to the flight, and so he had to
read the coordinates in to Gump verbally rather
than simply throwing a disk in. It wasn't much of a
hardship, though it took a bit longer since the computer replayed every number in its precise but slow
synthetic voice.

"You ready back there, Captain?" Garcia asked
over the intercom when he was done. "Our orders
are to get out of here yesterday, if possible."

He had to tell James which button to push to get
the intercom to work. Before he could reply, the
tower boomed in with a runway assignment and a
priority clearance.

Things were cranking now. Garcia edged forward
on the ramp, heading toward the runway like a
sumo wrestler approaching the mat.

He was just swinging toward the runway proper
when a humvee shot out of the hangar area in his
general direction. He ignored it, sliding into position, manually checking his nozzles—though Gump

had already set them—and asking for a final go.

"Cleared for takeoff, Eagle One," responded the tower. Garcia's left hand grasped the throttle. The plane rocked as he plucked the engine from standby idle to takeoff boogie, the Pegasus nipping at its bridle like a colt at the starting gate. She began slowly at first, but quickly started high-stepping down the track.

"Object ahead!" shouted Gump in his ear as the Pegasus began rolling freely. "Object ahead! Avert takeoff."

Garcia overrode the computer, grabbing at the vertical flight controls to clutch the huge fan behind him into action, adding lift as the humvee careened wildly into his path. With Gump bitching its head off, he jerked the computer out of the circuit and yanked the Pegasus nearly straight into the air. The plane whipped up so awkwardly that he had to bend the stick to level off.

The controls were a million times more responsive than the Harrier's, and the plane pitched wildly, overreacting to his commands. Garcia just barely managed to hold it stable as it stuttered forward in the sky, the column of air from its powerful engines bailing the pilot out.

Back in charge, Garcia banked to his right to take a pass at the runway and find out what sort of lunatic had almost killed him.

The sort who stops his humvee in the middle of the runway and jumps up and down like a crazy madman.

Scott McPherson. With two marine MPs aiming rifles at the plane.

"What the hell's going on?" James asked in the back seat.

"Damned if I know," said Garcia, pushing the plane into a hover to land. He set it down a few yards away from McPherson, who ran forward as Garcia popped the top on the double cockpit.

"What is this?" Garcia shouted.

McPherson waved his arms at the plane.

"Out!" he demanded. "Get the fuck out of there." Behind the CIA agent, the MPs were dropping to one knee, aiming their weapons at the backseat.

Garcia heard James cursing in an hysterical voice and struggling to yank off his helmet. He turned just in time to see him pulling his service pistol from its holster.

Scotty dove to the ground, then rolled back up as the plane's engine revved and it began wheeling away. By the time he reached the jet, Scotty realized the captain was trying to shoot himself, not anyone else. Garcia, maybe to shake James off balance, had started rolling the plane.

"Don't fire, don't fire," Scotty yelled to the MPs, and in the same instant he vaulted onto the large delta of the rear wing, barely avoiding a blow to the chest as the Pegasus suddenly jerked toward him. Scotty jumped onto the smaller front stabilizer, then dove toward the wing root as the plane whirled, grabbing for the fuselage like a cowboy boarding a runaway stagecoach.

Had he hesitated one more second, he would have been sucked into the central fan, whose window flap snapped open with a pneumatic hiss. As it was, Scotty barely managed to hang on to the edge of the cockpit as Garcia whipped the Pegasus twelve feet off the ground and then back down hard, like a huge, angry fist.

The blow loosened James's grip on his gun, but this wasn't clear from the ground. Nor was it obvious that he was trying to kill himself. As the plane slammed to the ground, one of the marines finally had a clear view of the army captain in the rear cockpit compartment.

He put three rounds through his face.

The plane was soon swarming with mechanics, MPs, and medical people. Before they even loaded James into the ambulance, though, it was obvious he was dead.

The Pegasus, on the other hand, was fine, if slightly bloodstained.

Garcia, still seated in the cockpit, had the plane's computer review its critical systems while he caught his breath. Scotty, his nose bashed and his forehead bleeding, held one of the medic's towels to his head as he rested on the platform of the mobile ladder truck that had been scrambled out to the plane.

"You should have radioed me," Garcia told him. "I didn't know what the hell was going on."

"I forgot I needed permission to save your life."

"He wasn't trying to shoot me. He was trying to kill himself."

"Yeah, well, my friends saved him the trouble." Scotty pressed the towel against his forehead. He could feel his nose already starting to swell—he was going to look like one serious clown in the morning.

"What tipped you off?" Garcia asked.

"Among other things, it was James who told Porta about your father," Scotty answered as he climbed unsteadily to his feet.

"Thanks."

"For saving your life, or for keeping my mouth shut about your dad?"

"I think he volunteered for the mission because he felt guilty. Like he wanted to make up for screwing up. Maybe he wasn't that bad."

"You're welcome, Junior," said Scotty with a scowl. But he, too, guessed that James had volunteered for the mission so he could have a part in destroying the guerrillas he'd helped.

Of course, the asshole would have done better not to help them in the first place. There was no telling how much damage he'd done, though it would soon be evident enough.

Maybe he hadn't warned them. Maybe he'd tried to throw them off. If the goddamn marines hadn't been such good shots, Scotty might know by now.

Of course, they wouldn't have been able to trust him anyway.

"If you were in the damn hangar, none of this would have happened," Scotty told Garcia. "What the hell were you doing taking off? It's only a little after ten."

"We got the order that H-hour has been moved up to midnight. I'm supposed to get up and out ASAP."

"Yeah, well, good thing I came along. Asshole probably would have flown you into the wrong site, even if he ended up deciding he was on our side," Scotty added. "He had the luck of a dead cat."

"What do we do now?"

"We go have a beer."

"I don't think so."

"Yeah, well, that's what I'm doing." Scotty patted him on the shoulder. "Give my buddy Carla a kiss for me, will you?"

"Whoa, there—you're coming with me."

"Like hell I am."

"I need someone to look for the missile while I fly. This is a two-man gig."

"No way, Junior. I do not fly. Especially in something that looks like a clothes iron. Unlike our brave captain, I'm not even going to lie about being able to work the equipment."

"The plane's computer will show you the pictures. All you need to do is look real close at the monitor. Sergeant, we need a flight suit and a helmet, on the double," Garcia shouted, leaning over the cockpit. "You know, McPherson, I really wish you wouldn't call me Junior in front of the men," he added. "It sets the wrong tone."

Chapter Nine

Same Day, July 25
Over The Atlantic. 11:01 P.M.

The hi-tech cockpit looked like something out of a sci-fi movie. Besides the three large multiuse display terminals directly in front of him, Scotty could turn the clear glass of the cockpit windows into display panels, slaved either to infrared or optical video inputs. It was like sitting in the middle of his own personal theater.

The action he was interested in unfolded on the center screen in front of him. Connected to the ground-penetrating radar pod in the plane's belly, it provided a picture of the terrain so detailed that Scotty felt as if he was looking through an electronic microscope. The unit's computer could freeze-frame and zoom; add a sound track and popcorn and it'd be a box-office smash.

At the moment, all they were looking at was water, but that was about to change. The jet's extremely annoying computer voice—no wonder it had been named after Forrest Gump—chimed in his ear that land was approaching. Scotty glanced at the map in the right panel that blipped their position and path with neat little blue lines. They were supposed to take a turn around here somewhere, he remembered—just as the Pegasus whipped into a ninety-degree, five-g-pulling right angle. Despite the pressure pockets in his suit, several of his internal organs relocated themselves three feet outside of his body.

"Pilot to backseat, how you coming back there?" crackled Garcia over the intercom.

"You're fuckin' lovin' this, ain't you?" Scotty replied as he recovered.

"You're not too scared, are you?"

"Look, I'm not scared of flying, okay? I just don't like it. Not the same thing."

"Yeah, right. Listen, if you feel like you're going to puke, remember to take off the mask. You can drown in your vomit. Comfortable with those controls yet?"

"A fuckin' chimpanzee could work this thing."

"If the shoe fits . . ."

"You're too quick for me, kid."

"Plane's pretty cool, huh?"

"Cosmic," Scotty answered.

"Too bad we couldn't find a wizard hat for you. The visor projects data like a HUD no matter where you look. You can float through several modes, have Gump turn it on or off, even change the image colors."

"Gee. How can I live without it?"

"We'll be over the Sierra Maestra Mountains in ninety seconds."

"I'm holding my breath."

After the ancient Harrier, flying the Pegasus was like slipping a skintight glove over his mind. The minimal difference in the handling characteristics of the one- and two-seat versions was wiped away by the control computer. Garcia saw where he wanted to fly, and he was there. The only annoying thing was that he kept reaching his left hand up as if to adjust the nonexistent Harrier radar; some of the old-fashioned phosphorus had obviously been permanently burned on his brain.

The adventure on the runway had put them behind schedule and he'd had to blow off the scheduled refuel. It wasn't a critical problem—except that it meant he'd have to land in Cuba. San Pietro could accommodate him; he'd already had Gump help him program a course that would give him exactly the same amount of time over target he would have had under the original plan.

The thick clouds in the sky unfolded before him as the plane's sensors made up for the lost sun. Garcia slid the throttle ahead as the leading edge of the mountains, some twenty thousand feet below, loomed like a dark, intriguing mass in the ocean, a woman reclining in bed, waiting for her lover. Her eyes turned toward him slowly, their Cheshire glow begging him forward, promising him everlasting love if he would just hurry to her. He could feel her soft kisses on the wind, and his blood began pumping with the anticipation of having her.

The IRAD—infrared radar acquisition and detection system—was clear, and he set the plane into a descent to start the business end of his run. The Pegasus was a silent ghost haunting the mountains.

"It's show time," he told McPherson.

M-26 headquarters, Sierra Maestra. 11:10 P.M.

Standing on the roof of the building, Romano was silhouetted against the silvery glow of the klieg lights, watching as the giant erector assembly was pulled via tractor from the underground tunnel a short distance away. Men were running in every direction, each with a specific task to perform. Just thirty minutes earlier, the space to the left of the building had been so elaborately camouflaged that even Carla thought it was part of the jungle. Now fake trees and boulders lay in a heap at the far side, removed to reveal a hard-packed plateau next to an artificial hillside housing the underground fuel tanks. Wires and hoses snaked from the hill, illuminated by two large lighting arrays on trailer beds. A sharp ravine fell off to a creek. Elaborate antiair defenses were located about a half-mile away to both the north and the south. The most astounding thing was that Romano had very few men at the complex—far less than a hundred.

"It is like a dance, don't you think?" Romano taunted her. "A complicated ballet."

"You're mad, Romano. Insane." Her handcuffed wrists strained as against all logic she tried to pull the chain apart.

"No, it is the Americans who are insane, sister. You will see."

"I'm not your sister."

Romano laughed as the two soldiers flanking Carla caught her before she could lunge toward him. As they pulled her back, she wondered at their stupidity—surely they must see that he was mad.

"You know, our fates are still entwined," he told her. "Had you not ordered the missile removed from the mountain bunker hours ahead of my schedule, there would never have been enough time to set it up. If it weren't for you, the American satellites would have caught me."

"What a pity."

"They are attacking us at six A.M."

"How do you know that?"

"From one of your own sources, the man you bought with your counterfeit dollars. This is more information than he ever gave you, is it not? But you see, I am bold where you are timid. That is why we had to come together for this."

"How do you know he's not lying?"

"Sister, I believe you underestimate me as severely as the Americans do. I have bought many people. Even the Russians have helped me. My air-to-air defenses are the newest available."

"The Russians would sell you if the price were high enough."

Romano shrugged. "We will launch our missile one second after midnight," he told her. "The mechanism has already been set; all we have to do is watch. I cannot afford to wait for the attack," he added, almost as if he were apologizing to her. "The world will know that the Americans planned to come after us; that will be enough. Our people will know."

"The blood of millions of people will be on your hands. Our people. You must not launch the missile."

"Sacrifices, sister, must be made." He turned to the two soldiers holding her. "Bring her down to the launching area. I want her to see the missile go off before I kill her."

Over the Atlantic. 11:15 P.M.

In the end, he'd decided he had to fly himself. It was an obvious decision, and it had nothing to do with ego. Talic realized that three or four of the young squadron members were probably better at flying the Pegasus than he was. But none of them had been in real combat before, and none could command the group's instant respect in an emergency that he would. It was a no-brainer.

Talic approached the big, lumbering KC-135 like a kid tiptoeing toward his teenage lover's bedroom window. The 135 was running dark—instead of the veritable stadium full of lights that normally lit a tanker doing nighttime refuelings, it had exactly one red twirlie under its rear end. That wasn't a problem for the Pegasus, though—the computer chips in the windshield rendered a view as clear as if the sun were shining overhead.

Assuming it was a green sun. Talic swung in from the left side of his target, aiming for the refueling hose and basket trailing at the back of the plane.

It had been a while since Talic had sipped from the straw of a KC-135. The air force plane used slightly different refueling gear than the standard marine and navy tankers, which meant the Pegasus had to get a bit closer to plug its straw in. There was a brief second of confusion now as the tanker slipped back ever so slightly to the north. Talic rode the Pegasus steady, the jet slipping upward like a calf anxious for its mother's milk. The A/V-32A's probe, extending from a panel in the right-front quarter of the fuselage, licked at the air and caught the basket with a thirsty slurp. In seconds, fuel began gushing into the attack fighter's tanks.

Talic and his squadron had been equipped with a number of weapons and tasked for several roles; their actual mission would depend on what Garcia or the troops found. They were prepared to be called in as air support in a firefight, suppressing ground troops with their cluster bombs. Or they might be asked to hit a silo—which was why Talic's plane, alone in the group, was carrying a pair of Paveways in its belly. The GBU-24/B 2,000-pound laser-guided penetration bombs had been designed to penetrate concrete reinforced bunkers. First used during the war with Iraq, the weapons could blow through a hundred feet of dirt or twenty feet of cement as easily as a pickle sloshing through mayonnaise.

The other planes could, if needed, follow on, the

computer "flying" more conventional Paveways
down the blast holes. If the Cuban missile were
found on an erector at the surface, those munitions,
optimized for general rather than penetration du-
ties, would be directed against it. Talic's would then
be directed against a secondary target, a bunker believed to be the local guerrilla HQ. They had code-
named it Plato Base, and Gump had a prebriefed
strike plan for it all ready to go.

Talic had some doubts about how this enormously complicated plan was going to come together, but at least he and his kids were working
with a coordinated group of marines. The four Pegasus attack planes—they were calling themselves
"Raven One," etc., an appropriate nod toward the
plane's dark bodies—had been matched to marine
assault group Ajax, which ought to be launching off
the USS *Wasp* south of Cuba any second now. The
other assault teams were army units, with air force
and in one case navy fighters for support. Those
planes were all to stand off Cuba until the assaults
were well under way, since they lacked the stealth
characteristics of the Pegasuses. And because of
strict radio silence, the groups weren't even allowed
to talk to one another until sixty seconds before the
start of the assault phase.

It was bound to be even more confusing than it
sounded. And if that weren't bad enough, no one
knew for sure which site they were hitting yet.
Though they had default targets, each team was
waiting for final priorities to be set by Sierra One—
the command group headed by General Jake Finley
aboard an E-8A Joint-Stars aircraft somewhere in
the darkness above. Ajax would get the number-one
site—which to Talic's thinking was only natural,
since they were, after all, marines.

Weber was angling in from the west, preparing to
sidle up for her turn to refuel. Talic, remembering

his long-ago experience at night "tanking" in the Gulf War, had told his pilots to come in at an angle to make it easier to link up; trying to parallel park could easily send you into a never-ending whiffer-dill, a kind of Gordian knot of endless orbiting.

The two other planes in the group had already topped off; their green shadows filled the right quadrant of the LED-laden cockpit screen, which was in full night-vision mode, twenty-times enhancement.

Gump told him the plane was so full it was ready to burp. He let the computer disengage the probe and pop its cover back on, rigging for stealthy flight. As Talic slipped down from the tanker, he watched Weber come in so precisely her hookup could have been used in a training film.

Gump, who could think in kilometers as well as nautical miles, declared that there were exactly 432.7 between the target area and the plane.

Okay boys and girls, Talic said to himself as he saw Weber pull away from the tanker. Time to rock and roll.

Over the Sierra Maestra Mountains. 11:15 P.M.

The mountainside came at him faster than he expected. Garcia had to slam the Pegasus to the right, pulling into a bank to avoid crashing. McPherson groaned behind him as the g forces shot up.

"See anything?" Garcia demanded.

"How the fuck can I see anything the way you're flying? I'm gonna puke my balls out in a minute."

"Just watch the damn tube," Garcia barked, pulling the Pegasus to the left as they whipped through the valley toward the third site. So far they hadn't seen anything more threatening than a chipmunk. He hunkered in as close as he dared, hoping the sensors would be more effective. The mountain currents kicked at the plane, rocking it like a rowboat on an angry ocean. In stealth mode, he couldn't use the vertical thrust directors, and since the plane didn't have conventional flaps, Garcia had to rely heavily on Gump's help to muscle the Pegasus across the angled terrain. To make it easier for the radar to do its thing, he moved very slowly, barely two hundred and fifty knots, and every so often the computer warned him that he was within inches of stalling.

"Nothing on this damn screen," said McPherson as the Pegasus winged back over the target area. "Go on to Site Three."

"I'll take another pass just to be sure."

"We don't have all day, Garcia. Move on."

The pilot smiled to himself—at least he'd gotten McPherson to stop calling him "Junior."

As he banked out toward Site Three, Garcia took a long glance at the projection Gump conjured from the infrared and radar sets. There were no extraneous heat sources, nothing larger than a pebble was moving, and if the ground had been disturbed within the last half-century there was no sign of it.

Scotty had his nose practically in the middle of the screen, staring at the purplish-orange scan as it moved from left to right. His fingers went back and forth over the slider controlling the feed rate; whenever he thought he saw something he slowed the display to a crawl.

There was nothing beneath the mountain's rocky surface but more rocks.

He leaned back and took the paper map from his lap. Pulling back the resolution on the scan, he looked at the map and screen, aware that there must be a way to get the computer to superimpose its own map on the scan but not wanting to waste time trying to figure out how to do it.

Where the hell was the silo?

The damn thing had to be down there somewhere, unless the kid had been hallucinating.

Maybe it had been a setup. Everything—the bombing at Ave, de Souza's offer to let the pilot go, the tapes. Maybe it was a nice, ribbon-tied package designed to scare the piss out of the Americans and get them to negotiate.

Not to negotiate, but to invade. The second that American troops landed on Cuban soil, everything would change. The United States would be the enemy again. The people of Cuba would rally against the imperial invaders as they always had. Castro's heirs would win again.

An elaborate long shot, but if you were losing anyway, you might try it. De Souza especially—she was so confident and cocky she'd figure she could escape from the invasion force.

Especially if the missile site didn't exist.

"Site Three ahead," said the pilot. "Sorry about the bumps."

"Hardly noticing them," Scotty lied, punching the screen controls. This mountain came at him like all the others—a thick orange turd.

He saw the purplish-brown lump as the plane banked hard back to the north. It wasn't much of anything—just a splash of color he hadn't seen before. He was like a dentist, examining a set of X rays and finding an unexpected cavity.

"Go back, go back," he told Garcia, desperately trying to realign the radar. His gloved fingers slid off the control onto a rocker button, inadvertently changing the resolution. He yanked the glove off in frustration and started diddling the dial around, trying to get the blob back.

Garcia brought the plane in for a second pass and Scotty saw the blotch again. He pushed the resolution tighter, focusing in to see what was there.

Nothing.

Which was the point. He'd found a cavity in the mountain, one that shouldn't have been there. The readout on the left was spitting up technical details about the depth of the earth's surface, measuring the hole. There was a girder structure beneath nearly thirty feet of dirt; a steel-and-concrete roof. The radar wasn't powerful enough to see to the bottom of the cavern, but it was deep, very deep.

"Take another pass, kid, take another pass."

"I thought you weren't going to call me 'kid' anymore."

"Just take another fucking pass."

"Do you see the missile?"

He didn't. But there was no doubt that this was the spot. Farther down the side of the mountain there was something man-made in the smooth filling of the rock.

"This is it," Scotty told the pilot. "Tell Sierra One."

"Gotcha," said Garcia. "Transmitting now."

The location was marked precisely, thanks to the plane's geo-positioning system. The transmission took only a nanosecond. Garcia used the telemetry circuit only; its burst of encoded electrons would pass as insignificant noise to even the most sophisticated snoop.

"Now I'll have that beer," he told McPherson in the backseat.

"No way—we have to go ahead and check the other sites, just in case."

"I thought we nailed it."

"I didn't see an erector, or the missile. Come on, let's go to the other sites."

"You don't think they have two hangers like that, do you?"

"Believe me, I don't like this any more than you do, but we have to check the other sites," replied the agent.

Garcia cast a nervous eye at his fuel supply as he pushed the Pegasus onward. The repeated low-altitude swoops around the suspected missile sites didn't exactly raise his mpg. The plane's engine wasn't nearly as thirsty as the cantankerous Harrier power plant, but she wasn't anorexic either. They were going to cut it very, very close.

But Gump had factored that in and said they could make it. He could rely on that.

Right?

Garcia took two passes at each of the next two sites. Lining up for the sixth and last, he told McPherson that he was getting nervous about the fuel situation.

"I'm going in as low and slow as I dare," he said to his backseater. "Look real good, and if we don't see anything, I say we call it quits after one pass."

"Fair enough," said McPherson.

Garcia nudged the Pegasus around the side of the hill like a ninety-year-old taking a tour of a shopping mall. The plane didn't like it much—left to her own devices, she would have slid open the panel over her maneuvering fan and done the job right. But of course that would have been noisy as hell, to say nothing of presenting a hunk of heat and a radar profile fat enough for even primitive equipment to spot her. Garcia held the stick gently, nudging instead of manhandling, walking her through the mountain currents like a three-year-old approaching the gate at the Preakness.

"Nothing, kid. Take her out."

"Done." Garcia pulled the Pegasus level and began climbing. San Pietro was a good three hundred kilometers west. Kicking the plane out of stealth mode would increase the fuel efficiency; he'd do that as soon as possible.

Very soon. Gump whined that they were into their reserves.

It was 2335 military time, less than a half hour to go before the first troops were due to step off the helicopter and surprise the crap out of the guerrillas.

The school and underground bunker where Garcia had been held lay almost dead ahead. They suspected that there were at least primitive air defenses there. Garcia had Gump do a quick calculation that showed they could still make San Pietro with a slight jog to the north just to be safe. He was just pulling the jet onto the new course and preparing to knock off the silent-running routine when McPherson began shouting in his ear.

"Shit, there's something down there—looks like a fucking tunnel. I can see train tracks coming up to the surface. Hold on a second, Garcia."

"What do you mean, hold on?"

"Hey, fuck—hold on—go back—holy shit!"

It was all there on the screen, a million times clearer than anything they'd just seen in the mountains. An underground tunnel—the damn thing was enormous—surfaced several hundred yards away from the school building that hid the guerrilla headquarters. It ran in an exact straight line back to Site Three, several miles away. There was a flat field next to the building—a field that hadn't been in the satellite photos and wasn't on the topo map.

And right in the middle was a rocket and missile launcher. Being loaded with fuel.

His view was cut off as the plane banked around the far side of a steep mountain.

"Kid, call in that location. Direct the attack here," Scotty screamed. "Call it in. Get a verbal acknowledgment. Make sure they hear."

"Against orders. The guerrillas might have something that can pick us up."

"It doesn't matter now, Junior." Scotty's watch

said 11:36. The assault helicopters would still be far off. "Get everything here. Everything, you understand?"

How long had those air force wizards said it took to fuel one of these things and launch? Twenty-four hours?

Or twenty minutes. Take your pick.

"Take the plane around again," Scotty demanded as the pilot continued to the west. "If I switch this thing to infrared I can see how much fuel is in it. Then we can figure out how much time before they're ready to launch."

"Man, we're running lower than shit on fuel," Garcia said. "I ain't lying."

"Kid, this isn't a training exercise. Go back."

Scotty felt the plane swinging around beneath him. He hung on, hit the switch—the wrong one, then the right one—and got an infrared-enhanced image of the ground in front of him. There were tanks of some sort—rocket fuel or oxidizer or both—underground near where the erector was parked. Staring at the images, Scotty realized that the shadings in the images indicated how much fuel was in the tanks. He diddled with the controls and saw that the underground tanks were all between half and a third full.

And the rocket was nearly topped off.

"We have to go now," said Garcia as he circled away.

"No. Fire up your cannon and let's get that thing. It's filled with fuel."

"There's no cannon in this plane."

"What the fuck do you mean, there's no cannon? Are you shitting me?"

"The two-seater is for training only. The cannon would have been an added expense. Besides—"

Scotty didn't listen to the rest of the explanation. Most likely the stupid-ass general who had the damn thing designed didn't want it getting dirty.

"Turn around," he told the pilot.

"Are you nuts? I've already made two passes—we're really pushing our luck."

"Kid, the invasion force is a good half hour away. They've already fueled the thing. You want to gamble on them waiting to launch until our guys get here?"

"There's no way we can take it out. We're unarmed."

"Crash into the fucking missile."

"Are you shitting me?"

"Come on, kid. Don't chicken out on me now."

"I ain't chickening out, asshole. We're part of an operation, and we don't just go off and save the world by ourselves."

"That the marine motto?"

"Fuck you. You're the one who was making fun of me for being too gung ho, for chrissake. Look, we've already directed them here. There are probably a hundred fighter-bombers on their way."

Scotty looked back at the thick, greenish-purple log caught in a freeze-frame on the screen.

They had no choice.

"Take the plane back, Garcia," he said in a low whisper. "Get the fucking missile. Now!"

Aboard Sierra One, Over the Atlantic. 11:30 P.M.

Ambassador Steele, standing above the communications console in the flying situation room, turned and watched General Finley as the operation commander put on a headset. Steele had known Jake Finley for years; not only did he have a long, distinguished army record, but he remained austere in his personal habits, running several miles every morning, something Steele could no longer boast of doing. Both points weighed about evenly in the former general's estimation of the head of the assault team.

They had just been given the coordinates for the missile silo via the encoded telemetry communicator. It required only a minor deviation from the default priorities, and coded orders had quickly been flashed to the assault groups. Acknowledgments had been received. Finley was now communicating the location to the Pentagon.

A total of sixteen operators lined the long central area of the reworked 707; each was charged with a specific task relating to the assault. There was enough electronics gear crammed into the jet to keep a chain of discounters in business for months.

"The Patriot battery is just arriving at Homestead. With luck, they'll be set up by three hundred hours," Finley relayed to Steele.

"With luck we won't need them."

Finley nodded. Neither man had had time to exchange much in the way of pleasantries since boarding the plane. The news about James and the mission's security possibly having been compromised had sent everything into a fast-forward frenzy. The plane was now approaching the coast of Cuba, its sensors sharpening up for a view of the battlefield. Besides its own multimode side-looking radar, the Boeing took in data from a multitude of sources. The most significant was a U-2R with a near-real-time COMINT system in its wing pods; it was due to arrive on station in about five minutes. Finley had tactical control of the overall operation; Steele was, in effect, the eyes and ears of the President.

While Steele had commanded an armored unit in the Gulf War and had helped plan for Panama, he had never felt as responsible for the life and death of a group of soldiers as he did now. It was a helpless feeling, because he was so far removed from the action. Better to be one of the men stepping off the

Jim DeFelice

chopper in the night, bullets bursting around you, sweat and puke rising up in your chest, than to be standing on a steel-mesh floor bathed by the green and orange glow of screens that told you so very little about what was really going on.

A set of clocks near the ceiling clicked off the seconds. The one on the left showed Washington time; the one on the right declared there was exactly forty-one minutes before H-hour, 0012—the time when the assault teams would touch down. A third clock was set at zeros; it would count up the mission time, taking over from the clock next to it. Behind Steele, a screen showed the locations of all the units involved in the assault, with the exception of the Pegasus that was undertaking the advance scouting mission.

Steele had been wrong about James, very, very wrong. The mistake might well have doomed the mission.

He wasn't sure what he would do if it had. His son and daughter-in-law lived in Alexandria, not far from downtown D.C.

"Sir, we have a fresh transmission coming in," shouted the operator in front of him. "They want— Shit, the missile is located at the school building, the guerrilla headquarters, not one of the prebriefed sites. They want everything sent. Immediately. Sir, God—" The young specialist turned and looked up at Finley and Steele. "They say the missile is erect and prepared to launch."

Over the Sierra Maestra Mountains. 11:30 P.M.

Gump gave him another warning about the fuel— they were down to about ten minutes of flight.

Crash into the missile?

Garcia's intestines began tying themselves together.

364

Countless times he'd been presented with the chance to do his duty, to risk his life, and he'd never flinched.

But this was different. There was no chance involved, only dead certainty.

He'd taken an oath when he'd joined the Corps. He'd talked about it, several times, with his drill instructor, his first officers. Being a marine, being in the service—you didn't like to think about it, but there were some circumstances where you went ahead, knowing you were going to die, but also knowing it was your only choice.

They had to stop the missile any way they could. It was what he must do. Otherwise, he would be living a lie.

As his father had?

"Hang on, McPherson," Garcia said, pushing the throttle forward. "Gump, attack mode. Delete stealth."

"Acknowledged," said the computer. "Fuel re—"

"No more fucking warnings about the stinking fuel," he barked at the computer.

"Acknowledged."

He spun back around the mountains between himself and the launch site. He dropped the Pegasus toward the earth, looking at the red outlines of the terrain in the screen before him.

"I guess we ought to pray," he told McPherson.

Or he thought he told McPherson. Things were happening so quickly now that he had trouble distinguishing between thoughts and deeds. He hadn't programmed the target into Gump, he was going solely on sight—it ought to be almost dead ahead. He pushed the jet in, aware of his speed increasing, aware of how low he was, aware of how big the night was around him.

Gump screamed a warning. An instant later, the sky in front of him lit up with searchlights and millions of red tracers. The Pegasus began to wobble.

The target still wasn't in view, but they couldn't be more than a mile off. It must be right ahead, just beyond the stream and the hill. He pushed the plane in faster, leaning toward the screen, willing the missile to appear.

Suddenly the Pegasus leapt out of his hands, veering to the left with a jerk that must have approached ten g's. The force yanked his mask off his face, and for a long second Garcia hung in space, torn by Newton's laws of motion. In the next second he was screaming, pulling at the stick with all his might, so hard the electronic sensors were nearly crushed.

The plane was intact, but barely. It had no tail. The engine's central fan was rotating, thanks to Gump's help, but its familiar high-pitched *whomp* seemed more like the whine of a washing machine about to explode. Garcia wrestled the jet into semistability, trying to make his forward momentum bleed off in something close to an organized descent. He was piloting a pancake, nudging, begging, cursing it to stay flat.

There was a streambed at the bottom of the ravine ahead; it looked relatively flat.

Whether it was or not didn't matter. That was where they were headed.

"Hang tight," he yelled to McPherson.

It was the last thing he remembered doing for quite a while.

Scotty threw his arms stiff against the console just as the plane slammed into the earth. It made a funny sound as it landed—something like a dump truck losing a load of pebbles while getting squashed by a locomotive.

He might have laughed, if his teeth weren't too busy grinding together.

And then there was silence. The cockpit's instrument glow was sucked back into the dark glass and plastic of the panels surrounding him.

This is what I don't like about airplanes, Scotty thought to himself, struggling to find the release buckles on his seat harness. He ran his hands along the cockpit fairing, searching out the release tabs. He found what he thought was one and pulled; nothing happened.

A flicker of panic started in his stomach. He was afraid the plane might catch on fire, and this wasn't exactly the place he wanted to die. Crashing into the missile was one thing; pork-roasting in this high-tech trash can was another.

Crashing into the missile. What the fuck had he been thinking?

He jammed his fingers into every nook and cranny he could find near the canopy rim, pulling levers, pushing buttons. Suddenly the sides of the airplane exploded, as if someone had set off a dozen bottle rockets. The canopy flew off with a whirring buzz.

Good thing I didn't find the seat ejector, he thought as he climbed out.

Garcia's body was hulked in the forward seat, slumped to the side. When Scotty didn't see the pilot move, he started to reach for him, then realized he had more important things to do than give the poor kid a decent burial. The missile had just come into view when the plane went down; it couldn't be more than a half-mile away, up over the next hill.

Jumping off the plane's forward wing, he landed in a shallow stream. Water lapped at his boots. He took two steps and fell into a sinkhole; flustered and cursing, he lost his balance and got soaked before reaching the shoreline, which was only a few yards away. There, he undid the pouch where he'd put one of his Glocks. He thought of going back to the plane and retrieving Garcia's service pistol, but the noises behind him convinced him that was a bad idea.

Scotty figured they'd be sending half their army after him, with the other half waiting at the launcher. But he had no choice but to go forward, to take the one-in-a-million chance he might find a way to stop them.

Not that he really worked out the odds. He just started moving along the streambed in what he figured was the direction of the launcher, looking for a place to cross.

Maybe if Esma had still been alive, he might have been capable of thinking. Maybe if he hadn't screwed up in Angola, sent someone to his death when he should have been more careful, he might have actually considered the hopelessness of the situation. But now all he could do, all he was meant to do, was run toward the missile with a tiny gun in his hand.

Scotty turned a bend in the stream and saw a glow in the air about two hundred yards farther along. It must be coming from the launch site. He backtracked up the stream, then crossed quickly, not bothering to look for rocks or an easy place to get over. Nearly at the middle, the water lapped at his thighs; he thought for a moment he might have to swim, but with his next step the water was back down to his calf. The embankment here was extremely steep, but he reckoned that would be in his favor—it was so sharp an angle, anyone looking for him would probably conclude he couldn't climb it.

That wouldn't be a horrible assumption. Scotty slipped twice, and ripped his fingers to shreds pulling on the vegetation to get up. The brambles and bushes tore at his hands and face, sliced and ripped his clothes, but he stumbled upward. Almost at the top, Scotty heard a loud mechanical hum, the kind an electric transformer might make just before it went bad. He crawled the last few feet on his belly. When he peered over the top, he expected to see either more jungle or a phalanx of guerrillas pointing Russian-made rifles at him.

What he saw instead was something out of a 1960s Cold War nightmare. Down the hillside, a hundred spotlights illuminated the stiff gantry of a black, slightly modified SS-5 rocket, an obscene gesture toward the heavens. Condensation rose like an eerie fog from several spots on the rocket and the trailer, hot breath drifting into the night. An open fire flared on a small platform about fifty yards from the erector; figures moved around it, as if in a macabre dance inciting the devil himself.

Scotty had climbed a ridge over the launch site, so close that with a decent rifle and scope he could have picked off half a dozen guerrillas and probably the rocket itself.

But the Glock was useless, as was he. For the first time since he had crashed, Scotty glanced at his watch. He was amazed that it read 11:44.

The assault teams would be at least ten minutes away, if not more.

The missile must be close to ready. Were they waiting for something?

For midnight. Romano wanted to launch on July 26. Of course.

The insane bastard.

A rifle, that was all Scotty needed. Or a grenade.

He pounded the dirt in frustration, then started to launch himself forward, consumed by desperate fury.

Scotty had taken only two steps when the bullet caught him in the right thigh. He didn't realize he'd been shot at first, thought only that he'd stumbled. He fell in a headfirst tumble, losing his gun and sliding down long embankment. His hands suddenly felt space instead of dirt; before he could stop himself he dropped over a sharp embankment.

His fall was cushioned by a mound of sand.

Jim DeFelice

Though disguised to look like part of the jungle, Scotty had climbed up the side of the bunker's underground tank farm. He'd actually made it much farther inside the guerrillas' perimeter than they or even he would have thought possible.

Not that it was an accomplishment he could crow about. He looked up into the unsmiling faces of three teenagers holding rifles twice as old as they were.

"Up," one of them commanded in English.

Scotty started to comply. It was then that he realized he'd been shot. He stumbled back down.

The rebel soldiers weren't particularly concerned with his wounds, and began dragging him forward. The sand changed to a hard-packed clay; Scotty found his feet and managed to walk despite the growing pain in his thigh. Things jangled together in his head as if they were hallucinations; faces, odd noises, the large fire he had seen from above. A small crowd appeared, then parted; Scotty found himself standing in front of Hector Romano Moncada, the living incarnation of Fidel Castro.

The missile stood about fifty yards directly behind the Cuban, its nose lost in the night's darkness. In between the SS-5 and the fanatical guerrilla leader, rows of trailers and large boxes curled with wires sat in purposeful disarray. Closer to him, two chairs and what looked like a control panel had been arranged for a front-row view of the launch.

"So, Yankee, you thought you would spy on us. And here we have shot you down."

Scotty took a hard breath through his teeth and struggled to clear his head. "Why are you doing this?" he tried to say, but even he could tell his words came out in a mangled blur.

Ramano, laughing, turned and said something in Spanish to someone Scotty couldn't see. The words flew by, with phrases here and there popping out

but making no sense to him. Then another face crys-
tallized in front of him—Carla de Souza.

"So you lied to me," Scotty said. Even as the words
formed on his tongue, he followed her eyes as they
glanced downward.

Her wrists were handcuffed together.

Scotty looked back up, and for a moment their
eyes met. She said nothing, and yet he instantly understood that she knew this was madness, that if she
could have, she would have done anything to stop
it.

De Souza glanced toward the panel on the nearby
flatbed, but Scotty couldn't tell if it was intended as
a signal or not. It seemed obvious the rocket controls were there. Before she could look back at him,
Scotty was pulled to his right. He found himself in
front of the fire. It seemed to be part of an altar;
there were odd shapes around it, cards and beads—
rosary beads. A large woman bent down, praying,
moving cards and tokens around.

It must be Zora, the infamous Santeria witch who
had presided at Fidel's deathbed. She had gone on
to become an important adviser to de Souza, and
now, obviously, to Romano.

She took up a glossy photo of someone—to
Scotty, it seemed as if it were of President D'Amici,
but his vision was too hazy to tell—and put it into
the fire.

"Shit, do you really believe this crap?" he shouted
at her.

The soldier next to him jabbed him in the side.
The old woman turned and glared at him with disdain.

"Do not insult us, pilot," said Romano. "And do
not denigrate what you do not know. In less than
three minutes, when the clock hands pass midnight,
our fates will be realized. There is nothing you can

do now—the timer has already been set. Destiny awaits us all."

Crazy fucks, Scotty thought to himself. Where the hell are those assault teams?

Over the Caribbean. 11:39 P.M.

The voice startled him so much that Talic turned his head to the side, as if someone were in the cockpit with him.

They weren't. It was a transmission from Sierra One.

"This is Raven One," he snapped. "Proceed."

"Your target has been changed to Plato Base. Repeat, target changed to Plato Base. Acknowledge."

Plato Base?

"Gump, open the tactical target screen," he told the computer. "Highlight Plato Base."

The computer flashed a small asterisk in the mountains. Gump calculated it was a little over three hundred kilometers away, just over twenty minutes if they pushed their speed to maximum supercruise.

Plato Base was the guerrilla headquarters to the northwest of the suspected missile sites. Disguised as a school building, it was supposed to be hit in the second wave of assaults, not the first.

Had they just been demoted?

"Sierra One, this is Raven flight leader. Please repeat you message."

"Your target is Plato Base. You are to proceed there as quickly as possible. Use prebriefed plan Plato One for your attack. Take out the bunker. The missile has been located at the site."

"Affirmative." Talic reached for the C^3's mission-profile switch. The bombing run had been mapped out as a solo event, with Talic hitting the bunker and then orbiting in case the follow-on assault needed support.

Just as he wondered what had happened to their marines, Sierra added, "Ajax will join you after your strike. You are authorized to break radio silence to communicate with your group and Ajax on an as-needed basis. Godspeed."

Shit, he thought to himself as the transmission snapped off.

It wasn't the authorization to break radio silence that threw him; it was the phrase "Godspeed."

He hadn't heard that since his next-to-last mission in the Gulf.

The one where his wingmate had been shot down.

Godspeed. What kind of curse was that?

Sierra Maestra Crash Site. 11:40 P.M.

It began with a cough, a deep hack that shook his lungs and finally, slowly, brought him out of the dark hole of unconsciousness. Garcia nearly jumped from his seat as he opened his eyes. As if he'd been transported back to the moment just before the crash, he grabbed for the panel in front of him, trying to brace himself.

With a start he realized he was already down. Still coughing, he reached to blow the cockpit glass.

Again, he was surprised to find it already gone.

Fumbling, he undid his restraints. Dust, jet-fuel vapors, gunpowder, and the charged metallic smell of alloy mixed with the humid Caribbean air as he struggled to breathe freely. When he finally recovered, he realized McPherson had already left the plane.

It took him a moment to get oriented. He'd crashed into the stream at the foot of the ravine; the missile site must be ahead a few hundred yards. Pulling out his Beretta, Garcia jumped from the plane and began splashing along the streamside. Every so often, he hissed for McPherson, though the agent would have had to be within three feet to hear him over the steady hum of what he took to be generators at the nearby missile site.

Hearing a commotion above the ravine to his right, Garcia crossed back to the other side of the stream and trotted east several hundred yards, until he was sure he had gone past the base. The stream had veered off toward the north, and after he crossed it he found himself climbing a rock-strewn hill. He was almost at the top when a figure moved in the shadows before him. Ducking quickly, he realized it was a guerrilla whose back was turned to him.

Creeping up the ten feet that separated them seemed to take forever. Garcia held his breath and kept the Beretta pointed at the man's shadow. He was afraid that if he fired, he would alert other guerrillas nearby—and more important, he had no confidence that he could kill the man in the dark.

He was just about to launch himself at the rebel soldier when he began to stumble. The soldier turned and Garcia threw his arms forward, grabbing the man's legs. There was a quick, sharp burst of rifle fire before the soldier collapsed on top of him, a writhing, cursing banshee who smashed at his face as he fell.

Garcia lost the Beretta as they slid down together. He pulled his enemy to him as if he were reeling in a mammoth fishing line; they fell pushing and punching, until Garcia managed to jam his fist into the man's groin. The first punch had no effect, but with the second a fierce scream erupted from the guerrilla's mouth. Garcia punched again and again, then scrambled up, grabbed the rifle a few feet away, and went back to smash the stock against the man's head. The body jerked, then lay still.

Expecting that the gunfire would bring other troops running, Garcia took a step back up the hilltop. Then he got another idea. He bent quickly to the man, checking his size—he was a little shorter but much heavier than Garcia.

It took forever to get the man's green fatigues off, and still longer, an eternity, to pull them over his own clothes. At every second, Garcia expected the jungle around him to light up with the deadly whistle of machine-gun fire.

Or to hear the fatal rumble of the rocket launching.

Pulling the shirt to his chest but not bothering to button it, he climbed up the hill. There was no one nearby. There was no one, in fact, between him and the crowd gathered around a flatbed trailer a stone's throw from the missile launcher.

Scotty listened as the absurd ceremony continued. It was like something out of a perverse Dadaist play, a Mass almost, in which Zora was consecrating the missile as a giant harbinger of peace.

Peace?

Hellfire, maybe.

Blood seeped from his leg. It might not have been a serious wound, but the loss of blood, the lack of serious sleep for so many nights now, the trauma of this week of pain and death, drained the life from him. He was sleepwalking; he was spinning at the edge of consciousness. Zora the witch danced in front of him, waving her arms like one of Satan's friends.

One of the guerrillas poked him in the side with a rifle. Romano was talking to him. What did they want him to do?

"Kneel before the fire, pilot," said Romano. "Walk to it and perform your obeisance."

What the hell was he talking about? Scotty looked

Jim DeFelice

at him, turned, saw Carla. Her eyes flashed at him.

He heard words in his head as if she'd spoken to him: *Distract them. I will disable the missile.*

"Now, pilot. Kneel!"

Scotty felt one of the guerrillas pushing his shoulder downward. With his last ounce of energy, he lunged forward, throwing himself at the old woman, knocking her into the fire.

Carla felt something pass between her and the American, an understanding as their eyes met. She thought he was not a pilot at all, but McPherson, the man she had talked to at the ambassador's, the man she had made the tapes for. But that could not be, and if he bore some resemblance to the photos she had seen, it must surely be a coincidence. Perhaps it was only an odd sort of unconscious comfort that made her think of the CIA agent, the man who had lost his lover in the explosion meant for her.

It did not matter. Something passed between them. They were working together.

Whether it was all desperation and madness, it did not matter—they would kill her as soon as the missile was launched anyway. Better to make this one last gesture, better to die struggling to preserve her father's legacy, than to be shot with only tears.

She believed in her father to the end, despite the evidence before her.

Carla saw the American lunging forward, taking everyone's attention away. She twisted toward the panel, running three steps before leaping in an outstretched dive for the button marked "Destruct," hoping it would blow up the missile but not the warhead, realizing that in any event it would be better for her country, better for the Revolution. Her own death, the death of these men in the mountains, was nothing compared to the death of Cuba.

There was an instant before she reached the

panel, a moment of time when the earth hung around her, when she felt that Fate itself had given her a reprieve. The button, so clearly marked beneath its protective panel, glowed in that instant, a beacon to the future, to hope. Carla's body, beaten and battered by years of struggle, in that instant regained its youth; she was a graceful dancer leaping across the stage in a brilliant, final performance.

In the next moment, reality crashed into her, the 7.62mm bullets of an AK-47 slashing her chest and neck into grotesque ribbons.

Garcia let go of the trigger as the woman crashed to the ground half a foot from the controls. He'd stopped her.

He wheeled to his left and let off another burst from the rifle, scattering a small group of rebels. Bullets began wailing from the other side of the missile erector. Diving to his stomach, Garcia saw McPherson writhing on the ground not thirty feet away.

"The controls, the controls," McPherson was yelling, but Garcia couldn't understand what he meant. A man who looked for all the world like Fidel Castro jumped up and began running toward him, pistol in hand. Garcia squeezed the trigger, emptying the clip; the bullets caught the bastard in the chest.

The man smiled at him as he collapsed.

In the distance, Garcia could hear the helicopters coming. The rebels were scattering in the chaos. The assault had begun.

They'd made it.

He rose to his feet, looking for McPherson.

As he did, there was a low, guttural rumbling behind him. He ducked, his first thought that an Apache helicopter had swooped in to suppress resistance.

The trembling earth knocked him backward in a

tumble as the nuclear-armed missile left the gantry, heading for its target.

Over the Sierra Maestra. Midnight.

Slipping down from Mach 1.2 into subsonic speed, the Pegasus shuddered ever so slightly, as if the exotic horse was too temperamental to gallop at a mortal's pace. But she quickly settled down as Talic pointed the nose forty five degrees into the bomb run, her sleek black body once more accelerating in the darkness. The other three planes in the group began tacking to the east; they would attack only if he told them to.

Gump did the clerk work on its own. The Pegasus's bay doors slid open and the GBU-24/B's trundled into firing position. A white box slid across the cockpit's clear glass, walking over the liquid circuits of the embedded display as the Pegasus zipped toward the earth. The computer, with minimum intervention from Talic, had conjured and calculated the new data on the target as easily as a secretary changing an appointment in a date book.

The structure was dead ahead. But as he honed in, Talic saw the large shadow off to the side and realized immediately what it must be.

"Gump," he said, intending to tell the computer to change the targeting data and get the rocket.

In that second, the infrared sensors in his plane's nose exploded with a sudden burst of heat. Still nearly a mile off, Talic watched the Russian-made nuclear missile, so old, so outmoded, lift off its pad like a hawk escaping into the air.

The first thing he could think of—the only thing he could think of—was to fire the Paveways at the rocket. He pointed at it on the targeting screen, overriding the preset, and if Gump thought it was a ridiculous idea as he gave the command to fire, the computer never said so—immediately he felt the pop behind him as the two laser-guided bombs cleared the bay.

But they were bombs, not missiles, and as they glided in the direction of the rising rocket, Talic knew they would sail well clear, falling impotently into the Caribbean a few miles beyond.

"The missile has launched," Talic screamed. He yanked the Pegasus out of its dive, feeling the maneuvering thrusters kicking in as he jammed the throttle for more acceleration.

To do what? His plane wasn't carrying air-to-air missiles. It had a cannon, but even if the Pratt & Whitney behind him managed to accelerate in time, the best he'd be able to manage was three or four shots.

"Gump, plot an intercept," he told the computer, pointing at the rocket. "Fly me to it. Now. Fly me to the intercept."

The course was computed and the Pegasus leaped forward in the same instant. Buzzers started going off; Gump had read his mind and didn't like it, not at all.

There was no time to think, just to do. Talic tightened his grip on the stick, leaned forward, and hit the C^3 kill switch, in case the computer tried to abort.

The A-4 had been such a pretty airplane. It started on the drawing boards as a turboprop, wound up a jet instead, and over three decades proved a tough little son of a bitch, stronger and fiercer than anyone had ever dreamed. They added all sorts of doodads to her as the years went on, gave her a hump and piled electronics into the cockpit, but through it all she remained an old-fashioned, guts-and-glory flier, just the thing for a stick-and-rudder man.

But Talic couldn't have done this without the computer. He wouldn't have known precisely where to go; he couldn't have pushed the controls quickly enough to make the one-in-a-hundred shot pay off.

Talic saw nothing in front of him, just knew he was on the course Gump had laid out. For a second he thought the stinking, suckful computer had missed; he started to curse the electronics, thought to himself how ridiculous it was to have computers fly.

Then United States Marine Corps Colonel Henry James Marshall Talic felt something deep inside his soul. He closed his eyes. In the next second, the left wing of his plane crashed through the thin metal surrounding the missile's oxidizer tank.

Chapter Ten

Malcolm Steele slid back in the seat, away from the console. Rather than feeling relief, all he could think was, Man, I am way too old for this.

He reached to his wrist and took his pulse rate, as if he'd just finished a session on his exercise bike. It was running about nineteen every ten seconds—under his workout rate, but just barely.

"You okay, General?"

"You know, Jake," Steele said, looking up, "I'm not a general anymore."

"You keep the title for life, I'm told," said the two-star, patting him on the shoulder.

"Unlike ambassador?" Steele smiled weakly. He'd never really been an ambassador in Cuba—he'd always been more of a general.

Which was the idea when the President appointed him.

There was going to be a lot more need for an ambassador than a general now. Someone had to ex-

plain to the Cuban people—and the government—
everything that had happened.

The troops had secured the M-26 headquarters
site, and were holding about a hundred captured
rebels for the Cuban police. A large number of guerrillas had been killed, including Carla de Souza and
the madman Romano.

The warhead had not yet been recovered, though
the J-Stars and an E-3 in the Caribbean south of the
island had a decent line on it in the shallow ocean
offshore, having tracked all of the debris from the
wreckage.

It they could find the warhead, they would have
proof. The people would find it easier to believe.

The details were still hazy, but from their data it
appeared that a Marine Corps colonel in one of the
assault planes had deliberately given his life to stop
the rocket, crashing his plane into it as it rose from
the gantry in a one-in-a-million shot. If it was true,
it was certain to become one of those incredible,
split-second feats of bravery that become rallying
points for generations of boot-camp recruits, the
sort of thing that lives on in legend for hundreds of
years.

Steele wondered if the man's family might find
that comforting. He wasn't sure his would.

"Ambassador Steele, I have Lieutenant Garcia
here patched through Ajax command. You had
asked about him, sir. He was the pilot of the Pegasus
that radioed in the missile site before it went down."

"I know the lieutenant very well," said Steele,
smiling as he pulled the headset up over his ears.

"The line is yours, sir."

"Garcia, what the hell did you do with that airplane?"

"It's kind of a long story, sir."

"I'm not going anywhere." Steele winked at Finley, signaling that he should listen in.

"Well, sir, when we found the rocket, we were running low on fuel, and so we decided to, uh, land."

"Were you going to take on the rebels single-handed?"

"Since you ask, well, we were going to crash into the rocket."

Steele was dumbfounded. What the hell was it with the marines?

"It was McPherson's idea, sir," continued the lieutenant. "He told me to ram it. And he was right. We could have stopped it."

"Scotty wanted you to ram it?"

"That's what he said. We got nailed by heavy flak and a missile, I think."

"Well, you can relax. The rocket has been stopped," said the ambassador.

"Major Lewis told us. Do you know who got it?"

"A colonel in a Pegasus. That's all I know." The line was so silent, Steele thought it went dead. "You still there, son?"

"Yes, sir, I am. Was it Colonel Talic, sir?"

"I'm not sure."

"He's the best pilot I've ever known, sir."

"You're not bad yourself."

There was another pause before Garcia continued. "It was a hell of a firefight down here, sir. We just barely escaped alive."

"We? Is Scotty there?"

"He's lying right in the back on a stretcher, sir. The rebels shot him before the assault. There's a slug in his leg and he got nicked in the face by a bullet. He's lost a lot of blood, but the medic here thinks he's got a decent chance."

Steele nodded, as if he were in the room with Garcia. At least he hadn't been wrong about Scotty.

"He's been bitching up a storm, sir," Garcia added.

"Oh." Steele laughed. "You had me worried—I thought he was really hurt."

The ambassador listened as the young lieutenant relayed the details of their personal "assault" after the two-place Pegasus crashed. The chaos surrounding the missile launch and its destruction moments later had apparently saved Garcia and McPherson; the lieutenant had literally thrown the agent over his shoulder and dived down an embankment, dragging him across a stream and into some heavy bush, where they were found about an hour later by the marines.

"You've done very well, Lieutenant," said Steele, conscious of how big an understatement that was. "Get some rest now, you hear? We'll talk when this is all over. Make sure you come see me, no matter what happens."

"I will, sir. Thank you, sir."

Garcia, sore, bruised, beat all to hell—and with a bullet wound in his shoulder he hadn't bothered to tell the ambassador about—handed the radio set back to the Sea Stallion crewman. He gave the chopper pilot a pat, then squeezed back to check on Mc-Pherson.

The wounded agent was boiling with a fever, cursing and mumbling to himself. The corpsman had hooked up an IV and given him an antibiotic against infection. They were headed for a hospital in Havana, which had the best trauma center on the island.

Garcia leaned down on his haunches next to the agent. Among McPherson's assorted wounds were first-degree burns—he had disrupted some sort of ceremony by pushing one of the guerrillas into a fire and holding her there. The marines found that the woman's face had been burned off; it was, said the corporal who told him about it, the most hideous thing he'd ever seen.

Actually his description had been much more terse: "I puked my liver out when I saw her."

Garcia slipped his feet down and sat on the helicopter floor. The rhythmic hum of the motor was making him tired.

"Got any coffee, corpsman?" he asked the medic.

"Sure thing, sir." The corporal retrieved a thermos and gave Garcia a cup. He had to hold Garcia's hand as he poured—the pilot was shaking worse than an eggbeater.

"I'll be okay," said Garcia. "I just need a little rest. Been a hell of a couple of days."

"You married, sir?" asked the man, making conversation.

"No. But I got this girlfriend—I have to tell you, Corporal, she's beautiful. I know everybody says stuff like that, but this isn't bullshit. She's gorgeous. I can't wait to see her. She's waiting for me in Havana. At least, I hope she is."

"Sounds like she's the one, Lieutenant."

Garcia nodded, sipping the coffee. It wasn't exactly hot, but it tasted pretty good. "She's Cuban."

"You know what they say about Cuban women."

"What's that?"

"I don't know, sir," said the corporal. "I thought you did."

Garcia laughed at the lame joke. Hell, he would laugh at anything from now on.

Maria would be waiting. She'd told him so. And he believed her more than he believed anyone.

"Hey, kid," groaned McPherson in the stretcher. "That you?"

"You okay, McPherson?"

"I been better." The agent strained for a second, as if he wanted to rise. Then he gave up all pretense of rising. "Listen, kid, you talk to your father yet?"

"No."

"I want you to. Soon as we land."

"Jesus, McPherson. Why don't you relax, huh?"

"Listen, I want you to talk to him."

Garcia shot a glance at the medic, who was tactful enough to pretend he had something to do up front in the chopper.

"Relax, Scotty."

"You know, I was just thinking about this. No shit, I was. You feel ashamed he was a criminal in Cuba."

"You told me it might not be true," Garcia said.

"Yeah, I know I said that. It might not be." McPherson grimaced; Garcia could see a wave of pain take hold of his body, shaking it. When it passed, McPherson continued. "Whether it is or not, you ought to talk to him about it."

"What the fuck am I going to say?"

"Nothing. Just that it's not the thing you think about him, one way or another."

"Oh yeah, right." Garcia felt his anger writhing up, even as he reminded himself that the agent was most likely delirious. "You weren't raised by him. You don't understand. If this is true, then everything he did, everything he said, was a lie."

"No, not at all. Whether he was or wasn't a criminal, only he can tell you. Maybe Fidel jailed him as a dissident and made up the crimes. Maybe he did do something he's ashamed of. But the bottom line isn't what he did in Cuba, it's how he raised you."

"What? With lies?"

"You were ready to let James off the hook, for chrissake. Like you were his fuckin' shrink."

"This is different. This is my father."

"You didn't turn out so bad, cocksucker."

"Why'd you have to bring this shit up for?"

"I'm right, ain't I? He didn't do all that bad."

"Screw you."

"Don't curse a dying man, Junior. It's not polite."

"You're not going to die."

"Dying men always tell the truth, kid. Besides, I get a last request. Listen to me. Call your father."

"You're not dying, asshole."

"Who the fuck taught you how to curse, scumbag? When I met you, you were a sweet, innocent numbnut. Now look at you. Somebody's gonna have to wash your fuckin' mouth out."

Garcia patted McPherson's chest. He could feel the helicopter starting to descend; they were maybe ninety seconds from the hospital.

Probably he'd call his dad. It wasn't the sort of thing you should do over the telephone, though. Maybe he'd tell him to come down, meet him in Miami.

Or Havana.

He'd come to meet Maria. His dad would like her. So would his mom.

Probably Carla had lied to play with his head. Any way you sliced it, though, McPherson was right.

Dying men always told the truth. Even when they weren't dying.

Havana. August.

Scott McPherson, not entirely healed but no longer sick enough to be confined to a hospital room, sat down on the white sand of the Cuban beach and felt the warm rays of the sun soaking through his clothes. He wasn't sure precisely how he came to be here—literally as well as metaphorically. He tried, for a while, to find an answer to both dimensions of the quandary; tried, then gave it up.

He squinted at the rough surf, glistening in its fury. His mind waded out, testing the depths, losing itself in the vastness of the ocean.

There was a time he'd thought of himself as a soldier, fighting against the dark forces of the world.

He'd fought blindly for his country, blindly for the Agency. He battled on the side of Good against Evil, and if it was the sort of thing he'd never be caught saying out loud, still he felt it, and knew it was true.

Gradually, he began to see himself as a leader, a man who could advance to the highest levels of the CIA and the government. A man who worked with generals and presidents. Part of it was ego; part of it was a genuine belief that he could serve his country better than most other men. The righteous soldier hadn't vanished, though his battles had become increasingly obscure. Sometimes—like when he headed the team assigned to recover the stolen Russian warheads—the goals were clearly good but the methods were admittedly dark.

And then came Angola.

For the longest time, he'd blamed himself for screwing up. Everyone did. Or he thought they did.

Maybe they didn't. Isha didn't seem to, at least not anymore. She sounded as though she'd found some sort of peace.

Good for her.

When things were bleakest, Steele surprised him with the offer to work as an assistant. He jumped at it, assuming he'd remain dead-ended in the Company. He'd been right about that.

But he spent the first six months in Cuba still moping. Drinking a hell of a lot. Doing his job, yes, but not exactly applying himself. He and Steele had had words several times. The ambassador, who'd gone out on a limb, was disappointed, maybe wanted to can him.

And then Scotty met Esma. She was like no one else he'd ever met. Never, ever had he loved a woman like he loved her.

Had he even loved anyone else? It was as if she invented the feeling, created the force that blossomed inside him. Yet if someone asked him now what it was about her, what the quality was that set her apart, he would never find the words.

Scotty leaned back on the sand. He closed his eyes against the sun and saw her again, saw her fade in the relentless light of noon.

He was something like his old self at the job after he fell in love with her. He was fighting again, not so much for Good, as for her good, her vision of Cuba. More cynical, maybe, trusting even less—but still a soldier, still a believer in devils and angels.

The waves at his feet crashed, riderless horses plunging their heads in fury as they charged against the shore. They seemed for a moment like the world coming against him in frenzied madness, as if the only thing to do was leap up and rush at them, beat them back with sheer will.

A useless gesture, but no more useless than any other.

Scotty had meant it when he told the kid to crash into the missile. He'd meant it like he'd meant nothing else in his life. To have died saving Cuba—saving Esma's vision of Cuba—even more than saving hundreds of thousands of Americans, that would have given his life meaning in a way nothing else could.

Scotty felt a light spray of the water against his legs. His job here was over. M-26 was officially defunct. Told the entire story, the Cuban people had more or less accepted the American assault as a necessary evil. Their acceptance was greatly aided by the fact that the temporary government had finally set a date for elections. Their future was finally their own.

The CIA was shutting down most of its operations; Fashona was already working somewhere else. The ambassador was talking about retiring in six months, at most. The deputy head of mission, a professional, was rumored to be the most likely re-

Jim DeFelice

placement, and had already as much as told Scotty he'd like him on his staff.

Scotty didn't want to stay in Cuba. He had come to see it through Esma's eyes as well as his own; her way would be the true way now. But that made it impossible to stay. Everywhere he went brought some other reminder of her, some fresh attack he couldn't protect himself against.

He remembered her funeral, holding her mother's hand. And the words he'd read.

"Cease from anger, and forsake wrath: fret not thyself in any wise to do evil. For the evildoers shall be cut off."

They didn't get cut off on their own, though, did they? Not without effort. Not without loss.

He couldn't go back to Washington. He couldn't work for the CIA—or on "loan" to state, for that matter. He was no longer a soldier.

The waves continued to crash, pushed on by the endless ocean. Scotty lay motionless in the hot sand, sinking into the infiniteness of an unquenchable sorrow. The promise he had read echoed in his head:

For yet a little while, and the wicked shall not be: yea, thou shall diligently consider his place, and it shall not be.

But the meek shall inherit the earth; and shall delight themselves in the abundance of peace.

A Note on Sources

While this is a work of fiction and should be treated
as such, the descriptions of the A/V-32A as well as
the other technologies, weapons, and craft included
in the book are based on a large number of (unclassified) sources. As they are products of the imagination rather than actual sheet metal, in some cases
their performance and construction is more idealistic than would be possible given present monetary
and time constraints. But that, after all, is fiction's
major advantage over reality.

The Pegasus specifically is inspired by work undertaken by, among others, the Lockheed Martin
and Pratt & Whitney companies. The fictional plane
is named after the outstanding power plant used by
the current-generation STOVL aircraft, the Harrier.

Those very familiar with both Cherry Point and
Jacksonville will realize that I've made some slight
alterations to facilitate the action. I figured that

since I didn't have to file an environmental-impact study, no harm would be done.

With the exception of historical citations, the marine aviators mentioned herein are fictional characters. If anything, their present-day counterparts are several times more heroic.

The CIA document cited at the beginning of the book is an authentic excerpt from the Agency's original briefings during the 1962 crisis.

As of this writing, Fidel Castro remains in power in Cuba. While there is widespread dissension over his rule, it appears unlikely that anything but death will end his oppression. He will never, however, destroy the true Cuban spirit, which thrives like a deep-rooted tree despite great trials and deprivations.

I have been privileged to know many Cubans and Cuban-Americans over the years, including several who struggled to carve new lives in the United States after arriving on these shores with nothing but hope in their pockets. I have learned much from them, and owe a special debt to my friends Jerry and Elsa Fernandez—not for information in this book, which they read in an early form, but for their friendship and love. The book's errors are my own, but its truths flow from the hearts of all my friends.

Since I'm thanking a few of the many people who have helped me here, let me add the names of my editor, Don D'Auria, and my agent, Jake Elwell of Wieser & Wieser, both of whom have given me valuable support and guidance. And I must also mention my wife, Debra, without whom I could not have written a word.

To all Cubans: May you live to see the day freedom returns in fact as well as spirit to the island.

WAR BREAKER
JIM DeFELICE

"A book that grabs you hard and won't let go!"
—Den Ing, Bestselling Author of
The Ransom of Black Stealth One

Two nations always on the verge of deadly conflict, Pakistan and India are heading toward a bloody war. And when the fighting begins, Russia and China are certain to enter the battle on opposite sides.

The Pakistanis have a secret weapon courtesy of the CIA: upgraded and modified B-50s. Armed with nuclear warheads, the planes can be launched as war breakers to stem the tide of an otherwise unstoppable invasion.

The CIA has to get the B-50s back. But the only man who can pull off the mission is Michael O'Connell—an embittered operative who was kicked out of the agency for knowing too much about the unsanctioned delivery of the bombers. And if O'Connell fails, nobody can save the world from utter annihilation.

_4043-3 $6.99 US/$7.99 CAN

Dorchester Publishing Co., Inc.
P.O. Box 6640
Wayne, PA 19087-8640

JIM DeFELICE
COYOTE BIRD

The president is worried—with good cause. Two of America's spy planes have disappeared. Soon he—and the nation—will face a threat more dangerous than any since the height of the Cold War. A secretly remilitarized Japan is plotting to bring the most powerful country on Earth to its knees, aided by a computer-assisted aircraft with terrifying capabilities. But the U.S. has a weapon of its own in the air—the Coyote, a combat super-plane so advanced its creators believe it's invincible. Air Force top gun Lt. Colonel Tom Wright is prepared to fly the Coyote into battle for his country—and his life—against all that Japan can throw at him. And the result will prove to be the turning point in the war of the skies.

__4831-0 $5.99 US/$6.99 CAN

BROTHER'S KEEPER

JIM DeFELICE

F.B.I. agent Jack Ferico has never gotten along with his estranged older brother, Daniel. But now their father is dying and he wants to see Danny before he goes. The trouble is, when Jack tries to contact Danny, he finds he's disappeared—without a trace. The search that Jack begins simply for his father's sake soon uncovers secrets, hidden agendas, and a danger far more serious than he ever imagined. Danny—Dr. Daniel Ferico—is working with an international think tank as a specialist in stealth technologies, and his disappearance raises some major red flags. If any of the classified technologies were to fall into the wrong hands, national security would be threatened and the balance of power could shift. Suddenly Jack's not the only one looking for Danny. But if he wants to save his brother and end an international crisis, he'd better be the one who finds him . . . and fast.

CHARLES WILSON

NIGHTWATCHER

"A striking book. Quite an achievement."
—*Los Angeles Times*

The staff of the state hospital for the criminally insane in Davis County, Mississippi, has seen a lot in their time—but nothing like the savage killing of Judith Salter, one of their nurses. And with three escaped inmates on the loose, there is no telling which of them is the butcher—or who the next victim will be. Even worse, as the danger and terror grow apace, the only eyewitness to the nurse's death—a psychopathic mass murderer—begins to reveal a fearsome agenda of his own.

___4275-4 $4.99 US/$5.99 CAN

ROUGH BEAST
GARY GOSHGARIAN

"[Treads] territory staked out by John Saul and Dean Koontz...a solid and suspenseful cautionary tale."

—*Publishers Weekly*

A genocidal experiment conducted by the government goes horribly wrong, with tragic and terrifying results for the Hazzards, a normal, unsuspecting family in a small Massachusetts town. Every day, their son gradually becomes more of a feral, uncontrollable, and very dangerous...thing. The government is determined to do whatever is necessary to eliminate the evidence of their dark secret and protect the town...but it is already too late. The beast is loose!

_4152-9 $4.99 US/$5.99 CAN

ATTENTION
BOOK LOVERS!

Can't get enough
of your favorite **HORROR**?

Call **1-800-481-9191** to:

— order books —
— receive a **FREE** catalog —
— join our book clubs to **SAVE 20%!** —

Open Mon.-Fri. 10 AM-9 PM EST

Visit
www.dorchesterpub.com
for special offers and inside
information on the authors you love.

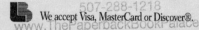